Catarina's Ring

BY LISA MCGUINNESS

bonhomie  press

ISBN: 978-0-9905370-2-1

Library of Congress Cataloging-in-Publication
data available upon request.

Manufactured in the United States of America.

Design by Elysse Ricci.
This book has been set in Adobe Garamond Pro & Bodoni Old Face.

10 9 8 7 6 5 4 3 2 1

Bonhomie Press is an imprint of Yellow Pear Press, LLC.
www.yellowpearpress.com

Distributed by Publishers Group West

Chapter 1

CATARINA IN PERDIFUMO:
A PICTURESQUE-BUT-IMPOVERISHED
SOUTHERN ITALIAN TOWN, **1913**

"Catarina," Mateo called.

Catarina Pensebene opened the heavy, black wooden door and squinted against the bright sun. She shook her head and laughed when she spied her brother Mateo, leaning against the crumbling wall of a stone house across the narrow cobblestone street and waiting for her to emerge at the usual time, on shopping day. Just seeing him brightened her mood. She hooked the straw market basket over her left arm and approached her rakishly handsome, mischievous brother while patting her side pocket to make sure the grocery list was safely tucked inside.

The two made a striking pair. Even in her faded brown dress and dingy apron, Catarina's vivid sky-blue eyes and dark brown, wavy hair attracted looks of admiration.

Going to the market stalls was a task she enjoyed—especially when her brother accompanied her. It was nice to be out from under the eye of Signora Carlucci, her employer, and Signor Carlucci, her employer's plump, balding, sweaty-palmed husband.

"*Come stai?*" she asked Mateo, deeply inhaling the fresh spring air. It was late morning but the sun already warmed the day and gave a hint of the heat to come as spring sashayed its way to summer.

"*Bene,*" he said, his eyes crinkling with humor as he fell into step beside her. His face was the first pleasant thing she'd seen since she arrived at the dimly lit, very formal Carlucci home early that morning. It felt good to be back outside, walking instead of soaking and scrubbing heavy clothes in scalding water since the break of dawn. She looked down at her red, chapped hands and sighed.

"Come on then," she nudged her shoulder against his as they headed towards the vegetable and fruit stalls. "Where do Mama and Babbo think you are this time?" she asked. Her eighteen-year-old brother should have been helping their papa with the olives, but he somehow managed to get out of more work than she and her sisters ever could.

"They both think I'm out on an errand for the other," Mateo said with a smirk.

Catarina cuffed him lightly on the side of the head. "Impossible," she laughed. "How is it that you never get caught?"

Catarina longed for the life Mateo led, but instead of being the favored son, she was the youngest of five sisters. Her family was struggling to put food on the table and couldn't afford to formally educate her, although she was proud that she could at least read, write and work simple sums. She was lucky to be only one year younger than Mateo, because when they were growing up, she sometimes got to sit at the table when her babbo was teaching her brother, whereas her older sisters were already busy doing farm work and barely knew how to read or write their own names.

When there was time in the evening, Mateo taught her more of what he was learning. She knew she should be pleased to know anything at all, considering how few grown men from the region were even partially literate. Good men who were busy trying to put food on the table each day, doling a percentage of their crops to the land owners, leaving little time to worry about education. Her family was fortunate to own the acres they farmed. They had their own grapes and olives to sell, and a kitchen garden to work, but Babbo kept saying changes were coming. Catarina wasn't sure what he meant exactly, and felt a vague sense of unease when she let her mind linger.

When she turned sixteen, her mama had announced that she was old enough for a job and informed her that she would begin working as a maid. Catarina was devastated. She loved working on the land with her family, but her protests were quickly silenced when her sisters whispered that the family needed the money Catarina would earn. Now, days were filled working for Signor and Signora Carlucci instead of helping out with the olives and vines. She missed being outdoors in the sunshine. She even missed the back-breaking drudgery of grape picking, which she preferred to scrubbing other people's laundry.

Day after day, she was stuck inside washing floors, ironing sheets, and cooking. She knew she should be proud to help her family, but the money she earned didn't stave off the tedium of her days or the clammy hands of her employer's husband.

Signora Carlucci was kind and lovely to Catarina, but was demure and kowtowed to the thick-lipped, hairy-knuckled Signor Carlucci, who was gradually becoming impossible by making untoward advances to Catarina and leering when his wife's back was turned.

Things were fine when she had begun working in the Carlucci house, but changed in an instant after an unexpected request. Signora Carlucci had left home for the day to take a meal to a sick friend and Catarina found herself alone with Signor Carlucci for the first time.

"Catarina," he told her, "la Signora has asked me to instruct you to change the sheets on our bed before she returns."

Catarina stopped sweeping the floor and looked up at him. There was something odd about the way he was gazing at her and her chest inexplicably tightened with anxiety. It was an unusual request. Signor Carlucci rarely spoke to her, and had never given her any type of work instructions, which he left to his wife. Signora Carlucci had her change the bed linens on Fridays, yet it was only Tuesday.

"It's not the usual day, Signor."

"It is not your place to question, Catarina."

"*Certamente, Signor.* I'm sorry," Catarina responded, even as the sense of unease further stole into her mind. She climbed the stairs to their bedroom and opened the door to the heavy, wooden armoire that held their sheets. The scent of the lavender water she used when she ironed calmed her nerves and she shook off the sense of disquiet. She appreciated the fine feeling of the fabric, which was much smoother than the coarse sheets they had at home. As she spread the bottom sheet across the mattress, she ran her hands over the material.

When she turned to reach for the second sheet, he was there, standing beside her. She gasped.

"Signor Carlucci, you startled me!"

"There's no reason to be frightened," he said. The look on his face was rapt—drinking in every detail of her. She froze with her arms still reaching for the top sheet, not sure what to do. And then he reached over, took a stray lock of her dark hair, gently twirled it around his finger, then let it drop.

"You have the most startling eyes," he said in a low voice, almost a whisper. He ran his hand gently along her arm and looked at her. "I'll watch you, to make sure you're doing it correctly."

"I assure you, Signor," she stammered, "there's no need. Your wife has taught me well."

But still, he stood against the wall and watched her while she continued. Finally, after the sheets were snugly tucked in, he turned, and without another word walked out of the room.

"*Oh, mio Dio!*" Catarina exhaled the breath that had been stuck in her chest, not daring to turn to make sure he was gone.

No men in her village would ever touch a young woman. It would dishonor them both. And she had never had a man stare at her like that—as if he were ravenous. She shivered, then grabbed the bedroom door with a shaking hand and quietly closed it behind him. She wanted to latch the lock, too, but thought he might hear the solid click and she wanted to call no more attention to herself. She leaned against the door's solid wood to give herself a sense of safety. She didn't want him to know she was afraid.

"*Cosa dovrei fare?*" she muttered. "What should I do?" she asked herself. Her instincts told her to turn and run home: to leave and never come back. But her family needed the lire she earned from this job, and Signor Carlucci was a respected man. What *could* she do? Speak out against him? She knew she couldn't tell Signora Carlucci. It would be too disgraceful.

Why would he do such a thing? she wondered. I've given him no reason to think he could approach me in this manner. He knows I come from a respectable family—that I am an honorable girl.

She sank down to the floor to think, but found no solution.

After a few minutes she stood back up and dropped her arms, which had been wrapped protectively around herself, back to her sides. She silently turned the doorknob and slowly slid the door open. She went to the armoire and closed the doors. With still-shaking hands, she put the linen-covered down comforter on top of the sheets, and fluffed the pillows to complete her task.

"Mama?" Catarina called when she opened the front door later that evening.

"In here, *mia cara*," she called.

Catarina walked into the tantalizing smells coming from the stove and the comforting embrace of her mother. Catarina held onto her tightly, drinking in the feeling of safety.

"What's this?" her mother asked, surprised by the intensity of her daughter's embrace. She leaned back and looked at her daughter's stricken face. "What happened today?"

Catarina could hardly look at her. She didn't want her to think she had done something to encourage Signor Carlucci's actions.

"Something strange happened today, Mama."

She told her about Signor Carlucci's request that she change the sheets and his appearance by her side, but she left out the part when he touched her. Even her father hardly ever touched her now that she was no longer a little girl, but something stopped her from including that detail when she spoke to her mother about Signor Carlucci's disturbing actions.

"He said I have startling eyes," she shivered.

"*Mia cara*. That's nothing, my darling. You had me worried. If I had a lira for every compliment we got about the beauty of your eyes we would be a rich family. It's nothing. You should not be worrying yourself or me with such things. Signor Carlucci is a respected man. A married man. He probably just got confused about what his wife asked him to tell you. And we need you to keep this job, *cara*. Do you think it's easy to feed the mouths of this family? Even having your sisters' husbands help in the field barely makes up for all the food they swallow." She clicked her tongue, shook her head, and went back to rolling gnocchi.

"But Mama, I don't think it was just a compliment. It was odd."

"Catarina, you need to ignore this and put it to rest. *Capisci*? He said you have nice eyes. Don't make nothing into something. I don't want to hear such complaints." She gave her daughter a little squeeze and a kiss on the cheek. "Now put your apron in your room and go help your sisters with the garden. The sage and rosemary are taking over along the south wall and need to be cut back."

Catarina slowly climbed the wooden steps up to the loft room she used to share with her sisters. They had gotten married one-by-one, so she now had the space to herself. She thought she would like it because the bed had always been crowded and her sisters snored, but instead she found herself lonely.

She couldn't believe her mother thought it was nothing. She had expected her to be enraged; to stomp her foot and rant against him. Her mother had always believed Catarina. She knew Catarina wouldn't make something up to stir trouble. She had expected her to march right over to the Carlucci's—dragging Catarina along by the arm—to give Signor Carlucci a scolding and have a thing or two to say to Signora Carlucci about how to run a household. But to tell Catarina to ignore it instead? She couldn't understand that.

Then it occurred to her that perhaps her mother was right.

"*Sono fessa*," she told herself as she slipped off her maid's apron to join her sisters in the garden. "Maybe it *was* nothing."

On Wednesday and Thursday, Signor Carlucci barely even glanced at her. He kept his head down, reading over a ledger. Accounting numbers from his tailoring store, Catarina noticed. He ate his meals and spent most of his time out of the house at his business. She gradually relaxed and became convinced that she had imagined something more than had happened.

Until Friday, when Signora Carlucci went over the daily list of chores with her.

Catarina stood at the kitchen counter, chopping raw tomatoes for the *salsa di pomodori a crudo* that Signor Carlucci favored, as the signora told Catarina what to do for the day.

"After you've finished preparing dinner, move on to the laundry and the ironing. I'm leaving the market list for you here, and of course, change the sheets."

Catarina stopped chopping and held the knife still over the tomato she had begun cutting. Without looking up she hesitated and then asked, "But, Signora, wasn't I to change them on Tuesday?"

"*Cosa stai dicendo*?" asked Signora Carlucci. "Why would you change them on Tuesday? Friday is the day to change sheets. I've been over this with you already," she said with a furrowed brow and a look of exasperation on her face. "Pay attention, Catarina."

Catarina glanced fleetingly at Signor Carlucci, who raised his chin and gazed at her with a level stare over his ledger.

Her heart pounded. She knew she should speak up and tell the signora that her husband had instructed her to change them on Tuesday, but she hesitated. Her voice caught in her throat. She felt afraid to speak up and her courage failed her.

"I'm sorry. I must have been mistaken," she turned back to his wife. "Of course, sheets are changed on Friday. I forgot for a moment." She was filled with regret and an odd sense of humiliation.

Catarina clenched her jaw and went back to cutting the tomatoes, paying careful attention so that she didn't cut her finger in her sudden surge of emotions. She knew right then that there was going to be trouble with Signor Carlucci. She almost put down the knife to tell Signora Carlucci what had happened, but she knew the signora was unlikely to stand up for her maid and stop her husband. And Catarina realized that her employer would be horribly embarrassed if she knew what had transpired. That in itself was enough to stop Catarina from speaking about it. But even if that hadn't prevented her, the look of warning from her husband certainly did. She took one small glance at Signor Carlucci and his eyes locked on hers. Before she could look away he changed his expression from one of warning to a conspiratorial smile.

After that, the situation gradually worsened. She couldn't walk down the hall without him subtly brushing against her. Serving him at mealtime seemed to be an open invitation for him to touch her thigh. The first time it happened she was so surprised by the unexpected touch that the platter of chicken cacciatore she held clattered to the floor.

"Catarina!" Signora Carlucci exclaimed. "Are you ok? What happened?"

"I'm so sorry, Signora," Catarina stammered. "I'm fine. I just lost my hold on the platter."

"Nina, Nina," consoled Signor Carlucci to his wife. "Don't worry yourself about this. Accidents happen and obviously the girl didn't mean it."

"It's true, Signora. I didn't mean to drop it. It was an accident. I'll be more careful from now on."

"Well, clean it up then." She looked at her husband. "I'm sorry, *mio amore*. She's usually so efficient."

"Not to worry, my dear," he smiled lovingly at his wife. "I'm sure it won't happen again."

In the kitchen Catarina leaned her back against the wall with a hand to her chest, breathing hard.

"This is *assurdo*," she muttered, absurd. This can't continue, but how will anyone believe my word against his? He'll tell everyone in the village I'm lying if I speak out against him. He'll make up some terrible tale. And if I quit, how will I ever find another position with no letter of recommendation? There are so few families who can afford to have help now.

If I stay though, she thought, it will get worse, until what? He gets me alone and dishonors me? She shivered, afraid it was simply a matter of time before the old troll tried something more.

She wiped her face on the one part of her apron that was free from the chicken cacciatore mess.

This is no time for weeping, she reprimanded herself, and wet a rag to go wipe up the ruined dinner.

Chapter 2

JULIETTE, AMILIA AND THE DAY
THAT CHANGED EVERYTHING

"Juliette!" Amilia waved to her daughter.

Juliette Brice took off her sunglasses, squinted against the sun pouring into the cozy bistro, and waved back as she made her way to their table.

"What happened to your finger?" Amilia asked when she sat down.

"Work casualty," Juliette answered, looking at her now stitched and bandaged index finger. "I got distracted," Juliette said, visualizing the kitchen door swinging open unexpectedly, as she—startled—sliced her finger with the razor-sharp chef's knife, cutting down to the bone.

She'd gasped, the shock of realization coming a fraction of

a second before the pain itself. Juliette's right hand had shaken as she tried to open the package of bandages to hold the cut together.

"Can you help with this?" she'd asked her boss.

"Hand it here," Elizabeth grabbed the packet of narrow, sterile strips from Juliette and then passed them to her one at a time to close the wound. Once it was closed, the two women paused and looked at the bandaged finger.

"Put on a finger cover, and get back to work."

Juliette had inhaled deeply to steady herself, grabbed a rubber finger cover out of the first aid kit and rolled it on.

Amilia listened to Juliette's account of how she spent the previous evening and smiled in spite of her attempted stoicism.

The two leaned their heads towards each other, temporarily oblivious to the hustle and bustle around them. Amilia, with her dark brown curls, was more petite and classically Italian looking than her taller daughter, whose light brown hair was long and silky smooth. But their eyes told the story of their connection. Both viewed the world through beautiful ice-blue eyes, the exact color of Juliette's grandmother Catarina's, and her mother's before her.

"Why are you smiling at me with that mischievous look on your face while I'm telling you about my work woes?" Juliette playfully reprimanded her mom who was obviously up to something.

"Sorry. It's just that I've been thinking a lot about your work situation lately and I have an idea."

"Funny you should say that, because while I was sitting in the ER at two o'clock in the morning waiting to get stitches, I also had a thought or two about my job situation."

"Then you go first," her mom said. "What are you thinking?"

"I'm thinking that even though working with the renowned Lucian Kidd turned out to be a disaster, it was a learning experience and it's time to stop licking my wounds and realize that there are different avenues to achieve what I want to achieve. Nonna used to say, grace and grit is what it took to get what you want in life and I think it's time for me to call on a bit more grit. I'm almost thirty after all."

"That's exciting, Juliette. I'm proud of you."

"I was just so hurt at the time. I didn't know it would take this long to get over it, but I think I needed time to heal and regroup."

"And now you have?"

"I think so. I could hardly even talk about it when it first happened. I had been so excited to work with him and everyone was happy for me, and then when instead of getting accolades for my inspired cooking and classical chef training I got fired, it was horribly embarrassing. I didn't know how to process it, let alone tell people what happened."

Amilia squeezed Juliette's hand. "You know hiding out and doing catering work for Elizabeth instead isn't the answer, right?"

"I know. She's practically as horrible as Lucian was, but figuring out what *is* the answer is the hard part. I feel paralyzed and I'm not sure where to go from here. Do I apply somewhere as a sous chef and start from the beginning? Try to get a job as a recipe tester? I'm just not sure."

"If you could do anything what would it be?"

"I would do what I've always wanted to do—open my own little café."

"What if you set aside all your fears and went for it?"

"I would in a heartbeat if I could get investors, but who is going to invest in someone who has next to no track record and has been fired by a well-known chef?"

"You *do* have a track record, Juliette. You were practically a legend at the Culinary Institute, which is why Lucian hired you in the first place."

"Spoken like a mom," Juliette smiled affectionately at the woman she loved more than anyone, "but *legend* is overstating it more than just a little."

"Well whatever, you were awesome!" Amilia said, looking over the menu to decide what she wanted to order.

Once the waiter brought them each a glass of wine, Amilia decided it was time to put her plan in place. Juliette couldn't have played into her hands more if she'd scripted the conversation herself.

"You know how you mentioned that thirty is creeping up on you?" Amilia asked. "And now you've said that you're ready to get back into the 'chef game' but you're not sure how to move forward? Well, I have the solution for you."

Juliette saw the twinkle in her mom's eyes and shook her head and laughed. "What are you up to? I'm a bit terrified already."

Amilia reached into her purse and brought out a shoebox-sized gift-wrapped package and set it on the table.

"What's this?"

"It's an early birthday present so we have time to make plans before the actual big day."

Her mom had wrapped the box in printed paper and tied it with a scarlet ribbon. Juliette carefully pulled back the tape and unfolded the wrapping, which was covered in red poppies against a sea of wheat. Inside she found an antiquated looking cardboard box.

Intrigued, she slipped off the lid revealing a neat row of letters that looked ancient. She gently pulled one out.

The postmark was San Francisco, 1914 and was from her papa to her nonna. Juliette looked at her mom.

"It's a correspondence. Mostly between your nonna and one of her friends, but it begins in Italy with your grandfather writing to her, trying to lure her to marry him. They're beautiful. I want you to read them to get yourself in the mood for this..."

Amilia handed her daughter another, small slim box wrapped in matching paper and ribbon.

"Mom," Juliette smiled. "What are you doing?"

"It's for both of us. Open it and see."

Inside, tucked under a row of tissue paper were two tickets to Italy—one for each of them.

Juliette's sharp intake of breath said everything Amilia wanted to hear and she smiled, knowing her idea was perfect.

"I've always wanted to go!"

"I know. Now we can go together. We'll celebrate your birthday and explore. Heck, maybe we'll even take a cooking class. Wouldn't that be fun?"

"Fun? It would be amazing! Thank you mom. This is..." Juliette was at a loss for words.

"I know," Amilia touched her daughter's cheek. "We're going to love it."

As they left the restaurant an hour later, Amilia glanced over at Juliette.

She was proud of the lovely young woman walking

beside her. She still couldn't imagine how her youngest daughter had gotten so old. Almost thirty. It seemed like barely yesterday she was thirty herself. "You know it's all going to be OK, right?" She said, harkening back to the conversation they'd had earlier at the restaurant about Juliette's job.

"Yeah, I guess so," Juliette said in a mock defeatist voice.

Amilia's own mother had taught her to *create* happiness in life. To change things up if she wasn't where she wanted to be, and Amilia intended to impart the same wisdom to Juliette.

"Let's go get some coffee," Amilia said, nodding to a coffee house just across the street and looking at her watch. "I could use a perk up before I head back to San Francisco."

The sidewalks of Walnut Creek, the bustling little cosmopolitan gem east of San Francisco, were filled with people relaxing in outdoor restaurants, shopping, some walking to meetings, others drinking coffee in cafes. It was a warm late-September day with a hint of fall in the air. It was one of those sublime instances of perfection that imprinted on Juliette's mind while they waited for the signal to cross the street. She would always remember it as her last pure moment of peace.

E ven after reliving the horror that unfolded over and over again—sometimes in slow motion, often in quick terrifying flashes—Juliette still couldn't wrap her brain around it.

The crosswalk light had turned green just as Juliette noticed her shoelace was untied. She bent to quickly retie it then hurried to catch up to her mom who was only a few paces in front of her. Amilia had been saying something over her shoulder about Nonna Catarina when they heard the squealing of the tires.

The hooded eyes of the drunk driver looked sleepy and unconcerned about the devastation he was about to inflict. If she'd reacted sooner, Juliette thought she could have yanked her mom back, but she hadn't. Instead, she'd frozen in terror as the car plowed into Amilia, who was flung like a rag doll against the thick plate glass of a high-end kitchen store.

Amilia could tell she was dying by the odd lack of feeling in her body and the look of equal parts terror and horror on her daughter's face. She wanted so much to be able to tell Juliette it would be OK, that she loved her and if she was going to die, having spent the last few hours of her life with her was exactly how she would have chosen to spend them, but for some reason she couldn't make her mouth speak. She reached for her and squeezed her hand.

"Mommy, it's going to be all right," Juliette tried to reassure her. "Hang on, please hang on," she said and squeezed her hand back. "An ambulance is on the way. I can hear it. It's almost here. Don't let go of me."

Amilia looked into the eyes that exactly mirrored her own. She wanted to smooth her daughter's long, silky hair away from her face like she used to when Juliette was a little girl. She wished she could tell her one last time that she was perfect. She wanted to tell her to allow herself to be happy, to find love, to chase her dreams and not to worry about her failures. She tried to tell her with her eyes, but she couldn't hold them open any longer.

"Stay with me," Juliette implored. "You're strong, Mom. You can do it."

Amilia tried, but no matter how hard she willed herself to do so, she could feel herself losing the battle to stay and instead of getting coffee with her daughter and then going home to her husband, she knew instead she was going to Catarina. How apt, she thought, feeling surprisingly peaceful, that she had just been talking about her.

Chapter 3

CATARINA, MATEO, AND
AN UNEXPECTED LETTER

Market days, especially when Mateo came along, gave Catarina a sense of freedom—at least for a short time.

"What does Signora Carlucci want today?" Mateo asked, snatching the list out of Catarina's hand.

"Let's see," he read, "calamari—that sounds *delizioso*—asparagus, that will cost *una fortuna* at this time of year, and *pugliese* bread.

"How they eat!" he said. "Like kings, while we eat the same thing over and over again. Pasta…minestrone…prosciutto…pasta…minestrone…prosciutto. Maybe I could get invited over for dinner, huh?"

Catarina snickered, "I don't think that's going to happen," as she shook her head.

Mateo's attention was suddenly grabbed by a beautiful girl passing by.

"*La Bella Bianca*," he said to the young woman by way of greeting and bowed deeply as she passed.

She smiled at him shyly and then turned to Catarina. "*Buon giorno*, Catarina," Bianca said as she passed.

Catarina returned her greeting, then as soon as she was a distance away turned to her brother and laughed. "Don't torture her, Mateo. I think she dreams about you."

The girl was only fifteen, but she had been pestering Catarina about her older brother as long as Catarina could remember, although she never had the courage to even answer his greeting when he passed.

"Torture her? You're not serious. One day I'll *marry* her, you just wait. Then who will be laughing?" Mateo said.

"You truly want to marry her?" she raised her eyebrows, then paused to consider. "Not a bad idea, actually," she conceded. "After all, her papa runs the dry goods stall; you'd never be hungry."

"Always practical," he said. "And who will *you* marry?"

Catarina snorted. "Maybe Old Signor Garvagio," she snickered as a vision of their eighty-two-year-old neighbor came into her mind. Mateo laughed with her. "Not a bad idea, either. You'd be a widow by the time you were twenty. Then you'd have your own vineyard and your choice of young men willing to marry you for your land."

The two couldn't stop giggling at the thought until Mateo abruptly halted and smacked his forehead with the palm of his hand.

"I almost forgot," he told her. "A letter came today to Mama and Babbo about you. It's from the Brunellis. Do you remember them? They moved to America when we were little but came to visit that time."

"What do you mean a letter about *me*?"

"I don't know. Mama asked Babbo what was in the letter, and he said 'It's about Catarina.' And then I said, 'What about Catarina?' and then they both clamped their mouths shut and didn't utter another word."

"You're such a *buffone*, Mateo. I'm sure they asked about us all," she scoffed. "I do remember the Brunellis, though. They were nice. They brought us sweets and had two teenage boys. Do you remember? The younger's name is Julian or something. I remember him being very serious."

"Not Julian," corrected Mateo. "Not even close. His name is Franco. I heard Babbo say it twice before I got kicked out of the room."

When Catarina returned home that evening she found her mother silently scrubbing artichokes, tight-lipped and tense. Her father was nowhere in sight.

"*Buona sera,* Mama. Did you have a good day?"

"*Ciao, mia cara.* It was fine."

Catarina wondered if her mother would bring up the letter. Mateo's words had stuck with her all afternoon while she prepared the evening meal for the Carluccis. What did it mean? She had no idea. But, no, of course Mama wouldn't bring it up. Leave it to Mama, Catarina thought, to never volunteer any information. It was *come tirare i denti*, like pulling teeth, when it came to getting information out of her mother.

"Anything interesting happen?" Catarina asked, deciding to bring it up herself. "Mateo said there was a letter from America."

"That boy. Always snooping. Always pestering." Catarina's mother shook her head and wiped her hands on her apron, but she couldn't help but smile a little bit, because she did adore Mateo—snooping and all.

"If you must know, yes, we did have a letter from America," she said sighing. She stopped scrubbing and turned to face her daughter. Catarina noticed that she looked weary. Her eyes, which were usually sparkling with life, seemed dull and tired.

"From the Brunellis," her mother told her. "Do you remember them? You haven't seen them since you were a little girl."

"I think I remember. Franco was the son, right?"

"*Precisamente*," she said. "One of them, at least. He's a grown man now. A good man, I'm sure, but a man who lives very far away."

The thought of America always gave Catarina a thrill.

"The land of opportunity," she muttered. She had always heard that, but couldn't quite fathom what it meant exactly. She tried to picture it, but all she could imagine were people beautifully dressed and dances full of smiling, handsome men and lovely women. Always smiling with big white teeth. And the men in suits . . . not in work clothes out toiling in the fields like her babbo.

"Opportunity. Yes. That's what they say. But too far away for my liking," said her mother with uncharacteristic intensity. "Italy is our country. I don't want my family spread across so much space like seeds flung to the wind." Her mother was impassioned and threw her arm out as if she was in the act of it herself, then shook her head and crossed herself.

Catarina laughed and shook her head at her mother's irritable response. "You don't have to worry about that, Mama. No one's going away. We love Italy, too. It's our home."

Catarina's mama turned away and looked out the window.

"But what was in the letter? Was it something about me? Mateo said you and Babbo said it was about me."

"No . . . no, *cara*. It was nothing." She told her, waiving her hand dismissively, but Catarina noticed she didn't meet her eye. "The Brunellis just asked after you is all. Now shoo upstairs to freshen up before dinner. You look tired out."

"I am tired out. Signora Carlucci works me like a dog. She's nice, but she loves to order me around."

"And Signor Carlucci?" asked her mother. "Any more problems?"

"He scares me, Mama. I don't like the way he looks at me. And..."

"Keep your eyes averted."

"If only that worked. He doesn't care if I'm looking or not when he touches my thigh under the table when I'm serving dinner or 'accidentally' rubs against me when I'm walking down the hall. It's always when my arms are full of food from the market or laundry and I can't sidestep him fast enough."

It felt good to tell her mother the ugly secret. She hadn't said a word to anyone about it since the one disheartening attempt she'd made with her mother months ago.

"What? Is this true? He touches you?" her mother asked, the alarm in her voice mixed with fury. "*Oh, mio Dio!* I'm sorry I didn't listen when you tried to tell me before. I didn't understand you when you told me earlier. But if what you say is true, it's unacceptable. I'm going to have to talk to your father about this." Her mother pursed her lips and started to pull on her apron strings and go talk to Catarina's babbo.

"No, Mama! I don't know if that's a good idea." Catarina grabbed her mother's arm in alarm. "You know Babbo's temper.

You know how he can be!"

Her mama paused for a moment and stared out the window.

"Maybe you're right," said Mama. "Maybe this is best handled between us. We'll think of something. We'll put an end to this, I promise," she wrapped her arms around her daughter and hugged her tightly.

"But for now, keep yourself clear of him as much as you can," her mother said gravely, and then, with the sparkle suddenly back in her eyes, "and put some lye in his underwear next time you do the laundry. Then you can smile to yourself as you watch him squirm all day."

"Mama!" Catarina laughed and gave her mother one last squeeze. It felt good to have her back on her side. She had felt alone when her mother hadn't understood before.

"Now go." She made a motion to push Catarina upstairs. "Rest before dinner."

When the family was seated at the long, dark wooden dinner table, Catarina could feel her father's eyes on her. She glanced through the window at the vine-covered hills in the twilight, then back at her father. Each time she looked up, his intent gaze was focused on her face. Had her mother said something about Signor Carlucci after all? Catarina hoped not.

Then she noticed her mother shooting her father secret looks as she passed the eggplant, and Catarina sensed a certain frisson. She gazed at a crack in the plaster on the wall while she tried to calm herself, then she gave her mama a look that said, "Why did you tell him?" but her mother had barely shaken her head when her father cleared his throat, effectively silencing the boisterous conversation going on among

Mateo and Catarina's sisters and their husbands who were trading good-natured barbs at the far end of the dining table.

"We've had a letter from America," he said, puffed up and full of importance. Catarina felt her heart skip a beat. So, it was something after all. But she hardly knew the Brunellis. Why was her father acting like a simple letter was suddenly a family matter?

"And?" dared Mateo. The only one who would even think of pressing their father who usually took his sweet time to get a story out.

"As it turns out, Franco Brunelli is looking for a bride."

"So are all the bachelors in the world," snickered Lorena, one of Catarina's safely married sisters. "But they don't write letters about it. They go and pick whatever flower they like from the bouquet."

"Lorena, don't be *sbocatta*. Your smart mouth always got you into trouble," said another sister.

"This is different," Babbo continued, combing his fingers through his increasingly sparse hair. "The Brunellis live in America—in a place called San Francisco—but their son doesn't want to marry *una Americana*, who will never know the Italian ways. He wants a woman who will remind him of his roots. Of his true home. Someone who understands Italian customs and speaks the language."

"So, he should come to Italy. Stay a while and meet a nice Italian girl, marry her, and bring her back to San Francisco," Catarina's mother chimed in, a tone in her voice implying that something about Franco's situation was *ridicola*. But Catarina didn't see the problem. So, this Franco wanted to come meet an Italian woman to marry. It wasn't uncommon. Lots of men came back to Italy to marry. What did that have to do with their family?

They all looked at Catarina's father. A table full of questioning looks. His lined, weathered face seemed to be full of mischief.

"Is that what he wants? To stay here while he looks for a bride, Babbo?" Catarina asked.

"Well, no," he said. "He can't afford the time away from the family business," her father answered. "They're jewelers and work is busy. Signor Brunelli can't let Franco leave the store for a few months. So they have written to us for help," he spread his palms as if his friend was at the table with them.

"How are *we* supposed to help?" Mateo asked.

"*Allora*, they inquired after one of my beautiful and talented daughters," explained Catarina's father, as he looked at Catarina. Her fork stopped halfway to her mouth and looked around to see all eyes on her.

"He must be desperate!" laughed Mateo, trying to lighten the suddenly tense mood, but he shot Catarina a glance as if to say he was sorry even as the words came out of his mouth.

"Shut up, *idioto*!" Maddelana said, and cuffed her brother on the side of the head. "What are you talking about, Babbo?"

"Well, as you know, our family and the Brunellis go way back. Vittorio Brunelli was like a brother to me when we were young. His parents were like my second parents. We grew up together and when he moved away it almost killed me," he added dramatically.

Catarina's mother rolled her eyes good-naturedly at her husband's melodrama. He felt everything so strongly.

"So now, his youngest, Franco, wants a wife. It only makes sense that he turn to me, his best friend since childhood, to find a respectable girl for him. We have five daughters. Four are married. One is not."

At that statement all eyes again turned to Catarina. She felt the blood rush to her cheeks.

"Surely you don't mean for me to go off and marry some boy I only met once as a child?"

"Of course not, Catarina," said Babbo, as relief rushed over her, but then he followed with, "but, you *know* Franco. Don't you remember him? And he's not a boy anymore. He's a grown man. He has a business. He makes a good living."

Catarina looked at her father as if he were a stranger.

"I met him once when I was a little girl. Surely that doesn't count as 'knowing him.' Not like I know the boys from our village. Are you going to make me marry him? Are you sending me away?" she asked, anger and terror simultaneously flashing in her eyes.

"Catarina, don't listen to him!" interrupted her mother, who slapped her palm onto the table—a look of exasperation on her face. "I will not have my daughter moving to America and marrying someone we hardly know," she turned to her husband, "even if *you* have known his father since you were toddlers running in diaper cloths through the orchards."

"We would never force you, Catarina," Babbo told her, "but it's something to think about. Something for us to talk about," his face showing her just how serious he was. "You don't have a good opportunity here. We don't have much to offer to you, *mia cara*. You live in a poor house with a small orchard and have to work as a maid. Whomever you marry here might get sent away to fight when the war breaks out—and war is coming. I wish it weren't so," he said, glancing around the table at his sons-in-law, "but it is. And even if it doesn't happen, then what? You marry the son of another poor farmer and move to his house and take care of his mother while you get poorer and poorer?"

"Emiliano! Why are you saying this?" Catarina's mother gave him a meaningful look with a nod at their other girls, sitting around the table with their husbands, who all worked on either their families' land or their own. "These men are good, honest, hardworking men. If Catarina does so well, I, for one, will be proud."

"Celestina," Catarina's father answered back. "You know I have all the respect for our sons-in-law, but in America Catarina wouldn't have to work so hard. I've heard the roads there are all paved instead of made with stones, unlike most of the roads in our village. There are markets full of food, and she could go pick what she wanted off of the shelf."

"I think it's a great idea," Maddelana chimed in, agreeing with her father. She took her husband's hand. "I love our life here," she smiled at him, "but if we could go to America, we would go *imediatamente*." She paused, as an idea popped into her mind. "In fact," she looked at her youngest sister with hope in her eyes, "if Catarina goes, maybe she could sponsor us once she's married."

"I bet she could," her babbo answered. "As I said, the Brunellis are jewelers," he continued. "They live well in San Francisco. Franco makes a good living."

"But this is my home" Catarina stammered. "I wouldn't know anyone there. And what about Anna and Maria Nina?" Catarina thought of her two best friends. They knew everything about each other. They grew up together and always knew that they would marry boys from the village and raise their own children where they, themselves, grew up.

"If I left here, if I moved to America, I might not ever see you again," she said. And then immediately regretted it when both her parents looked away from her, instead of denying that it might be the case.

"You're going nowhere, Catarina," her mother said, and then scraped her chair back from the table and started collecting the dishes. Catarina and her sisters dutifully followed her lead, and the conversation ceased for the moment. But Catarina knew it was something she would ponder during the long, sleepless night.

She told herself she would stay. She would refuse to leave her home to marry Franco—whom she could barely remember. She strained to pull together a vision of him. She thought she remembered brown hair and brown eyes. That could be anyone. She sighed, wishing she could picture him.

But if she wasn't going to leave and marry Franco, she wondered whom she *would* marry. She hadn't thought much about it. Anna and Maria Nina talked about the boys in the village incessantly, while the three waited in line at the pump to fill the water pitchers for their families, but there was no particular boy with whom she could picture spending her life.

Catarina visualized a few she knew. There was Dominico Pescatore—who had the most potential. He was handsome and kind, but he was the son of a fish monger, and she didn't think she could stand to marry a man who was covered in fish blood all day.

There was Armondo Deluca, who was funny and made all the girls laugh when they were at town festivals, but his family was even poorer than Catarina's, and his mother was difficult. She thought every girl was out to catch her perfect son, and that no one was good enough for him. She shuddered at the thought of living out her life stuck in that household under the dour eye of Signora Deluca.

Paolo Eliodoro could be a good man to marry, and Catarina liked him, but Anna had been planning to marry Paolo since they were both children, and she would never get in the way of that.

Besides the problem of marriage, she believed what Babbo had said about the war coming was true. At least that was what she kept hearing whispered in town. What if all the boys from home were sent away to fight? Who would she be left with then? That night she finally fell into a restless sleep, but when she woke up, in spite of her concerns she was resolved. She would stay. It would work out for her here. She would make it work out in order to be with her family. She didn't care if she never married and worked as a maid her entire life. It would be better than being sent away.

Signor Carlucci's face suddenly flashed in her mind, but she pushed that aside. She would figure that out, too.

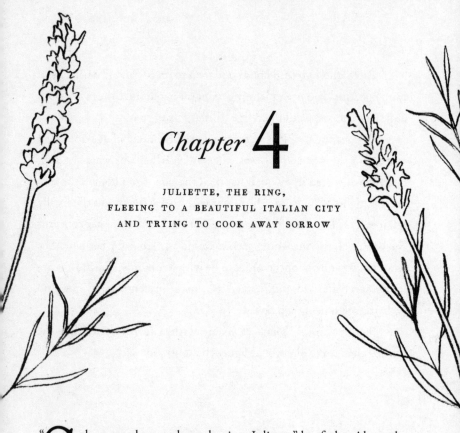

Chapter 4

"She wanted you to have the ring, Juliette," her father Alexander said, holding out the perfect diamond ring that had belonged first to her grandmother, then her mother, and now, horrifyingly too soon, to her.

Juliette looked over at Gina, sitting beside her at the table in her parents' kitchen, who nodded, obviously already having been told this news.

"Why me?" she asked, again looking at Gina who was older. Juliette had always assumed the ring would go to her.

"Mom left her share of the business to Gina," their father explained. "That's her heritage and connection to your grandparents. She left the ring to you so you would have a connection as well."

Juliette's hand shook as she took the ring from her father.

"I can visualize it on both of their hands," Juliette said, tears slipping down her cheeks. "I'm not ready for it to be mine. I want it to still be on Mom's finger."

"I know," her father said, and ran his hand over Juliette's long light-brown hair. It was shot through with gold threads and was a sharp contrast to her sister's loose dark brown curls that were so like their mother's. His two daughters were physically dissimilar and yet there was something that gave them away as sisters in spite of their differing looks.

Juliette was tall for the family—more lanky to Gina's petite frame that was like their mother's and grandmother's. Juliette took after the Brice side, whereas Gina looked like a Pensebene through and through. Except for their eyes, which they had each gotten from the opposite sides, to complete their heritage. Juliette's were the same as her mother, grandmother and great-grandmother, whereas Gina inherited her father's hazel eyes. The sisters were an interesting contrast, yet both beautiful in their own ways.

She had been feeling detached and numb since the accident. Sitting next to her father and holding hands with her sister Gina during her mother's memorial had felt surreal. The sorting and cleaning out of her belongings was even worse. It made the loss jaggedly permanent. Choosing some of her favorite things to keep seemed wrong, but her dad and Gina insisted so that there would be no regrets later about things lost or given away hastily in a moment of rash grief.

It had felt almost businesslike yet Juliette had felt like she was drowning.

During the weeks following Amilia's death, Juliette's mind often drifted towards the box of letters her mother had given to her. She had tucked the plane tickets inside the box with the letters when she had gotten home from the hospital after the accident, but hadn't been able to bring herself to open the lid since. The box sat on her bedside table, under a stack of novels, and she invariably found herself glancing over at it every night before she clicked off her light until finally one night she reached for it and slipped off the lid.

Juliette scooted herself up until she was leaning against the pillows by the headboard, took the tickets out, and ran her fingers over them, thinking about her mom's beautiful face when she had given her the early birthday present. They had both been so excited to go and had talked through travel ideas while they had eaten.

It felt like the world had tilted on its axis since that warm moment in the restaurant. Juliette took out the same letter she had looked at when her mother had given her the letters to read. It was from her grandfather to her grandmother when she still lived in Italy before they married. She gently slid the letter out of the envelope and unfolded it, looking at the words written in Italian. She lifted the letter to her face and inhaled, but she only smelled paper and ink—all traces of her grandmothers' scent long gone.

Juliette had been fairly fluent in Italian when she was younger and her grandparents had spoken to her in the language. She had loved the sound of it and had taken it in college as well, but hadn't said a peep in Italian for years. Nonetheless, she was pleased to see that she could make out most of the words in the letter, even though the language style was from another era.

That night, Juliette only got through the first few paragraphs before the tears blurring her vision became too much to continue. She carefully replaced the letter in its envelope, making sure not to get the paper wet from her tears, and then turned out the light. A huge, full moon shined through the window and she wondered what life had been like for Nonna Catarina when she received the letter from her grandfather.

The door chimed as Juliette walked into the Pensebene jewelry store and waved to Gina.

"What a nice surprise," her sister said, and came to give her a hug. "Come in and sit down."

"I brought us coffee," Juliette said, handing her sister a latte from their favorite indie coffee place.

"Yum, thanks," she said and took a sip. "Mmmm, perfect."

Juliette set her bag down and plopped onto one of the stools at the counter while she looked around.

"The place looks great, Gina."

"Thanks, but I haven't changed anything."

"That's part of what looks great. I love the fact that I can come here and besides a few updates over the years, it always looks the same. How many times have I sat in this chair, for instance? I can't even count the number."

Gina looked at Juliette with a mixture of curiosity and concern.

"I used to love sitting here, watching Mom and Grand-dad working on designs. And now I can come and watch you, too. It's nice. Unusual in this day and age."

"Are you OK, Juliette?"

"What do you mean? I'm fine. I just stopped by because I met a friend for lunch at the Ferry Building and had some extra time to come by and say hello."

"Oh, nice," she smiled. "Have you been sleeping any better?"

"No," Juliette said, looking away. "The moon was really beautiful last night, though. I must have stared at it for hours."

"That's something, I guess," Gina gave her sister a sympathetic look.

"Do you remember the box of letters I told you about? The ones Mom gave me the day of the accident?"

"Yeah."

"I read part of the first one last night. It was amazing reading words written from Papa to Nonna, knowing it was from such a long time ago. How much life happens and then. . . gone."

Gina glanced at Juliette again, not at all sure her sister was coping. She sometimes worried that Juliette's neck and shoulder muscles had become completely rigid from the tension in her body since the accident.

"Do you mind if I keep them?" Juliette asked.

"The letters? Not at all. My Italian's horrible anyway, but let me know if you discover anything juicy," she smiled, thinking of their grandparents.

"Mom said it's mostly between Nonna and a friend of hers."

"Maybe Nonna was leading a double life. Or was a spy during World War I."

"I wouldn't put it past her," Juliette said.

Gina frowned again at Juliette's lost look and asked, "Why are you biting your thumbnail and staring into space?"

"I'm just having a thought," she answered, thinking about the plane ticket tucked inside the box of letters.

B efore Juliette told her family about her plans, she enrolled in the Italian cooking class she'd been coveting for ages so she had a justifiable reason to leave. She knew that would help convince her dad and sister that she would be all right and that she wasn't truly going off the deep end. It would give her days an anchor. She knew they'd been worried about her. They were convinced she was still in shock and Juliette guessed they were right, but whether she was or wasn't didn't make a difference as far as she could tell. It was simply a label; but what did it mean from a practical standpoint? It's not like she could jumpstart herself into feeling normal again. Nothing could bring her mother back.

At home she couldn't sleep because when she closed her eyes she could see the car coming and feel the same horrifying sensation of being rooted in place, watching it happen. She would turn, wanting to react, but would be frozen while the car careened toward her mother again and again. She saw the impact over and over. She hated being able to remember what was on display in the store, as if her mind cemented those details in place while she simultaneously saw her mother being hit by the car, flung at the window, and finally land on the ground.

So she'd decided to flee from the sympathetic eyes of her friends and family, her in-law studio, the catering job she hated anyway, and enrolled in a cooking class in Italy to get some breathing room. If she could breathe again, and sleep, she thought maybe she could come to terms with what had happened.

N ow, weeks later, while Juliette was still mourning the loss of her mom, the ring rested on the middle finger of her right hand as she swung open the heavy black door to the flat she'd rented in Lucca, Italy. Juliette had decided to wear it always as a symbol of strength and perseverance. She thought her nonna, who was the first to wear it, would have wanted it that way. She subconsciously twirled it for strength as she peeked through the open door. She was exhausted as she dragged her heavy suitcase inside and looked around the tiny apartment she'd be calling home for the next six months.

Juliette stepped over the suitcase and let her eyes adjust to the interior light of her subleased apartment. It was dimmer than outside, but sunbeams streamed through a window that opened out onto a metal balcony spilling over with scarlet geraniums. She walked in further and was relieved to see that the apartment was more than fine. It had a tiny kitchen with a two-burner stove that would probably be deemed an illegal fire hazard at home, but seemed a perfect fit here. The bathroom was miniscule and entirely covered—including the floor and ceiling—in orange seventies-era tile, and the showerhead stuck out of the side wall with no enclosure, but she didn't care.

The wooden floors of the main room were laid in a traditional herringbone pattern and the walls were an off-white plaster with photographs of the surrounding sights. Thankfully there were no bugs in sight. The furnishings consisted of a small, round, dark-gray marble table with two black-painted wooden chairs by the window, a red linen sofa and a tall, beautiful, dark-chocolate colored armoire that made the room look richly furnished, in spite of its small size.

The armoire was exactly the type of piece her mom would have loved. She sighed, running her hand along the smooth wood. When she tried to open it, she realized it had a false front. What looked like drawers at the bottom and cupboard doors at the top was actually one large door that pulled open and inside was a Murphy-style pull-down bed.

Tucked onto shelves at the top of the armoire were sheets and a heavy down duvet with a plain white linen cover that smelled of lilac and starch. The fluffy down was thicker than she had ever encountered at home and the thought of snuggling under it was exactly what she wanted to do in her travel-weary, emotionally-exhausted state.

She liked the look of the apartment. It would be a cozy place for her for the next half year, where she could avoid soothing words and pep talks.

She went back down the steep stone staircase and brought up two smaller suitcases, dropped them in the middle of the room, pulled down the bed, made it, flopped down in her clothes, and was asleep instantly and dreamlessly for the first time in the seven weeks since the accident.

She awoke, disoriented, to the sound of Italian being shouted outside her window and the realization that she was starving. The angle of the sun told her she'd slept for hours and it was now afternoon. She sat up and looked at the clock, then kicked off the covers, threw her clothes into the corner, and took a long, hot shower.

While she shampooed her hair, she did a quick calculation and realized that because of traveling and the time change, she had skipped breakfast and lunch altogether and was now way overdue for a meal. She remembered the pastry she'd eaten half of at the train station, which she could finish now to tide her over, but she wanted some real food and soon. She had seen an open-air market in the main piazza from the taxi window on her way from the train station to her apartment and hoped the vendors were still open.

She would need to set up her kitchen and make dinner, so once she was out of the shower and dressed, she used the back of her train ticket to scratch out a grocery list of milk, tea, coffee, garlic, thyme, artichokes, cheese, wine, and bread among other essentials.

She quickly dried her hair, then threw it into a ponytail and ventured out to stock her kitchen. She thought she might even pick up some flowers to make it cheerful inside. She meandered back to the market she'd seen with only two wrong turns, which for the directionally-challenged Juliette was a triumph. As she walked under the stone arch that formed the entrance, she noticed that the piazza she'd spied was not the main "square" at all, but a circle. It was surrounded by shops and restaurants, strewn with parked bicycles here and there, and hosted a large farmer's market, which was the perfect place to begin. It was good to be someplace altogether different where she could focus on new sights and sounds instead of on her sadness and unbridled fury at both the out-of-control driver and herself.

Chapter 5

CATARINA, HER FIRST DECISION
AND HER SECOND DECISION

Catarina hefted her heavy, brown, chipped, ceramic water jug and scooted it along towards the well. Hers was just one in a short line of vessels waiting to be filled at the pump. She, Anna, and Maria Nina got their best gossiping done while they waited to fill their families' water urns with the rest of the women in the village, who managed to pump water and visit with their closest friends at the same time. On hot summer days, they fanned themselves while they sweltered and chatted, and in the cold of winter they—wrapped in shawls, thin cloth coats and hand-knitted sweaters—exchanged confidences while extracting the water their families needed from the old, creaky pump.

"My eyes were open all night," Catarina whispered, after telling them about the letter with the marriage proposal. She had lain awake until she could sense the morning near and even then was only able to sleep fitfully for a couple of hours. She had mulled over each and every possible bachelor she knew of in the region, and although she acknowledged that her Babbo was right, her prospects were grim, she still came to the conclusion that she would rather stay and be with her family and friends in a poor village with no suitors, than go live among strangers in another country—even one she had heard was the land of riches.

When she woke from her fitful sleep, her eyes were red and scratchy, but she was resolute. She avoided Mama and Babbo for the morning, though, making sure neither could get her alone, and rushed to meet her two close friends at the well.

Even though she had no intention of accepting the proposal, Catarina enjoyed being the center of attention for just a little while. After all, there was hardly any excitement in the village, so why not give her friends something interesting to talk about for once?

The well pump and trough were attached to a stone wall at the village center and for the last three years it had been Catarina's chore to get up and out early each morning, rain or shine, to go fetch the water. She brought the family's hand cart and two large, empty ceramic urns, which she would fill and haul back to her house.

"I would never go," Anna insisted after hearing the proposition. "They couldn't drag me away!" She helped Catarina hoist the first of her heavy, now-full urns onto the cart.

"What if your babbo ordered you?" asked Maria Nina, who leaned against the wall awaiting her turn. "Never mind. It doesn't matter." She shook her head at Anna. "You're a fool, Anna, so why try to reason with you?"

Anna frowned while they watched Catarina pump water into her second water jug. Anna was mild mannered and quiet. She had fine, golden-blond hair that was unusual for a southern Italian girl. It contrasted beautifully with her warm olive complexion and light-brown eyes. Her demure personality, however, was at odds with her dramatic coloring: the thought of changing her life had never entered her mind.

"Catarina, you must go," Maria Nina implored. Her personality was the opposite of Anna's. Of the three friends, Maria Nina was the most outgoing, the quickest to find mischief to get into, and the boldest about flirting with the boys in the village. Like Catarina, she had dark, wavy hair and a slim figure, but her eyes were a warm chocolate brown and she had an elegant, Roman nose. Both Maria Nina and Anna were taller than Catarina, who somehow managed to appear strong in spite of her small stature.

"It would be a mistake to stay here," Maria Nina continued to encourage her friend. This time it was she who helped Catarina lift and place the second jug onto the cart. She then took her own turn at the pump, and began the laborious task of filling her own family's water urns.

"There's nothing for us here but some old olive trees and withering grapevines," she said as her arms moved up and down with the pump lever. "You could live an exciting life in America. You would be in a big city. I bet they have dances every night." Her eyes looked into the distance, visualizing it.

"Now who's the fool?" Anna laughed. "Dances every night! Ha. I'm sure Catarina would still have to work hard in San Francisco. But instead of taking care of the Carlucci household and seeing her family every day, she'd have to take care of some stranger's house and live with people she doesn't even know. What if they're cruel? What if they won't let her ever come back to visit?"

"It doesn't matter, so stop arguing," Catarina told them. "I'm not going. I'm staying right where I am, so I can become an old lady with you two. I'm not leaving my family. I'm not leaving my country. "

She looked around the square, beyond the houses and stores to the orchard and hillsides where the olive trees and grape vines had been planted hundreds of years before. To Catarina, they were beautiful. They dictated the seasons of life: whether it was the green leaves of spring, wet with raindrops; the heavily laden grape vines of summer; the autumn harvest and crush; or the bare, dormant plants of winter. They spoke to her and she couldn't imagine life away from their rhythm. While in the back of her mind she did feel excitement at the thought of a big city, that alone wasn't enough to sway her resolve.

It didn't matter, she told herself. She would stay. She knew it would be difficult to go against Babbo, but he said he wouldn't force her to leave and she intended to hold him to that. She would tell them right away, she decided, so she gave both of her friends kisses on their cheeks, took the handles of her cart and wheeled her water jugs across the cobblestone square and back to her front door.

On the way back home, her resolve began to melt. She pictured her sister's face when she brought up the idea of Catarina being able to help give other family members the opportunity to move there as well. Was she being selfish? She trusted her father's opinion. She knew he was worried about the family being caught up in the war. She wondered if she should respect his wishes about going. By the time she opened the front door and unloaded the water urns, she was thoroughly confused.

She had planned to tell them that she would absolutely stay. Now she wasn't so sure.

She decided to spend the day thinking about it and then brought it up again with her father at dinner. Instead of the calm, reasonable Babbo of the evening before, she found her father impassioned on the subject.

"*Oh, mio Dio*," he practically yelled while waiving a fork twirled with spaghetti. "You will be wasting your life here if you don't go! There are no suitable men for you to marry," he began, and then continued with, "War is coming. Mark my words; this will be no place for a beautiful young girl when that happens."

He huffed while Catarina and her mother waited for him to cool down. After his final onslaught of, "Even if you find someone to marry here, he will probably be killed in the fighting," Catarina's mother, Celestina, had put up with enough.

"For the love of the Virgin, Emiliano," she interrupted, "enough about fighting and death. Our girl is staying. Besides," she pretended to be objective, "there are good men here. After all, this is where I found the love of *my* life," she smiled, trying to cajole him back to being reasonable, "and I'm sure Catarina will, too."

She was equally determined. Her youngest child would stay.

Catarina knew she would disappoint her father if she stayed, which weighed heavily on her. She knew he wanted her to have more opportunity than she would if she stayed—even though he would miss her dearly. She also knew deep down that he was right. But her heart was at home with her family. She tried to convince him that she would be happy if she stayed, but as the days passed, she began to wonder if she was trying to convince him or herself.

Every time she decided to say "no" to the proposal a jolt passed over her heart. She couldn't help but wonder if she would be missing her one chance. But when she thought about saying "yes" her heart would pound with a sense of dread, especially at leaving her mother and Mateo.

"I don't know what to do, Mama," Catarina said one morning, while making herself a cup of strong *caffè* before leaving for work at the Carlucci's.

"We don't know what the future will bring. We can only do what we think will be best, Catarina." She smiled at her daughter and gave her arm a squeeze as she poured milk into Catarina's *caffè latte*.

"How could I ever leave you?"

"I don't want you to, but no matter what happens I know you'll make a happy life, whether you stay or go, because you are a happy person. That's one of your gifts."

"Thank you, Mama," she said and hugged her before leaving.

It would definitely be easier to be happy, she mused, as she reluctantly walked to her employer's house, if only I could change this one circumstance. She sighed as she arrived, and slowly turned the knob to enter. The Carlucci's home, which was connected to the other houses on the street, was tall and narrow, with windows facing out to the curved cobbled lane. There were boxes of flowers in the front windows and a dour black-painted front door. It painted a sharp contrast with her stone farmhouse. The Carlucci residence was dim and formal with heavy carved furniture, woven rugs and ancestral paintings on the walls. The Pensebene home was sun filled and warm. There was no money for paintings on the walls, but to Catarina that was fine, because each window framed a view of the olive orchard or the hills, which she preferred to the stoic, unsmiling faces looking out from the frames in her employer's house.

As she entered, she involuntarily cringed when she saw Signor Carlucci sitting at the table with no sign of Signora Carlucci.

"*Buon giorno*, Signor Carlucci," she said.

"*Buon giorno,* Catarina," he replied with a formal air. "Signora Carlucci is away for the day. Her sister has fallen ill and she is tending her."

"I'm sorry to hear that, Signor. Did she leave instructions for me?"

"I see laundry," he said and waved his hand at a heap of clothes and sheets stuffed into a wicker basket.

"*Grazie, Signor.*" She picked it up and hauled it out to the courtyard. She poured water into the trough the family used for laundry and began to rub the clothes with soap. She hummed a tune while she scrubbed, content to be outside in the fresh air and away from Signor Carlucci, even if it was her least favorite task.

She rinsed one of the signora's nightgowns, picked up two clothes pins, and placed them in her mouth to hold them while she lifted it to the line. She turned to hang it and was suddenly grabbed from behind. She gasped clenching on the clothespins that were still between her lips.

Two firm hands were around her. One painfully squeezed her breast, the other hand roughly turned her face so she could see her assailant.

She tried to shriek when she met Signor Carlucci's eyes, but was stopped by the wooden clothespins stuck to her lips. She was able to spit them out but no sooner had they hit the ground than his mouth was covering hers. His breath was stale with coffee and his tongue thrust between her lips.

She gagged and jabbed her elbow into his ribs. He grabbed her wrist and twisted.

"Don't try to fight me, Catarina," he huffed with the exertion of trying to control her. "You might as well cooperate," he hissed. "And if you do, I'll see that the signora rewards you. But if you fight me, you'll lose anyway, and I'll tell my wife that you're *una putana* who flaunted yourself in front of me and you'll be out on your ear."

"No one will believe you!" she hissed back as she desperately tried to break free from his grasp. "Why would they?" She wriggled her wrist free of his grip and managed to slap his face and then lunged for the door.

He grabbed the back of her dress and she toppled down, smashing her kneecap against the smooth stones. Pain shot up her leg.

She gasped as he grabbed a handful of her hair and wrapped it around his fist, holding her in place.

The pain in her knee was searing and her head was being held back by his fist in her hair. She managed to arch her back enough so she could turn to the side to see his face, and what she saw etched on his features turned her insides cold. It was a smirk. As if he had already won. That look startled her out of her terror and turned her emotions to rage.

"I will not be your whore!" she yelled into his face.

Although he was still behind her, she twisted further to the side and crushed her elbow into his face. She could feel the cartilage in his nose give way and blood spurted onto her dress.

He involuntarily let go of her hair, and in the moment it took for him to grab his nose, she was up and running from the laundry lines outside, and back through the house to escape. She threw the twisted sheet she had been pinning up when he grabbed her as well as a basket with wet clothes into his path as she went by, and then ran to the front door and desperately fumbled with the lock. She could hear his footsteps rushing toward her but didn't dare lose time by looking over her shoulder. She threw open the door and slammed it as she passed to slow him down. She could hear Signor Carlucci yelling after her but all she focused on was the sound of pounding. She didn't know whether it was her heart or the sound of her shoes on the cobblestones.

She ran. Her one desire was to get home where she would be safe. She didn't realize she was crying until her vision blurred and she had to wipe her streaming nose. Her side felt as if a searing hot knife was piercing her skin and her lungs were heaving. She looked over her shoulder and saw that she wasn't being followed so she slowed and came to a stop, panting.

She ducked into a side alley and crouched for a moment to catch her breath, but kept hidden in case he came after her. She put a shaking hand on her chest to calm herself. Her breath and the pounding of her heart slowed, but as soon as she was able to catch her breath, she was out of the alley and running again. As she entered the main piazza she saw her mother in the distance walking among others across the square. It was like seeing an island of safety: the most welcome sight of all.

"Mama!" she screamed and her mother turned towards her, a look of shock on her face. She could hear the panic in her own voice but couldn't calm down. She ran to her mother and threw herself into her arms. And as soon as she was there, she began to sob.

"Catarina!" her mama shrieked. "What happened?"

She took in her daughter's appearance and immediately knew. Her disheveled hair was a tangle and her dress was ripped, askew, and splattered in blood.

"*Oh, mio Dio!* Catarina." She took Catarina's face in her hands and looked in her eyes. "Did he…?" But she couldn't bring herself to ask the question and immediately steered Catarina away from curious eyes. She couldn't stand to think of anyone violating her daughter. Her most precious girl. But she also had to protect her from town gossip—which could be almost as damaging as a physical assault.

"No…I got away from him. He grabbed me but I fought him, Mama. I think I broke his nose," she said, thinking of the crunch under her elbow and the splatter of blood.

"Let's get you home." Celestina wrapped her arms protectively around her daughter and walked with her, carefully blocking her from the view of people passing by.

When they reached their house, they went straight up to Catarina's room. Celestina sat her on the bed and went to get a basin of water. She came back with a cloth and warm water and with gentle hands wiped her daughter's tear-streaked face and scraped knees. She helped her out of her torn and blood-splattered dress and soaked it in the basin to loosen the blood. While Catarina sat in her slip, her mother gently combed out her hair and they began to talk.

"What will I do, Mama?"

"I'm not sure yet, but we're going to have to tell your babbo. That's clear to me now."

"He said he'd tell everyone I'm a *putana*. That I threw myself at him—and he, a married man. He'll shame us."

"We won't let that happen. We're a respected family, too." Her mother's words were firm, but Catarina saw that she looked away to brush aside a tear of her own.

"You know what I'm thinking, Catarina?" she said after a few moments of silence.

"No."

"I'm thinking that if we talked to Father Pinzano about this, just maybe he would say it's the sign we needed to finally make our decision about whether you should go. Maybe this is the Virgin hitting us over the head to say you shouldn't stay here. That you should go to San Francisco, where this won't happen to you."

"What? Let Signor Carlucci, that *porco*, ruin my home for me?"

"It's not just about this. Senior Carlucci's threats don't frighten me. We can take care of him, *cara*. I don't want you to go, it's true, but what I know deep in my heart is that you should go. It would be better for you there. I want what is best for you. You're the sunshine in my day. You're precious. And that's why I *have* to let you go."

"Mama…," Catarina started to speak, but paused to wipe another tear. "I wanted to convince myself that I should stay, because I don't want to be away from you. But deep down, I think you're right. I should go. I've been frightened, but then when this happened today . . . I think . . . maybe it *is* a sign."

She started to cry and hugged her mother as if she were being torn away at that very moment. The words she said were muffled against the cloth of her mother's dress.

"I should go."

After Catarina and Celestina talked, her mother settled her into bed for a rest and quietly left the house. She made her way to the Carlucci home and then lifted the heavy metal knocker and rapped it against the front door. Signor Carlucci opened the door—his eyes widening slightly when he saw Catarina's mother standing on the threshold, but he recovered quickly and kept his features bland.

"Signor Carlucci," she said, taking in his bruised nose with some element of satisfaction, "I'd like a word."

Signor Carlucci opened the door and motioned her in.

"Would you like a seat?" he asked, gesturing to a chair, his mask of superiority firmly in place.

"No, I would not sit in this home," Celestina spat out her words. "Instead I'll come right to the point. My daughter will no longer be working in this household."

"Catarina told me what you did. And I want you to know this: I know every woman in this village and we talk. And if you say a word against her, I'll tell every one of them what you did to Catarina today—starting with your wife."

"I don't know what you're talking about, Signora. I've done nothing. I'm a respectable man," he laughed mirthlessly and waved his hand as if dismissing her words.

"Maybe you're a businessman and I'm just a farmer's wife, but our family has been here for generations. I saw Catarina with my own eyes as she ran through the square trying to get away from you. And then, of course, your broken nose speaks for itself, " she gestured to his face— a falsely sweet smile on her lips and her eyebrows raised in challenge.

"What is it that you want from me, exactly, Signora?" he asked, as if giving in to a troublesome child, a sigh of resignation escaping him.

"What I want is for you to keep your ugly lies to yourself. Don't you dare speak my daughter's name in this village or anywhere. *Capisci*?"

"I'm sure I have no idea what you're talking about, but if you hear any talk against Catarina, you can be assured, it didn't come from me. I can't speak for any other man that little tease might provoke," he sneered.

Before she realized what was happening, Celestina reached out and slapped his face. It was as if her hand acted on its own, but it felt good to slap the sneer off of him.

"Don't," she said, and with that, let herself out.

She wiped her hand on her skirt as if to remove any trace of contact with the loathsome man. Catarina would be gone in a few months, and then, once she knew she was safely away, she would casually drop a word or two to her friends at the water pump about Signor Carlucci, just to make sure that this never happened to any other girls in the village.

She sighed and made her way home to start cooking dinner for her family. She thought about losing Catarina to America and Franco Brunelli, and for the first time felt not fear but hopefulness for the life her daughter would lead.

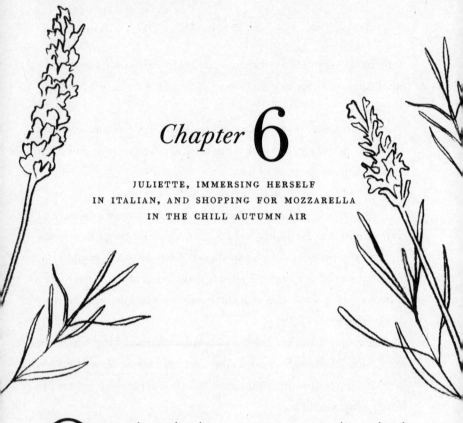

Chapter 6

O ut in the market, large crimson canvas tote bag in hand, Juliette wove her way along the market stalls. Taking in new sights and sounds was a welcome distraction—even exciting—but the smells were what she found intoxicating. The aromas of pungent cheese and heavy-scented flowers filled the chilly late-autumn air and woke up her senses. She was suddenly seeing things vividly again after the haze she'd been in since the accident: as if her senses had woken up when the plane touched down in Italy, during the train ride from the Florence airport to Lucca while passing olive orchards and vine-covered hillsides, and finally during her long, dreamless sleep.

She walked up to a cheese stall and stood back, observing the huge variety. She was shy to dive in and speak the language after realizing how rusty she'd been while trying to communicate at the train station.

As she hesitated, a man walked by, accidentally brushing her arm as he approached the vendor.

"*Mi scusi, Signorina,*" he said, turning to Juliette with a smile.

The response Juliette was forming in her mind immediately left her consciousness and only a confused sound came out of her mouth.

The man was absolutely beautiful as only Italian men can be.

"*Ciao, Roman,*" the cheese vender smiled and clapped the man on the back in a friendly manner. "*Come stai?*"

"*Bene, bene.* I need some cheese for my class this week, Vito," he said in rapid-fire Italian. "The new term is beginning, so we're going to start with something simple. I'm thinking about gorgonzola because I don't want to intimidate the students. Polenta with gorgonzola. How does that sound?"

Juliette stood to the side, trying to comprehend the words he was saying to get her brain into Italian mode. She enjoyed listening to the rich language being spoken all around her. It revived early childhood memories of spending the night at her grandparents' house and gradually wakening in the morning to the murmur of Italian being spoken in the kitchen, but that was more than a few years ago and she worried about being able to keep up with the torrent of words rushing at her.

She purposefully focused on the cheeses in front of her instead of looking at the two men speaking. They spoke quickly so Juliette didn't quite catch all of what they said, but the phrases she picked up, while pretending to look around the stall, seemed to indicate that the younger man buying the cheese was some sort of chef, which piqued her curiosity further.

While the gorgonzola discussion continued in Italian, a younger woman who also worked at the cheese stall—instantly reminding Juliette of Julia Ormand in one of her early films—stepped up to help.

Juliette had decided on some mozzarella. She was in the mood for crusty bread with mozzarella slices and olive tapenade to go with a roasted artichoke. Even though she was quite accomplished at sophisticated Italian dishes, Juliette's real love was basic peasant food.

She gathered her courage and spoke to the young woman in Italian, and was rewarded with a smile and plenty of encouragement.

The younger man stopped speaking and turned towards Juliette again with a look of interest before turning back to the vendor to finish his purchase.

She felt her face flush. She was afraid she had made a fool of herself with her imperfect accent, but she decided to keep going in Italian anyway.

She looked away from him and back to the woman who leaned towards Juliette.

"Watch out for that one," she whispered in heavily accented English and winked.

Juliette waved her hand to indicate that the last thing she was looking for was romance.

"He is handsome, no?"

"*Si*, in a different way than American men."

"*Sei americana?*"

Juliette nodded and reached across the stall to shake hands and introduce herself. "I'm Juliette Brice. I just moved here."

"A pleasure to meet you, Juliette. I'm Odessa Savelli."

"Nice to meet you," Juliette responded. "Odessa is a beautiful name, but isn't it French? How did you come by it?"

"Simple, really. My mother's French and my father's Italian," she smiled. "Maman's family also makes artisan cheese, so when my parents met at a seminar for cheese makers, it was a match made in heaven."

Juliette couldn't help but admire her accented English. The way Odessa spoke made everything she said seem more interesting.

"Well, I'm glad to have met you, and thank you for your help today," Juliette said as she tucked her mozzarella into her bag.

"It was my pleasure, Juliette. Hopefully I'll see you here next week." Odessa's natural warmth added to the invitation and Juliette felt like she'd made a potential friend. As she walked away, she wondered why some people were immediately drawn together with an instant sense of familiarity and companionship while others could be known for eons and yet remain distant. She instinctively knew Odessa was the former and that she'd be back to see her again.

She left the stall and worked her way around the market picking up artichokes here, bread there, flowers, soap, milk, tea and coffee. As the sun began to sink and the air to cool, she had two items left on her list and an aching shoulder from the weight of carrying everything she'd bought. She still needed olives and olive oil. She hadn't seen any stalls selling either, so she stepped into a corner store with a window display touting several olive oil varieties. When she emerged with her shopping complete, the square was emptying out. She saw Odessa from afar and gave her a smile and a wave, which was returned, as she headed towards her apartment. Then she saw the chef as well, talking and laughing with other local men. She smiled, wondering about him. He seemed nice, she thought. But, as she rounded the corner on her way back to her cozy home, her contemplation ended and she returned to her new kitchen to make dinner and unpack.

J uliette woke with a start. In her dream, the car was speeding towards them and she knew she couldn't stop it on time. She sat up covered in sweat, light shining in the window. Her alarm hadn't gone off yet and for a fleeting moment she had no idea where she was. But then she looked around the tiny apartment and a small glimmer of excitement replaced the initial confusion and emotional pain. She rolled over, liking the slightly coarse, foreign feeling of the starched white sheets. She stretched and peeked out the window from her bed and saw clear blue skies. She inhaled deeply, threw off the duvet, and stepped out of bed, pleased to be somewhere new instead of facing the same four walls she'd been bleakly staring at for the previous seven weeks. Her bare feet met the cold floor and she scrambled to the bathroom.

While she showered, she purposely shoved thoughts of the accident into a corner of her mind where she could squelch them as much as possible. Denial was her plan during her time in Italy. She hoped it worked.

Once she was out of the shower, Juliette dressed in comfortable-but-cute faded jeans and a long-sleeved casual tee shirt—her preferred "uniform" for the first day of cooking school so that splatters of food would be nothing to worry about.

Walking around Lucca the previous afternoon had been interesting. She felt like a veritable giant compared to the Italian women.

She could just see her mother and her grandmother fitting in perfectly among the population of this country, whereas at home they were tiny. In California, Juliette's five foot seven was nothing remarkable, but here it was quite tall.

She stepped into her diminutive sun-filled kitchen and put on the kettle to boil water. The strange coffee press that came with her apartment was more medieval contraption than coffee maker. Juliette spent about ten minutes trying to take it apart and figure it out and even then she wasn't sure that it was going to work, but she gamely spooned in the coffee grounds she had picked up from the market, put them in the top part, which looked like some tiny version of an old-fashioned percolator and drenched them in the scalding water. She steamed some milk and mixed the two together creating a passable *caffè latte*. An unabashedly heaping spoonful of sugar made it complete. Heady from her small victory, Juliette leaned against the counter and took the first large sip, then turned one of her chairs to face the window and sat down to enjoy her coffee.

She wished she had made the leap of faith to leave her job and pursue her dream of Italy and cooking school under better circumstances, but she believed her mom would have been proud that she had either way. She hoped her mom would have been happy she'd gone to Italy alone to at least make something good happen from something terrible.

Juliette glanced at the box of letters she'd brought with her. She had been intrigued by them from the moment she had opened the lid. Juliette planned to read them while she was in Italy, where her nonna had grown up. She was looking forward to getting a glimpse into her grandmother's past.

Because she'd woken at the crack of dawn, she was way ahead of schedule and was tempted to slip a letter out of its old, faded envelope, but she decided to wait until later when she could take her time with the Italian. Instead, she finished her coffee and blew her hair dry, then twisted it back in her standard work-style knot. She knew a few strands would undoubtedly escape by the end of the day, but at least it was secured to start. She put on a little makeup, and after eating her breakfast was ready to walk to the school. She knew from looking at the map that it was just inside of the ancient walled section of Lucca. The photo showed a white limestone building, with an arched entry. It looked to her like it was simply the first in a larger row of shops and businesses but she would know soon enough.

Juliette ventured out, map in hand, toward the address of the school. Along the way she peeked into numerous cafés with patrons lined up at the bar, sipping espressos out of tiny cups. The women were fashionable and the men were as coiffed and heavily scented as the women.

She turned a corner and came to an abrupt stop.

"Uh oh," she murmured, because she was sure she had walked by the same street before.

I hate this about myself, she thought. Why do I always get lost? A familiar sense of panic lodged itself in her chest.

Juliette looked at the street signs and studied the map. She had thought she was on track, and couldn't figure out where she had gone wrong. She took her bag off of her shoulder and set it down next to her while she leaned against a building to try and sort it out.

She finally saw where she had missed a turn so she started walking again, but decided to pick up the pace.

Pulling her cell phone out of her pocket to check the time, Juliette willed herself to remain calm.

What's the worst thing that could happen? she asked herself. She might be late, but it wouldn't be the first time and she would live through it.

Turning the corner, she saw the sign ahead for the street she was looking for and exhaled a breath she hadn't realized she had been holding. One more turn and then she would be there. Checking her phone again, she realized she had seven minutes left before class started, so she slowed her pace to a casual stroll to give herself time to stop panting before entering the classroom.

As she passed through the front door she was dazzled by a gleaming industrial kitchen with two long tables—one per side, set at angles, and surrounded by stools. The cooktop was set into a counter between the two tables and had a huge mirror hanging above it, so students could easily see the techniques being demonstrated. In addition, there were a few rows of stadium-type seats facing the kitchen, to allow for larger groups to view the cooking exhibitions. It was decidedly different from the old-fashioned kitchen she had expected, but she was delighted with it. If the instruction was as stellar as the equipment, she knew she was in for a treat.

Others had already arrived, so she followed suit and chose a seat next to a woman who looked about her age. She presumed she was a fellow student and nodded to her.

As soon as she settled into her seat, the door opened again and the teacher entered. Juliette immediately recognized him as the man whom she had seen in the cheese stall at the market the day before.

She surreptitiously snuck another peek, wondering how old he was. She had a difficult time determining the age of Italians. They all seemed more sophisticated and somehow more worldly than Americans, which she associated with being older.

"*Buon giorno, il mio nome è Roman Capello, e saro il vostro insegnante,*" he said in brisk Italian.

Juliette's pulse raced. She realized that she understood less than she anticipated. In an instant, she feared that the language was going to be more difficult than she had expected. She picked up the fact that his name was Roman Capello and that he was the teacher, but mostly because it was obvious from his actions.

"*Per cominiciare, ognuno mi dica che cosa voule imparare in questa classe.*" Let's begin by everyone telling me what they would like to get out of the class, he continued—again speaking rapidly. He gestured for a young man two seats away from Juliette to begin. Juliette felt the same blind panic she used to get when she was in high-school geometry and was about to be called on to solve a mathematical problem when she only had a vague sense of how to do it. As the student answered, she worked hard to concentrate on what he was saying and was relieved she understood most of it. She took a deep breath as he finished and all eyes moved on to the student who was next to her. Juliette could feel her face getting hot and cursed herself for the hateful blushing trait. It was the bane of the fair skinned, and she had inherited it from her father's side. Her mother's Italian genes would never have betrayed her so brutally.

Juliette was able to glean that the woman she was seated next to was saying something about taking the class because she worked in the family restaurant and wanted to expand her skills. Or at least something close to that.

When she finished, all eyes turned to Juliette and there was nothing to do but to dive in, so she took a deep breath and did just that.

"*Buon giorno,*" she began slowly, thinking about each word and pronouncing it carefully. "*Il mio nome è Juliette Brice e mi sono trasferita qui per migliorare la mia conoscenza dell'arte culinaria italiana.*" Hello, she said. My name is Juliette Brice and I moved here to improve my Italian cooking. She wished she knew how to say she was on an extended visit, but that was beyond her, so "moved" would have to do. At least that's what she hoped she said—although she wasn't entirely sure she had used the correct tenses and wondered if there were different verbs for "to move an object or move residences." She used to feel so confident in her ability to speak Italian and hoped desperately that it would come back quickly.

She decided not to worry about it and was just happy her turn was over. It must not have been too off base because a quick peek around the room told her that the other students didn't think she had said anything strange and the next student began to speak about why he was in the class.

She ventured another peek at Roman, and was startled to find him looking at her. On closer inspection, she guessed that he must be in his early thirties. He was tall for an Italian man, and had a slim build. He had dark, slightly shaggy hair, dark eyes and elegant features that seemed intelligent and serious. She smiled when she saw that his jeans were ironed so crisply that there was a perfectly straight line down the middle of each pant leg.

She wondered why he was still looking at her. Had she said something odd after all?

He gave her a slight smile and a nod, and she felt immediately relieved.

There were only about ten students so the introductions were quickly completed and the instructor began to explain the structure of the class. This time he spoke more slowly, she gratefully assumed, for her benefit.

She was listening intently with one part of her brain, while the other part was wondering about her teacher.

What had Odessa said about him? She searched her brain.

"*Signorina Brice?*"

Juliette looked up, suddenly aware that she had been caught thinking her own thoughts.

"*Si, Signor Capello?*" she tried to act as if she had been paying attention but was just confused by the language.

"Will you please answer the question I've asked the class?" he looked at her expectantly, but with slight humor because he realized he had unwittingly caught her mind wandering.

"I'm sorry," she replied in her slow Italian. "Could you please repeat the question for me once again? I didn't quite understand all of it."

"*Certamente,*" he said, and then elaborated, "How do you know if a gorgonzola is ripe?"

"Um," she stammered. She could answer in English no problem, but it wasn't so easy in Italian. It took three to five months after the cheese mold was added and the cheese was pierced to increase circulation, but saying "pierced" was beyond her skills in the language and she didn't think "poked" would do. Nonetheless, she took a deep breath and tried. She was pretty sure the class understood that the stabbing motions she made with her pencil were supposed to represent the piercing of the cheese rounds rather than the possibility that she had a violent streak.

From the encouraging look on her teacher's face, she guessed he understood what she meant, and soon she was so absorbed in the conversation that she was no longer embarrassed about being caught daydreaming and lacking in fluency.

By the end of the day, she was exhausted yet exhilarated. Thinking in and speaking Italian all day was tiring enough, but add standing while chopping, dicing, grating, crumbling and sautéing and she was ready to relax. Juliette was proud, though. She had made it through her first day, and aside from a few language mishaps and a misconstrued gesture or two, it had gone well. The polenta with gorgonzola they made was superb. It never failed to amaze her when simple foods transcended the everyday and became sublime. She didn't even like polenta much, but what they had made today was truly delicious.

She was almost to the door, trailing a couple of the other students, when she heard her name called.

"*Signorina Brice? Un momento, per favore.*" Roman called to her from where he was standing in the kitchen, so she turned back to see what he wanted. Her pulse quickened when she realized he was keeping her to chat a moment.

"How was your first day?" he asked her in English, not looking at her, but gathering printed recipes to put back in his leather satchel.

"*Meraviglioso, grazie,*" she answered in Italian. Wonderful, thank you. She smiled at him, wondering what else he would say. Roman was the perfect name for him, she thought, because his features were, in fact, classically Roman.

"Keep working on your Italian," he looked up at her and smiled, "and if there's something you don't understand, ask me in English. I can try to make it more clear for you. My English is far from perfect, but between the two of us, we should be able to stumble through."

"Oh, ok," she stammered, surprised at the generous offer and the unexpected breadth of his ability to speak English. "Thank you. *A domani,*" she said. See you tomorrow, and she smiled and waved as she walked out into the cool Italian afternoon.

Chapter 7

Catarina looked into the rickety wooden chest and then up at her sister.

"How am I supposed to fit everything I want to bring with me in this one trunk plus a suitcase?" she asked. "Babbo said he reinforced it, but it looks like this chest is going to fall to pieces."

"How practical you are, Catarina. Who cares about what you bring or whether this trunk becomes kindling wood. I'm more worried about what it's going to be like to kiss a stranger than how you're going to fit your things into this old trunk. And what about trying to make a baby with him? You don't even know him."

"Aurulia, don't talk of such things!" Catarina focused on the empty trunk, so she didn't have to look at her sister's face. She was shocked that her sister would bring up such a subject. But in truth, it was something she, too, had thought about many times. She could put it aside during the day, while she kept herself busy, but at night when she lay in bed trying to sleep, she couldn't put it out of her mind. She was terrified about it all. She was marrying a man who might as well be a stranger to her and leaving her home for an unfamiliar country. What if she couldn't stand him once she met him again? What if he had oozing sores on his face and bad breath all the time? There had to be some terrible reason he had to ask for a bride who couldn't remember what he looked like. She felt desperate, but she wasn't sure what she was desperate for. Desperate to know exactly what she was getting herself into? Desperate to stay? Desperate to get out of a promise she had made out of fear?

It had seemed unreal at first. They had written a letter to send to the Brunellis accepting the proposal. And then they waited. They decided to tell no one about it until it became official with the return post—which would take weeks. And then, as those weeks of waiting passed, Catarina was almost able to forget that it was happening at all. She labored in the garden, helped her father with the vines, and worked in the house alongside her mother, all the while staying far from the Carlucci house. She had no idea what lie her mother told her father about why she hadn't gone back to her job, but he never brought it up with her, so she let the subject alone. The only people who knew the whole story were her mother and her two best friends, who would never tell a soul. But, looking back, the moment of terror with Signor Carlucci had sealed her fate. She knew she would move to America and marry Franco.

The one noticeable difference in her routine was the sewing they did at night. Catarina and her mother began sewing things she would need for the marriage. Her mother put Catarina to work on a simple, white linen nightgown that was to be covered in white embroidery, while her sisters began to stitch a quilt for the marriage bed. Celestina set to work on Catarina's undergarments. No daughter of hers would be sent off for marriage in old, faded underthings.

Several weeks after they posted the letter, they began wondering when they would receive the awaited response. The daily trip to the post office became agony, and because she was no longer working for the Carluccis, the task had been given to Catarina. The pimple-faced boy who delivered the mail to the general store trudged to the village each day around three o'clock in the afternoon, a beat-up leather satchel over his shoulder. He was surly and rude—filled with self-importance—but at least he was punctual.

Catarina didn't want to appear to be waiting for something important, so she made sure to arrive just before the store closed each day—as if it were an unwanted burden to collect any letters that arrived for the family. When she stepped up to the counter, she made sure to put a bored expression on her face. The last thing she wanted was talk from the village. And then, when there was no letter, she made sure to hide her disappointment. It took six weeks of daily agony from the day they mailed the letter to the Brunellis until the response was finally placed in her hand. Remaining calm was almost impossible, but Catarina forced herself to reply with a simple *"Grazie"* when she saw the Brunelli name on the thick envelope. She walked at a restrained pace through the square, the letter gripped in her suddenly clammy hand.

"Mama, it's here!" she yelled as she opened the front door.

Celestina came bustling from the kitchen, wiping her hands on her apron. When they tore open the envelope, they found two missives: one letter for Catarina's parents and another for herself.

Catarina wanted to take the letter upstairs to her room to read in private but she knew her mother would never allow it. She felt her heart beating nervously. She watched until Celestina became engrossed in the first letter before she began reading the one to her alone. The writing was small and gently sloped. It was written in blue ink. The vague vision she had of Franco came to her mind. She could almost see him sitting at a desk, composing the words. She wished she could remember his voice and his face more clearly.

Cara Catarina,

May I call you Cara? It's presumptuous, I know, but I feel that it follows the presumption of asking you to marry me based on my memory of a girl. How shall I begin this letter? By telling you first of all how pleased I am that you said "yes." Are you wondering why I chose you to ask? I can easily tell you. It's because of a certain memory I have of you and your brother, Mateo. You two were sitting at the table in your kitchen when my family was there for a visit. You were working on learning your sums. Mateo couldn't remember how to work one of the sums and you not only reminded him how to do it, but looked over at me with a fierce expression while you did so—daring me to say something that would slight your older brother. I wouldn't have, but I admired your nerve, as I was much older than you. That image stuck with me. Your intelligent blue eyes and the fierce expression on your face. When I decided it was time to marry, I didn't want to marry a girl from America. I wanted to marry a girl who would remind me of Italy. Who would speak my language and understand what it means to be Italian. My father said he would ask your babbo if there was a suitable girl in the village. While we were talking about it, your face flashed through my mind. I asked my father how old you would be now, and once I knew you were of marrying age, I asked him to talk to your father about it. I know it's strange that we don't know each other well—that we haven't seen each other for years. But then again, my parents met only days before they were due to be married, and it has worked well for them.

My family has booked passage for you on a ship. The letter to your parents contains the details of your departure. I want to assure you of some things myself, though. The first is that I promise to take good care of you. My family has a successful jewelry business and soon we will have an apartment of our own. Until then, we will live at my family home.

I will come to New York to meet your ship and travel with you by train to San Francisco. We will be married there in a cathedral near our home. It has a beautiful glass window made of different colors, so when the sun shines through, it's like looking at a rainbow. I know it sounds like make-believe, but wait until you see it.

I will write more later, but for now, please know that I look forward to our marriage.

Yours,
Franco

That had been more than a month ago. Now Catarina had a small bundle of letters from Franco tied up with a ribbon. It was the first thing she placed in the wooden chest.

She was due to leave in a matter of days. The plan was to travel with Babbo by cart to Salerno, where she would board a ship to cross the Atlantic Ocean. The most important thing, Franco had said, was to stay healthy on the ship if she could, because they were very strict about whom they let into the United States. She would have to go through a place he called Ellis Island, where those who wanted to immigrate had to be checked over and cleared before they could enter the country. He wrote that even when she arrived in the United States, there would still be a risk that she could be sent back, even with a fiancé waiting for her. She hoped that wouldn't happen. It would be humiliating to be found unfit and have to return home after telling everyone that she was going to America to be married.

He had booked her into a berth she would share with one other girl. She hoped she liked her, because they would be spending a long time together aboard the ship.

The next item Catarina placed in the wooden trunk was the quilt her sisters had made for her. It was the color of the old bricks that made up the oven where they baked their bread. A deep, rich brownish red that they trimmed in cream-colored crochet. The fabric was heavy and the feathers they filled it with were thick and fluffy. Franco told her that the evenings were cold and foggy in San Francisco, and her sisters wanted her to stay warm. She couldn't imagine living somewhere where the evenings, even in the summer, were cool. Summer evenings at home were the best part of the day—after the heat had receded to sultry warmth. Would she have to wear a coat in the summer there?

She couldn't imagine that. She looked over at her thin, old coat. It had been tight on her last winter and she knew she had grown more since then. She decided to leave it at home for her sisters. Even if that meant she was cold during the voyage, at least her coat would be something she could leave behind to help. Even though Catarina was petite, they were even shorter, so she knew it would go to good use.

She couldn't bring herself to pack any more yet. Instead, she walked outside and sat on the stone wall that surrounded *la cucina giardino*, the kitchen garden, which faced out to the olive orchard. The air was warm and still and it felt good to be out of her stuffy attic room. The leaves were grays and verdant greens. The lavender stood sentry at the entrance to the orchard, with its spiky, purple flowers. How would she leave it? But the decision was made. She would see it through. She would exchange the sights and sounds of the countryside for the noise and bustle of an unfamiliar city.

Babbo called her stubborn, but Catarina knew it wasn't that. She had the inner strength to forge ahead in spite of the pain she felt. She had gotten that trait from her mother. *È inutile piangere sul latte versato*, no crying over spilt milk, she said. Lift your head high, and walk forward. And Catarina would do that. But she would miss home. And she would miss her family.

Although she could bend her will, she couldn't control the tears that silently slid down her cheeks. She wiped them away with her apron, swinging her feet as she had since she was a little girl, and tried to memorize every detail of what was before her.

As the last few days passed before her departure, she and her mother performed an intricate dance—never mentioning the diminishing time they had left together. Celestina asked her questions about what she had packed and what was left to do, as if she was simply going to visit her aunt in the next village. She didn't mention marriage or Franco, but instead gently chastised her for not filling the water jug enough for the day, or doing a bad job of sweeping.

But on the morning of her departure, they could no longer ignore the facts. When Catarina came downstairs dressed in her simple gray traveling dress with red-rimmed eyes, Celestina handed her a *caffè latte* and then immediately took it back, setting it down on the table, and wrapped her arms around her daughter. Catarina could feel her mother's shoulders shaking as she silently wept. She held her mother tightly and for the first time allowed herself to cry unchecked.

"I'm scared, Mama," she whispered, so only Celestina could hear.

"There's nothing to be afraid of, *mia cara.*"

"What if I never see you and Babbo again? How will I live in this world without you? I can't bear the thought of it."

"Shhh. Don't talk like that. I will still be in this world, and you will see me again. That was part of the marriage contract Babbo insisted upon. Franco will bring you home to visit us. And until then, look out at the moon each night, and know that I am looking at the same moon. We won't be so far apart."

Catarina let go of her mother and wiped her face. Celestina handed the coffee back to her daughter and sent her back upstairs to drink it and splash water on her tear-stained face.

When she came back down the rest of the family was waiting for her and the tears began again. She hugged each of her sisters and brothers-in-law goodbye. They insisted they would all write constantly, but Catarina knew letters would be a poor substitute for seeing them every day as she had her entire life.

It was a relief that Mateo and her father were both taking her to the ship, so she could postpone those farewells at least for a while.

When Catarina climbed into the cart and sat down on her trunk, it was almost a relief to be underway at last. Mateo jumped onto the cart as well, tucked her suitcase under the bench seat, then sat facing his sister. Catarina's father stepped up to the driver's seat and took the reins of the Pensebene's workhorse before taking a seat on the wooden wagon bench. Celestina handed a basket of food up to Catarina so they could eat breakfast and lunch during the journey to the port. Catarina gave her mother one last hug and then her father clicked his tongue and the horse started off.

She watched her mother's form recede as the cart and horse picked up speed on the road out of the village, then she yelled one last time, "*Ti amo, Mama!*" I love you. She stood up and waved both her arms and blew kisses to her mother.

"*Finiranno mai queste lacrime?*" asked Mateo theatrically, leaning over to their father. Will these tears never cease? This is what it must be like at an opera."

Then he turned back to his sister and said, "I, for one, am happy to be rid of you." He smiled at her mischievously. "I intend to take over your room as soon as Babbo and I return. I don't know how you ended up with the best room in the house, but it will be mine soon enough."

Catarina burst into laughter through her tears, thankful for her brother's sense of humor.

"My husband and I will kick you out when we come to visit," Catarina retorted, as she blew her nose into a handkerchief. But she was happy to think of Mateo in her room.

"When I get married, my wife and I will live in your room and make a baby right in your bed."

"Mateo!" Babbo cuffed his son on the ear. "There will be no talking like that in front of your sister."

But Mateo just laughed harder and winked at Catarina, who shook her head at him.

They were hungry, so they ate while they passed the time in the cart. The day was glorious. Sunny, but not too hot because it was early. Mateo and Babbo would be sweltering on the return journey, but for now it was as if Italy were giving Catarina a perfect farewell.

When they arrived at the harbor, it was like nothing Catarina had imagined. There were people everywhere. Carts and horses clogged the streets. The port was crowded with people loading supplies onto the ship, shouting to one another. The whole spectacle overwhelmed her, but the main focus for Catarina was the ship. It took her breath away. It was bigger than the orchard at their house. It was bigger than the town square in their village. It was huge and hulking, but what shocked her even more than the size was that she had expected a wooden ship like she'd seen in paintings. Instead, it was made of steel.

"Babbo, how will it stay afloat?" Catarina asked. "It must weigh so much it will sink to the bottom of the sea."

Babbo laughed. "Don't worry, child. It will stay afloat and get you all the way to America. It's much safer than wood. It's a steamship. Now, let's get you aboard and find where you'll be sleeping."

Mateo quickly tied up the horse and cart and helped his father with the trunk. He was eager to explore the ship. He, too, was in awe of its enormity and could hardly believe it would only take Catarina nine days to reach New York. She and Mateo looked at each other with matching expressions of wonder etched across their similar features.

They walked up the gangway, Catarina holding the suitcase in the lead and Mateo and her father behind, hefting the trunk between them. When they reached the entrance, they were stopped by a young, uniformed man who asked for their tickets.

Catarina opened the first purse she had ever owned, extracted her ticket, and handed it to him.

"My daughter's traveling to America to get married," Babbo told him.

The man looked up and met her eyes.

"Lucky man," he winked at Catarina and punched a hole in her ticket, then handed it back to her. His accent was from northern Italy and his hair was golden and curly, which made his dark eyes almost confusing. Catarina felt heat rise to her face and looked away.

"Can you tell me where she will be sleeping?" asked Catarina's father.

"*Si, Signore,* on level two you'll find a door with the same number as the ticket. And if you would like, I will keep a special eye on your daughter while she is aboard ship. My name is Gregorio Villa, and I have a sister who must be the same age," he smiled.

"*Grazie mille.* I would appreciate it," said Babbo, and handed him a coin which he casually pocketed.

As they walked away from him, Catarina glanced back over her shoulder and saw that Gregorio was watching her, too, an amused expression on his face. Her sharp intake of breath startled her father. She quickly turned back and acted as if she were simply looking around.

"What is it, Catarina? Did you hurt yourself?"

"No, Babbo. I'm only looking at the ship. What an amazing thing it is!" she said, but in truth, the face of Gregorio Villa was immediately fixed in her mind.

W hen they got downstairs, they easily located the berth Catarina was to share. Inside was the girl whom Franco had written to her about.

"*Buon giorno,*" they said in unison and then smiled at each other.

"*Il mio nome è Catarina Pensebene.*"

"Nice to meet you, Catarina. My name is Maria Crostina."

Catarina introduced her brother and father as well, stored her suitcase and trunk, and then told her that they were going to look around the ship.

"Would you like to join us?" she asked.

"*No, grazie,*" said Maria. "I'm going to unpack, but I'll see you later."

So they left her to explore the different levels of the ship. They found the dining area, the outside decks, and even snuck a peek into the first class accommodations, until they were asked to see their tickets, then shooed out when they couldn't produce them. They stood against the rail looking out at the dock below. Mateo stepped away to look off the bow and Catarina's father took his daughter in his arms.

"I will miss you," he said, "but this will be best for you."

"I know, Babbo."

He reached into his pocket, pulled out an envelope, and handed it to her.

"This is for you. Keep it safe. I didn't want you traveling with no money, should anything happen."

Catarina had never been given money for herself before, and the thought of it alarmed her.

"What would happen? Why would I need this?" she asked.

"I'm sure nothing, but this way if Franco's train is late or you need anything, you have some money."

"*Grazie, Babbo*. I will keep it safe," she said, and tucked it into her purse without looking at the amount. She peeked discretely around to make sure no one was watching. She felt conspicuous having money. She felt a sense of pride, too. She was a grown woman. Her father trusted her with money.

Suddenly, the horn sounded and they both jumped. Catarina almost dropped her purse but caught it just in time, averting embarrassment.

"We have to go now, Catarina. That's the signal."

"Ok," she said, this time determined not to shed more tears. She smiled bravely at her father, who hugged her and then held her at arms length to study her face. Mateo appeared at their sides and quickly hugged his sister as well.

"*Ti amo*," she said to each of them in turn, and forced her face to keep smiling. "I'll stand here and wave to you. You find me from shore, ok? Look, we're near this big cable. Look for that and you'll find me."

"*Si* Catarina, we'll find you from shore," said Babbo, his voice strained with the effort of keeping composure. And then they stepped away and left her staring from the deck.

She bit her cheek and breathed deeply. She reminded herself of everything she was excited about. She would have adventures in America. She would ride a train from New York to San Francisco, so she would have time to get to know Franco before they married. She would be the wife of a jeweler instead of the daughter of a farmer. She went through the list in her mind until she spotted her father and brother ashore waving madly at her. She waved back until her arm got tired. Finally the ship sounded two more times, and then she felt a lurch under her feet as they pulled away from the dock and headed out to sea.

Chapter 8

JULIETTE, LEARNING TO DRINK
ESPRESSO THE ITALIAN WAY

When she got back to her apartment, Juliette tossed her bag on the still-unmade bed, kicked off her shoes, and poured a glass of red wine even though it was only four in the afternoon. She sank onto her love seat and called her sister on her now internationally equipped cell phone.

"Hi," she said once Gina picked up. "It's me."

"Juliette? The connection's so clear, it sounds like you're just down the street. How are you? How's it all going? I miss you already!"

"I'm fine. And Lucca's gorgeous."

"Did you have your first day of class today? How was it?"

"Yes, and it was amazing. I think it's going to be an excellent class, but man did I have to stay on my toes. It's difficult to try to keep up with what I'm supposed to do while it's being taught in Italian."

"Trial by fire, as they say."

"Trial by skillet in this case, but being here and surrounded by the language brings back so many memories of when we were little and spending time with Nonna and Granddad."

"That must be nice."

"Yeah, I wish I knew what it was like here when they were young," Juliette said wistfully.

"We should have asked them more about it, while we still had them. But now it's your turn to be young in Italy. So try to enjoy it. Don't think about what happened before you left, if you can."

"That's my plan, actually. Sometimes deep denial is best, don't you think?"

"At least for now. So, tell me," Gina said, trying to move her little sister into a more life-affirming frame of mind, "is there anyone interesting in your class? Any appealing men?"

"Juliette realized what her sister was trying to do and appreciated her effort.

"My instructor is definitely interesting," Juliette noted.

"Do tell."

"Well, the first thing you should know is that Italian men have some sort of indefinable sexiness that American men don't. Well, not that they don't, but it's definitely different. Like being sexy here is expected in the same way it is for women at home. They dress better, make more eye contact, and I don't know. . . there's just something. I've only been here two days and have already been scrutinized with frankly sexual undertones more than I think I have during my entire adulthood at home."

"Maybe they're just more obvious."

"Maybe. Anyway, my teacher definitely has that frank Italian undertone of charisma. Not that it matters. He's way too handsome to be my type. But it'll be fun to take my class from him, that's for sure."

"Don't discount him just because he has a pretty face, Juliette. After all, who knows, maybe he's the Italian version of the dorky guys you usually go for at home. "

"That may be true!" Juliette chuckled in spite of herself. "Maybe he's a complete dork and I just don't know because it's a different kind than American dorkiness. Either way, he seems like a great teacher. And he's nice! And he speaks English, so he let me know that if I get confused he'll help me sort it out. But that's not even the best part—we made mouth-watering polenta today . . . and you know how I feel about polenta."

"Yes, I believe your stand on polenta is 'boring: might as well be grits.'"

"Exactly. But this was different in a fundamental way. It was extraordinarily flavorful and rich."

"It's good to hear you sound excited. It seems like this is going to be as great as you hoped."

"I hope so. I feel far away from home, though, and terrible about leaving you and Dad with so much to deal with. I'm kind of lonely and freaked out, but I'm trying to be tough."

"Don't worry about us. The police let me know yesterday, though, that because the driver has been charged with criminal drunk driving and manslaughter you'll have to make another official statement at some point. But for now, the police said they can talk to you by phone if they need to."

"I still can't believe she's gone. How could this have happened?"

"I know, but for now try not to dwell on it."

"I'm trying not to, but sometimes I need to. You know, to process it. Does that make sense?"

"It makes complete sense. When I miss her, I try to focus on one of my favorite memories of her. It seems to help."

"At home, my friends were trying too hard to cheer me up. I needed to get some space away from that," Juliette paused, then Odessa popped into her mind. "I met a woman here who I can see becoming friends with. Her family sells cheese."

"Of course, back to food. Leave it to you to find a friend who makes cheese. It would never be someone who, say, works at a bank."

She had to agree that her sister was probably right.

After their conversation, Juliette felt the time change dragging her down and wanted nothing more than to climb into bed, but she knew she needed to go get some dinner. In fact, she knew exactly what she was in the mood for: minestrone soup.

She doubted if there was such a thing as take-out in this town, and it was only six o'clock. Restaurants wouldn't serve dinner for hours yet, so she decided to shut her eyes and rest a little bit. Over the next hour, she kept jerking awake, afraid to fall into a deep sleep, so she finally forced herself to get up off the couch and find a restaurant and that bowl of minestrone.

Juliette's minestrone quest wasn't as simple as she'd hoped. She searched several narrow cobblestone streets off the main square, peeking into the windows of restaurants and checking the menus posted at the door of several trattorias with no luck. Finally, she found a cozy venue that looked promising. The windows were steam covered because of the sheer number of people packed into the small eatery. It was casual and welcoming, filled with candlelight and color. Long tables were crowded with locals talking animatedly, with their hands moving as rapidly as their words, and eating with gusto. Some people were in groups. Others were alone. Her feet were tired and she felt worn out and hungry so she decided to go in, minestrone or not. She didn't even bother to look for a menu outside. She entered the little cafe and stood by a table featuring samples of the evening's offerings. She looked through the dishes, spying some favorites and others that were new to her, drinking in the sight of the local delicacies.

"Juliette? . . Juliette?"

She was engrossed by the food on display and didn't hear her name being called at first, then jumped when she felt an unexpected tap on her shoulder.

She turned and saw Odessa's smiling face.

"*Ciao!* I was eating dinner with my boyfriend, and saw you standing here. Would you care to join us? I recall you're new here, yes?"

"Odessa! It's such a nice surprise to see you. I don't want to intrude, though. I just came in for a bowl of minestrone. I had my first cooking class today and I'm exhausted and starving."

"It wouldn't be intruding at all. We just sat down ourselves, and I would love to introduce Antonello to you. Please? We always enjoy meeting new people."

"If you're sure I wouldn't be in the way, I would love to join you."

"It's settled, then. Come."

Odessa took Juliette's arm and led her through the crowded space to where they were seated. She pulled out a chair and waved Juliette in, so she gratefully sat down.

"Juliette, this is *mio ragazzo*, Antonello."

"It's a pleasure to meet you," Juliette said and shook Antonello's offered hand. She liked his looks. He had longish dark brown hair and heavy eyebrows. He looked like her idea of a stylish journalist and she later learned she wasn't far off base.

"Thank you for letting me crash *tuo appuntamento*," she said, then wondered if "crash" your date meant the same thing in Italian as it did in English. Probably not, she decided, but Antonello laughed and assured her that she was welcome, so she guessed that she hadn't insulted either of them.

She smiled as she glanced around.

"I love this place already and I haven't even tried the food yet."

"It's actually my favorite restaurant. How did you manage to choose this one of all the restaurants in Lucca?" Odessa asked.

"I walked around to find one that looked good. This one was the most crowded, so I thought, if all of those people want to eat here, it must be good."

"I never would have thought of that." Antonello said, as he waved to the waiter to come to their table. "From now on, that's how we should always choose restaurants," he said to Odessa.

When the waiter arrived, Odessa and Antonello both broke into such rapid fire Italian that Juliette couldn't follow what they said. She did hear Odessa say the word "minestrone" with a wave of her hand toward Juliette, so she assumed that her soup had been ordered. She enjoyed watching them together. They seemed completely at ease with each other and on familiar terms with the waiter, who somehow managed to listen to both of them talking to him over each other. They all laughed at something and then the waiter turned to Juliette.

"*Vino, Signorina?*"

"*Si, grazie. Rosso, per favore.*"

"*Certo.*"

He left to get their wine, which gave Odessa time to explain what she had ordered.

"We asked him to bring us a sample of his favorites tonight," she said. "But don't worry, I made sure to include a request for minestrone."

Juliette was happy to be in Odessa and Antonello's care. She knew instinctively that she was in for a treat, and was happy she hadn't ended up sitting by herself eating only a bowl of soup.

She wasn't disappointed. At the end of the evening, Juliette tallied thirteen different little dishes with tastes of this and that. Each one was superb. They had started with cups of minestrone, which was perfect. Next came a few spoonfuls of the most delectable, savory, delicate white beans she could have imagined. She wondered how something so basic could melt on the palate in such a way. The waiter told them the beans were cooked in a clay pot for days with salty ham.

The beans were followed by three morsels of lamb—the meat so succulent it fell off the bone. And then next came breaded eggplant, which had been pounded to a tenderness she'd never imagined could be achieved, followed by diminutive artichokes baked in a wood oven, and on and on. The meal ended with *un digestivo* and a serving of tiramisu.

"I don't think I've ever been so full in my life. And that's saying a lot for me," Juliette told them. "But I think that was the best meal I've ever had, which is one of the reasons I came to Italy. This is what

I want to do."

"And what were the other reasons you came?" Odessa asked.

"I'm running away a little bit, to be honest," Juliette admitted.

"Ah, we Italians can understand that. What are you running from? A lover?"

"No, a different kind of heart break actually, but let's not talk about that," Juliette gestured to them with her wine glass. "Let's talk about food and you two. I can't thank you enough for inviting me to your table."

"Now you know why it's our favorite restaurant," Odessa told her, graciously taking her new friend's lead to change the subject.

"I'll order us some coffee," Antonello said, raising his arm to the waiter.

"None for me, please," said Juliette. "I don't know how you Italians can drink such strong coffee and still sleep."

"It's in the genes, I guess," he smiled at her.

"It can't be that. I've got the genes. Well, half of the genes, at least."

"Well, I guess half isn't enough. Odessa can do it, too, because the French are as serious as the Italians are about coffee."

"It's true," Odessa agreed. "I guess you just have to build up your tolerance."

Juliette looked at her watch. She wasn't surprised to see that it was almost eleven o'clock. The dinner scene in Italy was decidedly later than at home, and she was amazed at even how many children were still awake.

"Well, I'll leave you two to have coffee," Juliette said, and reached for her purse to pay her share of the bill, but Antonello waved her off.

"It's our treat," he said.

"No, that's ridiculous. You were wonderful to me tonight and you kept me from being lonely. You don't have to buy me dinner, too."

"We insist," said Odessa. "We were happy to introduce you to our restaurant. You can have us over to dinner sometime—once your class is finished."

"Ok, but I'll have you over long before that. In fact, maybe I can practice on you."

"*Bene*," said Antonello, and Odessa nodded.

"Good night then," said Juliette, and gave them each a kiss on the cheek before putting on her jacket and scarf. She was still smiling as she walked back to her apartment.

"Enchanting," she said, thinking of the evening, "*affascinante*." She loved the Italian language. What a beautiful sound. And she enjoyed listening to her new friends talk to her in a mixture of Italian and melodic English, with their lovely accents. She turned the key in the center set doorknob and entered her temporary home.

Juliette awoke with a muted scream just as the car was hurteling towards them in her dream. Her heart was racing, and she was sweaty and disorientated with the picture of her mom's frightened face burned into her sleep-hazed mind. When she looked at the clock, she saw that it was just after two a.m. and she knew she wouldn't be going back to sleep for a while.

She threw off the covers and switched on the light. She padded to the bathroom in bare feet and splashed cold water on her face, realizing she was still a little tipsy from the wine she had at dinner. She sighed and looked at her face. It looked exhausted and older than her thirty years. The skin around her blue eyes looked like crinkled tissue paper to her. Last spring, on Juliette's twenty-nineth birthday, her friends unanimously commented that she looked younger than her age, but no one would make that mistake now, she thought.

She knew she'd just stare at the ceiling if she tried to go back to sleep, so Juliette picked up the shoebox of letters she'd brought with her and climbed back in bed. The odd thing was that both sides of the correspondence between Nonna and her girlfriend were together in the box, as if someone had carefully organized them chronologically. Juliette slipped the first letter out of the envelope for the second time. She scanned over the first two paragraphs to refresh her memory of where she had left off and then continued. It was yellowed with age, but the writing was still legible. The formation of the script had a distinct European style to it in spite of the fact that her granddad had lived in the United States for two decades, if not more, before the letter was written.

It was a beautiful letter: full of longing and desire. She stumbled over some of the words, so she grabbed her old, well-worn Italian dictionary to help with them. Forget flawed online translators; Juliette viewed her dictionary as an old friend.

As she submersed herself in the prose, she could visualize the two of them young and her grandfather in love with her beautiful grandmother from afar. She could see her nonna sitting on the low stone wall near their olive orchard and imagining the long future they would have together. Although at that point, Nonna wouldn't have truly understood the journey they were about to begin.

Juliette wondered if she would have been as brave if the choice to leave her own country forever had been hers. What would have been so dire to cause her to leave home?

W hen she finished reading, Juliette tucked the letter back into the box. Their love had begun here in Italy, she mused. She was glad she'd come.

She snuggled back under the covers and closed her eyes, hoping for a peaceful sleep, and was relieved to see rows of ripe grapes growing on sun-filled hillsides in her mind's eye instead of an out-of-control car racing towards them.

It seemed like moments later when she awoke to the blare of her alarm. She was tired, but she knew the excitement of day two of cooking school would get her through. The antiquated espresso maker worked enough for her to eek out a cup and she was on her way.

When she walked into the classroom, she already liked the familiarity of it. She greeted her classmates with a smile and a nod and took a seat, wondering what was in store.

Three hours later the question was well under way to being answered. The subject being taught was how to debone a rabbit. They were learning to make *coniglio ripieno di salvia e formaggio*/sage and cheese stuffed rabbit. She had always found the act of tearing meat from bone disgusting, and working on the rabbit made her consider becoming a vegetarian. But at least she was learning something new to do with it. She vowed next time to try to be included at the prep station where they were busy chopping herbs and grating cheese, instead of the meat station.

"*Come va*? How's it going?" Roman walked around the class, observing progress and answering questions.

Juliette wondered what the Italian word for "yuck" was, but

decided to be brave and stick with "*Bene*" instead.

"Good technique," he said, nodding to her rabbit. "You have deboned rabbit before?"

"*Grazie, and si*, I went to the Culinary Institute of America."

"Ah," he said, with a tone of respect. "In New York or California?"

"California. That's where I'm from."

"*Bene*," he said. "You learned good technique there." She felt a sudden sense of triumph.

The *coniglio ripieno* was consumed as the finale of the day. The students sat on stools surrounding one of the islands and purposefully swirled the pinot noir that they'd poured into their respective glasses to accompany the rabbit. They discussed the merits of the meal and exchanged preparation tips and pitfall warnings to each other. She liked the camaraderie of cooking with other students. She hadn't realized how much she'd missed it since her time at the Culinary Institute.

Juliette admitted that the rabbit was succulent and delicious, but she didn't include it in her mental list of what she would serve in her own café someday. There were too few Americans who would order it, and frankly it wouldn't be something she'd enjoy making on a regular basis. She smiled as she swirled her wine, thinking about what she *would* do when she finally opened her own place. Even being here and taking the first step towards her dream was exhilarating. It was almost surreal to have begun the process with this important step after fantasizing about it for so many years. She planned to spend her time here doing research in her down time to fine-tune her plan so when *someday* came, she'd be ready.

When the meal was over and the kitchen cleaned, the students collected their things and left for the day.

Juliette strolled slowly back towards her apartment in the waning afternoon sunshine. She peeked into the windows of the boutiques along the *corso*, and enjoyed the simplicity of being in the incredibly picturesque town. She liked the low key beauty of Lucca. It was a "real" town where people lived and worked. It wasn't a glitzy tourist destination, so it had an unassuming feel and a certain quaintness about it. There were many small piazzas to be found and lots of gardens. She was looking forward to going for her runs along the wall, which was wide and lined with trees. She was determined to be present in every moment she spent in Italy, and promised herself that she would savor them.

Not long after she left class, Juliette was surprised by her teacher who suddenly appeared by her side.

"I've been to Napa before," he said to her in English, as if they were in the middle of a conversation. She was confused at first and then remembered her comment about the Culinary Institute.

It was a relief that he had spoken in English instead of Italian. Her brain was exhausted from thinking and speaking in another language all day.

"How did you like it?"

"I liked it very much. The area reminded me a bit of here, no?"

"I agree," said Juliette. "Of all the places in the United States, the wine country is the most like the hill towns of Italy."

"Are you a chef back at home?"

"I was, but things went badly so I have been working for a caterer—someone who cooks for parties—," she explained, "but I want to open my own small café someday when I have enough money. I'm here to study a bit more for now; so at least I'm taking small steps, you know?"

"Ah, yes. I understand," he said. "The kitchen in our school is beautiful, no?"

"Very beautiful. I can only dream of having something like that at home."

"I set it up myself," he smiled at her.

"This is your school?" Juliette asked.

"Yes, mine and my family's. We have a restaurant in Florence as well. Quite a well-known restaurant," he smiled, and although at home if someone had said that, she might assume he was bragging, in this case she could tell that he was just being matter-of-fact. "I work there sometimes, but I love to teach cooking as well as do the cooking."

"Well, you're very good at it."

"*Grazie*. Would you like to stop for an espresso with me?" he asked, nodding to a coffee bar they were passing. "I usually end my day here."

"I would love to," she smiled. "I could use an espresso. I was out late last night. I had a wonderful dinner out with new friends at a restaurant called *Salvia*. Do you know it?"

"But, of course. It's a wonderful restaurant. You'll have to tell me about your meal," he said, after he ordered espressos and settled them both at seats along the window. He watched as she stirred in her lump of sugar and took teeny sips of the delicious hot coffee.

"No, no," he laughed, after he scrutinized her for a moment. "This is not good at all," he said, his eyes twinkling with mirth.

"What's not good?" she asked, laughing with him, why, she didn't even know. "My espresso is delicious," she said, nodding to the little white porcelain cup holding the rich, dark brown liquid.

"I'm sure it is, but you are not drinking it in the Italian way."

"The Italian way? I didn't know there was an 'Italian way' to drink espresso."

"Oh yes. Espresso is very Italian and you must drink it properly. What you have to do is stir in the sugar very slowly," he said.

He dropped a lump of sugar into his own cup and demonstrated how to stir it in by barely moving the spoon back and forth. He was completely serious and the way he stirred was almost sensual.

"And then you drink it very fast," he continued, and then drank his espresso in one large gulp, as if he was tossing back a tequila shot.

"Interesting," she smiled. "I'll try it. Then you can try my way and we'll see which we enjoy most."

He chuckled, "Not a chance," he said. "You're in my town, and while you're here, you drink it the Italian way," and then went to the counter for another.

"You're right and thank you for teaching me. I want to learn all these subtleties. "

"Then I'll take you 'under my wing' as you Americans say. But now, tell me about the meal you had last night," he said. "I want to hear all the details."

So she did. He listened intently, as only someone who shared a passion for food would do.

"It sounds delicious." He took his eyes off of her and looked out the window at the early November dusk settling in. "*Oh, mio Dio!* How did it get so late? I'm sorry, Juliette, but I must go."

"Oh. Sorry. I didn't mean to keep you."

"No, not at all." He seemed suddenly distracted. "I would love to stay longer, in fact, but I have a meeting I must get to," he said.

"Ok, well, I'll see you tomorrow, then."

"*Si, a domani.*" He met her eyes. "Until tomorrow."

She watched him go from her spot at the window.

Wow, she thought. What an amazing, unexpected afternoon. She knew she could get used to his company. He was gracious, warm, and kind. Why do the perfect ones come along when you're not looking? She wondered, hoping that today's coffee wasn't going to be a one-time event.

When she emerged from the café, the temperature had dropped considerably and Juliette noticed her breath turning to vapor. She wrapped her pumpkin-colored wool coat around herself tightly as she began to walk home, and felt warm in spite of the chill. She tucked her hands into her pockets and reminded herself to bring gloves the next day.

Chapter 9

C atarina couldn't stop from shedding more tears as the boat departed and her father and brother slowly slipped out of sight. The heat of the day was immediately replaced with a brisk wind that, although still warm, whipped her hair and dress. Nonetheless, she stayed up on deck until she composed herself and then she made her way down to her berth to unpack her suitcase. She found Maria right where she left herself in the small, stuffy cabin, except Maria's trunk was now empty. While Catarina took her turn unpacking herself, the two got acquainted before it was time to go to the dining room for dinner.

Like Catarina, Maria was on her way to America to be married.

"I've never met him," Maria told Catarina when she asked about her fiancé. "I have no idea what he looks like. My mama said he is handsome, but she described my sister's husband that way and believe me, it's not a word I would use to describe him, so I'm not very hopeful. I know that I'm plain," she shrugged, putting a hand to her cheek, "so I'm not worried about that. I just hope he's kind, and not too poor, you know?"

"You are not plain," Catarina smiled reassuringly. "How old is he?" she changed the subject.

"Thirty-two! Can you believe it?"

"But that's so old!" Catarina exclaimed. "I'm marrying a man who is twenty-six, and even that seems older than I can imagine. My sisters married men who were at the most twenty and as young as eighteen. That's what I always thought I would do. But now this," she said, and shrugged one shoulder as if to say, "Whatever will be will be."

"I have no choice in the matter," Maria continued matter-of-fact-ly, turning down the corners of her mouth. "My papa arranged it. After all, what was he to do with another daughter? Eh?"

"You had no choice at all?"

"No," she paused. "Did you?"

"Yes. My babbo said he wouldn't force me to marry Franco, but I wanted to because I think it will be wonderful in San Francisco." Catarina had said that so many times she had begun to convince even herself.

"Well, you're so pretty, I'm sure you could have found a husband at home," Maria said, "but who would want me? Not even the poorest farmer asked for my hand."

"That's ridiculous," Catarina looked at her. "You're very pretty, too."

"Thanks for trying, but I know what I know. I just hope my fiancé isn't too disappointed."

"He'll be lucky to have you," Catarina smiled at her.

The bell rang to indicate that dinner would be served in fifteen minutes, so they freshened up, emerged from their cabin, and made their way to the dining room—not really knowing what to expect. What they found was a pleasant surprise. It was large and filled with round tables, covered in cloths even in second class. There were candles lit in sconces along the walls of the room, and the conversation amongst the travelers had an air of excitement. It was contagious. Catarina glanced at the men in uniform to see if any of them was the one who took her ticket when she boarded the ship. Even before Catarina's eyes found Gregorio, she was filled with a sense of anticipation. But when their eyes met, she felt an intensity.

Her friends and their older sisters talked about that type of thing happening when they met at the well, but Catarina hadn't put much stock in it. After all, she had seen all the boys in her village since they were small and none had ever caused such a reaction in her.

"Love will take your breath away," her sister once whispered dramatically while they were folding sheets. Catarina scoffed. Especially when she set her eyes on that same sister's husband. Catarina was the practical one. So, when her eyes finally met Gregorio's the feeling was unexpected. She watched him say something to the uniformed man he was standing next to, and then he made his way towards her.

"*Signorina Pensebene*, would you and your companion care to join us?" He motioned with his hand to a table filled with officers and other passengers.

Catarina looked over at Maria and raised her eyebrows in question.

"*Si, grazie*," Maria said for them both.

"How do you know him?" Maria whispered to Catarina as they made their way through the dining room.

"I met him as I boarded. He took my ticket," she whispered back.

"He took my ticket, too, but that doesn't mean he would have asked me to dine with him."

"It's nothing. My father asked him to keep an eye on me. That's all. He's just being kind," said Catarina as they approached the table.

When they arrived, Gregorio introduced the two young ladies to his friends and other passengers, and indicated that they should sit on either side of him.

"You found two young ladies this evening, 'eh Gregorio?" one of his friends chided him good-naturedly. Gregorio laughed but didn't respond.

"*Volete un po' di vino?*" Gregorio asked them. Would you like some wine?

"*Si, grazie*," Maria answered, again for both of the girls, before Catarina could decline. She was allowed to have wine at festivals and special occasions, but she wasn't at all sure her parents would approve of her having it now. Then again, she reminded herself, she was a grown woman, no longer a girl. She was unaccompanied on a ship and destined to be married, so why shouldn't she sample some wine?

"*Si, grazie*," she said as well, smiling at Gregorio.

As the evening wore on, Catarina found herself laughing more than she ever had in her life. Gregorio amused her with little stories—

all of them humorous—about his past. Her favorite was about a time when he borrowed his father's fedora without his knowledge to impress a young lady in his village. They were strolling through a meadow on the way to a picnic when it flew off his head in a gust of wind, and before he could pick it up, a goat rushed at it and took a bite right out of the brim. Catarina could just imagine it.

"And was your father angry at you?" she asked.

"Yes, it took months of extra chores for me to repay him." Gregorio told her.

Each anecdote was like a little jewel he placed into the palm of her hand, one after another.

"And what about your younger sister?" she asked. "Are you close? You must miss her when you're away."

Gregorio laughed, "Actually, *bella Signorina,* I have to confess. I don't have a sister. I made that up as an excuse when offering to look after you."

Catarina was shocked.

"You lied to my father?"

"*Si,* but please don't hold it against me."

His eyes twinkled with humor and she felt her shock die away.

"I'm incorrigible," he told her.

"I see that," she said, and allowed herself to laugh with him.

At some point in the evening they set up a dance floor and he asked her to dance.

She gazed at the dancers before answering, feeling awkward because the couples already on the dance floor were considerably more sophisticated than she was, with her conservative mid-calf dress and sensible shoes. She had changed out of her traveling dress before dinner, but even the fabric of her best dress showed signs of wear and was plain when compared to the more elegant dresses worn by the other women in the room. She guessed, by looking at the light catching on the richly-colored fabrics of the other female dancers, that at least some of them were wearing silk, whereas she, until now, had only heard about that type of cloth. She herself wore pale blue wool that, although finely woven, was itchy when she got hot and definitely didn't catch the light in the same way. She also noticed the conspicuously lower-cut bodices many of the women wore. She found it embarrassing, but also intriguing. Although she knew she would feel naked revealing as much chest as some others, she was interested in the new fashion. She wondered if she would ever be brave enough to dress in that way.

"I'm afraid I can't dance with you because I don't know how," she told him, tearing her eyes away from the dresses she had been admiring and back to Gregorio.

"There's nothing to it. I'll show you," he said and then coaxed her out into the middle of the floor in spite of her protest. There was a small band to the side of the dance floor and when they began a new piece of music, couples around them began moving.

"This is called a waltz," he instructed. He took her right hand in his and placed her left hand on his upper arm. She felt the warmth of his hand on her lower back and realized she had never been so close to a man who was neither her father nor brother—except for, she reminded herself, Signor Carlucci, and had to stifle a shudder at the thought of him.

I don't have to worry about him anymore, she reminded herself. I've left and he'll never be able to bother me again. And then she looked up at Gregorio and gave in to the moment. He began to teach her the basic mechanics of the dance. She stepped on his feet several times when she got mixed up about which direction to turn, which embarrassed Catarina but Gregorio didn't seem to mind. He was patient with her and laughed good naturedly at her mistakes. By the end of the evening she was getting better and could dance a few of the steps fairly well.

At some point Maria came over and touched Catarina's arm.

"We should go back to our room," she whispered. "It's getting late." She took hold of Catarina and gently pulled her towards the door.

"You're right," she acquiesced, "but I should at least say goodbye."

She stepped back to Gregorio, who was standing still amid the moving couples, and told him she was leaving.

"No, stay. Why let Maria tell you what to do?"

"She's right. I should go back to our room. It's late." Catarina looked around and saw that the room had emptied considerably without her noticing.

"Well, will you have dinner with me again *domani*?"

"*Si*," she said, although she was afraid her father would disapprove of her eating with a single man two nights in a row.

"Until then, Catarina," he said and then walked back to the table to rejoin his friends.

"Catarina!" Maria urged her back off the dance floor. "*Andiamo!*"

"Here I come!" she said and then took her new friend's arm and walked back to their berth.

"He invited us to dinner tomorrow night, too," she told Maria.

"That sounds fun, but you better be careful with him. I saw the way he was looking at you and I don't think your *fidanzato* would approve one bit."

Catarina had to acknowledge that Maria was probably right. Though, what harm can come of it? she asked herself. After all, we'll be aboard such a short time.

Chapter 10

JULIETTE, AN UNEXPECTED DINNER,
AND A WELL-COIFFED ITALIAN MOTHER

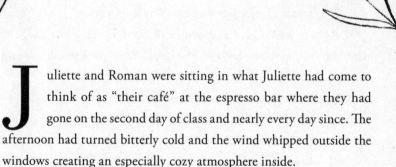

Juliette and Roman were sitting in what Juliette had come to think of as "their café" at the espresso bar where they had gone on the second day of class and nearly every day since. The afternoon had turned bitterly cold and the wind whipped outside the windows creating an especially cozy atmosphere inside.

They had quickly fallen into a routine of having espresso together when class ended, talking over the day and the recipe they'd made. He was true to his word and taught her any and all Italian cultural tidbits he could think of. Increasingly, the talk had moved on to the more personal natures of their lives.

"Is everything all right, Juliette? You don't seem happy today."

"Today would have been my mother's birthday," Juliette told him, a far away look out the window, "but she passed away recently. It's hard."

"*Mi dispiace tanto.* I'm so sorry, Juliette. I understand the pain. My father has also died. It's strange, isn't it, once they're gone."

"Very strange."

Roman took Juliette's hand and stroked it.

"Was she ill?"

"No, she was hit by a drunk driver. I was with her when it happened. That's part of the reason I came here. I had to get away."

"*Merda.*"

"Yes."

"We should celebrate her life. That's what we do here, no? I'll take you to dinner and . . . Why do you smile at me?"

"No reason. You're just an incredibly kind person."

Roman waved his hand dismissively. "I'm not. I'm a cad," he paused trying to remember a phrase he wanted. "Be worried," he said in a false intimidating voice.

Juliette laughed. "I think you mean 'Be afraid'," she replied, in the same feigned voice and then, "Somehow I doubt I have to. And, yes, I would love to have dinner."

"Is there any particular place you've been wanting to try?" he asked, his warm brown eyes meeting hers.

"You choose," she said, her mood lifting a little bit, preferring the prospect of spending the evening with him instead of alone. "After all, you know all the best spots."

"*Si*, ok, yes. I know just the place," he said with a mysterious half smile while he wrote down directions to her apartment.

Roman picked her up in a black Alfa Romeo coupe. She had expected him to arrive in a somewhat beaten up small Italian car like so many she saw driving in Lucca. Maybe faded red and a bit dented, smelling of exhaust. The difference between her imagination and the sleek black version waiting for her at the curb, with Roman holding the door open, was surprising and pleasant. The luxurious brown interior leather was the warm hue of a well-used baseball glove and she sank into the comfortable seat. It was the first time she had been driven in Italy, aside from her first cab ride, and she was a decidedly nervous, having seen the way Italians operated their vehicles. As he pulled out and maneuvered his car inches from the cars parked along the streets, she realized he was the exact kind of Italian driver she'd come to both fear and respect. They seemed to have no qualms about missing both pedestrians and other cars by a hair's width. Their aggressive style was something to behold.

She tried to relax and give herself over to one more quintessentially Italian experience, while clandestinely doing the deep breathing exercises a therapist had taught her to help cope with the panic attacks she'd had after the accident.

"Where are we going?" she asked, purposefully keeping her voice light and forcing herself to loosen her intense grip on the door handle.

"I know it's a bit out of the way, but I thought I would take you to my family's restaurant in Florence," he said, oblivious to the fact that his driving was causing ripples of terror to roll through her body.

"Really?" Juliette was surprised. Florence was more than an hour away by car. She was dressed in faded jeans with black, low-heeled boots and a simple, pale-pink V-neck sweater. This outfit was more casual than she would have worn had she known she was going to meet his family. She absentmindedly twirled her nonna's ring, relieved she had it, as well as a stylish, chunky silver and stone necklace Gina had designed, to dress her up a bit.

"*Si*, you'll love it. We make *carabaccia*, which is exactly the type of thing you're looking for. It's rustic. Simple. Just *zuppa di cipolle*, onion soup, no? But it is made in a way that will leave you begging for more. We have a family secret that I'll share with you." Roman paused to add drama, then continued. "We add a cinnamon stick to the broth while it's simmering. You'll see. We will start with that and then see what you would like to sample."

"It sounds wonderful. Thank you."

Their conversation was easy and comfortable and the drive went more quickly than she imagined. The traffic increased as they approached Florence, slowing them down, and then they entered the maze of the city through a huge, ancient gateway.

"She looks like she must have quite a headache," Juliette said, pointing out a statue of a woman with a massive block of marble on her head at the entrance to the historic part of town.

"Indeed," Roman said. "I have often wondered why she's depicted that way," he smiled. "It's definitely not how I would like to spend thousands of years."

If anything, the level of driving became more intense as they entered Florence proper. Even as the crowds increased Roman didn't slow down for pedestrians or to pass by parked cars on narrow streets, and yet they seemed to confidently escape hitting side mirrors, curbs and even people without missing a beat. Roman turned down an alley, stopping his car behind a restaurant, which she could identify only because of the telltale cook leaning against the wall in a chef's apron, smoking a cigarette.

"*Mario, come va?*" asked Roman. How are things?

"*E pazzesco.*" Everything's crazy. How did you get here so fast?" he asked.

"What do you mean?"

"Antony's sick and Nicco is nowhere to be found. Mama wants you to cook tonight. Even if you can, though, we'll still be shorthanded. But forgive me. Who is this *bella* with you?"

Mario threw down his cigarette and stubbed it out with his shoe before blowing smoke out of the side of his mouth and approaching Juliette.

"Mario, this is Signorina Brice. She's a student in my class. Juliette, this is my youngest brother, Mario." She could see the resemblance in the eyes and nose. Although Mario was taller and more muscular, he was equally handsome, and Juliette was curious to meet the woman who had given birth to such gorgeous men.

"*Piacere di conoscerti,*" he said. Nice to meet you. Then he nodded his head toward the door to the restaurant.

"You better get in there and talk to Mama," Mario told his brother.

Roman steered Juliette through the back door and into the restaurant's kitchen.

"Wow!" Juliette couldn't keep herself from practically yelping when she saw how small and antiquated the kitchen was. It was nothing like the modern, expansive kitchen of the cooking school.

The chefs hardly had a place to turn around in here, she thought as she surveyed the space. It was spotless though. Gleaming copper pots and pans hung from hooks above the stoves and the stainless counters were wiped clean. As they passed through, there were only two prep cooks on the line—one frantically chopping onions and parsley while the other sautéed a vast quantity of mushrooms. He and Roman nodded to each other, but neither stopped to talk, so Juliette assumed they weren't family members. She inhaled deeply while she followed Roman through the kitchen. The aroma of sautéed mushrooms was one of her favorites.

"It smells delicious in here," she said as he led her through the swinging door and into the main part of the restaurant, which was still empty. Knowing they were short of help, she understood the tranquil atmosphere was like the calm before a storm.

Unlike the kitchen, the dining area was exactly as Juliette imagined. Cream linen tablecloths and a rich brown polished floor. There was a huge Deruta urn on a table in the middle of the room filled with olive branches dripping with black fruit. She made a mental note of it. It was exactly the type of thing she would like to decorate her own café with someday. Next to it on a plate, was a chunk of parmesan cheese wrapped and tied in a linen napkin with a fine cheese grater sitting next to it. The room was warm and inviting. Standing at the front near the door was Roman's mother. Juliette knew right away. She was rail thin and wore a perfect suit with not a hair out of place. She turned when she heard them enter the room and Juliette looked into the same brown eyes as her son's.

"Roman, how did you get here so fast? I just left a message for you five minutes ago."

"I didn't get the message from you. I was on my way here anyway. I brought a friend," he indicated Juliette with his hand "to show around Florence and have dinner here. Then I saw Mario and he told me about

Antony and Nicco."

"*Si,* well, I'm afraid we're going to need you tonight," his mother said, giving Juliette a tight little smile, which clearly indicated that she found her nothing more than another problem in her day.

"*Buona sera, Signora,*" Juliette said to Roman's mother and continued in her most formal Italian. "I'm also a trained chef, and I'd be happy to assist if you need help."

"Don't be ridiculous," Roman's mother answered in English, and looked to Roman to put a stop to Juliette's embarrassing offer.

"She's talented, Mama," Roman told her. "And you shouldn't refuse a gift, no? You yourself have told me that many times."

"Can she truly cook?" she asked her son, giving Juliette an appraising look, as if she was at worst an imbecile and at best a child.

"Like a goddess. And if you want me, you are going to have Juliette cook as well, because I've run that kitchen shorthanded, and it's *un incubo,* a nightmare, no?"

"Fine. Get her an apron and show her around," she said with a dismissive wave of her long-fingered, diamond-covered hand and then turned back to the reservation book.

Juliette was surprised by her cold demeanor and wondered how she could have raised such a warm, kind son.

Roman frowned at his mother and grabbed an apron out of a pile of linens.

"I'm sorry," he whispered, "she can be brusque sometimes." He exaggerated a grimace and rolled his eyes good-naturedly, which put Juliette back at ease.

They went back into the kitchen where he quickly showed Juliette around, then printed off the menu for the evening and posted it above each work station. He gave Juliette the recipe for the items he assigned her to cook and suggested she do a quick run through of each dish while he began prepping.

Juliette grinned at him as she tied her apron strings, suddenly glad she had dressed casually after all.

"This is going to be fun," she said. After taking down a large skillet she began to peruse the recipes. Roman smiled conspiratorially back at her and touched his lips to hers before walking into the refrigerator and bringing out boxes of ingredients.

"*Eccoci,*" he said. Here we go.

Juliette's heart leapt, surprised and pleased by the light kiss.

Mario walked out of the refrigerator right behind Roman, saw Juliette in an apron, and asked Roman if he could have a word with him. Juliette tried not to notice as the two men had a discussion in whispers and hand motions.

When they returned, Mario smiled warmly at Juliette and said, "Our *bella* savior."

"Hopefully," Juliette smiled. "We can decide at the end of the evening."

The dinner rush hit and the kitchen became a hive of activity. Roman kept an eye on what she was doing and yelled out instructions and encouragement on occasion. Juliette made a few missteps here and there, but managed to keep up with the items that were ordered from her station in the kitchen—even if she occasionally had to improvise when she wasn't sure how they prepared specific menu items. After she got used to the small size, she actually came to enjoy the kitchen's economy. There was no shuffling back and forth for ingredients. Everything was within reach. The prep cook also did the garnish, so Juliette didn't have to worry much about the presentation. Her job was all about preparing the dishes as they were specified. She was happy for the years of training she had under her belt.

Occasionally she and Roman would catch each other's eyes. There was a new intensity between them. His deep brown eyes held hers and turned her insides to warm, melted chocolate. She had to tear her eyes away and force herself to stay focused in order to keep up with the deluge of dinner orders being hooked on the thin, metal line that stretched across the shelf between Juliette and the dining room. She realized that her lips were curved into a perpetual smile in the midst of the chaos and was again happy that she wasn't spending her mom's birthday alone. She felt giddy and light—energized in a way that she hadn't felt in a long time.

Finally things started to slow down and Juliette stepped outside to take a break and get some fresh air. She leaned against the wall in the precise place she had first seen Mario hours before. She took a deep breath and then looked over as she heard the sound of the door swing open.

"That was the best date of my life," Juliette smiled at Roman as he walked through the door, meaning every word. It had been incredible working together.

Roman walked up to her, placed his palms on either side of her face and kissed her. The kiss began softly at first and then deepened. She put her arms around his neck and she felt him move his hands into her hair, which had come loose from the twist she had fastened.

Finally they broke apart, both of them trying to gain control.

"Thank you for helping out tonight," he murmured into her lips.

"Is that how you always thank the help?" Juliette asked him, tipping up her chin and holding his eyes.

"*Certo*," Roman said playfully. "Is that not customary in your country?"

"Of course it's customary," Juliette bantered back. "I just didn't realize it was the same in Italy."

Roman snorted. "Come on," he said, giving her another quick and playful kiss. He took her hand and steered her back inside, grabbing a stool for her to sit on. "You rest while I clean up the kitchen, and then at least I can take you out for a drink before we go back home."

Juliette set aside the stool and started to clear the dirty pots and pans, but Roman took the pile from her and pointed her back to the stool.

"Sit," he ordered. "You've done enough already."

Juliette tipped the corners of her mouth up. "I will gratefully say 'yes,' but would it be ok if we had a drink here instead of going somewhere else? Maybe we could make ourselves something to eat and have a glass of wine."

"*Oh, mio Dio!* I never gave you dinner! You must be starving, no? I suddenly realize I'm hungry, too."

"I am actually. Can we make something?"

"Of course. After all the help you gave us, we can make anything you want."

"I would settle for some of the *carabaccia* you told me about with some bread and a glass of wine."

"*Perfetto.* Why don't you go relax at the bar while I finish up here and then I'll bring out the soup and wine, ok? I'll meet you at the bar in a couple of minutes."

"That sounds great. Thanks," Juliette said and then slipped into the bathroom with her purse to freshen up.

Juliette looked in the mirror. She was relieved to see that she didn't look too bad. A bit flushed and a little greasy from all the cooking, but she had powder and lipstick, which were the only two truly necessary cosmetics in her opinion. She took down her hair and brushed through it with her fingers. She contemplated putting it back up, but decided it looked better down. She splashed her face, then dried it, powdered it, and put on a touch of lipstick.

When she made her way to the bar, she found Roman there with two glasses of Pinot Grigio, bread, cheese, olives, and two steaming bowls of onion soup.

She tipped her face toward the bowl of soup and inhaled deeply, catching the tantalizing aromas and the clean scent of herbs. She was ravenous. She wanted to rip off big hunks of the bread and dig in to the soup, but she could see Roman's mother surreptitiously glancing their way so she forced herself to be dainty about it.

The chemistry between them, so evident in the kitchen, was still at a simmer. They couldn't stop looking at each other as they ate their meal and rehashed the unexpected evening they'd had.

When they were ready to leave, and went to say good-bye to Roman's mother, the spell was only slightly broken. Juliette hoped for a bit more warmth than when she first met her, and she was rewarded by a genuine smile. His mother said all the right things. She thanked her, said *ciao*, even kissed her cheeks, but while her mouth was expressing the kind words, something in her face let Juliette know that she was not entirely welcome in her son's life. The hard pinch she gave her son's cheek left her curious as well.

"Ouch, Mama!" Roman laughed at her and playfully slapped her hand away. "This, for the man who saved the night?"

"I don't know what you're up to young man, but watch yourself, do you hear me?"

"*Si, si,* how could I not?" He purposefully stood over her small frame.

"You're a terrible boy, Roman." She shook her head, but with a look of love for her son. "Be careful of this one, young lady," she said to Juliette, then waved them away with a good natured shake of her head.

Back in the car, Juliette replayed the scene in her mind. It was slightly odd, but she didn't want to ask Roman about it and break the spell they were under. Instead she sank herself into the comfortable leather seats and turned to look at him. She couldn't seem to tear her eyes away. She loved the way he listened when she talked, the humor in his eyes. His was a perfectionist in class but she knew that was part of the reason he was stretching her cooking skills. He demanded more from her than the other students, but she could tell she had earned his respect and that gave her a surprising sense of pleasure. She knew she was dangerously smitten and that she had better be careful. She couldn't remember the last time her feelings for a man had become so intense in such a short time.

He kept his eyes on the road for the most part, occasionally looking over at her. He kept his right hand in hers, his fingers stroking her palm as they drove, talking a little, but mostly listening to music, lost in their own thoughts. The sound of the motor and the comfort of the seats lulled her into a sleepy state. Her eyes burned with the desire to close, but she didn't want to miss a moment of her time with him.

He was unguarded and real to her in a way she loved. Roman reached over and twisted a loose lock of hair absently and then gently stroked her cheek.

"It's ok, rest," he whispered. "I'll wake you when we arrive back at your door." His car was a small coupe, with a low console, so she leaned right across it, put her head on his knee and dozed, but didn't drift all the way to sleep.

By the time they reached Juliette's apartment, Lucca was dark and quiet. The city was bathed in moonlight. Roman hated to wake up the beautiful complication who dozed with her head on his lap. He knew he was wading into deep water with her but didn't want to stop. He gently shook her awake and then walked her up the stairs. He smiled at her sleepy face and rumpled hair. It made her look vulnerable and appealing. She was unlike any of the women he knew. She unlocked the door and then turned to thank him for the unusual but perfect evening. But when she opened her mouth to speak, he moved towards her and without even a second of hesitation they were kissing again.

Juliette was lost in the sensation. It was intoxicating, warm, sweet, and left her wanting more. When they finally broke apart, Juliette leaned her forehead against his collarbone. She breathed in deeply and then lifted her eyes to his. They didn't speak, but the communication was clear. She reached behind herself and opened the door. They both stepped in.

Chapter 11

CATARINA, THROWING LOVE
AND EMBROIDERED HANDKERCHIEFS
INTO THE SEA

Catarina lay in bed in the stuffy cabin under a thin blanket for a long time before sleep came. Maria snored softly beside her and the ship rocked gently, which should have lulled her to sleep, but even that couldn't quiet her churning thoughts. She played and replayed every moment of the most exciting evening she had ever had. She could hardly believe how wonderful it had been. Even the festivals at home weren't as much fun. She wished she could stop the ship from continuing on to America so she could stay right where she was. She discovered that she loved dancing and enjoyed wine with dinner. She felt giddy and knew that the wine she'd drunk was only one part of it.

Before she dropped off to sleep she thought of Franco. She wondered what he would be like. Surely not as wonderful as Gregorio, she thought. She wished she could switch the two men and that when she got off the ship Franco would have miraculously turned into Gregorio. She tried for the thousandth time to picture Franco's face from her memory. All she could conjure was dark hair and a thin face. It wasn't much to go on, but nonetheless, she tried to push Gregorio out of her mind and focus on Franco. When she finally dropped off to sleep, her dreams betrayed her efforts and Gregorio's face was the one she saw.

When morning came, Maria gently shook her awake.

"*Fa giorno,*" she said. It's morning.

Catarina sat up groggily, rubbed her eyes, and wondered how it could be morning already, when she felt as if she'd just fallen asleep.

How many days were left? she wondered. Her thoughts immediately went to Gregorio, and this time she didn't push them away. Instead she got ready with special care, in case she ran into him during the day. She wondered what he did on the ship. They had been so wrapped up in talking about his childhood and where he grew up that she had completely forgotten to ask him about his job.

The day passed slowly. A cold sea wind arose and the sea was the color of steel. It churned, rocking the boat relentlessly. Many of the passengers felt ill. Maria was among those who did, so Catarina brought damp cloths to her throughout the day. She couldn't bear to stay in the swaying cabin for long, though, and spent most of her time wrapped in a blanket on deck.

By dinnertime, Maria felt worse than before so Catarina had to venture to the dining room alone. She wasn't sure what to expect. Would the kitchen be closed because of the lurching of the ship?

Would Gregorio be there as he said he would?

She had only two nice dresses, so she wore the one he hadn't yet seen. It was the same blue as her eyes with a fitted bodice and a lavender sash that cinched tightly around her waist. The slim skirt made her feel taller than she was.

Gregorio was there waiting for her. Maria's absence made the meeting feel forbidden. In her mind's eye, she could see Babbo's eyebrows knit together and a frown on her mama's face. He wore his black crew uniform, which made him look elegant and sophisticated. He was speaking with one of his shipmates and they were laughing at something he said. She enjoyed watching him unawares for a moment. He seemed so at ease with himself and others. She admired that about him.

He must have felt her gaze because he turned towards her and she saw his expression change. It was a mirror of her feelings: excited and full of anticipation. He patted his friend on the shoulder and then turned and walked towards her. She met him in the middle.

"Catarina."

"*Buona sera.*"

"You're as beautiful as I remembered. Your face is like the Madonna and it was in my mind every second of the day."

Catarina felt her face flush.

"I should remind you that I'm engaged to be married. You shouldn't speak to me like that," she said properly, but she was pleased to know that he had thought of her as much as she had thought of him.

"You're right. *Scusi!* My apologies. But what am I supposed to do? I meet the girl of my dreams but her hand is already spoken for."

Catarina decided to laugh, as if it were a joke, so that they could go on being friends, but her face showed that she shared his regret.

"Perhaps I can entice you to run away with me instead of getting married," he bantered, allowing himself to say what he wanted under the guise of verbal play.

But Catarina wasn't skilled at that kind of interaction and simply looked down at her shoes for a moment.

When she regained her composure, she said, "Let's not talk like this. Let's have dinner and dance again. It was so much fun last night. But, I can't stay too late and I have to bring some bread back for Maria. The rocking of the ship is making her queasy."

"You're right. I'm sorry for being too forward. We have eight days left. Let's just have fun," said Gregorio, and then he took her hand and led her to the same table as the previous night.

The next eight days were by far the most exhilarating of Catarina's life. The sea air agreed with her and she stayed healthy throughout the voyage. Maria recovered once the sea calmed and the two became inseparable. She wrote letters to her family each day and collected them in a ribbon to post upon her arrival in New York. She and Maria washed out their clothes together each morning and hung them to dry in their cabin. They sat on their bed and up on deck for hours while they stitched borders on handkerchiefs for their future husbands. They talked about their fears and about missing their families, about whether a war would come and whether Italy would fight in it if it did. They talked about what it would be like to be a soldier and what it would be like to be a mother someday. They talked about what it was like to marry unknown men, as they were both planning to do.

The one thing they didn't talk about was Catarina's feelings for Gregorio. To speak about them out loud would be to acknowledge them as real. That she could not do. She thought about the words Gregorio had spoken during the second evening they were together. At night when she was supposed to be sleeping, she took them out and polished them in her mind to save forever: "Perhaps I can entice you to run away with me instead of getting married," he'd said. She knew she would remember those words and his face forever.

Even though she'd known him such a brief period, she wished she *could* run away with him. She would like nothing more, because although she'd known him such a short time, in the depths of her soul she believed she loved him. She couldn't allow herself to take those feelings out and nurture them. Instead she trampled them down like the grapes in the crush. She was a dutiful daughter and would go through with the marriage to Franco. She would embrace her new life, even if it would be painful.

For now, she allowed herself to enjoy her time. Every evening she, Gregorio, Maria, and a group of passengers and crewmen dined together. They quickly became her friends. The older women were her protectors, the young men her dance partners. The conversation was exciting and different because it had to do with the whole world instead of grapevines, olive trees, family, and people she'd known all her life.

Most of all, she reveled in her time with Gregorio. She had feelings no words could describe. She felt as if she were surrounded by a golden glow. They fit together perfectly. He continued to teach her to dance and even when they were dancing with others, they were aware of each other's presence. He was alive and charming to her in a way she hadn't encountered with young men at home. They talked and talked without tiring of each other's company.

The music was like nothing she had ever heard. There was a live band each night and the sounds were rich and mesmerizing. At home the music usually consisted of a mandolin and other string instruments, but nothing as stylish and graceful as the piano she heard aboard the ship. It was one more thing she came to love.

On the night before they were due to arrive in New York, Catarina felt as if her heart would be ripped out of her chest if she were forced to leave. She and Gregorio danced to song after song and then he took her hand and asked her if she would step out on to the deck with him. She knew she shouldn't. It wasn't proper, but her head nodded and her legs seemed to have ideas of their own. She followed him without a word of protest.

As soon as they were away from everyone else, he took her into his arms and kissed her. Her first kiss. His lips were warm on hers. She felt herself melting into him. She knew they should stop, but she didn't want to. When he stepped back from her, she started to silently cry. She looked out to sea, her face an expression of sorrow and pain. Everything she was doing was wrong, but she decided she could speak her mind, just this once. For this moment, she would tell the truth and then she would lock the words away.

She was about to speak when Gregorio beat her to it.

"Catarina, I promised myself that I wouldn't say this to you—that I wouldn't interfere, because I know that you're promised to someone else. But I love you. And the thought of you with someone else is killing me. How can you do this?" His voice was ragged, and he too was fighting back tears. "I want us to be together. *Ti prego*," he pleaded. Please.

"I want to be with you, too," she admitted. "But what am I to do? Franco is the son of my father's best friend. It would shame my father if I ran away with you. My mother would never acknowledge me again, and I couldn't stand that. I would be dead to them."

The wind whipped her hair and her teeth began to chatter. Gregorio tucked her into his warmth, her face turned against his chest.

"I wish I had never met you," he said. "I was happy before and now I'm crazed and filled with jealousy. It's terrible. My life is ruined." Gregorio ran one hand over his face while he kept the other wrapped around her.

"Don't say that. This has been the happiest nine days of my life. It's been the best time for me, and I will remember you always. I will love you always." It was easier for Catarina to be honest about her feelings, because tucked into his arms, she didn't have to see his face.

"If you truly loved me, then you would choose to be with *me*. Don't marry him, Catarina. We'll be happy together."

"I can't, Gregorio," Catarina looked up at him. "I wish I could. Believe me. I'm sorry."

"Then go," he said and stepped back away from her—the cold wind making her shiver. "If you're so afraid to disappoint them and to be dead to them, then fine. Instead, you're dead to me," Gregorio said.

"Stop. Please, I can't bear it if you despise me. I love you," she said.

Gregorio grabbed her forearms and then dropped them. He stepped towards her and then stepped back again and turned away.

"Please don't leave like this. Don't end it like this," Catarina pleaded.

"I don't want to end it at all," he shouted at her. "You're the one ending it," and then he strode away from her and didn't turn back.

Catarina waited for him to return, but he didn't. She was freezing out in the night wind coming off the ocean. She couldn't stop herself from crying. She took one of the handkerchiefs she had been working on out of her pocket and wiped her face and nose with it. She looked at Franco's initials in the corner of the cloth and then crumpled it up and threw it into the black, frothing sea.

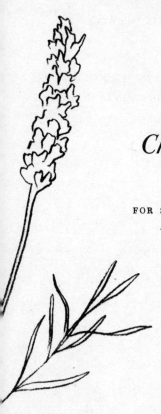

Chapter 12

"He's smart, and he loves food and cooking as much as I do. He's Italian—my ultimate fantasy—and he's even handsome which is a nice plus," Juliette told Gina, recounting the details from the night before to her sister.

"He's probably sick to death of Italian women. He probably thinks you're exotic."

"Who knows? Either way, you should have seen us, Gina. When we were cooking together in his parent's restaurant it was like some crazy aphrodisiac."

"The last time we talked, you said that you were having espresso together every day after class."

"We still do. Amazingly enough, I've finally met a man who actually talks about food more than I do."

"That's a miracle."

"I know. Oh my gosh, though. I have to tell you about his mother," Juliette said, then gave her a recap of the slightly odd treatment she'd received.

"And what was his take on it?" Gina asked when Juliette was finished with the story.

"I didn't ask. I didn't want to burst the bubble we were in."

"Well, I wouldn't worry about it. I've heard Italian mothers are particularly protective of their sons. Hey, speaking of parents and children, have you talked to Dad lately? There's something he wants to talk to you about."

Juliette's mind immediately went to the accident.

"Is it something about Mom?"

"It's kind of about Mom, but it's not bad, so don't worry. He discovered something that could be helpful to you."

"Helpful to me? How? What do you mean?"

"It's not for me to say. You'll have to talk to Dad."

"Seriously? Don't be weird. Just tell me."

"I can't. Sorry." Gina changed the subject. "Have you been inspired about opening your own café while you've been there?"

"You're infuriating, Gina," Juliette complained. "I can tell you're changing the subject, but fine, if you're not going to spill the beans, I'll humor you. The answer is yes, I keep seeing stuff that I'd love to incorporate into the look of my theoretical restaurant. There's one little café here that has light purple stemware with air bubbles inside. It's gorgeous and I've never seen anything like it. And Roman's family restaurant has the most beautiful rustic table with a huge pottery jug filled with olive branches. I'm putting something like that on my mental 'to do' list."

She picked up the folder she'd labeled "Café Inspiration" that was sitting on one of the cushions. It had never occurred to her that she would adore Italy quite as much as she did. And now this unexpected relationship with Roman had her reeling.

Over the almost-two months she'd been in Lucca, the folder she'd started had become jam-packed with recipes and ideas she'd hastily scribbled on pieces of paper as they came to her. She thumbed through the pages as she talked.

"Being here has been incredible. I've been making a folder with all of my favorite recipes, and I discovered a local restaurant that serves food that would make you weep. I wish I could take you there. It's going to be my model." She told her about *Salvia* and the amazing meal she'd had there with Odessa and Antonello, and then finally forced herself to say goodbye.

She missed her sister the second she hung up. They both had plenty of friends, but they had been each other's closest confidantes since they were in diapers. She wished Gina would meet someone and fall in love, too. She wanted her to feel the same rush of excitement she'd been feeling with Roman. And then the thought struck her that she was already labeling herself *in love*. It was scary but seemed right. She had dated a lot throughout her life, but had never felt this giddy sense of love before. It was exciting and she decided to not overthink it. She would just see where it took her and be grateful for it.

As Saturday morning crept toward afternoon, Juliette got a little stir-crazy so she made herself a cup of coffee and brought down the box of letters. She slipped the second letter out of the envelope. It was from someone named Maria Crostina.

As Juliette began to read, she realized the letter must be from the girl who had traveled by ship to the United States with her grandmother. Her words were filled with longing for home and struggle as she tried to get to know her new husband. Juliette couldn't imagine how strange that must have been. She wondered how old Maria was at the time. She would guess quite young. And her new husband seemed much older.

The letter was intriguing and Juliette poured over it, then sucked in her breath in surprise when Maria mentioned two names: Gregorio and Franco. Why two men? She recognized her granddad's name, of course, but who was the other, and how did he figure into Nonna Catarina's story? Juliette searched her mind for an answer but nothing came to mind and the letter abruptly ended. Before she could reach for the next to satisfy her curiosity, her phone rang. She ran to grab it, thinking it must be Roman, then saw the familiar number of her father on the screen.

"Hey Dad, how are you? Gina said you'd be calling. Is everything ok?"

"As ok as it can be right now. There's no new new information about what will happen with the drunk driver or when the trial will be. Besides that, I've been keeping busy at the university and doing some work around the house."

"Am I going to recognize it when I get home?"

"I'm not sure," her dad sighed, and ran his fingers through his gray hair.

"Has the same contractor been helping you? Ian, right?" Juliette asked, thinking about the man who sat beside her outside the hospital room where her mother's body had been taken.

"Yes, he's been great."

"I need to thank him when I get home," Juliette paused, "for helping me."

"With what?" Alexander asked. "Did you have some work done on your studio?"

"No, I need to say thank you because he was kind to me," Juliette told him. "He stayed with me at the hospital until Gina got there. He sat with me and held my hand, even though he had never even met me before."

"I didn't know that," Alexander said. "To be honest, I hardly remember the details of the day beyond the shock of it."

"Me too."

"I'm actually calling because I have some news."

"What's that?" Juliette braced herself.

"It's about your mom's estate."

"Estate?" Juliette asked. "What do you mean?"

"Your mom left you some money, Sweetheart."

"But you're still alive. I mean, not to state the obvious, but wouldn't you keep everything?"

"There's family money and the family business. It's always been set up that you and Gina would inherit directly."

Juliette was having trouble taking in what he was saying. Since when had there been family money? No one had ever said anything about it.

"I'm confused," she told him.

"Your mom and I always had money that we comingled. Mine

from my professorship and hers from working at the jewelry store, but your mother came into the marriage with a share in the business and it has always been understood that it would go directly to you and Gina when she died. It's a family business, Juliette, and I'm just the guy who married in," Juliette's dad said with good-natured humor.

"But that's why I got the ring, right? Mom left the business to Gina, but you already gave me the ring."

"That's correct except for the division of the finances. Gina got Mom's share of the business and the earnings from it going forward. That's her legacy and you have the ring, but the two of you share equally in the value of what was your mother's share of the business at the time of her death. I needed to sort out the details of the estate before telling you about the money."

Juliette's heart was pounding against her chest.

"Dad, I can't possibly take it. It's the last thing I want given the role I played in Mom's death."

"Are you still torturing yourself with that?" Alexander paused to collect himself before continuing. "I thought we were straight on this, Juliette. You played *no* role in your mother's death. There's nothing you could have done. It was an accident. You didn't cause the drunk to hit your mom. And I'm sure as hell glad he didn't take out you as well."

A sob escaped Juliette, "I should have yanked her out of the way, but I froze. She would have saved *me*. I know she would have, but I just stood there like an idiot watching her get run down." The pain of it felt like her heart was being seared and Juliette subconsciously put her hand on her chest and doubled over.

"Listen to me. It is not your fault. You have to stop this. You're being irrational and it would have pissed your mother off. "

Juliette closed her eyes. Even if he was right, she couldn't hear it yet.

"It's a sizeable amount of money, Juliette," he continued. "You could use it to open your café. It's what Mom would have wanted for you."

"I don't want it, Dad." Juliette told her father. "I'm sorry, but I have to go now. I'll talk to you later, though, ok?"

"Juliette . . ."

"I love you. I'll take to you later. I've got to go, I'm sorry."

Alexander sighed. "All right, and I love you too, but we're not done with this," he told her before they disconnected.

Juliette sighed, held her head in her hands, lay down, and cried until she was all cried out. Then she stared at the ceiling while she tried to figure out what to do next. She knew her dad was right in that her mom wouldn't want her to wallow in her misery, so she forced herself to get up, pull herself together, and get out of the apartment.

She realized the day was mostly gone and she hadn't heard from Roman. She had expected him to at least call her or send a sweet text after spending the previous night together. She felt stir-crazy but didn't have a plan, so she decided to go to the market to see if she could find Odessa. She grabbed her coat and started out the door, almost tripping over a potted plant on her doorstep. It was filled with lovely purple blooming pansies, and there was a note tucked inside. In Roman's handwriting she read: *Mi sono svegliato pensando a te*. I woke up thinking of you.

She unconsciously placed the fingers of one hand to her lips and smiled a little in spite of her mental state. Maybe better than a phone call or a text she decided, and wondered when he had left the flowers there. She brought them inside and placed the pot in the center of her kitchen table. It added a homey touch to her tiny apartment and she was grateful for their cheeriness.

She buttoned her coat and wrapped her scarf around her neck. The weather reminded her of home. She guessed it was around 40 degrees, but in her opinion that counted as frosty. Christmas was close. When she decided to sign up for the class, she worried about being away over Christmas, but as it approached, she found that she was feeling fine about it. She'd bought gifts for her dad and Gina and had already sent them home.

She walked down the stairs and into the section of town where the weekend farmer's market was held. She browsed through the stalls and pondered what she would actually do on Christmas day itself. She decided on going to church and making herself dinner. Maybe she'd watch a Christmas movie on the computer. It wasn't ideal, but she knew she'd survive. While she thought about it, she kept shopping. She chose a crusty *ciabatta* loaf and some brie, along with a mixture of olives dripping with pungent oil and herbs to nibble with her dinner. She spied some delicate gem lettuces and added them along with a lemon to her shopping basket. She could already taste the fresh salad dressing she would whisk together made of lemon juice, virgin olive oil, and a pinch of salt. She finally spotted Odessa's stand from afar and made her way over. The booth was crowded, so she stood to the side until Odessa had a free moment.

"*Buon giorno*, Odessa."

"*Buon giorno*, Juliette! *Come stai*?"

"*Bene, grazie*," she told her friend. "*Posso convincerti ad uscire per un bicchiere di vino dopo il lavoro*? Can I lure you out for a cup of wine after work?

"*Si, ottimo!* That would be wonderful. Meet me back here at six fifteen."

"*Va bene.* See you then."

It was only four thirty, but Juliette's fingers were cold, so she decided to take everything back to her apartment and warm up before returning to meet Odessa.

Walking back towards a flower stall selling early-blooming paper whites, she spotted Roman an aisle away. She found herself smiling and started to make her way towards him. He turned and saw her coming and flashed her a heart-splitting smile in return.

When she reached his side, he wrapped her in a hug and rubbed her arms to warm her up.

"Thank you for the flowers and note. It was a nice surprise and perfect timing because I needed cheering up."

"Why did you need cheering up?" he asked, tucking her cold hands inside his coat and pressing them to his sides to warm them. "Would you like to go for an espresso or a *cioccolata calda* and you can tell me what's going on?"

"I would love to. Then I'm going to meet Odessa for a glass of wine, if you'd like to join us."

"I didn't know you were friends."

"I met her on my very first day here. The same day I saw you at her cheese stall."

"Ah yes, I remember well. The day my heart was stolen."

Juliette smiled at him. He took her hand and steered her towards a nearby espresso bar where they ordered *cioccolate calde* and grabbed a table.

"What's saddening you, Juliette?" Roman asked once they were seated.

"Just a conversation I had with my father about my mom."

"Ah, I understand. This is difficult for you, no?"

"It is. But I'm trying to focus on the positive. And speaking of that, I want you to know that I had a wonderful time last night. Thank you, again. I know it wasn't exactly what you planned when you invited me to dinner, but it was great. I had forgotten how much I enjoy the rush of cooking in a restaurant."

"It was a perfect coincidence that we arrived when we did. We couldn't have done it without you."

He lifted her hand and kissed it.

Juliette's heart skipped a beat.

"So, Signor Capello, tell me," she said, "are there any terrible secrets I should know about you? Any skeletons in your closet? Are you actually a criminal or something? Because you seem awfully perfect to me."

"Ha, far from perfect, but no, with me what you see is what you get."

"Hummm," she leaned over and kissed his lips, "so far, I like what I see."

"I'm glad to hear it," Roman said and then proceeded to entertain her by recounting a humorous snippet about the mayor of a nearby town who had been caught in a hotel with his son's tutor. "It's true," he laughed, "I read in the newspaper this morning."

He had Juliette laughing too, and before she knew it, she was in a much-improved mood and it was time to meet Odessa.

Once back in the market square, she scanned the few people who milled about as the vendors took down their booths. She headed towards Odessa's stall where she saw her waiting while her father finished the last bit of packing up.

"*Ciao*," Odessa said and kissed her on one cheek. "You look happy."

"Does it show?"

"Yes," she smiled. "Come on, I know just the spot to have a glass of wine and you can tell me what has you looking so pleased," she said and took Juliette's arm.

Juliette was looking forward to telling Odessa about the new status of her relationship with Roman. She wanted to find out how well she knew him and see if she had any insights. She felt surprisingly comfortable with Odessa already and they fell into an easy conversation while they made their way to a wine bar tucked into a side street. Juliette had never noticed it, but it was obviously known by all the locals because it was quite full.

When they were seated with wine, bread, and olives in front of them, Juliette asked, "Do you remember the handsome guy who was also in your stand the day I met you?"

Odessa frowned for a moment, thinking back, and then raised her eyebrows.

"Roman Capello?"

"Yes!" Juliette smiled at Odessa as if she was a star pupil. "He's teaching the cooking class I'm taking. We've been hanging out after class, getting to know each other, and then last night we spent the evening together and one thing led to another . . ."

"With Roman?" Odessa looked surprised.

"Do you know him well? What do you think of him?" Juliette asked.

"Of course I know him. In a town this size everyone knows everyone. He's wonderful. Smart, handsome of course, good family. Has he mentioned past relationships, though? Perhaps you should ask him if he has any entanglements."

"Entanglements?" Juliette didn't like the sound of that.

"Yes. I only mention it because I happen to know he was in a relationship with a journalist named Maddelena, but if he's involved with you, it must have ended."

"Hummm." Juliette looked down at her glass and gently swirled the wine. "I asked him if he had any secrets to tell me and he didn't say anything about a girlfriend or a break-up."

"Then you should take him at his word," she said, and then added after a brief hesitation, "Perhaps be cautious."

"Thanks, I will," Juliette told her, but she knew she wasn't going to be cautious. She had never felt such intense emotion about a man and she was enjoying the feeling. She wanted to leap right into the deep end of the pool with him and enjoy the swim. She found herself visualizing herself throwing her dreams to the wind and staying in Lucca, getting a cute bike with a basket on the front to carry her groceries and growing old with this man. It felt right with him in a way she had never experienced. But, for now she decided to keep that to herself. To Odessa, she said, "We aren't very involved yet anyway, so don't worry. Enough about me, though," Juliette said to change the subject. "I want to hear about you and how it's going with Antonello. I had such a good time having dinner with you two. In fact, I would love to have you over to my apartment soon. I'll have a little dinner party and practice some things I've been learning in class."

"That would be wonderful."

"*Va bene*," said Juliette. "Now, about Antonello . . ."

Later, as Juliette lay in bed, the word *entanglements* popped into her mind again. She pushed the thought to the back of her head and slipped into sleep.

Chapter 13

Catarina felt a jolt as the ship docked at Ellis Island. Her face was puffy from crying and the tears continued to slide down her cheeks as she folded her clothes and put them into her suitcase.

Maria snuck glances at her periodically, and after she buckled her own suitcase shut, silently picked up some of Catarina's things and started folding them for her. When there was nothing left to do, the two girls sat on the bed.

The waiting seemed interminable.

"Here," Maria said, and took a piece of paper out of her pocketbook. This has my name as well as Roberto's. I know you've heard about my *fidanzato* for days and days, but this way you won't forget. It also has the address of his family's apartment in New York, where we're going to live. Write to me, ok? You're the only person I know here. I know we'll be on the opposite sides of a vast country, but no matter what, or when, if we need each other, we can go to each other. *Va bene?*"

"*Si*," Catarina hugged her friend. "*Va bene.*"

"But this isn't goodbye yet. I've heard going through immigration is a long process here, so we'll be together for hours more, perhaps longer."

"Franco said it might even take a couple of days. But he said he would be waiting here, so he'll meet me here whenever I'm done."

"Are you going to try to see Gregorio this morning?"

"No." Catarina looked down at her hands. "He made it clear that he didn't want to see me."

"That might be for the better." Maria smiled empathetically at her friend.

"*Forse*," Catarina nodded. Maybe.

"Come on. Let's leave our bags here for a bit and go up to the deck and look across the bay at New York instead of waiting in a long line to get off the ship. It will take forever, so we might as well go look at the view."

"You're right," Catarina said and heaved herself up. "And let's try to stick together when we're at Ellis Island, *va bene?*"

"Like we're sewn together."

"*Esattamente*, like we're sewn together. And we stayed healthy! No lice. No fever or sickness."

Up on deck, the fresh, humid summer air felt good. The ship's rails were thick with people trying to get a glance at their new country.

At first the girls could only see the backs of other passengers who were stacked almost ten-deep along the side of the ship that faced the city. But eventually they made their way forward. Catarina was able to scoot through a gap and got to the front first, but she had Maria's hand and was able to pull her through the crowd beside her.

"*Oh, mio Dio!* It's so big!" Catarina exclaimed, and in spite of her sadness, had a flash of excitement. Even from afar New York was bigger than she had imagined. The buildings were taller than anything she had seen before and there were so many. The statue she had heard about— what did they call it?—Lady Liberty?—was immense, like nothing she had ever imagined. This is the world she had come to. This is what she had left her home and family for. She felt a spark of hope and she told herself to hold on to it.

Over the last weeks the combination of having to say goodbye to everyone she loved, and then meeting an amazing man whom she also had to leave, was heartbreaking beyond anything she had imagined possible. Until now, she hadn't known that someone's heart could truly feel as if it were being wrenched apart.

She tried to push her thoughts away from what she was losing and focus on what life would be like now that she had arrived. She wondered how San Francisco would compare to New York. Would the buildings be so tall? New York was larger than she had imagined and she wondered if that's how all cities in this new country would be. She felt overwhelmed but determined.

I will make this work, she said to herself. I will choose to be happy here. I will make it happen. She turned and hugged Maria again.

"We're here!" she yelled, and the new friends laughed together, overcome by emotion.

A ny exuberance they felt had gradually drained out of them by the time they finally disembarked at Ellis Island. It began with an inspection before they were allowed to leave the ship. Authorities checked their eyes, ears, tongues, teeth, hair and skin. They checked their foreheads for any fever, and if all looked healthy, they were allowed to walk down the gangway to the next line. Those who were found to be infirm were directed into another line. Catarina wondered what would happen to them. Would they have to leave? What about keeping families together? She was grateful she didn't have to find out.

She waited, barely breathing, as Maria went through the same inspection, and finally they were allowed to join the line, for those leaving the ship. She still hadn't caught sight of Gregorio. Although she told Maria she wasn't going to see him again, she had hoped to at least have a chance to say goodbye. She wondered if he had purposefully avoided seeing her or if his duties had kept him away.

As if she could read Catarina's thoughts, Maria caught her friend's attention. "Come on," she nodded down the gangway to the line onshore. "Let's see if what they say about sea legs is true."

So Catarina tore her eyes away from the ship and walked down the gangway. When her feet touched soil, she was surprised to find that she did feel a bit wobbly. She laughed in spite of herself. Just then, she felt Gregorio's presence and whipped around back towards the ship. She saw him on the lower deck, watching her. He saw her laughing and just as she began to wave to him, she watched him turn away.

"Let him go," Maria said. She saw the hurt on her friend's face. "There's nothing you can do anyway."

"But now he'll think I don't care about him." She despised the thought of him not understanding how she yearned for him.

"I think he understands, but he's not who you're here for. You have to let him go."

"I know you're right, but . . ." she stammered, torn, and searched the now-empty deck railing one more time before she turned back to her friend.

"It's a new life," Maria told her and squeezed her hand.

"*Si*, a new life," Catarina forced herself to stand up straight and smile back.

Unfortunately their "new life" began with a long immigration process. Hours and hours after they left the ship, they were still waiting in line. Catarina, like everyone, shoved her trunk and suitcase forward inch by inch. Workers came by with water and bread for everyone waiting, but the line moved forward at a snail's pace and they began to worry that they wouldn't even make it into the building by nightfall.

Fortunately they did make it through the doors, but just barely. Their first night in America was spent curled up on the hard floor, still in line, wrapped in blankets provided for them, and surrounded by their suitcases and trunks. Catarina was thankful to have Maria by her side. She hated to think of what it would have been like to go through this process alone.

When morning came after their fitful night, the girls tried to tidy themselves as best as they could. They scrubbed their mouths, brushed their hair, and splashed their faces with the water that had been doled out. Neither felt comfortable changing clothes while still in line so resigned themselves to meet their fiancés looking like wrinkled street urchins. At least they knew both men had also been through this process and wouldn't be surprised. Still, it was hard to meet the most important people in their futures knowing they were dirty and probably smelled bad, too.

Even the breeze off the water didn't help the crowded, hot, stuffy conditions inside the customs building on Ellis Island. Immigrants shuffled in and the slow moving lines caused disheartening delays. When it was time for their physical exams, the girls were separated. Neither knew how to protest their separation in English so they were at the mercy of the immigration officers.

Catarina was led down a long corridor filled with people. She looked over her shoulder and caught a glimpse of Maria's back as she stepped through a door Catarina had passed. She made a note of which door it was so she could go back to meet her friend after they were finished examining her. There was a nurse and a doctor in the room. The efficient middle-aged woman was dressed in a light-gray dress with a white apron, her graying hair tucked into a white cap. The man wore a brown suit and tie with a white coat over it and a contraption slung around his neck, which she later discovered he could use to listen to her heart and breathing. The doctor examined her ears, eyes, mouth, hair, and skin for infestations while murmuring to the nurse, who was checking boxes off of a form. He poked and prodded her more than she had ever been in her life. The nurse then asked Catarina in broken Italian for her name, wrote it on a line at the top of the card, stamped the form and then handed it over while ushering in the next expectant immigrant.

When she left, Catarina hoped to see Maria waiting for her, but was disappointed. Instead, there were more people moving along the hall with their bags and trunks, preventing her from going back to wait for her friend. They told her she had to keep moving forward down the hall. She told them she had to wait, but after it began to get heated, she lost her resolve and decided to keep moving to the next area. She wondered what awaited her there: More questions? She wondered if they even understood all of her answers. She frantically looked for Maria in the sea of strangers.

She turned a corner and then was surprised to enter a different section of the large, open room where they had spent the first night. It was blocked off from the newer arrivals, but Catarina scanned that area of the room anyway, just in case Maria had been sent back there for some reason. Catarina shuffled forward in the line, hoping she would catch up to her friend, but became increasingly worried when she didn't see even a glimpse of her. What if Maria hadn't passed the physical for some reason? What if she was going to be sent back to Italy?

The moving stream of bodies continued to push her forward, and by the time Catarina reached a desk that appeared to be the final document checkpoint, Maria was still not to be found. They asked her to produce her papers. She now had her coveted health form along with her Italian nationality papers, and the form stating that she was immigrating to the United States to be married. She took them out of her purse and they signed and stamped them in several places. Then they had her sign a large, numbered journal to record her entry into the country, and then shockingly, it was done. Her long ordeal was over. They indicated that she should go through the doors, and told her that there was a spot where fiancés were directed to wait for their brides, but she didn't want to leave without Maria. She waited to the side of the door for a while, dazed that the process was finished but reluctant to leave the building without her friend. Every moment seemed like an eternity while she stood there. Was Franco waiting outside for her? Was Maria's future husband there as well? Should she find him and tell him that she didn't know what had happened to his fiancée? She looked around to search for her one more time but when her eyes met only other immigrants, she finally picked up her suitcase and dragged her trunk through the door.

She blinked in the sunlight and looked around. Inhaling deeply, she took in the fresh air. She felt the distance of every mile that separated her from her family. Here she was in her new country and she had never felt more alone.

She looked around to find the area she had been told about and immediately spotted a group of men waiting behind a rope. The men looked different to her from the men she knew in Italy. Many of them wore suits with ties and hats, instead of overalls and clothing suitable for outside work. Some held signs with their bride's name written on them. When they spotted Catarina moving uncertainly toward them, they rousted themselves. Some held up their signs hopefully and others good-naturedly called out to her. She didn't recognize Franco in the group—not that she thought she would—but she continued to look, hoping he had a sign with her name. Then, she heard it— tentatively at first.

"Catarina?" Then it became louder and more sure. "Catarina Pensebene? Catarina! I'm here!"

She saw a man shove his way to the front of the group. And then she saw him. Relief flooded her. She ran towards him and hugged him as if it were Mateo who stood before her. The other men cheered. Some of them clapped Franco on the back. The atmosphere was charged with goodwill.

She let go of him and stood back, suddenly remembering that she hardly knew him, and a sense of formality overcame her sense of relief.

"*Buon giorno,* Franco."

"*Buon giorno,* Catarina. It's good to see you again." His eyes were smiling with warmth and happiness.

"*Grazie.*" While they spoke, she took in his face. It was nice-looking, but she couldn't stop herself from comparing it to Gregorio's. Franco's face, instead, was narrow and his nose was a classic Italian nose. His eyes were a rich deep brown, instead of the light green of Gregorio's, and his hair was straight and dark. He wore brown pants and a white button-down shirt rolled up at the sleeves, and a hat to keep the sun out of his eyes.

It's ok, though, she told herself. It's a kind face.

And then she remembered Maria and looked around once again for her.

Franco noticed an almost frantic look crossing her face.

"*Tutto a posto? Hai perso qualcosa?*" Is everything all right? Did you lose something?

"Maria. I have to find her. She's the girl who shared my berth for the crossing. It was perfect, Franco, because she also came here to get married. We became fast friends."

"*Si*, don't worry. We'll find her."

"We stayed together though immigration, but then we got separated at the end and I couldn't find her. I can't leave her. I need to know that she made it through and say goodbye."

"Don't worry," he reassured her again.

"Her *fidanzato's* first name is Roberto," Catarina said, opening her purse. "Let me find where I have his surname," she searched through her purse until she found the name and address Maria had given her before. "Penachi," she said and handed Franco the note with his name.

"Roberto Penachi!" Franco yelled into the crowd. And then louder, "ROBERTO PENACHI!"

"*Qui!*" a man yelled back. "Here!"

A stocky, homely man came forward and Catarina smiled with relief, because she could tell, just by looking at him, that he was nice. His face was sympathetic and open.

"*Buon giorno, Signor Penachi.* My name is Catarina Pensebene and I made the crossing with your fiancée, Maria. We got separated at the end of our time going through immigration, and I'm looking for her. I wanted to make sure she made it through. I don't know what could have kept her." She spoke rapidly, as if she needed to get the whole story out at once. "We went in to the examination rooms at the same time, and then when I was done, I couldn't find her again."

A look of concern crossed his face as he considered the different things that could have gone wrong. People were turned away all the time for many different reasons.

The three stood awkwardly for some time, staring at the doors, willing Maria to walk through them. Each time someone emerged they would look up hopefully. At least forty-five minutes passed while they made painful small talk and waited. Catarina told them an abbreviated version of their trip and about how much they enjoyed each other's company. And then finally, behind a large family, came Maria. Her face held the same tentative expression that Catarina's had when she walked through the doors, and then she saw her friend. They ran to each other and threw their arms around each other.

"What happened to you?" they said simultaneously.

"I couldn't find you after the examination," Catarina said. "When I got out, I tried to wait, and then other people in line pushed me forward until I was in the other room and I couldn't find you!"

"When I went in to get my exam, there was a large family still inside and I had to wait, and wait. I'm so glad to see you!"

"I was so worried when you didn't come out. I couldn't think of any reason they would turn you back, but when it was so long, I was sure there was trouble."

Finally the girls slowed down enough for Roberto to graciously clear his throat, so he could meet his future wife.

"Excuse me," he said quietly, then moved forward a step and took off his hat. "Maria, may I present myself? I am Roberto Penachi."

"Pleased to meet you," she said, looking down shyly. "I'm sorry I am so dirty. I wish I could have looked better to meet you."

He smiled at her kindly. "You look beautiful to me," he said shyly. "Besides, we know what it's like, don't we, friend?" he said to Franco. "I am eager to bring you home to meet my family."

"Yes, we should be going, too," Franco agreed.

"Promise to write to me," Maria said, hugging Catarina once again.

"I will. And you write to me, too. *Si*? And thank you for everything," Catarina gave her a meaningful look, knowing she would understand that she meant.

Maria smiled back at her. "You're welcome. Be happy."

"You, too."

The August day was humid and sweltering. Catarina's clothes stuck to her and she was desperate to rest after a night on the hard floor. Franco led her to the shade of a tree where he left her to arrange accommodations for the next ferry. He soon returned with a porter, who took her trunk and suitcase and delivered them to the dock. Once on board, they sat together along the rail of the boat, so she could see the city as they approached.

"It's strange," she said as they got closer." It's big. Much larger than I imagined."

"It is," he smiled, remembering how he felt when he first arrived. "I got rooms for us at a hotel for the next two nights, so you can rest and we can see New York, and then we'll take a train to San Francisco."

"Rooms?" she said, her tone unsure and nervous.

"Yes, separate rooms, so don't worry," he reassured her.

"Thank you."

"You're welcome. And guess what?" he asked her, as excited as a child showing off a new toy. "The hotel where we're staying has a water closet. Water comes out of pipes and you can have a bath in a bathtub right in your room."

"I don't understand," Catarina said. A vision of the water pump in the square at home coming to mind.

"You'll see." Franco recalled the first time he seen indoor plumbing and had a hot bath in a bathtub. He could fully submerge himself in the claw-foot tub at home. It was so different than the customary sponge baths when he visited family in Italy.

He turned towards Catarina. Her face was pink from the breeze coming off the water. She was as lovely as he'd known she'd be.

"Before we get there though," he said. "I have something to give you. It's something I made myself. It represents the fact that I will be good to you. I will always take care of you. It's a way to say thank you for taking this risk, and agreeing to be my wife."

Catarina looked up at him. His face was so serious and hopeful. Franco reached into the pocket of his coat, pulled out a box, and then carefully opened the lid. Inside was the most exquisite ring she had ever seen. It was diamonds in a platinum setting. The center stone had a line of three baguettes on each side and then those diamonds were surrounded in three fleur de lys of small diamonds.

Her hands were shaking, but he took her left hand and slid it onto her wedding-ring finger.

"It's *bellismo*, Franco. More than I could ever imagine."

"Each stone is flawless, like you."

Catarina choked back a small laugh. "I am *not* flawless," she said and guiltily thought back to throwing the handkerchief she'd made for Franco into the sea just two days before. And now, she was accepting this ring, which felt disingenuous.

But her mother's voice was in her mind. "Choose happiness," it said. Catarina had left home to find a better life. She had given up family and Gregorio and now here she was being presented with a flawless gift. She resolved to make sure she would live up to her wedding vows. She would embrace her life and her husband.

"*Grazie*, Franco. I don't know what to say. It's a work of art."

Franco smiled, obviously pleased.

"And this way, with a ring on your finger, no one will question us traveling together before we're married. I don't want any appearance of impropriety. My brother would have come as a chaperone to avoid any risk of gossip but we're so busy at the store, it was even difficult for me to get away. But be assured," he said, "I will behave honorably."

For the first time since she and Gregorio had parted, Catarina laughed. "I'm sure you will be honorable, or my babbo will skin you alive. All the way from Italy."

Franco laughed as well. "Yes, he would."

Chapter 14

O ver the next weeks Juliette knew she was falling hard. There were many things that attracted her to Roman: his wit, his sophistication, his *Italianness*. The time she spent with him felt supercharged, intense and exhilarating, like she was a more exciting version of herself with him.

Roman was generous with praise, listened to her thoughts and dreams, was a gentleman about little things like opening the door, following her up the stairs, and standing up when she returned to the table when they went out to dinner. He was a class act and she appreciated it. Completely aside from feelings of attraction, she adored him and he seemed to feel the same. They spent hours upon hours together and their interest in each other never seemed to wane. The fact that she was due to leave at the end of the class session loomed in her mind.

She had been falling in love with Italy as well. Not just the Italy she was in, but also with the Italy described in Catarina's letters. She poured over the correspondence during her downtime and was surprised by what she was learning about her grandmother and her life growing up. She'd had no idea that she had been the victim of an attempted rape until she discussed it in her letter to her friend Maria. And even then, she only talked about it to encourage her friend to find the good in her circumstances. She wanted her to search for happiness with her husband in spite of her homesickness. To see that good could come from something difficult in the same way she felt that the happiness *she* had found had been born from the terror of her experience, which prompted her to accept the marriage proposal instead of staying in Italy.

"She was such a strong woman," Juliette told Gina when they talked.

"Interesting that Nonna fled *from* Italy to get away from a terrible situation and you fled *to* Italy for the same reason."

"Hardly the same reason," Juliette countered.

"Not exactly the same, but interesting coincidence nonetheless."

"Yeah, I guess I can see that. So maybe I should ask myself what Nonna would do if she were me."

"I know exactly what she would tell you."

"What's that?"

"To use the money Mom left you to open your café when you get home."

Juliette sighed. She didn't want to talk about it, but she could see her sister's point. Then again, maybe she wasn't ready to go home yet.

Juliette had been spending almost as much time at Roman's apartment as at her own. It was on the second floor, just off the square, with stone walls and multiple twisted wrought-iron balconies. His furniture was luxurious and comfy—grays and dark browns. His couch was something she sank into and never wanted to get out of. But the best part was the mess. There were stacks of cookbooks, old newspapers piled up, and herbs drying along the window (something most American men would never do). It was the perfect combination of old and new world and she liked having some of her things strewn here and there amidst his stuff.

She couldn't get enough of his kitchen. There were copper pots and pans hanging above the stove and rustic wooden countertops. She wanted to live and die in his kitchen.

She often sat at his counter in the evenings after class with a glass of wine and a bowl of pasta, making notes on the iPad she bought once she realized her folder was getting bloated with too many scraps of paper.

Roman was full of ideas and often gave suggestions about what she could do if she opened a café. He talked about teaching techniques and his favorite recipes, produce, cheese, and equipment.

He often came behind her while she typed in her notes, lifting her hair and kissing her neck. Then he'd move away and pick up a book. He had thick black-rimmed reading glasses that somehow made his face even sexier.

Juliette sighed. "I'm starting to get confused," she said, turning to Roman and switching off her iPad.

"About what?" he asked, folding the newspaper and looking at her.

"My mom left me some money and I could use it to open my café, but I don't think using the money would be right. I mean," she clarified, "I don't think I could stand to use the money."

"Why not?"

Juliette put her head in her hands. She hadn't elaborated about the circumstances of her mom's death since the abbreviated explanation she'd initially given Roman. Her plan of deep denial had been working and she was loathe to rock her newly-acquired boat of contentment. It had been a relief to keep it to herself, but now she needed to talk it through with him.

"Because I don't want the money. I want my mom back. I know that sounds juvenile. I just want to undo the whole terrible thing. I want to relive the moment and shove her out of the way of the car. Just to shove her out of the way and undo it."

Roman scooted next to her and took her hand.

"You told me your mother was hit by a car in front of you. Maybe you should tell me exactly what happened. Therapy, no? Aren't you Americans fond of telling everything?" He smiled and nudged her with his shoulder in an attempt to cajole her into talking about it.

So she did talk to him about everything that had happened— including the nightmares, finding the letters and plane ticket her mom had given her the day she was killed, escaping to Italy, and finally the inheritance that was emotionally ripping her apart.

When she was done she smiled, "That actually was thera-peutic. *Grazie.*"

"*Si*, American through and through."

"What do you think I should do?"

"I can see how painful this has been, but unfortunately there's nothing to be done, *mia cara*. That's the terrible tragedy about life, no? It moves forward *solamente* and we can't change our mistakes."

"I know. I mean, I know that intellectually, but I'm having trouble coming to terms with it."

"Clearly," he smiled sympathetically at her. "What would your mother want you to do?"

"Use the money." Juliette said without hesitation.

"Then, perhaps that's what you should do," he said gently.

"That's what my dad and sister think, and sometimes lately I've been thinking the same. But then, my mind switches gears. I think about the guilt I feel, and I think about you and about how much I love it here. I can't even imagine leaving. How can I be so at odds with myself? I feel like a ping-pong ball."

Roman rubbed her arm and touched her face.

Juliette looked at his face and knew that she had fallen in love with this kind-hearted man: he was opinionated and funny, shared his dreams and details about his family and friends.

So how could she leave in another couple of months whether she wanted to open a café or not? But then again, how could she not leave? She knew her dad and sister wanted her home.

She snuggled next to Roman.

"What am I going to do?" she asked him.

"I'll tell you what you're going to do, *bella*. You're going to learn everything there is to learn while you're here and stop worrying about the future. It will take care of itself. Stop being a—what did you call it? Ping-pong ball?"

"That's easier said than done," she kissed his cheek. "But I'll try."

"*Esatamente*, that's good." Roman put his arms around her, pulled her to him, and kissed her until her mind was on to new thoughts entirely.

In the spirit of enjoying her time in Italy instead of ruminating, Juliette decided to plan the dinner she had spoken about with Odessa ages before. It had slipped her mind in the intensity of her relationship with Roman, but she finally set a date to cook for her friends.

She envisioned an extension of the dinner she, Odessa, and Antonello had at her now-favorite restaurant. She splurged on a couple of bottles of exceptional wine and cooked *pici con salsa alle noci*, thick handmade egg noodles with walnut sauce. They had learned to make the rustic noodles in class, but it was the first time Juliette tried to craft them on her own. The creamy walnut sauce was one of her favorites and she knew it would be delicious and worth the hours the meal took to prepare.

She set her small table and added flowers and candles as a centerpiece. It looked inviting. Roman arrived first, which was perfect. She wanted to have a few minutes alone with him before Odessa and Antonello came.

"Welcome," she said and handed him a glass of wine. He stood at the counter while she finished grinding white pepper into the sauce.

The noodles caught his attention.

"*Pici*?" he asked, and picked up a noodle from the batch that was set out on a cloth.

"I thought I would give them a try. What do you think?" Juliette was proud of them.

"They're quite good, Juliette. For someone who isn't a native Italian you pick up on our culinary arts quickly. You're one of the best students I've ever had."

"Really? You're not just saying that?"

"I'm not just saying it."

"Thank you," she pressed her lips to his. "Hopefully you'll like the sauce, too."

"I'm sure I will," he said, and wrapped her in his arms.

"You know, I could get used to this. Maybe I'll never go home," she tried out tentatively. "Maybe I'll stay here with you." Juliette tilted her head back and looked at him.

"*Voresti restare?* You would stay?" he asked. "But what about getting back to your father and sister? And maybe opening your café?"

"You don't like the idea of me staying?"

"It's not that at all," he said, smoothing her hair back and kissing her forehead, then looking away with an expression that seemed almost furtive to Juliette.

A ripple ran through her stomach. She wanted to ask him more about his feelings, but just then Odessa and Antonello arrived.

"*Benvenuto!*" she said, putting aside her sudden apprehension as she opened the door and ushered them in.

"Roman, you know Odessa and this is Antonello."

"Of course, Odessa," he said kissing her cheeks, "it's nice to see you. And Antonello, nice to meet you," Roman said, while Juliette also gave each of them a kiss on the cheek.

"Your apartment is charming," Odessa said. "You have made it feel like a home."

"*Grazie*. It's small but perfect for me."

"And how much longer do we get to have you in Italy?" asked Antonello, as she handed them each a glass of wine and brought out some antipasti to snack on before dinner.

"We were just talking about that," Juliette answered. "Six weeks, unless I decide to stay on longer."

Odessa smiled. "I would love to have you stay, Juliette."

Juliette said, "I've grown so attached to Lucca."

"I'm guessing you've grown attached to more than just our fair city," Odessa said with a nod toward Roman, who Juliette noticed looked a bit uneasy with the direction of the conversation.

"I think we're frightening him," Juliette laughed and changed the subject. "Odessa," she said, "I'm using some of your delicious *mascarpone* cheese in the walnut sauce. I tasted it, and the flavor is heaven."

"I noticed it looked a little bit drier than *mascarpone* is usually," Roman commented, suddenly distracted as if he couldn't think of anything to say.

Juliette was stunned. Criticizing wasn't like him. Was he serious? She wondered if she was missing a subtlety of the language as she sometimes still did.

But Antonello came to the rescue when he said with a laugh, "Ah, Odessa, it looks like you have a critic. But don't worry. I'm sure you'll show him what an artist you are when he tastes it." Then he turned to Juliette and asked, "What is it that you Americans say? 'The proof is in the pudding?' I guess we'll have to wait and see," he winked.

Juliette laughed too. She was grateful for Antonello. He lightened the strange mood Roman was suddenly in. She was further grateful to Odessa and Antonello as they proceeded to regale them all with humorous stories and witty anecdotes that kept the evening light.

Roman, on the other hand, wasn't acting like the man she'd come to know. He joined in the conversation and laughed at their comments, but Juliette picked up on a shift in him with a sense of unease.

When the evening was over, the door had no sooner latched behind Odessa and Antonello than Juliette turned to Roman. "Is everything all right?"

"What do you mean?" Roman turned from clearing the dessert dishes from the table.

"You just seemed more quiet than usual. Don't you like Odessa and Antonello?"

"I like them very much. It was especially nice to get to know Odessa better after years of knowing her more as an acquaintance."

"Well that's good. So, there's nothing wrong?"

"Nothing at all, Juliette." He smiled and pulled her to him. He kissed her lips and her neck and then turned back towards the cluttered table. "Unfortunately I have to go home after we clean up, though. I'm expecting a call."

"A call? This late on a Saturday night?"

"Yes, I'm sorry. My mother said she needs to talk to me about something and insisted that I call her when I get home."

"Are you worried?"

"No. She just gets this way sometimes."

"Too bad," she turned back towards him. "I had some plans for you later."

Roman laughed and kissed her again. "I guess those plans will have to wait for now," he said and gently pinched her chin before leaving.

Juliette leaned against the closed door after he left, furrow lines between her eyebrows. Something was off, she thought. She didn't like the chill she suddenly felt deep in her bones.

Chapter 15

CATARINA, THE JOYS OF TAKING
BATHS WITH INDOOR PLUMBING, AND
AN ITALIAN LANDSCAPE PAINTING

C atarina and Franco walked into the most ornate building she
had ever been in. The hotel's architecture was her vision of a
palace, with high stamped-plaster ceilings, carpeted floors,
and fabric-covered walls. She couldn't stop herself from gaping. Franco
left her sitting in a beautiful, velvet-covered chair with her belongings
while he talked with the man at the front desk. He returned with two
keys and a porter to take her luggage. They had rooms across the hall
from each other. Catarina's room had a green carpet with entwined
roses patterned around the border. The walls were the palest pink. She
felt like a princess in a jewel box. Before he left her alone to freshen
up, he showed her how the plumbing worked, helping her to draw a

bath. It was the first one she had ever taken that didn't involve filling pot after pot of water that had been heated on the stove.

He instructed her to lock the door behind him as he left, and told her that he would knock again for her in two hours, so she could have a bath and a nap before they went out for dinner.

After he left, she undressed and carefully hung her clothes on real hangers instead of pegs. As she walked across the room to the bathroom, she could feel her feet sink into the carpeting—a sensation she had never experienced. She climbed into the bathtub and sank under the water. The hot liquid embraced her in warmth and calm and she felt the tension she had stored inside her release. She allowed herself to let down her guard and before she knew it tears were streaming down her cheeks. She hadn't realized just how exhausted she had been. She was worlds away from her family, and unexpectedly feeling the full force of a love she had had to give up. She had been afraid of being turned back while going through the immigration process while secretly almost hoping it would happen. After all, if she was unfit to immigrate, then going back and being with Gregorio would have been in the realm of possibility. But then the face of Senior Carlucci flashed in her mind and she shivered with disgust. Going home wasn't an option.

But she had made it through, and now here she was. In this iron thing called a bathtub, in a hotel in New York City in the United States of America. She knew her life would never be the same.

While Franco was not as handsome as Gregorio, she did like the way he took charge and was considerate. She felt safe with him. After almost two weeks of depending on herself, it was nice to have someone look out for her. She knew at seventeen she should be strong, but sometimes she wished she could go back to being a child, eating a pear just plucked from a tree in her own garden.

Catarina looked at the sparkling diamond ring on her finger. Her hand looked like a grown woman's hand. The ring was the most beautiful thing she had ever seen and she couldn't believe it had been given to her. She would take strength from it from now on.

Catarina shampooed her hair and scrubbed herself clean. It was the best she had felt since she left Italy. The soap was more fine and the suds more silky than any she had used before. And the scent was fresh. Like milk and honey.

Before slipping into the water, she had taken a look at herself in the mirror and was dismayed by how disheveled she was. Her face was shiny, she had a smudge of something on her cheek and her wavy hair was looking decidedly rumpled. She hoped Franco hadn't been disappointed.

Once the water became tepid, she got out of the tub and dried off. She was determined to make herself look beautiful for their first dinner together, but before that, she wanted to lie down and rest for just a few minutes. She put on her nightgown and slipped between the sheets. She could hear unfamiliar sounds outside the hotel; people speaking in an unfamiliar language. The sounds rushed around her and she closed her eyes.

There was a loud knocking at the door in what seemed like an instant later. Her heart hammered in her chest as she realized that she had fallen completely asleep. How long had it been? She didn't know, but based on the change in light, she saw that the day had turned to evening.

She jumped out of bed, opened the door a crack, and was met with Franco's worried face.

"*Oh, mio Dio!* Thank God you're in there. I have been knocking and knocking and when there was no answer, I was afraid you'd left the hotel."

When Catarina saw that it was Franco, she opened the door further.

"I'm sorry, I must have fallen asleep. I didn't realize how much time had passed."

"It's ok." He put his hand to his chest and breathed a sigh of relief. "Don't worry. I'm sure you were exhausted. When I arrived here for the first time . . ." then his voice stumbled because he realized she was standing in just a thin night shirt and he could see the outline of her body clearly. He tried to look away before she noticed his embarrassment, but then she realized what state she was in and turned red.

"Excuse me! I'm sorry," she stumbled over her words and moved behind the door.

"Yes, well. I'll wait for you downstairs in the lobby," Franco stammered. "When you're dressed and ready, come meet me and we can go to dinner."

"*Grazie.* I'll be right down," Catarina said, then closed and locked the door again. Her face felt hot. She looked at herself in the mirror. This time she was clean, but her curly, dark brown hair had dried while she slept and was now in a mass of uncontrolled waves around her head. She splashed water on her face and cleaned her teeth, then opened her suitcase and got out her best dress. The blue fabric looked faded and tattered to her eye and one of the sleeves had lost a button. Fortunately, the rounded pearl button served no purpose except for ornament, so the three-quarter-length sleeves were still nicely fitted to her forearms. She shook it out in order to get rid of the worst wrinkles, wishing she had something new and fresh to wear, but everything she owned had been worn aboard the ship and washed out in a basin several times over. She slipped it on, brushed her untamed hair, then pinned it back at the nape of her neck. She pinched her cheeks and bit her lips to add color to her face. Slipping on her shoes, she took the small purse her father had given her, and locked the door behind her.

She walked down the stairs. Finding her way to the lobby, she saw Franco standing by a window, waiting for her. He was lost in thought. She stopped where she was, so she could look at her future husband while he was unaware. He had a wiry frame, and the looks of southern Italians, with almost-black hair and dark eyes. He seemed to have a certain elegance about him. A ready smile. A kind face.

He must have been able to sense her there because he turned and his face lit up at the sight of her. He began to walk towards her. She met him halfway and he took her elbow.

"Come, I'll take you to the first restaurant I ate at when I arrived here. It's in a section of town where many Italians live and the food will feel like home to you. I'm guessing you could use a little bit of that about now."

Catarina smiled at him. "*Sono affamata*," she said. I'm famished, so that sounds perfect.

As soon as they walked through the doors and into the city, Catarina was struck by the noise. It was a warm summer evening and there were more people out in the single block of the hotel than one would find in her town square during market day. Where were they all going? she wondered. And the buildings were incomprehensibly tall and majestic, like sentinels overlooking a kingdom. She was intrigued by the walkways, along which people could stroll. They were smooth, unlike the rutted dirt paths or cobblestones at home.

Franco took her elbow and guided her to the restaurant, while she took in the sights around her.

"I think you'll like this one," Franco told her. "Hearing Italian spoken and eating a plate of spaghetti helped me when I was a home-sick boy."

"You didn't want to leave Italy?"

"No, I loved it there. But I was a child and had to go where my father chose. I ended up liking this country, though I still miss Italy sometimes."

Once they were settled at a table, she closed her eyes and inhaled, "Ummm, it smells like home here," she said. "You know, I've never thought about food being specifically 'Italian' or anything else. It was just 'food.' But on the way here, I saw restaurants with menus that look different and some of the smells coming from the open doors were like nothing I've smelled before."

"*Certo*," said Franco. "Here there are many things to eat—as many as the nationalities of people who have come."

"Have you tried many?"

"*Si*, I like to try food from different cultures. We can do that together while we're here if you want. This city has a great variety of ev-erything. One of the most amazing places is Chinatown. It's as different from Italy as you can imagine. Would you like to go there tomorrow?"

"That sounds wonderful. I want to try lots of new things." Ca-tarina paused and thought back to the day by the well, when she told her friends about the marriage proposal. She thought back to her vision of America. "And is there much dancing here?" she asked. "I always thought there would be lots of dancing."

"I imagine we could find somewhere to go dancing. We could even go dancing this evening after dinner, if you want."

"*Si*," Catarina smiled.

"*Bene.* We'll find somewhere to dance," Franco smiled back. It was the least he could do for someone who had braved leaving home and family to start a life with him.

He couldn't help but assess her now that she was sitting at a table with him.

Her eyes were intelligent and took in her surroundings with a sense of inquisitiveness, which is what had caught his attention so many years ago. She had become beautiful in the years since he had seen her, as he had suspected she would. But it wasn't just that. The way her light blue eyes contrasted with her dark hair and olive skin was striking, and it was the spark in her eyes that made her stand out from other girls. He knew from experience that beauty attracted, but it was wit that kept him interested.

Their conversation was easy and comfortable. He asked lots of questions about her family and about home and in turn told her about his family and what it was like in San Francisco. He described arriving in New York as a young boy and then traveling by train.

"This time I'm looking forward to the trip," he said. "It will give us a chance to get to know each other better before we marry. And I think you'll be amazed by the countryside. It's vast."

He reached out and took her hand.

When he did, she hoped to feel an instant spark as she had with Gregorio, but was disappointed. But she liked him and that was a start.

Franco asked the waiter if he knew where they could go dancing. He told them about a little café, still in the Italian section, called

Delucca's. If the mood was right, and the wine had been poured generously, they were likely to find dancing there.

They decided to search it out. When they found it, they were met by the sound of musicians playing and a crowd of boisterous people spilling outside. The balmy evening invited lingering. There was a mix of Italian and English being spoken, and Franco thought it would be a fun way for them to spend their first evening together.

He spontaneously took her hand and spun her around while they waited to get inside. He was rewarded with not only a seamless twirl but an unexpected smile. Franco had imagined she would be shy and he'd have to draw her out, but instead she was lively and easy to talk to, which pleased him.

They inched their way in and were finally able to find a table. He ordered them each a lemonade, which they sipped while listening to the music. It was loud enough that conversation was difficult, so after a song or two Franco asked her if she'd like to dance. As they walked to the dance floor, Catarina was happy she had learned some steps on the ship.

He took her in his arms and led her around the dance floor.

"How did you learn to dance so well?" he asked.

"Aboard ship we danced every night," she told him, omitting whom exactly had given her the instructions. "Maria and I sat with the same group of people during the voyage and we all took turns dancing. I didn't know how at first, but I got a bit better after a while. It was great fun," she said, turning her face away from Franco, lest he see the mixture of happiness and wistfulness cross her features.

He moved back from her, spun her around, and she found herself laughing. She looked up at the man she was going to marry and felt a sense of unexpected peace. It would be ok after all. She tried to push all thoughts of Gregorio to the back of her mind. She stored them there for safekeeping, but she would try to love Franco instead.

They danced until the café closed and then walked back to the hotel. Catarina was exhausted and kept envisioning the hotel bed. She could hardly wait to sink into its soft mattress and sleep.

Franco walked her to the door of her room and waited with her until she opened it and was safely inside. Before she closed the door behind her though, he caught her hand and turned her back around. He smiled at her for a fleeting moment and then moved forward and softly kissed her lips.

"*Buona notte.*"

"*Buona notte,*" she said back to him. "See you in the morning." And then she paused and added, "If you don't mind, though, I would like to take another bath before I come down to breakfast." The corners of her mouth turned up in a shy smile. "That was the most luxurious thing I've ever done."

Franco laughed. "*Certo.* After you've taken a bath, why don't you knock on my door when you're ready, and then we'll go down to breakfast together."

"*Fantastico, grazie,*" she said and then turned again to go. Then she added, "Franco?"

"*Sì?*"

"I had a wonderful evening. Thank you."

"You're welcome," he gave her a half smile, then turned and went into his own room.

Catarina locked the door behind herself, then took off her dress and for the first time in her life, left it in a heap on the floor. She knew her mother wouldn't approve, but she'd never been more tired. She didn't bother even taking the tie out of her hair, she just climbed into bed in her slip and let sleep envelop her.

T he next morning, after breakfast, Franco asked Catarina if she'd like to go shopping for a few new dresses.

"There are dresses we can buy that have already been made," he said. "We can go into a dress shop and you can try them on and then they will alter them to fit you. It's amazing—not like at home where everything is made by hand. We'll pick them up tomorrow before we catch the train. Would you like that?"

"I would love it. I've never had a dress that wasn't sewn by either Mama or me. I can't imagine being able to buy a dress that is already made. How do they do that? They don't even know me." Franco laughed. It was interesting to notice how many things he now took for granted: indoor plumbing and ready-made clothes just scratched the surface.

She started to speak and then looked away.

"What is it?" Franco asked her, when he saw her hesitation.

"I was just wondering," she said. "Are you happy you brought me here? Now that you've met me again, I mean. Do you regret choosing me? Because I'm sure you could have someone much more elegant, not a farmer's daughter you have to buy clothes for."

He took her hand across the table and looked directly into her eyes. "You're exactly as I had hoped. And I didn't mean to make you think that I was offering to buy you new dresses because yours aren't good enough. I simply thought you'd like it. Now, come on," he said when they finished up. "Let's go see the sights."

They spent the day walking around New York, and Catarina found herself in awe of the vibrancy of the city. The buildings were tall, the streets were wide, and there were more people than she had ever seen in one place. Everyone seemed in a hurry. They walked up to Central Park and strolled along the meandering paths. She found the acres and acres of quiet and beauty a strange contrast to the bustling city, but she liked being surrounded—even temporarily—with green lawns, trees, and flowers.

When they were hungry, they bought sausages from a street vendor who hawked sizzling links from a grill on the sidewalk. The sausages were spicier than those at home, and she enjoyed the heat they left in her mouth.

She told Franco about the money her father had given her when she left, and asked him to help her exchange some of it for dollars to buy his family a gift. She and her mother and sisters had sewn a tablecloth for them, but after seeing the finery of their hotel, Catarina worried that it wouldn't be enough. She wanted to arrive with something more special.

They found a local bank to do the exchange and Franco explained about the value of the American bills she now had. After poking through store after store, they settled on a small painting of the Italian countryside as a gift for Franco's family. Catarina fell in love with it immediately because it captured the colors and light on the vine-covered hills beautifully. It captured the essence of Italy and she hoped they would love it, too. Catarina gave Franco her money so he could handle the negotiations with the vendor, but she was unaware that Franco surreptitiously added to her funds. Once the purchase was complete, the vendor wrapped the painting in burlap and secured

it with twine so it would be safe on their trip. When they walked out
of the little shop, Catarina was pleased with their efforts and was filled
with a sense of lightness.

"Do you know what I just realized?" she asked Franco.

"What?"

"I haven't done any work in two weeks. I haven't helped Mama
with dinner or helped Babbo in the vineyard or orchard. I haven't
scrubbed floors or brought in the well water. I have been dancing and
eating and shopping instead."

"How does that feel?"

"Strange, *certamente, ma mi sento bene*. It's been a nice change.
I will always remember this time."

They walked silently for a distance, both lost in their own
thoughts. Then she asked, "What will it be like in San Francisco? Will
I help in your store?"

"Possibly. My brother Carlo and I work at the store Monday
through Saturday with my father. Mama sometimes comes in to help
out. Sometimes Carlo's wife Gabriella comes in to help as well if we're
busy. But usually she's at home with their children. We have a large
apartment above the store, so we are all close by. It's crowded, though.
Gabriella is expecting another baby and I am marrying, which will
add two more, so I've asked Mama and Papa if we could move to our
own apartment nearby."

"Your letter said that. Would we live alone?"

"Lots of people in San Francisco do that—live in houses separate
from their parents, I mean."

"It would be so strange to live with just us. At home my sisters
live with their husbands' families, and Mateo and I are home with

Mama and Babbo. Well . . . now it's just Mateo I guess, until someday when he gets married."

"It is different. But I think we would get used to it. If we don't like it, we can always shove our way back in," he smiled.

"I'm sure I will like it," Catarina said, but in truth the thought of only the two of them living together sounded lonely.

The rest of their time in New York sped by, and after another night's sleep and one last bath, Catarina and Franco were due to board the train that would take them all the way to the other side of the country, where they would catch a ferry for the last part of the journey to San Francisco.

When they got to the platform, Catarina took one fleeting look around her before climbing up the steps to enter the train, just on the off chance that she would see Gregorio. While she had been in New York, she sometimes wondered whether he was in the city on leave before the ship returned to Italy, but now that she was leaving, she knew without hope that she would never see him again.

Franco boarded ahead of her to stow their bags, and as she climbed the steps she kissed the palm of her hand and waved it to an absent Gregorio as a final farewell.

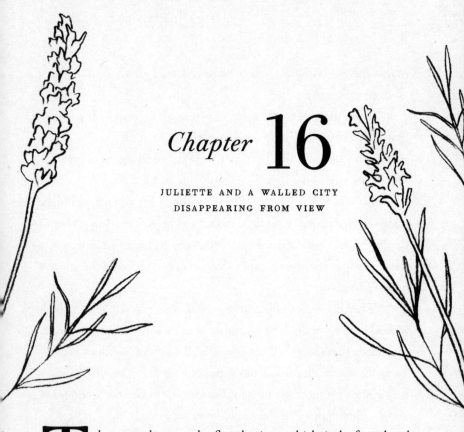

Chapter 16

JULIETTE AND A WALLED CITY
DISAPPEARING FROM VIEW

The next three weeks flew by in a whirlwind of weekend traveling, cooking classes, and spending time with Roman, while Catarina's letters were temporarily abandoned in their ancient shoebox.

Juliette felt the gradual knitting back together of her heart— the gaping wound of her mother's death growing more bearable even though she knew the wound would never be entirely healed. At least the pain had grown slightly less raw.

Just live and don't think became her temporary mantra, and she repeated it to herself whenever the accident vividly flashed through her mind, or the turmoil she had over the money her mom left to her seeped into her consciousness. She thought about her mother every day, but tried to take Gina's advice and visualize her within the confines of a lovely childhood memory.

The only monkey wrench thrown into her newfound *gioia di vivere* was the fact that Juliette was beginning to get the sinking feeling that she loved Roman more than he loved her. She couldn't understand what was going on. He still seemed to dote on her, but in a more distracted way than before and he never even hinted that he wanted her to stay. She gave him every opportunity, but he seemed to have mastered the art of subtly changing the topic or ignoring the subject entirely. He steered the conversation so smoothly, often Juliette didn't notice it had taken a new direction until they were deeply entrenched in a new topic.

"I'm beginning to question myself," she told Gina when they talked. "I don't know what to do. I love him. He seemed to love me too, but lately it's like . . . " she hesitated, trying to think about what was different. She couldn't put her finger on it.

"Just ask him, Juliette," she said. "What do you have to lose?"

"Let's see," she hesitated, "how about my pride and my fragile happiness? And what if he's planning some surprise and my American directness ruins it?"

"I don't know. I wish I had the answer, but I don't."

Juliette sighed. "What if I've been wrong about his feelings for me and I get my heart broken?"

"That's the thing about love, isn't it? There's always the chance of that."

Still, with one week to go before her departure date, she realized he wasn't going to be the one to bring the subject up. Maybe he didn't want to be the one to ask her to give up her country and proximity to her family. She didn't know, but she decided to stop fretting about it and take matters into her own hands.

They were sitting on his couch, sipping homemade hot cocoa they'd concocted with blocks of dark chocolate, while a frigid early-spring rain sheeted against the window. They were situated with mugs in hand, feet on the coffee table, and the newspaper strewn across their laps.

Juliette was suddenly nervous, but she didn't want to be the type of person who doesn't get what she wants because she's too afraid to ask for it. *Be brave,* she silently reminded herself.

"Roman?" she folded the paper she had been looking at.

"Umm hmmm?" He was deeply entrenched in an article about the speed of wireless internet service in Italy.

"How would you feel if I were to stay here?"

"What?" he asked, making his face neutral, but Juliette caught a glimpse of nervousness she didn't want to see.

"I can't stand the thought of leaving you. And Lucca. I love it here. I didn't expect to have this happen when I came, but it did, and now I don't want to go home."

"Juliette, the reason you're here is to heal and to learn Italian cooking to take back home. That's what you've always said."

"I know, but I didn't realize I was going to fall for you."

Roman looked away, a pained expression in his eyes, and suddenly she knew.

"You don't feel the same, though," Juliette shook her head. Trying not to choke up.

"It's not that Juliette. I am crazy about you. You know that. You're incredible and I've never known anyone like you." He leaned forward and rubbed his hands over his face.

"*But?*"

Roman paused.

"There is a '*but*' right?" Juliette prodded.

Roman nodded. He looked out the window, away from Juliette's face.

"The last thing I want to do is hurt you. You've been through so much." He tried to take Juliette's hand, but she gently pulled it away. "I didn't think I would have to tell you this, but it's Maddelena. She's coming back."

"What does that mean? Who's Maddelena?"

"We were together for years. We were talking about getting married but then she got an opportunity to work for a while in the Middle East. She's a journalist. I didn't want her to go. I thought it was too dangerous. She accused me of being controlling. She insisted we take a break, and left. She's been covering the unrest there but now she's coming back."

"And you've talked to her?"

"*Si*, the first time was the night you had Odessa, Antonello, and me over for dinner."

"The night you said you had to go home because your "mother" needed to talk to you?" Juliette motioned with her fingers to indicate quotations marks around the word *mother*.

Roman looked away, giving her the answer she already knew. "We had spoken earlier in the day, but I had to talk to her again to resolve things between us. Please understand. Her family and mine have been connected. You understand? I've known her since we were this high," indicating that they'd known each other since childhood.

"But what about us? What was *this*, then?" Juliette asked, gesturing between them.

"I fell for you, too, Juliette. Don't think I didn't. But I knew you were leaving. We've had such a good time."

Juliette nodded and fought for composure, suddenly feeling incredibly foolish.

"I'm sorry," Roman told her. "I didn't mean for you to fall in love with me. I adore you. I never meant to hurt you."

"I'm such an idiot."

She felt an actual acute pain in her chest. She always thought it was a metaphor until this year. Now it seemed to happen to her repeatedly.

"You're not an idiot. You mean a lot to me, but I have a history with Maddelena. Our families have a history. I've always known I would end up with her someday."

He looked confused and maybe for the first time she'd seen, at a loss for words.

Juliette wiped at her cheeks with the back of her trembling hand.

"I don't think you should stay, Juliette."

"Yeah, I guess not. I didn't realize the situation," she paused, trying to keep her emotions under wraps, because she didn't want to start to sob while she was still with him. She fought with all her strength to maintain her emotions. Juliette looked around for something to focus on besides his face. Finally her eyes fixed on her coat, so she grabbed it, quickly slipped her bare feet into boots, and started for the door.

Roman stood beside her, his face betraying how badly he felt about hurting her.

"I'm so sorry," he reached out to give her a hug, but she stepped closer to the door.

"Can you bring anything I've left to class tomorrow? I've got to go. I can't get my stuff right now."

"*Si*, I'll bring it."

She fleetingly looked around the room while she stepped backwards towards the door. She searched his face one last time. How could this have happened? She couldn't believe he had been in the process of getting back together with his girlfriend while spending time with her. She *loved* him. She put her hand on her chest to collect herself, then moved it to the doorknob when a realization struck her and she turned back.

"That's why your mom was strange about me being there, wasn't it? It wasn't me. It was the fact that you showed up with another woman. I thought she was a bit chilly at the time, but now I have to hand it to her. She was extremely gracious under the circumstances."

"Yes, she would be. Which I was counting on."

"But why would you do that?"

"I enjoy your company, Juliette. I just wanted to show you the restaurant."

"Was it that? Or was it that you knew it would get back to Maddelena? Maybe make her jealous? Get her to come home?"

"I don't know," he sighed. "Maybe both," he looked introspective and remorseful. "But please, don't doubt my feelings for you Juliette."

"At this moment, I have no idea what your feelings are for me. I . . . I guess I thought you were someone else."

"I didn't mean to mislead you," he said, and ran his fingers through his hair.

She wanted to throw herself in his arms and have it be a bad dream but instead he was telling her he didn't love her and letting her walk away. She slipped through the door and closed it behind her, trudging the short distance back to her flat in the rain, with silent tears streaming down her face. When she finally had her apartment door closed behind her she couldn't hold it in any more. She sat on the couch, her face in her hands. She was back to feeling wretched and desperately wanted to just go home. In that moment she would have given just about anything to miraculously be back at her little in-law studio with her friends sitting next to her. She couldn't believe he'd been amusing himself with her to pass the time.

She squeezed her fingers together to feel the pressure of Catarina's ring, and through it, to feel the strength of her grandmother and mother. Juliette wasn't sure she could take any more heartbreak. She looked down at the ring, remembering something her nonna had told her when she was little. She had said the ring symbolized the choice to be happy, no matter what circumstance she found herself in, but at that moment, even the idea of happiness seemed like a foreign concept.

She splashed cool water on her face, then leaned on the sink and inhaled three shaky, deep breaths to try to regain her equilibrium, and then crawled under the covers in a fetal position and pulled the blankets over her head.

She didn't realize she'd fallen asleep until she was jarred awake by the sound of a car door closing beneath her window. She looked around, groggy and confused, and then she remembered what had happened, and before she knew it, tears were sliding down her cheeks again. She wiped them away as she walked to the window to peek out.

The unexpected sight of Roman standing behind the open trunk of his car stopped her in her tracks. Her first sense was elation. Maybe he'd changed his mind. Maybe he realized the moment she left that he couldn't live without her after all.

Then he pulled an open box of things out of his trunk and looked up at the window. When he saw her, he crushed out his cigarette and exhaled the smoke.

He waved, but the wretched expression on his face told her he wasn't there to tell her he'd made a mistake.

She went down to unlock the door for him.

"I couldn't stand how that ended." He walked past her into her apartment and set the box on the table. He put his hands on her shoulders.

"Please forgive me, Juliette," he said. "I truly didn't mean to hurt you. Here," he gestured to the box, "I brought your things. I didn't think it would be right to bring them to class."

She looked at him and then did allow herself to be wrapped in his arms to get the comfort he was offering.

"Shhh," he whispered when he heard her crying.

"I guess this is goodbye," she said.

"I'll see you in class, though, right?"

"I don't know. I don't know if I can stand to go."

He tilted her chin up so she was looking in his eyes.

"Of course you can, you're tough as nails. Isn't that what you Americans say?"

She sighed and tucked her face back to his chest. She didn't feel tough and couldn't imagine facing him in class and pretending he was something less than he had been to her.

The weekend passed in a painful haze. It seemed ridiculous to do ordinary tasks in the midst of heartbreak. She'd had the same feeling after the accident. How could everything continue on as if nothing had changed? Standing in line at the post office seemed almost ridiculous. Choosing ripe fruit, absurd. The only thing that felt good was reading Catarina's letters and running along the wall that surrounded Lucca. Just running. Not thinking, not dreaming about the future. She let herself be held up by the centuries-old stone. She wondered how many other people throughout the thousand-year history of the hewn rock had passed along the same path feeling a similar sorrow and she took comfort in thinking that she was just one in a sea of humanity who had loved and lost.

After Roman had dropped off her things, she'd spied the neglected box of letters and opened the lid. During her time in Italy, her fluency had improved and it had become easier to read through them.

She had come to feel a deep attachment to Maria and was intrigued by the many new layers that had been revealed about her grandmother. She had always known and loved her simply as her nonna, but to read the letters from a young, passionate Catarina revealed the complex life she'd led. She witnessed the compassionate friend she was when the two women wrote about Maria's difficulty in getting pregnant and was fascinated to read the recounts of her falling in love with her grandfather. So much had happened that she had never known about.

A shipside romance? Juliette could hardly stand the suspense of what had happened and passed hours escaping into the correspondence. In the letter she had just finished, Catarina had told Maria the ring saved her life. Juliette wondered what her grandmother meant by that and couldn't wait to find out what happened in the next letter.

When the alarm went off on Monday morning, Juliette moaned, burrowed back under the covers, and went back to sleep for hours. The thought of seeing Roman made the prospect of getting up and out impossible. Instead, when she finally dragged herself out of bed, she spent the day sprawled on the couch, drinking tea and reading the letters.

Strength, Juliette noticed, was one of Catarina's underlying and ongoing messages to Maria. Strength and choosing to create a full life. Choose happiness. Grace and grit. It was sweet to see that even a young Catarina espoused the same wisdom as the nonna she knew.

It got Juliette thinking about her own life circumstances in light of her grandmother's. Catarina had courage in spades. She took risks. She left her country to get away from a would-be rapist and the almost certain knowledge that a war was coming, and moved to San Francisco with the worry that she may never see her family again. But she did it. Juliette thought about the money her mother left her and the fear and regret that were holding her back from using it.

She sighed and stared out the window, unconsciously biting her thumbnail. Juliette moaned with the realization that she was holding herself back. *Merda,* she said under her breath. She twisted Catarina's ring on her finger and could almost hear her mother and nonna giggle joyously from beyond at the realization that Juliette finally got it.

"Thank you, Nonna," she said aloud. "Thank you, Mom." She had the sudden urge to throw the correspondence around herself like confetti, but came to her senses before doing any damage to the frail paper and instead gently tucked them back into the box and stretched. Her limbs felt stiff, as if she had been sitting for days instead of hours. She did a few knee bends then decided to throw on her running clothes and run the wall.

"Forget Roman," she continued the conversation with her mother and grandmother while she laced up her shoes. "I'm choosing my own happiness. And something good *will* come from your death, Mom. I'm going to open my café. I know that's what you would want," she wiped a stray tear that had escaped, locked the door behind her, and headed to the outskirts of Lucca to run a victory lap.

On Tuesday, she decided to try out her newfound strength and go to class. It was the last week, after all, and she had come here to learn everything she could. On her way through the door, she kissed her ring for courage. Once she settled in, she attempted to focus on the singular task of dicing the onion in front of her and shutting her mind completely to everything except perfect chopping technique. She decided if a tear or two slipped down her cheek, her classmates would assume that it was because the onion was burning her eyes.

She wanted to learn what Roman had to teach, but it was incredibly painful to be in the room with him. She was determined to be courageous though, so she forced herself to suck it up and went back the next day and the next. She wanted to touch him and she couldn't stop looking at him, but the real agony came when she left class each afternoon alone, and walked by the espresso stand where they had wiled away so many enjoyable hours.

She got together with Odessa a couple of times and filled her in on what had happened, but mostly she spent hours and hours working on the plans for the café she now knew would be a reality. She poured herself into the details in hopes of dulling the heartbreak and was happy to discover that under the blanket of despair was a glimmer of excitement.

It would have a service counter, as well as several tables and an eating bar with stools for people who came in alone. She would serve pastries, sweet frittata, tea and coffee in the morning; a variety of gourmet sandwiches on homemade foccacia bread, minestrone soup, pasta, salads, and specials at lunch and dinner. On certain nights, she would open up the kitchen to hold classes where she and her students could prepare and then eat a meal. All she had to do was find the right space.

She thought about three different cities. San Francisco was the first that came to mind because she had grown up there. She had been around the family jewelry store since the time she was in diapers. And, it would be nice to be close to Gina, who still worked at the store that had been located in the same spot for generations.

Berkeley was another thought. It was the heart of the Slow Food Movement. She would love to be in the Gourmet Ghetto where other venerable foodies had restaurants. Her one concern about Berkeley was that her place might be lost among so many great venues. Of course that could be a problem in San Francisco, too.

She also considered staying close to home in Walnut Creek; a suburb, yes, but one with a genuine, flourishing downtown, where her café might be more of a standout. In the end, she decided to look in all three places and keep her options open.

S he found herself desperate to see her dad, Gina, and friends again. She needed to be with them while she licked her wounds, and now that she had decided to take the plunge she was dying to talk to them about her ideas. Talking on the phone from afar just wasn't the same.

Packing up her Lucca apartment proved more daunting than she had imagined. She had collected more things than she realized during her weekend jaunts around the countryside. A Deruta pitcher here and an antique stone bowl there had added up to many more boxes than the ones she arrived with. She had bought her dad and Gina presents, as well as bottles of aged balsamic vinegar from Modena for several of her friends.

Her favorite acquisition by far though, was an oversized ceramic urn that she planned to display prominently with long stems of blooming branches in her café. She had meandered through an antique market in Bologna filled with all kinds of treasures. She had to limit herself to the urn and a few tiny silver pillboxes she couldn't resist, but if she had the money, she could have spent buckets of Euros there.

The Friday before she left was spent at the shipping agent's office and then Juliette met Odessa and Antonello at *Salvia* for one last dinner together.

Juliette had become a regular while in Lucca, and over the last week had talked to the owner several times to get advice about her café now that she was getting serious about it. She told him that she was planning to include several of his specialty dishes on her menu, which

LISA MCGUINNESS 193

made the jovial old Italian proud. He felt a special fondness for his American protégée, so when they came in on her last evening in town, he showered them with little tastes of each of his specialties and brought them Juliette's favorite wine, staunchly refusing to accept a single Euro.

The evening was much like the first dinner Juliette shared with Odessa and Antonello and ended with hugs and cheek kisses to say goodbye.

Juliette spent her last night in Lucca in the little apartment she'd treasured. Even though the evening was chilly, she wrapped herself in blankets and sat on her balcony thinking about her time there until the wee hours.

Her plane didn't leave until late afternoon, so she was able to sleep in before she went out for her last taste of *bombilini* and espresso, then bring her suitcases down to meet the taxi to the train station, and close up the rental she'd made her home.

When the train left the city, Juliette looked over her shoulder to get one last glimpse of the walled town she had come to love. She would miss being in a city of such history and architectural beauty. She was suddenly afraid that leaving was a huge mistake. Maybe she should stay and fight for him. But then she remembered he loved Maddelena, not her. She was still confused about how she could have misjudged the situation so terribly.

She sighed and watched the scenery speed by.

At least she would be home soon. She tried to focus on that.

During the two-hour train ride to get to the airport, Juliette immersed herself in thoughts of home and getting back to her familiar life. When the train neared the station, she checked her purse again for her passport and ticket, finding comfort in seeing them tucked into the pages of the novel she was reading.

She hoisted her shoulder bag up higher and then headed to the check-in gate. She joined the fray and stopped on the outskirts for a time. The Italian passengers crowded the counter. There was no sense of lining up in Italy. It was all about discreetly elbowing your way to the front. Juliette eased into the crowd and tried to make her way up in line without being too aggressive. She reminded herself that it was just part of the culture as she gently leaned her shoulder into a young man who was trying to casually shove his way in front of her. She gave him a sweet smile when she reached the check-in counter in front of him and placed her ticket on the counter.

Chapter 17

The cross-country train ride took four days, but Catarina didn't mind. It gave her a chance to get to know Franco better and to see her new country. She had a difficult time grasping how vast it was because her frame of reference was so small, but she realized it was expanding daily. On the train, one entire day went by and all she had seen was flat prairie land.

Finally that landscape gave way to desert and rock formations that seemed like strange dreamscapes. But she was most in awe of the mountains. She imagined they rivaled the beauty of the Italian Alps she had heard about, but never seen.

"Tell me again what it's like in San Francisco," she requested.

"There are lots of hills and the houses are painted many different colors. It's very different from Italy. There's a huge park, kind of like Central Park in New York, which we can walk through. And there's a downtown area with paved streets and wide sidewalks. Our jewelry store is on a side street off of Market Street downtown. And if you walk toward San Francisco Bay, there's a huge building called the Ferry Building with a clock tower that keeps the time. You'll see it when we arrive."

"Is the water warm? Do people swim?"

Franco laughed. "The water is cold, frigid really, so people don't often swim in the bay. But sometimes people go to a beach that faces the ocean to swim. I can take you there someday. But San Francisco isn't hot like it is at home."

"What do you mean?" Catarina couldn't imagine summers that weren't sweltering.

"It's foggy lots of the time in San Francisco."

Catarina looked back at him with an expression of dismay. She didn't like the idea of fog day after day. "It sounds dreary," she said.

"It is sometimes, but I think you'll get used to it. We live in the most sunny section of town," he reassured her. "And," he went on, "we're going to get a new library. So once you learn to read in English, you can check out books from the library and stay in and read if it's cold and foggy."

"I could go to the library?" Catarina asked, because she was sure back home that would be something only men were allowed to do. She was one of the few females in her village who even knew how to read.

"*Certamente*," Franco said. "I'll teach you to read English myself."

Catarina liked the sound of that.

"Do you have books in Italian?" she asked. She wondered if she could begin reading books as soon as they arrived.

"Yes, Italian and English. I love to read, and if you do, too, then you'll find no shortage of books at home."

It was odd to think of someplace she'd never seen as "home," when home to her was an orchard and vineyard with her family around her.

"Why are you getting a *new* library? What's wrong with the old one?" One of the things Catarina noticed from his stories is that things seemed to change more and faster in this new country. At home, buildings stayed in the same families for generations and new ones were rarely built.

"The old one burned down," he replied. "There was a big earthquake six years ago and a lot of the city burned down. Even though it's been a while, there's still some rebuilding to be done."

"A very big earthquake?" she asked. Between earthquakes and fog, Catarina wasn't sure she had made a good decision in agreeing to move to San Francisco.

"*Sì*. But it's over now, and I doubt we'll have another big one like that," Franco told her.

Catarina tried to be reassured, but the idea of the ground shaking was frightening. They occasionally had earthquakes at home, and the rumbling feeling terrified her.

"There are also some small islands in the bay," Franco changed the subject. "One of them is called Angel Island. Someday we can take a boat there and have a picnic. It's a beautiful spot. And the view of San Francisco from there is interesting to see. Would you like to go with me?"

"*Si*, of course," she answered.

"And there's a small beach there. Perhaps we could dip our feet into the water." Franco raised his eyebrows at her, to ask her if she liked the idea.

She did like the idea. She imagined cool water against her bare feet.

She suddenly pictured herself there with Gregorio sitting next to her. She knew she should shove the image away, but instead she allowed herself to dream about him for just a moment.

Thinking about Gregorio made her wonder about Franco and why he asked her to come to San Francisco instead of marrying a local girl. She had asked him a little bit about it in New York, but it still seemed odd to her—especially now that she saw how kind he was— that he wasn't already married.

She felt shy about asking him for more details, but finally her curiosity got the better of her.

"I keep wondering, because it seems so strange to me," she began timidly, "why did you decide to ask for me to marry you instead of marrying someone who already lives in San Francisco?" And then she stammered, "I'm sorry, it's none of my business."

Franco laughed. "Well, first of all, I think that it is your business. We're each other's business now; after all, we are going to be married soon."

Catarina hadn't thought of it that way, but laughed too because his laughter was contagious. When he stated it so plainly, she saw that he was right. They would be each other's business for the rest of their lives. It was strange to think of it that way.

"Well?" she prodded.

"Well, there's not much to tell, really. Even though my parents have forced me to go to every single Italian festival and social gathering for the last ten years at least, there hasn't been a young lady whom I wanted to marry. And now, I'm glad I didn't." He looked into her eyes.

Catarina unexpectedly started to tear up. She nodded at him and then looked out the window while she tried to regain composure. She didn't like to cry in front of other people and had no idea what would cause her to tear up now.

He didn't interfere with her attempt to get her emotions under control, but he smiled at her and reached into his pocket and handed a clean, folded handkerchief to her.

She smiled gratefully in response.

Franco had booked a sleeping car for the trip. Each night as the train sped on, they took turns changing alone in the room, then unhooked the bunks that folded up during the day so they were able to stretch out while they slept. Catarina was lulled by the rocking and clacking of the train. She enjoyed the motion and the feeling of distance being travelled while she slept. It was also a nice way to get used to sleeping in the same space as Franco. Although she knew once they married they would share a bed, this was a nice in-between step. The thought of sharing the marital bed was still a bit terrifying to her. On one hand she wasn't looking forward to it, on the other hand, she mused, at least she would know what all the gossip was about.

When she awoke on the last morning of their trip, Catarina was treated to the view of the Sierra Nevada mountain range. She looked out the window from her bunk as they emerged from a tunnel and saw a pristine jewel of a lake below them. Franco was already awake and saw that she was looking out the window. He got up and opened the window just a little bit.

"You have to smell this," he said. And before she could laugh at how strange that sounded, the scent of pine invaded her senses. It was unlike anything she had smelled before. The fragrance was fresh and clean with a hint of vanilla. She wished her mother was with her so she could smell it too. She would have to remember it, so she could describe it to her parents in the letter she was writing.

She closed her eyes and inhaled deeply.

Franco took in the look on Catarina's face and knew she appreciated the scent as much as he did. He went over to her and touched her face and smoothed back her sleep-tousled hair. Catarina opened her eyes and smiled.

After giving her a quick kiss on the lips, he turned to hook his bunk up for the day. He knew in a few hours they would be home. His family planned to meet them at the ferry, so these last few hours were the last ones he'd have alone with Catarina until after they were married, and he intended to use them well.

He left her to get ready while he went in search of some milky coffee and rolls. When he got back, she was dressed and her bunk was put away.

He handed her coffee that he had fixed to her liking with lots of milk and sugar, and set out the rolls and jam on the small table that folded down from under the window.

"We should be in Oakland in around five hours," he told her. "Then we'll take a quick ferry ride. After that, we'll be in San Francisco."

Catarina blew on her coffee and looked out the window while

she contemplated the reality of being met at the ferry by the entire Brunelli family. It seemed fitting to begin and end her journey on the water. She wondered how they would treat her. She remembered them as boisterous and a bit overwhelming, but of course she'd been a child. Perhaps now she wouldn't find them as intimidating. She knew her parents trusted them and that Franco's father and her father were like brothers growing up. Still, that doesn't mean they would automatically like her, Catarina reflected.

"Did your parents mind that you wanted to marry me instead of someone here?"

Franco paused for a moment before answering. The truth is that his mother thought he was being ridiculous and had told him so many times, whereas his father couldn't have been happier to finally join the two families. His mother had picked out the daughter of one of her dear friends for him to marry. The problem was that Franco wasn't interested in her. In his mind, she seemed more interested in the diamonds the family could offer her than in Franco himself. He had a hard time keeping a conversation going with her, which his mother brushed off as a temporary problem. Franco doubted that very much. If there's nothing to say when you're getting to know someone, how much worse would it be when you already knew everything there was to know? So, he dug in his heels, which was no easy task against his determined and stubborn mother.

In the end, though, Signora Brunelli realized her husband and son had joined forces. Outnumbered, she acquiesced. But she had still harrumphed loudly and often during the plans and arrangements. Franco was slightly concerned about how she would receive Catarina once she was actually here; a worry he had no intention of passing on to his betrothed.

Catarina smiled. "And now remind me about your brother's wife. I remember your brother a little bit from meeting him when you were in Italy, but tell me about his wife. Do you expect that we'll become friends?"

"Do you remember that my brother, Carlo, is named after your father?"

"Of course. My father has always been proud of it."

"Carlo's wife is named Gabriella. You'll love her. She's funny and kind. They have two *bambini* and she's in the family way again. She gets as big as a house," Franco laughed, but the fact that he was truly affectionate towards his brother and sister-in-law was apparent. "Their children are Anna and Anthony. I've told them that they better not name the third child a name that begins with 'A' or it will sound too strange. Don't you think?"

"Definitely. When we have children, we'll make sure their names aren't too matching. I don't like that either," Catarina said.

Franco took her hand and squeezed it. The thought of having children together made them both smile shyly.

"Wait until you see the church where we'll get married. It's a beautiful Catholic church right in the heart of the Italian section of the city. Mama took the liberty of inviting everyone we know. She wants to show that she was finally able to marry me off, I think." Franco winked at Catarina.

"Mama and I made the dress I'll wear." She could picture it folded neatly in her trunk, as if it were waiting patiently to be worn. She wished her parents could be at the ceremony.

They sat side by side in their compartment, watching the landscape turn from mountains to rolling hills and then to small populated towns as they talked about the details of their wedding day. Catarina felt as if her life were moving as rapidly as the train they were on: hurtling down the track toward a destination that she both wanted and feared.

She felt closer to Franco than she would have imagined after spending only a week in his company. She was determined to make the two of them into a family. She had escaped signor Carlucci, and a coming war. She wanted to make saying goodbye to her life in her beloved Italy worth the sacrifice of leaving the family and land she loved.

Finally, the train wheels stopped turning and they gathered their belongings while the metal screeched. The train, dragon-like, bellowed a hiss of steam and pulled into the Oakland station.

The doors clanged open and people began unloading. Franco leaned out the window to see if his family was on the platform. He had a feeling they would surprise them at the train instead of waiting for them to take the ferry to San Francisco. He was right. He burst into laughter, shouted and waved, calling out their names, but Catarina, standing behind him, couldn't see the group that had gathered.

"I hope you don't mind," he told her, "but it looks like they decided to surprise us and meet us here."

"What?" Catarina was momentarily frozen, having thought that she still had time to prepare before meeting them.

"Don't worry," Franco squeezed her hand reassuringly. "They're going to love you."

Franco's father sent a porter in along with Carlo to help Franco with Catarina's suitcase and trunk. Carlo threw the door open with a bang and stepped into the compartment. He hugged Franco, slapping him on the back, then grabbed Catarina and hugged her, too, as if they were long-lost friends.

"Look who's all grown up," he exclaimed, making her feel not only welcome, but showing he was ecstatic to have her join the family. It was the best greeting she could have imagined.

"I feel that it was just yesterday that we were running around your orchard together," he said, as he hustled them off the train.

Like Carlo, Franco's father grabbed each of them separately in bear hugs and welcomed Catarina.

Franco's sister-in-law and their two children stood back respectfully waiting to be introduced, which Franco did as soon as his father released them. Catarina knew right away that Franco was right, she would like Gabriella. She was lovely and had a ready smile. Anna and Anthony seemed shy but interested in Catarina and said a formal *buon giorno* to her.

While the hugging and greeting took place among the rest of the family, Franco's mother stood slightly separate. Finally, she came forward.

"*Buon giorno*, Catarina," she said, and placed her hands on each of Catarina's shoulders. "*Benvenuta nella nostra famiglia.*" Welcome to the family. She kissed her on each cheek and smiled into her eyes. Franco felt himself exhale a breath he didn't realize he'd been holding. His mother was warm and plump, and had the same nose as Franco. Her eyes also held the same kindness and Catarina could tell she would be safe with her. It wasn't as good as having her own mother here, but she immediately felt that she could trust this woman.

"Thank you, Mama," Franco mouthed above Catarina's head and his mother winked at her son in return.

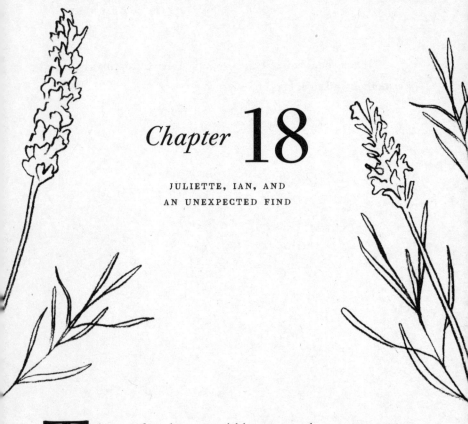

Chapter 18

They sat for what seemed like ages on the tarmac, waiting for a jet with a mechanical problem to be relocated. Between that and the eleven-hour flight with an extremely large, snoring seat companion, Juliette had never been happier to get off of a plane in her life. On the way to the baggage claim, she popped into the bathroom to brush her teeth and splash water on her face, then joined her fellow passengers at the carousel to retrieve her bags.

While she waited, she turned her phone back on and checked messages. There was one from Gina letting her know that she and their dad would be waiting eagerly for her outside of Customs, and one from Roman asking her to call him so he would know she had arrived safely.

She wanted nothing more than to pick up her phone and hear his voice, but for her own sense of self-preservation she instead texted a quick "arrived safely" to him, then tucked her phone back into her purse.

As her mind drifted while she stood beside the luggage carousel, her dad's contractor, Ian, suddenly popped into her head. Now that she was back, she wanted to get in touch with him to say "thank you". She made a mental note to ask her dad for his contact information just as she spotted her bags coming down the ramp and clunking onto the rotation belt. Slinging her shoulder bag on and edging her way through the crowd, she was in a good position to make a grab for them. Then, after waiting in a line that seemed to be inching forward at a sloth's pace, and having her suitcases repeatedly smelled by drug-sniffing beagles, she was through Customs and searching for her dad and sister.

She stared blankly around her, lost in an island of strangers before hearing her name being called. Gina was rushing towards her as fast as she could while pushing their father in a wheelchair, his leg sticking straight out and a huge grin on his face.

Juliette's face went ashen.

"Oh my God! What happened to you, Dad? Why didn't anyone tell me you were hurt?"

"He's okay," Gina was quick to hug and reassure her while simultaneously her dad said, "I'm going to be fine."

Juliette untangled herself from her sister's embrace and bent down to give her dad the best hug she could considering the awkward maneuvering around the outstretched leg protruding from the wheelchair.

"What happened?"

"It looks bad, I know, but it could have been worse, believe me," he told her.

"Dad fell off a ladder and busted his leg. He was in traction, but he's on the mend now."

"But…?"

"I know, I know…we probably should have told you, but Roman had just told you about Maddalena, we didn't want to give you an excuse to run home instead of finishing your class."

"What were you doing?" Juliette looked at her dad.

"I was working on the sky light. It's leaking again and I was up on the ladder holding the window up while Ian bolted it in place."

Gina chimed in, "Fortunately he didn't break his neck on the way down, and Ian called an ambulance right away."

"Your poor contractor; he was probably freaking out after being with you when you got the call from me on the day of Mom's accident, and now this. He's going to be afraid to work for our family."

"Geez, that's true," Gina said. "I hadn't even thought about that."

"How long were you in the hospital? Was this just last week?" Juliette asked.

"Just a few days, Sweetie. No big deal."

"Well, broken heart or no broken heart, you should have told me. I can't believe you didn't."

"We've been fine, right Gina?"

"It really was ok once we knew he'd be good as new. It was a little scary until then, but you were going through your own stuff and we didn't want to add to your stress."

"Sorry," her dad looked properly chastised, "but you can't be mad at us now because we're too happy to see you!"

"True, and good strategy, I guess. But," Juliette's mind immediately went to the worst-case scenario, "you could have been paralyzed or killed! Look at you. Are you in pain?"

"I'm not in pain, so don't worry about me," he said. "They've got me on great pain meds."

"I tried to get him to stay home, but he was extremely uncooperative. Finally, I took pity on him, shoved him into the car, and brought him with me."

Juliette laughed and her father shook his head as if to deny the whole story while Gina rolled her eyes and sighed theatrically.

"This way we got to park in the handicapped parking area, which is way closer."

Juliette laughed. "You guys, it feels *so* good to be home!" she said. "I've missed you!"

The three of them talked nonstop all the way to the car. They barely broke their stream of conversation while they wrangled Juliette's dad into the back seat and got him buckled up.

"I can hardly wait to start looking at spaces to rent, " Juliette said, speaking about her café, hiding her emotions about Roman behind a curtain of cheerfulness.

"Actually, Juliette," Gina piped in, "you've already been looking, unbeknownst to you, because Dad's been a little bored since he's been laid up."

"At least once they took me off the Percocet," he said. "Until then I was laying in a warm sunbeam of contentment."

"He's not joking. He actually said, 'I'm having such a nice afternoon' while he was in traction." Gina laughed. "Anyway, once the fog cleared, he started scoping out venues."

"It's true, but no pressure. I gathered some information for you online while being forced to convalesce, but I don't want to get in your way."

"I'd love to see what you've found." Juliette knew her dad had been lonely with too much time on his hands since her mom's death. She could only imagine how much being stuck in a cast would add to that, so if helping her find a restaurant space interested him, she was happy to oblige.

"And," her dad told her, "If you're going to move forward with this, I'll have to reintroduce you to Ian."

"I actually want to get his contact info from you for another reason as well," she said. "I want to say thank you to him for driving you to the hospital and staying with me until Gina got there when Mom died."

"That would be nice. I'll text you his info right now," Alexander said, pulling out his cell phone. "He'll be perfect to use when you find the right place."

Suddenly the memory of Ian sitting next to her in the hard, plastic chair at the hospital flashed through her mind. She could almost feel the rough texture of his callused palm, holding one hand while she hugged the box of letters to her chest with the other. A ripple of tension shot across her body when she remembered that day. She hadn't had a panic attack about it in months and hoped the tingling tightness wasn't a precursor to one now.

"You could even meet with him and tell him what you have in mind ahead of time," Alexander said, not noticing the subtle deep breathing Juliette was trying to do without her dad or Gina seeing, nor the relief on her face as the feeling passed.

On the drive home, Juliette drank in the familiar sights and was filled with a sense of peacefulness.

The wheels crunched onto her gravel drive and she sighed with relief at the sight of her little in-law studio. The red geraniums blooming in the flower boxes fleetingly reminded her of the flowers on the balcony of her apartment in Lucca. It felt distant already. She noticed the sage was overwhelming the flagstones of her walkway and made a mental note to trim it back.

The windows were open, letting in the cold spring air, but it was lovely to walk into a fresh house.

"I hope it's all right," said Gina. "Christine thought it would be nice to open the windows and let in some fresh air for you. I didn't think you'd mind."

"Are you kidding? It's just one more thing to love about my best friend. I can't wait to talk to her and catch up."

Juliette noticed more things Christine had done, including a bouquet of flowers left on her kitchen counter and fresh milk and her favorite yogurt in the fridge.

"First things first," Juliette said, after she dumped her luggage into her room, texted a thank you to Christine, and they'd gotten her dad situated onto the couch. "Presents!"

She unzipped the larger of her suitcases and took out a few things she had brought home for each of them, which they oohed and ahhed over appreciatively. Then, while Juliette took a quick shower and cleaned up, Gina picked up dinner from Juliette's favorite sushi place so they could eat together before Juliette completely crashed from jet lag. She already felt a bit spacey, but knew she could at least make it through dinner with her family.

It had been too long since she had eaten sushi, and Juliette savored every morsel as she regaled them with stories of Italy. She swirled wasabi into her soy sauce and happily endured the heat. But after a while, her eyes were burning and she knew she couldn't keep them open much longer.

"I'm sorry you guys, but I have to get to bed. I feel like my head is actually going to fall off my shoulders and roll across the floor."

"You do look exhausted, Sweetie," her dad said.

"Get some sleep then," Gina told her. "I'll get Dad home." She kissed her little sister on the cheek. "It's great to have you back."

"Even though I loved Italy more than I ever imagined, which is saying a lot, I am very relieved to be home. It was hard to be away from you guys for such a long time. And once Roman broke up with me, I literally had to tell myself each day that I could get through it; and then another day would come and I'd tell myself the same thing."

Gina squeezed her sister's hand.

"Yeah, that last week was not so fun," Juliette said and hugged her again. "But you know what? If it hadn't happened, I would have been spending every spare moment with Roman instead of pouring over Catarina's letters, and I wouldn't have noticed the recurring theme of strength they were infused with: the promise of being able to take charge of life, make it a full one no matter what, and choose to be happy. It was like . . . I don't know . . . like suddenly waking up. I felt freed from my paralysis."

Juliette thought about those feelings once again as she climbed into her pajamas and snuggled in bed with her book, enjoying the fact that she was in her own bedroom. She read for about two minutes before her burning eyes got the better of her and she clicked off the light.

She stirred briefly at around five a.m. and peeked open an eye to check the time, but refused to give in to wakefulness, rolled over, and went back to sleep. When she awoke again, the light was streaming in her window. A quick glance at her clock showed that it was already eleven thirty in the morning. She stretched in bed, feeling beautifully rested, and then threw back her covers. She picked up the folder her dad had left for her. It was filled with sheets of paper detailing listings of various retail spaces for rent. She climbed back in bed, and started looking through them.

It was Sunday, she reminded herself, and she wasn't sure whether the listing agents were available to answer questions. She often saw "open house" signs around the neighborhood on Sundays, but she had no idea whether commercial real estate agents worked that day as well. She could hardly believe it was only Sunday. Had she really been in Italy just one long day ago?

Her cell phone chirped. She picked it up and looked at the text.

It was from Roman, and said: *"Buying mozzarella and thinking of you."*

She sighed and turned the phone over on her bed. Why would he do that? Didn't he understand how hurt she is? Besides, it was a lie anyway. He wouldn't be buying cheese at nine thirty at night, so why send some funny, sweet text?

"Argh!" she grunted, resolved not to respond, and then climbed out of bed.

She wanted to forget about him, no matter how hard it was, and get on with her day. The thought of getting dressed, doing her hair, and putting on make up seemed overwhelming, but she wouldn't allow herself to have a pity party, as her mom used to call it.

She had presents for several of her friends and wanted to catch up with everyone, so she sent out a group text inviting her friends to meet her for cosmos and appetizers. She was looking forward to eating food that wasn't Italian in any way. Then she spent the day catching up on mail, bills, grocery shopping, and laundry. All the things that make the world go round.

Juliette hadn't been in a supermarket in months and was slightly overwhelmed by the size and selection. It seemed a bit over the top, compared to the outdoor market and tiny grocery stores she'd frequented in Lucca. She chose a bunch of things she'd been missing while she was away, including some of her guilty pleasures: Nathan's hotdogs, buns, and sauerkraut, as well as slice-and-bake cookies, which she hid in her cart under a loaf of organic bread while furtively looking around.

After she loaded the groceries into her trunk, Juliette decided to take a quick walk downtown before she went home.

It was good to be back, and the April day was gorgeous. The sun was shining and the tree-lined streets were filled with shoppers and late lunchers. She had missed it. In the evening, she knew the trees would be lit up and looking cheerful with white twinkle lights. She strolled by one of the fountains and watched some kids running around the edge, tossing in pennies to make wishes. She headed up Locust Street then cut over to walk back down Main. Her plan was to go around one more block to Broadway, but she stopped short when she saw that one of her favorite buildings was vacant. It was one of the few original brick buildings in town. It had housed a little clothing boutique before she left, but was now empty. She looked for a "for rent" sign, or any sign at all, but didn't see any indication that it was available. Her heart drummed in her chest. This was exactly the type of space she had envisioned, but surely it was too good to be true.

She reminded herself that she hadn't even decided in which town she wanted to open her café, but this space was too promising not to be considered.

Her mind spinning, she remembered something her mom used to say: Success is about luck and timing as well as hard work.

Juliette realized that if this building *were* available, it would not only be perfect luck but impeccable timing as well. She looked again for any sign with contact information, but came up empty, so she decided to go to city hall first thing in the morning to inquire. She was sure they would at least know where to direct her.

She hardly remembered walking back to her car or going home and unloading her groceries. She could practically feel the synapses in her brain firing as it worked through the possibilities.

Juliette felt an incredible sense of anticipation all evening. Over drinks and appetizers, she told her friends about Italy, Roman, and the vacant building she saw downtown. She was surprised to realize that of the three topics, she was the most excited to talk about the third.

On Monday morning, Juliette was outside city hall at nine a.m. waiting for the doors to open. She decided to start at the city planning office and was happy to discover that they did have ownership information available for all the retail buildings in town. From her coat pocket, she pulled the rumpled piece of paper on which she'd hastily scrawled the address, and handed it to the man behind the desk.

"Oh, I know exactly which building that is," he said, and punched the address into his computer. "I think it needs a lot of work, though," he added and raised one eyebrow at her as if to appraise her ability to handle the task.

He tore a piece of paper off of his scratch pad, wrote the contact information for the owner, and handed it to Juliette.

"Good luck," he said and then turned dismissively and called up the next person waiting.

She didn't want to wait to get home to make the call, so she sat outside on a bench and dialed the number. She took a deep breath to calm herself. She knew the search was just beginning, but couldn't stop being hopeful anyway. After a brief conversation with the owner, she learned that the building was indeed available, but that it truly did need considerable work. She made an appointment to look at it anyway and then scrolled through her contacts until she located the one for Ian Matthews.

J uliette arrived at the coffee house early because she wanted to be there before Ian. She grabbed a table by the door and was stirring sweetener into her latte, wondering whether she would recognize him, when he walked through the door.

When her father had originally told her about the fantastic contractor he'd found to help with the structural changes they were making to the house, he had said nothing about a hunky, but kind of lanky, young, handsome contractor. She had expected a paint-stained, jeans-wearing, paunchy, middle-aged contractor. But Ian Matthews was definitely the former.

She hadn't been able to conjure his face in her mind, but as soon as he walked in she knew it was Ian. This time she registered his appearance in a way she hadn't been able to process when she met him on the day of her mom's accident.

Juliette stood up and came around the table with her hand out stretched.

"Hi," she said by way of introduction.

He took her hand, but instead of shaking it he gently leaned towards her and kissed her cheek in a warm, familiar manner.

"It's good to see you looking so well," Ian said.

"Thanks for meeting me." Juliette, surprised but not put off by the familiar gesture.

"I'm glad you called," he said, then nodded to the counter. "I'll be right back," he smiled and headed towards the register.

"What's your coffee of choice?" she asked when he got back, coffee in hand.

"Triple shot Americano," he said and took a sip. "Ah . . . that's good."

She liked the unapologetic contentment on his face. Something about him put her immediately at ease.

Once they were settled in, Juliette said, "I've been wanting to say thank you for sitting with me at the hospital. I was so out of it, I don't think I remembered to tell you how helpful it was to have you there."

"You actually said thank you several times."

"I did?"

"You did. I think you were in shock, and so inside yourself you were hardly aware of what was going on."

"Do you mind telling me what happened from your perspective? I keep reliving the accident itself and then . . . I don't know . . . it's weird. The memories are crisp and yet illusive. Like I see some details under a microscope but can't seem to see others at all," Juliette said.

"Sure," Ian paused for a moment, recalling the sequence of events. "I was with your dad at his house when you called him," he began. "I could tell something terrible had happened from his voice and then he frantically started looking for his keys. He was in no shape to drive, so I just grabbed my keys, said 'Let's go,' and we jumped in my truck. He told me about the accident on the way to the hospital. I stayed with him to make sure he could find the room, and when we opened the door we saw you there with your mom and I knew I needed to stay."

"I think I was in a daze. It was like my brain stalled because none of what had happened was in my version of a possible reality. We were on our way to get coffee together. She wanted to talk to me about something," Juliette closed her eyes for a second. "But the car came out of nowhere and then I was sitting with her body in a hospital room and . . ." Juliette still couldn't say the words.

"You were holding her hand and you looked completely lost. I wasn't sure what to do, but your dad was so overwhelmed he couldn't help you, so I came in and led you into the hallway so your dad could be with your mom and talk to the doctor. I didn't do anything, really, but find a couple of chairs and sit with you."

"I remember you held my hand."

Ian smiled.

"It helped."

"I'm glad. I wish I could have done more."

"I could feel you trying to give me your strength. That sounds weird, but I could feel it."

Ian watched her. She was as lovely as he had remembered.

"Your dad told me you went to Italy to recuperate."

He and Alexander had spent numerous hours together in recent months, renovating this and replacing that. Ian's theory was that Juliette's dad was trying to keep himself busy so he didn't have to dwell on the new version of his life, and as far as Ian was concerned, if he could help with that, then so much the better.

Alexander was definitely a talker and his favorite subjects were work and his daughters. Ian didn't think Juliette would necessarily be pleased to know that her father had told him about her trip to Italy, cooking school, and even her broken heart, so he just asked the question to see where it would lead.

"I did go to Italy. I had to get away. I'd been alternately trying to convince my dad, sister, and friends that I was all right, and secretly cooking compulsively. Hours and hours at a time. I couldn't stop. I made so much hand-rolled gnocchi I started to bring batches of it to the homeless guys who live down in the creek. They found me very confusing."

"I bet they did."

"And then one night when I couldn't sleep, I started to read the first in a bunch of letters my mom had given me. I was supposed to read them before she and I took a trip to Italy together, because they were a correspondence between my Italian grandmother and one of her friends from Italy. Anyway, that night, I opened the box, saw the letters and plane ticket, and I suddenly knew I needed to go."

Ian was engrossed. He put his elbows on the table and leaned closer, curious to hear what came next. Juliette noticed his eyes had the beginnings of smile lines that would grow deeper as he aged. He was looking at her—really looking at her as if he were trying to memorize her face.

"Why's that?" he asked.

"The day of the accident, Mom had a heart-to-heart with me about the fact that I should quit my dead-end job and refocus my life. I knew she was right, so I finally did it. I quit my job the next day, signed up for a cooking class in Lucca, and then fled with the shoebox full of Nonna's letters. I'm not usually that impulsive."

"Desperate times call for desperate measures, right?"

"I came to terms with a lot of things while I was there, which leads me to the second reason I asked you to coffee," Juliette said, and then filled him in on her plans and the space she'd found downtown. "I'm hoping I can lure you into being my contractor if this pans out."

"I'm guessing," Ian said, "it wouldn't be too hard to say yes."

Two days later Juliette peered into the building, checking her watch each time she moved from one window to another. She was scheduled to meet the owner in five minutes and she was hoping Ian would get there on time to meet with them. He told her he had a city planning meeting first, but promised to come as soon as possible. She looked up and down the street again, and then spied him hurrying towards her. He was wearing a suit with no tie and was even more handsome than she remembered, in a casual businessman sort of way. He was very different from Roman, she noticed. Where Roman was a crisply dressed Italian metrosexual, Ian had a casual, loose-limbed sort of home-grown sexiness to him.

"Am I late?" he asked.

"No," she said.

He stood next to her and peered into the window.

"I was wondering what would eventually go in here." He smiled and raised his eyebrows conspiratorially as if to say, "Now, I know," then continued, "When the owner gets here, let's just have you visualize the space out loud and we can talk about what your ideal set up would be. I'll take some notes and draw some sketches, and then we can meet again once I've given some thought to what we'd be looking at. Does that sound workable?"

"That sounds perfect," she said. She liked his sense of confidence and ease.

When the owner arrived, she unlocked the door for them and went inside. Ian held the door open for Juliette.

"After you," he said, as if they were already in this together. "Let's have a look."

Chapter 19

The bells rang in the large Catholic church that was decidedly different from the small, stone chapel she was used to at home. Franco had described the stained-glass windows perfectly. With the sun shining through them, the guests were bathed in color. The doors opened and after Franco took Catarina's arm, the newly married couple walked back up the aisle, smiling at the clapping, whistling guests, and stepped out into the sunshine. It felt strange to be married without her family and friends in attendance. But, much of her life was so different now, that she was getting used to her new circumstances.

The weeks since they had arrived in San Francisco had been a whirlwind, filled with preparation. Moving to a home filled with virtual strangers had only been the beginning. She'd hardly had time alone with Franco since they had stepped off the train.

Instead of talking to her future husband, the time had been spent getting to know her mother-in-law and Gabriella while they cooked, chose flowers, and prepared for the wedding.

As far as Catarina could tell, the Brunelli family had invited every Italian in San Francisco as well as many of the customers and neighbors they'd become friendly with over the years. The marriage ceremony would be in front of a huge crowd. She knew the party after the ceremony was going to be large and boisterous. Franco's parents, Vittorio and Isabella, rented out a large restaurant in the north end of town. The family had been up at daybreak, decorating the church and restaurant with flowers and streamers, so both looked especially festive.

At home, weddings were simple affairs. Here, the weddings were more elaborate as far as she could tell.

When the moment came, she was terrified and yet strangely calm. She was aware of herself walking, on the arm of Carlo, to meet Franco at the front of the church. And was aware of her voice repeating her vows as the priest led her through the ceremony in an odd, somewhat detached way. She pushed herself to stay present. She looked into Franco's eyes and made her promises before God. But even while doing so, she had to push away a flashing memory of Gregorio and the look on his face when she told him she couldn't run away with him.

She tried not to think about how she would feel if he were marrying someone else today. She made herself smile at Franco and when the time came, met his lips for their first kiss. And then it was done.

The crowd clapped and their applause brought her back into herself. She smiled at her new husband and said a silent prayer to God asking for Him to help her be a good and loving wife.

Catarina looked back at the church as guests emerged while she and Franco waited on the steps for everyone to follow behind them. And then, en masse, the festive group walked to the restaurant to celebrate, with the bride and groom leading the way. As they walked down the street, well-wishers called out to them and waved from windows. Catarina and Franco smiled and waved back, laughing at the unusual feeling of being the center of attention.

The experience continued to feel somewhat unreal to Catarina, as she walked in the beautiful, beaded shoes her new mother-in-law had insisted she buy in honor of the occasion. She was wearing the same long-sleeved, ivory dress her sisters had worn to their weddings. But she and her mother had painstakingly altered it to fit before she left home. It stopped just above her feet, which made Catarina happy because it would have been a shame for her shoes to be hidden. They had repaired a tiny tear in the dress's lace and added stitches in a swirling pattern along the waist to accentuate Catarina's lean form.

The scene was different than Catarina had imagined while she and her mother had sat working on the dress. The city where she now lived was larger, noisier, and colder than she thought it would be. The people were more gregarious than people at home. Everyone had been incredibly kind, especially those who had moved from Italy themselves, rather than the children of those immigrants, who had only heard stories of the old country. They had no idea what it had been like to uproot and move halfway across the world.

Catarina could tell her feet were going to be in pain by the end of the day. A blister had already formed on the back of her heel as they walked, but it was worth it, because never in her life had she owned shoes that were so elegant.

As they neared the restaurant, the San Francisco Bay shimmered in the distance. The September day was breezy but lovely and Catarina knew it could have been perfect if only her family were there to celebrate with her. She knew they were thinking of her, though. She could almost see them sitting at the dinner table, talking about her while they ate. She wondered what sassy comment Mateo would have to say about it. She smiled wistfully at the thought. *Dio*, she missed her brother.

As they approached the door, she could hear music playing and several men rushed ahead, linking their arms to form an arch for the newlyweds to pass under on their way in. Everyone cheered as they entered.

Catarina's new parents-in-law came in behind them, and as the rest of the guests approached the restaurant, they cheered again.

Each took turns kissing Catarina and Franco on the cheeks, then the rest of the guests jostled their way in, and trays of food and drinks appeared. Tables had been covered in white cloths, and pale-pink rose bouquets and white candles made the most elegant center pieces Catarina had seen. At home, wedding parties were often held outside with much less decoration and fuss. Here, the evening was filled with laughter, dancing, and feasting. Catarina had never danced with so many gentlemen in her life.

She could seemingly hear Gregorio whispering dancing instructions. No matter how many times she tried to stop thinking about him, he still crept into her mind. She would not allow herself to think about what the day would be like if it were

Gregorio and not Franco whom she had just married.

Instead, she focused on being grateful for marrying into the Brunelli family. They had made her feel like one of them from the moment she arrived. They didn't exclude her from decisions and made her feel comfortable among them, even though she knew her presence was forcing Gabriella and Carlo to share a room with their daughters until the wedding night, when she would switch from her own room into Franco's.

Her cheeks burned when she thought of that and how the entire family would know what was going on in Franco's room that night. She already wondered how she would face them in the morning. For now, she decided not to worry about it as she turned around the dance floor once again.

She met so many new people that by the end of the evening all she was capable of saying was, "*Grazie mille per venire, è stato un piacere conoscerti.*" Thank you so much for coming and it has been such a pleasure to meet you.

Franco circulated and talked with the other men who had come to the party. Occasionally she would catch his eye and he would give her a warm smile and a wink. She smiled back, amazed that he was her husband.

I am a married woman, she told herself. It felt strange, as if she were just playacting as she did with her sisters and Mateo when she was a little girl.

After several hours of eating and dancing, Franco's mother called Catarina and Franco over to cut the cake. It was three tiered and covered in white frosting with white filigree adorning the side. Pale-pink rose petals covered the top and were sprinkled on the table surrounding the elegant confection. Before they cut the first slice, Franco's father made a generous and kind toast—welcoming her to the family, and talking about the long friendship between the Pensebene and Brunelli families, and what joy he felt to have them joined as one family at last. Catarina, proud to be a part of it all, raised her own glass of champagne to join in a toast with the guests.

After his toast, she went over and kissed her father-in-law's cheek.

"Grazie, Papa." She turned and gave Franco's mother a kiss as well, then whispered to both of them, "You have both made me feel very welcome and I truly appreciate all of your kindness. I know my parents would have loved to have been here for this, but in their absence I want to say thank you."

"*Eviva!*" a bunch of people called out. "Cheers!" and then Franco and Catarina cut the cake.

Shortly after that, Franco came up and whispered in her ear that he thought that they should sneak away.

Catarina felt both a sense of thrill and fear at the prospect. Her feet ached and she was exhausted, but she wasn't sure she was ready to end the day. And a tremor went through her body at the thought of going home alone with Franco and what that would mean.

"How could we sneak away?"

"I'll dance you right to the back door and then we can sneak out. Once we're outside I can cover you with my coat, so you won't be so noticeable."

"Wouldn't your parents be angry?"

Franco laughed. "I assure you, it's done all the time. Expected really. The group has had enough of us, and we can make our departure without them knowing. Come, we'll slip out. I already left my coat by the back door."

"Are you sure?" she asked. "I don't want to embarrass your family or upset them."

"Trust me, it's customary," Franco urged her.

Catarina looked around nervously, wishing there was someone there to guide her in this matter. At home, it would never have been done, but she knew things were different here. She caught Gabriella's eye. Gabriella could see what was going on right away. She remembered being snuck out on her own wedding day, and smiled encouragingly at her and gestured with her hand that it was all right to scoot along.

"Go," she mouthed. "It's ok."

Catarina bit her lip in one more moment of hesitation, then allowed herself to be led onto the dance floor by Franco. They stopped once or twice to chat while they made their way casually to the door that led to the kitchen and then out onto an alley. Were the other guests in on Franco's intentions? She wondered. She could swear she saw the hint of a conspiratorial smile on the faces of a few of them.

As soon as he saw an opportunity, he grabbed her hand and pulled her through the swinging door. She started to giggle, and he shushed her then wrapped his coat around her shoulders to hide her dress.

He peeked out the back door and, taking her hand again, led her out onto the street. They ran down the block and then turned the corner onto a side street that went in the direction of home.

"If this is customary, as you said, why do we have to run?"

"Because it's part of the fun," Franco answered, pulling her along.

"My feet are in great pain," she said, as she tried to keep up with his fast pace.

He stopped running. "I'm sorry. I didn't know. Perhaps you should take off your shoes," Franco suggested.

"And ruin my beautiful stockings? Never!"

"Then I guess I'll have to carry you," Franco said, and before she could protest he lifted her into his arms and ran with her for almost a block before he had to put her down because they were both laughing so hard. They stood on the corner for a moment so he could catch his breath, and then they continued walking along, but at a slower pace so Catarina could go easy on her feet.

When they arrived home, the apartment seemed too quiet. Catarina realized it was the first time she had been there without the rest of the family.

"Perhaps you should go change," Franco suggested, "and then meet me in my room. I'm going to bring us in some food. I don't know about you, but with all the talking and dancing, I hardly had time to eat and I'm famished."

"Now that you say it, I'm hungry too. I hardly ate all evening even though there was so much food," she said over her shoulder, while she made her way to her bedroom to change out of her wedding dress and shoes. She unbuttoned the heavy dress, hung it on a hanger, and then slipped off the hose and looked at her feet. They were red and there was a large blister on each heel and each small toe.

What Catarina wasn't sure about, though, was what to put on. The formal nightgown she and her mother had made in anticipation of this moment somehow seemed silly and old-fashioned with its high, lacy collar. Should she put on a nice dress? That didn't seem right either. But her regular house dress was dirty, and she wanted to look pretty for Franco on their wedding night.

She chewed on her lower lip as she looked through her things. Finally she decided to wear a simple nightgown and a robe. She hoped he wouldn't think she was too forward, but she knew that he would have one thing in mind when she got to his room anyway, so why not make it easier on herself, she decided with more confidence than she felt.

The simple white linen nightgown her mother had made for her before she left was beautiful. It had a graceful V-neck and her mother had sewn a pearl at the bottom of the V and at the base of the straps she made to hold it up. It hung to her ankles and was almost as beautiful as her wedding dress, Catarina thought, except much more plain. She wrapped her robe around her and then brushed out her hair, which Gabriella had pinned up for her. It felt good to have her hair free of the pins.

She looked at her face and decided to put on a bit of powder to get rid of the shine, then she slipped out and gently knocked on Franco's door. Her heart was pounding. She was afraid he would be naked and she wasn't ready for that. She breathed a sigh of relief when he came to the door wearing the pants and shirt he had worn to the wedding. He had removed his tie though, and untucked his shirttail.

"Come in," he smiled. He seemed completely at ease, which helped Catarina feel more relaxed.

"Here, sit down," he said, indicating a chair he had placed by a small table that was covered with food. "You must be tired." He poured a glass of wine and handed it to her.

She sat down and looked around his room. She hadn't seen it before. It was bigger than she had imagined with a wonderful bay window.

Franco sat on the bed opposite her and put some food on his plate.

"Have some food," he said, so Catarina helped herself to some antipasto.

"Do you think everyone will be home soon?" she asked.

"No, I don't think they'll be home for hours," he told her. "Wedding parties go on well into the night here. It's only the bride and groom who are allowed to sneak away."

Catarina nodded. She was nervous and afraid her voice would give her away. She took a sip of wine and nibbled on some sliced prosciutto and olives.

Franco sipped his wine as well, and then met her eyes, "Listen Catarina, nothing has to happen tonight if you're not comfortable."

Catarina took a moment before answering.

"It's all right. We're going to be together at some point, yes? And it is our wedding night. So, we should be together, don't you think?"

He came to her and kissed her as his answer. It was a different kiss than he had given her before and she tried to give herself over to it in spite of her nerves.

She smiled at him, shyly. "I have to admit, I am nervous," she said.

"That's natural," he told her, and kissed her again.

She wondered whether Franco was also a virgin and whether they would be sharing this new experience together, but she couldn't bring herself to ask.

"How are your feet?" he inquired.

"They're killing me," she told him. "Look at these blisters."

"Here, give them to me. I'll rub them," he said and patted the bed.

She leaned against the headboard while he rubbed her feet. It felt amazing. No one had ever rubbed her feet before. Between that and the wine, she was feeling entirely relaxed.

She took another sip and then set her glass down and moved so she was kneeling on the bed next to where he was sitting. His shoulders were strong even though he was thin, and she could see his wrists below the rolled-up cuffs of his shirt. His face was becoming increasingly handsome to her as she got to know him.

She reached out and touched his arm and he kissed her again. She allowed herself to feel the sensuality of his mouth and his hands touching her. She was just getting comfortable with kissing, when he lifted her arms and took off her nightgown. She feigned confidence at first, but seeing his face while he looked at her naked body was too much, and she turned her face away.

He took her chin in his hand and looked into her eyes.

"You're beautiful, Catarina."

"*Grazie*," she said, and forced herself to hold his eyes. He shifted and removed his own clothes. She could feel the pounding of her heartbeat, even at her throat. She touched his chest, but couldn't bring her hand to venture further.

"Don't worry. It's just me. It's going to be fine," he told her while he gently explored her. "And this is definitely more fun than pruning olive trees, right?"

"We'll see," she laughed.

His comfort and humor lightened the tension for her. He kissed her to divert her attention from being naked with a man for the first time, until she was able to relax and be drawn along with his passion. He tried to be gentle when he finally did enter her, but her sharp intake of breath let him know to wait a moment. He stopped and looked into her eyes until she nodded at him and he continued his gentle motion for their first time together.

Afterword, she curved herself into the crook of his arms and enjoyed the feeling of being entwined with him. He ran his hands over her hair for a moment.

"Are you ok?" he asked.

"*Si*. I'm fine. Are you ok?"

He laughed. "More than ok," he said leaning up on one elbow and kissing her cheek. He then got up and brought her a basin with water and a cloth.

"I'll be right back," he said, kissing her quickly and excusing himself so she could have some privacy.

They were asleep with Franco's arm wrapped around her when she awoke in the wee hours of the night to the sound of the rest of the family coming into the apartment. They seemed to be purposefully noisy, she thought. Either that or they had all had a lot to drink and were unsteady on their feet.

Franco didn't wake up, but he did turn over in his sleep. She had a chance to see his face by the light of the moon.

I'm married to him, she thought. It was strange how much her life had changed in such a short time. But she was too tired to reflect further. Instead, she tucked herself into the curve of his body and fell back into an exhausted sleep.

When she woke up the next morning, Franco was already up. She could hear his voice in the kitchen talking animatedly to his mother. He seemed to be recounting some humorous incident from the wedding party.

Catarina snuck out of bed and went to the bathroom to tidy herself, brush her teeth and comb her hair. Then she padded silently down the hall to get dressed in her own room before she went into the kitchen. She was embarrassed to see everyone, knowing what they knew, but she couldn't put it off forever.

She held her head up and walked into the kitchen. She tried to act as if nothing was different, but when she was walking by, Franco pulled her to him and wrapped his arm around her. He kissed her on the lips, which startled her. Isabella stood at the counter making coffee and she smiled at them.

"Leave her alone, Franco," she said to her son. Then she came over to Catarina and took her face in her hands. "How are you, sweet girl?" she asked.

"I'm fine," she said, embarrassed by the implications of her question. "Your son is a gentleman."

"See, Mama? I'm a gentleman," Franco smirked at his mother.

"How was the rest of the party?" Catarina asked. "Franco dragged me away. I hope you aren't upset that we left early."

Isabella waved her hand as if to say "It was nothing," and then regaled them with stories of who drank too much after they left, and who she saw kissing in a corner. Gradually the rest of the family made their way into the kitchen: the adults looking a bit hungover and the children subdued by the late night and excessive amount of cake consumed.

Once the initial embarrassment of facing them wore off, Catarina was able to laugh at their stories and even add a story or two of her own. As they reminisced and drank coffee, Franco moved behind her and wrapped his arms around her shoulders while they stood together. It was a nice feeling. One that she knew she could get used to.

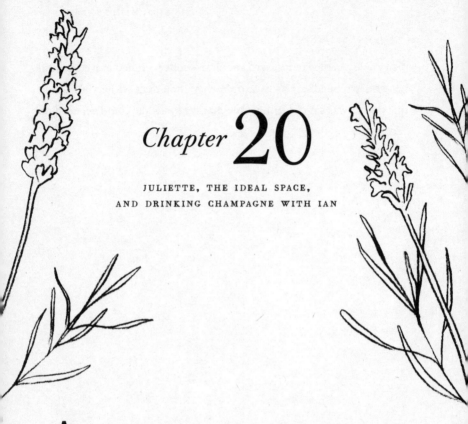

Chapter 20

JULIETTE, THE IDEAL SPACE,
AND DRINKING CHAMPAGNE WITH IAN

As she surveyed the space, Juliette could see dust motes floating in a sunbeam, which she found oddly appealing. The space had been gutted, so seeing what it could be was fairly easy for her. It wasn't terribly big, which she considered a plus because she wanted to keep the atmosphere feeling energetic and almost crowded. That could be difficult in too large an area. There were windows at the front of the building facing the street, but none to the sides. It was deep and somewhat narrow. One side shared a wall with another business but the other brick side did not. She wondered if it would be possible to open it to the outside with a door and windows.

Ian watched Juliette take in the space. She looked thoughtful and intelligent and also seemed to possess the dreaminess that occurs when a person is seeing what *could* be. She didn't speak for a few minutes.

He stood aside, looking at the space with a contractor's eye. He was curious to hear her ideas but didn't want to disrupt her wheels from spinning. He could practically see the gears clicking into place behind her eyes.

The owner walked to the back of the building to unlock the rear door so they could see the loading dock behind the space. When she was out of earshot, Juliette whispered to Ian.

"I think this is a great space. What do you think?"

"I agree," he replied, in a soft voice. "It could be incredible. I like the brick walls. And the windows would be fairly easy to change out, if you wanted something with more character. Tell me what you're thinking."

"Changing the windows would definitely help. These are so plain," she nodded towards the front of the store.

Then she continued, "I think it would be great to have a counter that ran along one side. It could start around a third of the way back and then cut back to the wall and extend all the way to the front window with tall chairs. Then we could have tables along the opposite side and toward the middle with some space left open for traffic. And I like the idea of an open kitchen in the back."

"Sounds entirely doable to me. Not complicated at all," Ian said, while he turned slowly to examine the space from all sides. "What types of materials are you thinking of using?"

"I love an industrial look, but not too modern or cold. It has to be mixed with warmer touches. The brick already gives it warmth. I picked up some wonderful, huge pottery pieces when I was in Italy, and I'd love to incorporate them. I'm thinking about stained concrete for the counters and wrought iron paned windows."

"Sounds great." Ian reached into his satchel and pulled out a sketchbook and pencil. He started by drawing a rectangle roughly in the building's shape, then added in a counter. "Is this what you had in mind?" He tilted the sketchbook so she could take a look.

She leaned in to see.

"Hmm, I think I would want it to come out farther and then curve around here," she ran her finger along the counter he had drawn and then over to the sketched wall.

He changed his drawing to reflect what she said. "How's this?"

"Exactly," she smiled at him.

"Ok, let's look back here and you can tell me what you're thinking about for the kitchen."

They walked towards the back of the space while the owner busied herself, giving them time to talk. Juliette gazed around her.

"It's amazing, I can see it already. What I would want is an island cook top here. A big square with lots of counter space." She paused and looked around her. "And a large fridge here with a bank of ovens next to it. Then a separate walk-in fridge and freezer right there," she pointed. "The dish area would also have to be enclosed." She turned around wondering what would make sense.

"Maybe there?" he pointed.

"Yes, I think that would work. I wonder if I could pick up some of that stuff secondhand."

"I'm sure you could. It's just a matter of searching it out."

They talked through more details and took a look behind the space. Juliette grew increasingly excited, but tried to rein herself in and not show too much. She knew she didn't exactly have a poker face, but she reminded herself to at least keep up a cool façade if possible.

"I think I have what I need," Ian said, putting his sketchbook and yellow legal pad back into his satchel. "I'll put my thoughts together and then we can meet to talk about what it would take to make it happen."

"Thanks. And thanks for coming on such short notice," Juliette said and walked him to the door. "Remember, I'm just a poor girl with a dream, so if you could think about how to make this fabulous while not breaking the bank, I'd appreciate it!"

"Will do," Ian laughed. "Extraordinary on a budget. Not to worry. Consider it done."

"Perfect. And you'll call me about it soon?"

"As soon as I possibly can, if not sooner," he smiled again and waved while he walked backwards away from her. "In fact, practically immediately," he smiled his farewell.

Wow, how great is he? Juliette thought, as she turned back to talk to the owner. A contractor who not only shows up, but takes notes, sketches, is incredibly nice, and looks great in a suit. Then she shoved that last bit under the rug.

Stop it, she told herself. He's probably another heartless guy who seems nice but would trample her heart given half a chance. Then she reprimanded herself for that sentiment as well. She had never been a bitter man-hater and was determined not to let herself become one because of what Roman did. Nonetheless, she was far from ready to jump back in, no matter how charming her potential contractor was.

She brought herself back to the situation at hand. The space *was* perfect. She only hoped she could afford it.

After talking with the owner about a few more details, Juliette inhaled deeply and asked about the rent. The property owner jotted a number down and handed it to Juliette.

"Ouch," Juliette said when she took a peek at the figure on the page, but in truth a sense of relief flooded her for two reasons. The first was that the number wasn't as high as she'd feared it would be. The second was that Juliette found negotiating stressful and was happy to be able to jot down a lower number than say she wanted to pay less out loud. "Any chance this is negotiable?"

"Not much. What did you have in mind?"

"Well, I have to talk to my contractor about what it would take to make the renovations that would be required, but I was thinking more along the lines of this," she handed the paper back with a number that was several hundred a month lower.

"Possibly," she said. "Why don't you talk to him and then we can chat again."

"Sounds good," Juliette said shaking her hand. "I'll be in touch soon."

After Juliette left, she casually strolled down the block until she turned the corner. She looked over her shoulder to make sure she was out of sight, then ran to the nearest bench, grabbed her phone out of her bag and speed dialed her dad.

"Hey," she said when he picked up. "I just looked at the building and the space is amazing! It's exactly what I want, but..."

"But?" Juliette could hear the smile in her dad's voice.

"It's the first space I've actually looked at. Would it be wise to jump in before looking at other stuff?"

"If it's everything you want, what's the problem?"

"What if it's not a good deal? And I don't know that it's not a good deal because I haven't compared it to other places?"

"Well, why don't you take a look at all the rentals in the file I gave you. They all show square footage and the rent amount, so that should at least give you an idea of whether you're in the right ballpark. You can even drive by some of them to get a better sense about them. How did the price she gave you seem?"

"That's the thing, maybe I was just assuming the worst, but it wasn't actually as high as I thought it would be."

"You should put some numbers together and we'll do some feasibility work and create a business plan. You'll have to take a good, honest look at how much you think you can bring in every month and then look at your expenses."

"I've done that over and over already. Maybe you could come over and see what I've done and let me know what you think."

"OK, but you know, your mom was the one with the business sense. Why don't we have Gina come, too? She's used to looking at monthly profitability reports. She'll have good insight."

"Maybe I could cook you guys dinner, and we can talk about it. I'll see if Gina's free, then call you back."

"Sorry," Gina told her when Juliette got a hold of her. "I can't tonight. I've got a date."

"You have a date? You didn't say anything about it."

"I'm saying something now."

"Shoot," Juliette said. "How about getting together tomorrow instead? I'll cook."

"Sounds great. Can we have eggplant *parmigiana*? I've been

having a craving lately."

"Done!" Juliette said. "I'll see you tomorrow." Then she hung up and finalized the plan with her dad, too.

J uliette would have loved to talk with Roman about the space. She desperately missed him, but when she did think about him she inevitably visualized his girlfriend snuggled up with him on the couch that she had so recently vacated. She sighed and put her hand on her chest. It still hurt, but at least she was home and diving back into her life. She had to admit, she was extremely excited about the building she had found, and was happy to have something new on which to focus.

She spent the rest of the day checking websites for used appliances to get a sense of the price of things. She also looked at some incredible new industrial stoves and refrigerators, because a girl's got to dream, and then she focused on floor treatments. What would go well with brick walls and cement counter tops? She thought through several options then finally narrowed it down to either wide-plank wood floors or a dark-gray slate. Or maybe wood floors stained dark gray. That could be nice, too. There were going to be so many decisions to make.

She knew exactly what kind of windows she wanted. The ones on the building now were boring and nondescript, and they made the facade look like a bank. The fact that Ian had noticed the same thing made her feel hopeful about his design sensibility. Juliette knew that large paned windows with black metal casings would look perfect. She wanted ones that opened to let in fresh air during the warm months.

She'd paint the ceiling the color of butter or maybe sage. And buy brushed-aluminum chairs with wooden tables to juxtapose the warm with the cool.

She wondered how long it would take for Ian to work up an estimate for the project. She liked the questions he asked and felt that he understood her vision. He seemed sharp and intelligent, and so far she liked the prospect of working with him; however, a lot would depend on his estimate. And, she reminded herself, absolutely no getting emotionally involved with him. She would keep her distance. Keep it professional this time. No mixing work with pleasure.

Over the next few days she jumped with anticipation every time the phone rang and chewed the ears off of her family and friends until they were sick of the topic. But the person whom she most wanted to hear from was Ian. Finally, after an excruciating two weeks, he called to set up a meeting.

She was on pins and needles until the moment arrived. The feeling reminded her of childhood Christmas mornings, when she'd sit on her hands and bounce on the couch until it was time to open her presents.

He was waiting at the same table where they had met weeks before, his triple shot Americano in front of him and a large latte waiting on Juliette's side.

"You remembered my drink," she said, impressed.

"Photographic memory," he joked, pointing to his forehead while reaching into his satchel for the proposal.

Juliette looked through as Ian laid out his plan in detail. She had suggestions here and there, but for the most part, he had not only gotten the sense of what she wanted, but improved upon it. He even surprised her by designing an outside eating area on the side of the restaurant. He had surrounded it with a heavy trellis and planters around the edges to create a sense of defined space. She was almost as excited at the prospect of that as she was about the inside. It would add table space and ambiance.

The cost was jarring, but she had expected as much. The reality was, because of her mother's generosity, she could afford it, even though it would mean putting her inheritance on the line. She hoped she was correct in her newfound belief that her mom would have wanted her to do this. Juliette looked at the ring and thought about Catarina's bravery in getting on the ship when she was much younger than Juliette was now.

"Let's do it," Juliette said, looking at him with eyebrows raised as if to say "So, are you in?"

Ian laughed. "That's it? Just, 'Let's do it' with no revisions, no complaints, nothing?"

"Trust me," she reassured him. "I've obsessed over this ad nauseam. I've questioned the project, I've questioned myself and whether I'm up to the task, the feasibility of it, everything I can imagine going wrong, over and over again. I've been thinking about this for years. Now I'm ready to jump in. So, yes, let's go for it. I mean . . . you know . . . not to say that we won't want to change things here and there." She nodded towards the design.

"I'm in," Ian said, and reached across the table to shake hands with Juliette. "I'm looking forward to it. I think we can make this great."

"Me too," Juliette said, laughing nervously, hoping her mother would approve. It was truly going to happen.

"So, maybe we should go out for champagne instead of drinking coffee," Ian suggested.

"Unorthodox, but an excellent idea! Let's go," Juliette said, closing the estimate and tucking it into her bag to review later.

"I know exactly where we can get a nice glass of champagne at this hour," Ian told her.

"I won't even ask how you'd know that," Juliette said.

She noticed Ian took several large sips of his coffee before standing up.

"So I don't get a headache," he explained.

"You did confess to being an addict when we were here last time," Juliette reminded him.

When they arrived at their next destination they sat by a window that was open, even though the fire in the fireplace was ablaze to stave off the morning chill. Ian placed the order.

"Special occasion?" the server asked them with a smile. "Did you two just get engaged, perhaps?"

"You could say that," Ian laughed, before Juliette could get out her earnest, "No."

"In that case, the champagne is on the house."

"No, no, you really don't need to do that," Ian protested, and shot Juliette a look that said, 'Uh oh, now I've done it!'

"It's our treat," she said, and walked over to the bar to place the order.

"Oops," Juliette said, and nodded to the bar, where the server and the bartender were obviously talking about them and smiling. In truth, she couldn't imagine feeling any more euphoric if she *had* just become engaged. "We can leave her a big tip to ease our consciences," she said, and then continued, "So, do you always go out drinking with clients when they say 'yes' to your bids?"

"This is the first time, actually. It just seemed fitting," Ian said as the champagne arrived. "Cheers!"

They touched glasses. "Cheers," she responded.

As they settled in, Juliette took a closer look at Ian. She noticed his brown hair was wavy and had a slightly shaggy look. His eyes were light green, flecked with gold, and she could tell that he was prone to a five o'clock shadow. He was wearing jeans and a button-down instead of the suit today, but he looked just as good. She caught herself gazing at him too intently and turned to look out the window.

"So, since we're going to be spending so much time together, why don't you tell me more about you," Ian prompted. "Tell me your story."

After two more glasses of champagne, Juliette felt as if she and Ian knew the bones of each other's life stories. She started to laugh.

"What's so funny?" Ian asked.

"I just realized that I'm too drunk to drive and it's still before noon. I'm so ashamed."

"I'm in the same boat. I think we need to either walk this off or each take cabs. What's your preference?"

"Let's walk it off," Juliette said, gathering her purse and following Ian outside. "Then I'm going home to take a nap before I call my future landlord to tell her I'll take the space. I'm a bit of an irresponsible entrepreneur already, aren't I?"

"At least you know to sober up before making business calls," he raised one eyebrow at her. "You have that going for you."

"You're right. I guess I'm not so bad after all. Listen, we have to make some important decisions."

"Always a good idea to do after drinking," Ian chuckled. "What do you have in mind?"

"Let's talk timing."

"Well, I'm in the middle of a project right now—although I think I have to take the rest of today off," he smirked at her. "My project should wrap up in about a month and a half. That's about right for dovetailing in with your project, because it's going to take at least a couple of months for us to make working plans, get all of the permits, and have everything signed off before we can start hammering away on the building."

"Two months? . . . All right. Can you still work on plans with me while you're finishing the other project?"

"Sure. We can meet during lunch or in the evenings if we need to."

"Great," she said. They were in front of one of Juliette's favorite stores, so she decided it was a good place to make a graceful exit. "I think I'll say goodbye here," she said, indicating that she was going to go in.

"Seriously, no driving home until you're sure you're fine."

"I promise. And that goes for you, too."

"Bye then," Ian said, and reached out to shake her hand. But instead held it while he leaned forward and kissed her cheek the way he had when they had met for the first time at the café.

Between their extraordinary meeting the day of the accident, having coffee weeks before and champagne today, they had begun a comfortable friendship. She smiled at the thought of their unexpected morning. She browsed around the store in somewhat of a daze before stepping outside to call her friend, Christine. She couldn't wait to tell her the news. As she unlocked her phone, a vision of her giddily drinking celebratory champagne with Ian, coupled with the departing cheek kiss, flitted across her mind. So much for not getting emotionally involved, she chided herself. But, she decided, there was no harm in becoming friends. They would be spending large quantities of time together, but it *was* business. She reminded herself of that as she scrolled down her contacts then dialed the number.

Chapter 21

CATARINA, LEARNING TO READ,
SPILLING COFFEE,
AND SEEING GREGORIO AGAIN

Catarina spread a picnic blanket out on a gently sloping lawn in Golden Gate Park. The park was vast, sprawling, and beautiful, with trees, meandering pathways, and vibrantly colorful gardens. The day was unusually warm. October had been a month of sunshine for which she was grateful. She'd found the weeks of fog and cool breezes had put a damper on her appreciation of her new home. She longed for the sunshine and heat of Italy, and warm summer nights when her family ate dinner outside. Here, by evening, she had to add a sweater to keep warm and she was quickly learning to knit out of necessity.

She was content to sit on the frayed lemon-yellow blanket she and

Franco had brought. She unpacked the food and sliced some cheese to snack on, along with cured green olives and fresh, crusty bread. Franco pulled a book out of his pocket and held it up for her to see.

Catarina lifted her hand to shield her eyes from the sunlight so she could see which one he'd brought. It was a child's nursery rhyme collection that he was using to teach her to read in English. The stories were silly and nonsensical, but she loved her reading lessons. They had taken to conducting them in the park or in their room in the evenings.

Franco enjoyed teaching his new wife to read English. They went together every week to check books out of the library. Catarina loved the dusty smell of the paper and the old cloth stitched together to form bindings. She liked to open up books at random and put her face against the pages, inhaling deeply. Franco laughed when she did it, and sometimes shook his head in amusement, but his mirth didn't stop her. She found the scent appealing. There were so many words. Sometimes she would run her fingers along the lines of printing. For now, most of the words were a mystery to her, but she knew someday the combinations of letters, now foreign, would make sense.

Catarina took the book Franco held out and looked through the pages. The illustrations helped her understand what was going on, but there were still fewer words than she would have liked that she could read on her own. She ran her finger along the lines of the text on the first page and said "the" aloud every time she came to it. And then did the same with other words that she now thought of as "her friends": the ones she was comfortable with. Her group of friends was expanding every day.

Pondering her "word friends" made her realize that she needed to make some real friends. Gabriella was wonderful, but she was so busy with the kids. And Franco was at work Monday through Saturday.

She exhaled deeply and lay back on the blanket, letting the sun warm her face, and thought about Maria Nina from home.

"*Che c'è, Tesoro?*" What is it, darling?

"*Niente.* " I'm just missing home and my friends," she said, suddenly seeing the vine-covered hills and gossiping at the water pump.

She did like San Francisco. There was always so much going on, but she felt a bit trapped inside the apartment. In Italy, she had often been outside, working in the garden or off running errands for her parents. Whereas here, aside from going to the market, she was often inside most of each day. She sometimes stood in front of the small painting of the Italian landscape she bought for Franco's parents in New York, wishing she was there instead. She wanted Franco to be there, too, and smiled at the realization that she would miss him otherwise. She wondered if she was falling in love. She liked the phrase that the Americans used. "Falling." She watched Franco. He lay on his side. His gangly frame comfortable and his eyes sparkling with mischief at her.

"What?" he asked again.

"Nothing," she replied, in English this time, instead of Italian. She shook her head, but she smiled at him, to let him know that she found him wonderful, and then lay back on the blanket to let the sun's rays warm her face.

She thought of the words "falling in love" again. Unbidden, the face of Gregorio came to mind. Had that been love, and if so, what was she feeling now, with Franco? Was it companionship? She didn't think so, because her feelings for Franco were real, too. A different kind of love, maybe. With Gregorio, it had felt desperate and intense.

More like jumping off a cliff than falling. With Franco, it was more like the sun warming her cheeks.

In the evenings after dinner, she and Franco often left the apartment to go for walks around the neighborhood. That was the best part of the day. He held her hand and told her funny stories about what had happened at work.

She peeked her eyes open against the bright sun and looked at Franco.

"Let's read," she said lazily. "Will you read to me first, or do you want me to read to you?"

"I'll read to you," he said, scooting closer to her and laying the book open on the blanket between them so she could see the words. "You follow along with your finger."

"Perfect," she said, shrugging off her sense of listlessness, and edged herself over, so she could lean gently against him. "But do you know what we should read next?"

"What?" he raised his eyebrows in curiosity.

"A love story, I think," she told him, and ran her fingers through his hair. She could have sworn she saw his olive complexion turn one shade darker.

"If it's a love story you want, then a love story you shall have," he said, quickly kissing her. "But for now, you get nursery books."

"For now," she said. And then she ran her finger along the first line of text and listened to him slowly read the words. Occasionally she stopped him to ask for the meaning of one word or another, but she was coming along well. She always spoke Italian at home, but she switched to English when she went to the market and when they were out at restaurants. She knew she often butchered the tenses and that her speaking ability was choppy at best, but she could get her point across and she was eager to learn. Catarina knew it was just a matter of time before she could speak fluently and she looked forward to the day. She hoped she had plenty of time to get better before she became pregnant. She saw how limited Gabriella's time away from the family was, and wasn't quite ready for that herself.

Catarina definitely wanted *bambini*, just not so soon. Her mother-in-law already looked at her for signs that she was carrying a grandchild for her, but for the time being Catarina was happy; happy each month with the discovery that she, in fact, was not pregnant. Luckily, Franco didn't seem to be in a hurry either. Although she knew he would be excited if it happened, each month when she got her period, he would smile at her and say, "*Va bene*. For now I still get you all to myself."

Until then, she was content to help out with her nieces and nephews. Their apartment was already crowded, and adding another baby would make it more so. Franco still talked about getting an apartment of their own. On the one hand, Catarina liked the idea of making her own home and being the mistress of her own time and her own kitchen, but she had her reservations about being alone all day. She had always lived with a large family, and couldn't fathom what it would be like not to do so.

The possibility of moving to an apartment was their main topic of conversation on a rainy December evening, while they waited for cannoli at Flavio's, a tiny old-fashioned Italian café. Catarina loved it, not only because the gnocchi reminded her of her mother's back home, but also because the people who frequented Flavio's could all have stepped right out of her village.

They were contentedly facing each other and hashing through the idea, tucked into a tiny leather booth. Franco and Catarina relished the delicious, homey Italian food, and had just finished a large platter of gnocchi, which they had consumed with abandon, and were now sipping strong, thick coffee while they waited for their dessert to arrive. Catarina lifted the cup to her lips, let out a shriek, and suddenly found herself scalded and covered in coffee.

"What happened?" Franco asked her. "Are you all right? Are you burned?"

"I'm so sorry," she said, using her napkin to blot the wet coffee stain that covered the front of her dress. "I just got startled. That's all. I saw one of the people who was on my ship, and I was so surprised that I dropped my coffee," she stammered.

"Who?" Franco asked, looking around the restaurant.

"That man there," Catarina told him, pointing to the one man whom she had never expected to see again. He was wearing the clothes that the other waiters at Flavio's wore, which confused her. Why wasn't he wearing the uniform of the ship? Her mind raced for answers.

Gregorio had an equally surprised look on his face. Catarina's heart lurched and she tried to regain composure as he walked over to their table. His look of surprise was quickly replaced by one of acute indifference, and Catarina found it cut her to the core. How can he feel nothing, she wondered, while she had to fight to keep herself from jumping up and running to him.

"Catarina," he said. "Or should I call you *Signora* . . . ?" his voice trailed off, as he realized he didn't know her last name.

"Brunelli," she added to help him. "And, this is my husband, Franco. Franco, this is Signor Villa. He was one of the men who worked onboard the ship I traveled on from Italy. We dined together several times, along with the others in our group of passengers, during the crossing." She felt herself stammering a bit with nervousness, but Franco didn't seem to notice how flustered she was.

"Nice to meet you," Franco said, and reached out to shake Gregorio's hand.

"Have you stopped working on the ship?" Catarina asked, happy that her voice didn't betray the turmoil she felt. His hair was different, too. Less closely cut, but his face was the same one she'd thought of so many times since she had last seen him.

"*Si*, I got tired of making the crossing. On my last voyage there was a tremendous storm, and I vowed if I made it to land I would never make the trip again. I was sure we were all going to drown." He smiled and shrugged, so she wasn't sure whether his story was true or exaggerated.

"Now you work here?"

"As a waiter for now. Just until something better comes along." He self-consciously brushed at a stain on the sleeve of his shirt. "Well, I better get back to work," Gregorio said hesitantly, as if he didn't want to.

"It was nice to see you again," Catarina said.

"You, too," he said looking away. She watched him walk to the counter and pick up plates to deliver them to the guests in his station. She was thankful he hadn't waited on them, which would have been more painful than she could have endured.

She turned back to her husband, who was studying her.

"He seems nice," he said.

"Yes, he was very nice to Maria and me," she smiled. "Now where were we," she asked, "before I threw coffee all over myself?"

"Waiting for our cannoli, I believe."

"Ah yes, and here it comes," she inclined her head towards the waiter coming their way with a plate of the Italian pastries and a fresh cup of coffee for her.

Catarina looked around the restaurant before they left, hoping to catch a glimpse of Gregorio again, but he was nowhere in sight. They walked out into the evening to begin their stroll home. The streets were quiet and although she kept up a conversation with Franco, her mind was on Gregorio the whole way home. He was as handsome as she remembered, although there seemed to be a new weariness around the eyes, and she thought he looked a little thinner. Neither change diminished her attraction to him and as much as she regretted it, she couldn't help but think again about what her life would have been like if they could have been together.

Those thoughts made her feel like she was betraying Franco, so she entwined her fingers with her husband's and smiled at him to try to make up for the guilt she was feeling. She was distressed even thinking about Gregorio, but she couldn't get him out of her mind.

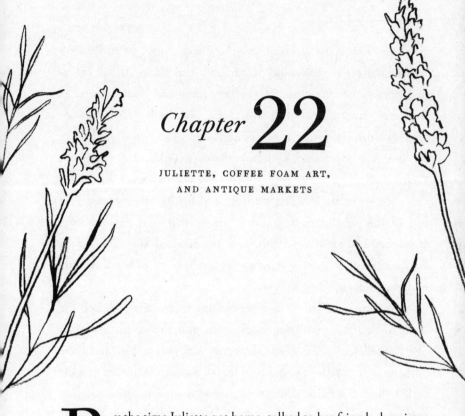

Chapter 22

JULIETTE, COFFEE FOAM ART,
AND ANTIQUE MARKETS

B y the time Juliette got home, talked to her friends, her sister, and her dad, she had a bit of a champagne hangover coming on from her crazy meeting with Ian. Although it was only midday, she couldn't wait to take a nap so she grabbed a blanket and curled up on her couch.

When she woke up, the afternoon sun was slanting through her window. She contacted the owner of the building and finalized the rental details. She smiled again thinking about Ian and the waitress who assumed they were newly engaged. She splashed her face and brushed her teeth, then plunked herself down in front of her computer to look at some styles of windows. She loved thinking about the possibilities the space could offer. Juliette had a good eye for color and design, an artistic trait she had inherited from Nonna Catarina. Her in-law studio had several paintings from her grandma. All of them featured lush Italian landscapes or scenes of the California wine country. She sighed. She would love to have her mom and grandma there to talk color and show them samples.

She spent the evening reading, and finally, she dropped into bed in the wee hours, and didn't stir until late in the morning. It was odd not having a job, and she realized she should face facts and work on getting some sort of gig to bring in money to tide her over before opening the café.

She made herself a latte, got out her laptop, and checked the "help wanted" ads under waitresses, cooks, and catering on Craigslist. She wanted someplace where she could just pull a shift and leave without any aspirations or drama. Her hope was to find work in some little indie coffee house where she could serve up specialty coffees, so she started her search there. She responded to several ads online, and then decided to kick it old school and opened the newspaper to the "jobs offered" section to check that out as well.

Several weeks later, Juliette was racing around, picking clothes up off the floor, and gathering miscellaneous mail and papers into a pile. Her place was a bit of a wreck and Ian was coming over to review the café plans.

She had spent several nights at her dad's house to help out while he healed, and it was nice to be home again. He was improving daily, much to Juliette's relief. His physical therapist was somewhat of a drill sergeant, but she seemed to be getting the job done. Juliette was relieved that he would be walking without crutches soon and was ready to care for himself for the most part.

Things were in order enough to spare her embarrassment by the time the doorbell rang. Juliette brought Ian outside to the table in her tiny backyard garden. It was cooler then the previous day, almost crisp.

While Ian rolled out the plans, Juliette filled him in on the new job she'd found.

"It took me a couple of weeks to find it, but now I get to work on my skills at creating little pictures in the foam on the top of lattes and cappuccinos," she joked and handed him a latte in a white ceramic mug with a curly heart in the foam. "So far, the only shape I've mastered is a heart, but it's only been a couple of days and I'm working on expanding my horizons."

"Nice," he smiled. "What other pictures are you working on?"

"I was thinking of trying to create landscapes, but that seemed a bit ambitious, especially given my limited time frame, so I've settled on attempting a tulip in addition to the heart. I've had some good results, but sometimes things go awry."

Ian laughed at her mock seriousness.

"Hey, don't knock the coffee art," she laughed, "or next time you'll get a frownie face."

"Duly noted," he said, reaching for his briefcase and bringing out the latest version of the plans. "I'll behave. Just don't hex my coffee."

In the weeks since they began working on the project together, they had formed a companionable friendship. Now, at the final stages before they submitted the plans for permits, they wanted to go over them one last time. It was the first time Ian had been to Juliette's home.

Ian dove right in. "Before we move forward, let's review everything while we can still make changes easily."

"It's going to be a beautiful space," Juliette admired the plans like a doting new mother. "I keep trying to picture myself working there and when I go over my movements in my mind, I can't think of anything I would change."

"Once we're working on the interior of the building, as long as it's within the footprint of the structure, it's no problem to shift things around if you do decide you want to tweak something."

She peeked at Ian's profile, appreciating his quiet confidence. He seemed completely comfortable in his skin.

Forget it, she told herself. Best not to even go there.

When the meeting was finally over, Juliette picked up their coffee cups while Ian packed up his stuff. She put the mugs in the sink and turned to walk back out, but saw Ian following her in.

"I love this place," he said, looking around her kitchen. "How long have you lived here?"

"About four years. I moved in not long after I finished culinary school. I was lucky to come across it when I was out running one day and noticed the "for rent" sign. It's small, but it's perfect for me."

"It's got a great aesthetic. I like your sense of style. It suits you." He casually leaned with one arm up against the doorjamb and surveyed her face with the same interest he had when he surveyed the room.

Because it was Saturday he hadn't shaved and the dark stubble gave him an appealing scruffy look.

Juliette met his eyes and then looked away, trying to casually hide the sudden unexpected blush she felt in her cheeks. She busied herself putting the cups in the dishwasher.

"I'll give you a call after I make these changes and submit them for the permits," Ian said.

He turned towards the door, absentmindedly tapping the rolled up plans against his thigh.

"Sounds good," Juliette said and walked him to his truck.

Ian opened the driver-side door and tossed in the plans and his briefcase, then leaned over and gave Juliette a kiss on the cheek.

"Bye, see you soon."

"Yeah," she said. "See you soon." She turned and walked back to her cottage door, then turned and waved as Ian backed his truck out of the driveway.

She sighed and ran her fingers through her hair then looked at the clock and realized it was almost time to pick up Christine and their friend, Saraya for their début foraging expedition to the San Francisco Antique Market on Treasure Island. Milling around flea markets and antique markets was one of her favorite ways to wile away a weekend afternoon. And this was one she'd never been to before. She hoped to find something interesting for her café.

She grabbed her purse and coat and then headed out. As she backed her car out of the driveway Ian had so recently vacated, she couldn't help but focus on how excited she was to be on the cusp of fulfilling her dream. For the first time since Roman had shredded her heart, it occurred to her that maybe his defection was for the best. If he hadn't broken up with her, she'd still be in Lucca instead of here. Being in love with him in Italy had been amazing, she couldn't deny that, but being back and opening her own café was incredibly exciting too. She tried to stay focused on that.

Saraya picked up a bracelet and dangled it from her fingers while considering. It was made from old typewriter keys and she loved it immediately.

"What was that old saying your grandmother had, Juliette? The one about weeds and flowers?"

"She had a million sayings but I'm guessing the one you're thinking of was, 'If your garden's full of weeds, pull them out and plant flowers.' It sounds more exotic in Italian, though."

Juliette guessed it was some sort of Italian version of "If life gives you lemons, make lemonade."

"For some reason that's what this bracelet reminds me of," she said.

"If life gives you typewriter keys, make a bracelet?"

"Exactly."

"I think she might have a thing or two to say about your current situation," Christine added, picking up a bracelet as well.

"What do you mean?" Juliette asked, "The *I'm excited and terrified about risking all of my money to open my own café* one, or the *I'm a loser who got her heart broken* one?"

"Neither, exactly. I'm thinking something along the lines of the *even if your heart is broken, when life gives you a contractor like Ian, you might as well hook up with him* one."

"Hum," Saraya said, pondering. "I'm not sure about that, Chris. I mean, from what Juliette says Ian's cute and all, but I'm thinking not *risk the construction of your restaurant to get involved with your contractor* cute or anything."

"Maybe," Christine admitted, "but from what I'm hearing from Juliette, he may be worth it."

"The reality is," Juliette told them, "It's not about whether I like him or not. It's just that ever since Roman broke up with me, I've been acutely aware of the fact that we can't control whom we lose and I'm tired of losing people. Whether it's death, friends moving, or getting dumped, or people who had become a huge part of your life, are just no longer there. That's it. Another one gone. You don't have that person anymore."

"That's why we have to love people with abandon while we do have them," Saraya took Juliette's arm.

"I just don't know if I'm ready for that. I have great friends, and you two are *not* allowed to break up with me. I have my dad and Gina, and maybe that's enough for now."

"That's fine *for now*," Christine agreed, "but not forever. You have to keep yourself open."

"I promise I will, but let's drop it for now. Besides, I think I'm going to buy one of these darling bracelets."

"If life gives you typewriter keys . . ."

"Exactly," Juliette smiled.

After poking around the antique market, they decided to head over to Fillmore and then to the Legion of Honor to see if they could get into the Picasso exhibit.

Fillmore Street was one of Juliette's favorite spots in San Francisco. Funky shops and restaurants abounded, and it had always been a home away from home because her grandparents had lived in the neighborhood the entire time she was growing up. She still popped into some of the long-time establishments to say hello.

Juliette was thrilled she'd been able to twist Saraya and Christine's arms so easily into seeing the Picasso exhibit. After stopping in to rejuvenate at Coffee Bar, they headed over to the Legion of Honor. The show featured his paintings and ceramic pieces. She'd always been a fan and had loved visiting the Picasso Museums in both Paris and Antibes when her family had traveled to France when she was in college.

Chapter 23

Catarina stole many more glances at Gregorio before she and Franco left the restaurant, but she never caught his eye. She wondered whether he had seen her before she dropped her coffee cup, directing attention to herself, or whether it was the commotion that made him notice her. His face had registered surprise, but she didn't know whether it was surprise at seeing her unexpectedly or surprise at being seen by her.

If he had noticed her first, she wondered whether he would have let her leave without saying a word. The thought of that tormented her. Had he already seen her around town or even at the restaurant another time? Maybe he had seen her several times and hadn't said anything because he didn't care anymore. After all, she reminded herself, she's the one who said "no" to him. And more than a year had passed. He probably no longer gave her any thought. He probably loved someone else. Maybe he was even married to someone else. She searched her mind. Had there been a ring on his finger? She was sure she would have noticed.

Her thoughts swung wildly between never setting foot into Flavio's again, and going there as soon as possible to see him, even though she knew it would be wrong now that she was married to Franco.

She didn't want to do anything to hurt Franco. He was so good to her, and he was a wonderful husband. But thoughts of Gregorio continued to fill her mind.

She told herself not to go back to the restaurant. She knew it wasn't a good idea to see him again.

Yet, somehow she found herself sitting at the counter of Flavio's late Monday morning sipping a coffee with clammy palms, nervously looking around for a sign of him. She wore her most prim dress so she wouldn't give him the wrong idea. She just wanted to talk to him without Franco there so she could speak plainly. After an hour of pretending to read the newspaper and having her coffee refilled twice, she saw him walk through the door, tying on an apron. His curly hair was damp, as if he had just bathed. She wondered where he lived and with whom. A group of bachelors? Or did he live with relatives? Probably a wife, she told herself. If he *did* have a wife, it would be good. She would be happy for him. Anyway, she would know soon enough.

She tried to calm herself before she spoke to him. She folded the page of the paper again and tried to focus on the advertisements so she didn't appear too eager. She suddenly felt flushed and had the instinct to flee, but just then he caught sight of her and walked over. He stood behind the counter facing her. He brought coffee and filled her cup without saying a word.

"*Buon giorno*, Catarina."

"I'm sorry to bother you here," she said. "It's just . . ." she stammered, "I wanted to talk to you again. It was a surprise to see you the other night."

"I didn't think you would notice me and then when you did, it surprised me almost as much as it surprised you, I think."

"You knew I was here?"

"From the moment you walked in. You were here one other time while I was working, too. It almost killed me, but I tried not to catch your attention."

"Why not? You could have said '*ciao*'."

"I have been looking for you since I got to San Francisco. Every time I saw a dark-haired girl with your stature, my heart stopped. I can't tell you how many times I have run up to someone only to startle a stranger."

"You were looking for me?" she asked. "But when I came in, why did you hide from me?" She had told herself she just wanted to know how he was doing, but she couldn't help allowing herself the happiness of knowing he had been looking for her.

"I regretted the way I acted when you left. To be honest, I had hoped you hadn't gone through with your marriage after all. I had to find out. I couldn't stand knowing that you might be in San Francisco on your own. But then I saw you here, with your husband, and you obviously had gone through with it. Not only that, but you looked perfectly happy together. Content. You had forgotten me and I felt ridiculous having even come to find you. But for now, I'm stuck here."

"It's not like that, Gregorio. You have to believe me. I did get married. I told you I couldn't back out. But I didn't forget you. Please know that. I have been lucky, though. The man I married—Franco— he's a good man, a kind and honorable man. I shouldn't even have come to see you; I know he wouldn't be happy, but I wanted to hear how you are."

"Well, now you know my story and I know yours," Gregorio said, with a tone of resignation. "Listen, I have to get to work. But I'm glad to know you're happy, Catarina."

"Gregorio . . . "

"*Si?*"

"Nothing. It just feels strange, to have you here only to walk away again."

"Yes, but that's how life is, no?"

"*Credo che si,*" she said. I suppose you're right, and stood up to leave. "Would it be alright with you if I came back to say hello sometimes?"

"Of course. I would like that, *signora,*" he said, emphasizing the fact that she was married.

"*Arrivederci* then. See you."

"*Si, arrivederci.*" He picked up a tub of utensils and a stack of napkins and vanished through the swinging doors to the kitchen without looking back. She folded the newspaper and left with a vague sense of regret and guilt at having come, but also a happiness that she had seen him again. She knew she would have to be careful, in order to guard her heart.

She spent the rest of the day trying not to think about Gregorio, but her mind drifted to him constantly while she folded the laundry and did the dishes. What would her life have been like if she had run away with him? At the time, she had been overwhelmed, confused, and couldn't have imagined. But now, she could imagine them together in a tiny apartment. She pushed it to the back of her mind and focused on ironing Franco's favorite shirt. She lifted it to her face and inhaled the scent of him she could faintly detect through the clean soap smell. She had come to love her husband, so why think about someone else? She wouldn't, she told herself.

She knew the smart thing to do would be to tell Franco everything about what happened on the ship and confide in him. It would be the safe thing to do, because then it would be out in the open. As long as it was her secret, she knew she was ever so slightly in danger of doing something that would ruin her life with Franco. Something *pazzesco*, crazy. But she just couldn't bring herself to tell him.

As the days passed, she realized she was becoming preoccupied and conflicted so she was especially careful to be funny and charming with Franco. She stored up little anecdotes to tell him about her day and talked him into reading a love story to her. Her favorite was *Portrait of a Lady* by Henry James. She loved listening to Franco read to her. She especially enjoyed hearing about the heroine of the story, Isabel Archer. Catarina could understand and sympathize with her indecisiveness.

In spite of the angst it was creating in her, she found herself making excuses to leave the apartment to visit Flavio's for a cup of coffee and to see Gregorio. While she sat at the counter sipping her coffee, he stood on the other side, rolling silverware in napkins as he prepared for his shift. When their eyes locked, she forced herself to look away. She never stayed long. Still, she found herself confiding in him, telling him the details of her new life. She enjoyed the way he turned half of his mouth up when she told him something amusing. He confided in her as well. She enjoyed hearing about the other bachelors he lived with and about his dream of working for himself one day. He wasn't sure what he wanted to do, but he knew he didn't want to work for someone else forever. He was tired of taking orders and wanted more freedom.

His desire to change his life made her think about her own. What did she want to do? She had never thought about that before. When she was young, she lived the way her parents lived—did chores, was lucky enough to learn to read and write a little with Mateo. And then she went to work for the Carluccis. She was never asked what *she* wanted to do. Not by her parents or herself. Life was what you were given. But now, talking to Gregorio about his dreams, she realized that people—even some women—could do what they wanted in life. In a way, she had already done so by leaving Italy and marrying Franco, but she had never given a thought to shaping her days once she was here.

She and Franco had been living with his family for more than a year and most of the time she did chores and errands.

She often found herself looking at the painting she bought when they were in New York. The scene made her feel a connection to home. It made her wish that she could paint, and one day she mentioned it to Gregorio.

"You want to become a painter, eh?" he said with his half smile, as if she were about to launch into an amusing story.

"*Si*," she said, "I think I would like that." She realized, as the words left her mouth, it was entirely true. She didn't expect to become a *real* painter—a professional—but it could be something just for herself. She felt an unexpected sense of excitement at the prospect of putting paint to canvas. She had always noticed colors and textures. She had loved to sketch as a child but it had never occurred to her, until now, that she could develop that part of herself. It would give her a chance to recreate the colors and vistas of her childhood. It would be a way to bring that part of her life—a part that she dearly missed—back.

"Well, good luck, *principessa*," Gregorio said. "Maybe you can become a painter while the rest of us toil."

"You don't understand, Gregorio, it's boring cleaning an apartment all day. I love talking with my mother- and sister-in-law, playing with my niece and nephews, and gossiping with the shopkeepers, but it's . . . I don't know how to explain it," her voice faded away.

"It's not what you want? Because . . . " he slipped his hand on top of her hand, which had been resting on the counter, and wrapped her fingers in his. His hand was warm and calloused. It was larger than Franco's hand and heavier. She knew she should pull her hand away, but she didn't.

Her heart skipped a beat. This wasn't what she had meant to happen. She looked at his hand on hers and then looked up at him and saw a look of longing. She was afraid that her own face was a mirror of his. After a moment, sitting paralyzed, she forced herself to slide her hand out from under his. She placed it on her lap and stammered, "I'm not saying it's so hard . . . I just wish . . . maybe . . . that . . . "

She didn't know what she had been saying. They had been talking about her desire to paint, but now he seemed to think she was talking about something else. Was she? She felt confused. It was dangerous territory and she needed to steer the conversation away from where it had drifted.

"You wish what?" he asked, giving her a smoldering look, as he wiped down the counter where their hands had just been clasped. She was sitting in what had become her regular spot. Then he looked up and nodded to a table full of people who had just entered and sat down. He walked over with his order pad. His movement gave her a moment to think and she knew she had to leave before she did anything regretable.

On the walk home she felt like her life was going down too many roads at once and she didn't know how to decide which one was the right one. She wanted to be with her husband, be a part of his family, raise children, and learn to paint; at the same time she wanted to run away with Gregorio. She wanted to feel his lips on hers. She yearned for him. She could visualize both lives. She knew if she gave Gregorio one word he would be with her.

She sat down on a bench she passed en route back to their apartment and put her head in her hands. She knew her parents would be ashamed of her and she felt the weight of that on top of everything else.

"I have to give him up," she mumbled. "I'm a good wife. I love my husband." She wished Maria Nina were there to remind her not to do something stupid.

She stood up and walked the rest of the way home, happy to be enveloped in normalcy when she entered and was greeted by her nieces and nephews.

It was easier to push Gregorio to the back of her mind while she went about the task of helping her mother-in-law get dinner on the table. Dinnertime was her favorite time of day. The family came together, sat, bantered, talked about the day, and berated each other good-naturedly. There was laughter and Catarina appreciated being comfortably ensconced in the familial scene.

While she pushed the thought of Gregorio from the front to the back of her mind, she realized the thought of learning to paint still remained and had deeply taken root. In point of fact, the physical prospect of putting paint to canvas thrilled her. She wondered how difficult it would be to learn and wondered if she would be any good. What if she didn't have the raw talent? She wasn't sure why she had suddenly become so passionate about it, but there it was. When she and Franco were getting ready for bed, she broached the subject.

"You know how I'm afraid of moving to our own apartment because I'm afraid of being lonely?" she asked. "Well, I think I may have a solution."

She dangled her feet off of the edge of their bed and talked to him while she watched him change into his pajamas. She always found this endearing. Maybe because once he was in his pajamas he was a different Franco. He was not the son, or the jeweler, he was just hers. It made it easier to share this dream with him.

"You see, besides Gabriella, I don't have any real friends here. I love your mama and your family, but I dearly miss Maria Nina and Anna from home. And, maybe if I could do something to make some new friends, that would help me, no? Then I wouldn't be lonely and we could move to our own little apartment."

"What kind of thing are you talking about doing, my *tesoro*."

"Well, since you ask," she said, and smiled at him. She crossed her legs and her face became animated. "I know this sounds strange, but I want to take painting lessons. I could learn to paint landscape paintings of home. That way maybe I won't miss it so much."

Franco moved over to her and lifted her chin in his hand. "That's not such a surprise, Catarina. I see how you stare at that painting. As though by looking at it, you are there for just a moment or two."

"Do you think it would be ok? I know it's a lot to ask, and I'm sure I won't be a good painter, but maybe with work I could paint something that would be nice just for our house."

"I think it's a good idea. We can find a class for you, and you can see whether you enjoy it. I'm sure you'll make a wonderful painter. And then when we have babies, you can teach them to paint." He smiled at the thought.

Catarina smiled as well and met his eye.

"Maybe we should work on that right now," Franco climbed up beside her on the bed and kissed her.

"Maybe we should," she smiled and wrapped her arms around her husband, content to be in his arms, the thought of Gregorio momentarily gone from her mind.

Chapter 24

JULIETTE, UP TO HER ELBOWS
IN PREPARATIONS AND PASTRY DOUGH,
HOT SUMMER NIGHTS, AND GUSTO

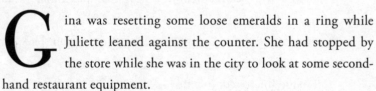

G ina was resetting some loose emeralds in a ring while
Juliette leaned against the counter. She had stopped by
the store while she was in the city to look at some secondhand restaurant equipment.

"How are things going on the café?" Gina asked, while focusing
her attention on the task at hand.

"Great, the plans are currently waiting to be approved but Ian
thinks it will only be a matter of days now."

"Exciting."

"I know. I've started trying out a bunch of pastry recipes to have
something to do, because I can't do what I'm really itching to do."

"Which is what?"

"I want to take a sledge hammer to something so I can start the demolition phase of construction. I'm dying to get going. All this waiting is killing me. And now, because of all the pastry sampling, I've gained several pounds and poor Dad is currently up to his eyeballs in *sfogliatelle* in case you want any."

"I love *sfogliatelle*. I don't think I've had any since Nonna passed away."

"I think that's why I started with that one. I was feeling a little nostalgic. When Nonna taught me to make it, it was the first time I thought about becoming a chef."

"I remember that," she smiled. "If you want a partner in crime when it comes to wielding the sledgehammer, count me in. I could bring a bottle of champagne and make a toast while *you* smash through a wall or something."

"What, you don't want to bust up a wall yourself?"

"I don't know if I could even lift a sledgehammer. I don't want to completely embarrass myself."

"You wouldn't have to be embarrassed in front of Ian. He's not the type to make fun."

"You sound interested, Juliette."

"I'm not. He and I work together."

"You've gotten to know him pretty well by now? What's he like?"

"Really nice, actually. Smart, funny in an understated way. You know, the type of humor that people miss unless they're paying attention."

Gina looked up from the ring she was working on.

"It doesn't matter anyway, because I'm all about business these days. Architecture and food, that's me."

"Do you ever hear from Roman?"

"He tried to keep in touch at first, but it hurt too much then and now I'm letting it go. That's for the best, I think. Besides, it's not like I'm ever going to see him again."

"I'm sorry that whole thing happened to you."

"I know. Me too. I guess misery is just part of the human condition, right?"

"Unfortunately, yes. It sometimes is. But you know what Nonna would say, 'If it's raining, all you need for happiness is a colorful umbrella.'"

"It's so funny that you say that, because Saraya, Christine, and I were just reminiscing about another one she had: 'If your garden has weeds . . . ' " Juliette began.

"Pull them up and plant flowers!" Gina finished. "She was full of them wasn't she? So many old-school Italian sayings."

Juliette laughed. "I don't know that they actually were Italian sayings. I think they were just stuff she made up that sounded more wise when she said them in Italian. But you know what? She lived it. She did find happiness no matter her life circumstances."

"That she did."

"Well, on that philosophical note, I have to get going." Juliette kissed Gina's cheek.

"Don't be a stranger. I'll see you soon for the exciting demolition of your café."

"Out with the old, in with the new," Juliette chimed in as she waved goodbye.

When Juliette got home she again submersed herself in pastry dough. She wanted to create something unusual in order to keep people coming back. She remembered a certain pastry she loved to pick up on her way in to work when she was holding down her first job out of the Culinary Institute. She was working as an assistant to a chef at a long-established San Francisco restaurant. When she got off the train at Powell Street, she either bought herself (or had to talk herself *out* of buying, depending on what the scale had said that morning) a raspberry ring from the Coffee Roastery at the station. It was flaky perfection with an exquisite balance of breadiness and sweetness. The day the establishment closed was truly sad for her. But, the memory of those perfect pastries lingered. That's what she wanted to create for someone else: the type of morning treat that kept them salivating all the way into work.

The permit process had drifted longer than expected with one hang-up after another slowing things down. Finally the approval was stamped by not only the county office, but the fire chief, the city planner, and, as far as she could tell, every civil servant in the city who happened to have a stamp pad on his or her desk.

When she told Ian about her sledgehammer fantasy, he laughed.

"Sounds fantastic Juliette, but what do you plan to smash up exactly? The building is already gutted, so unless you want to break through the exterior wall to open up the patio, I'm afraid you're out of luck."

"Shoot. How could I have not thought of that?" She looked around, trying to find something else to do, but nothing immediately presented itself. "Well, I'll figure something out, but just so you know, I'm definitely going to be here to help out when I'm not brewing coffee at my day job. I love this type of stuff and I don't want to miss out on anything."

"Duly noted," he said, his eyes still twinkling. "I'll put you to work. I promise."

The morning they were due to begin construction, Juliette parked her car in a reserved spot behind the building and lugged out the Capresso coffee maker she'd brought. She opened the back door and stepped through. The morning light streamed through the front windows and she felt as if she'd finally arrived home. The exposed brick walls were exactly what she'd wanted. The windows were still boring and functional, but she didn't see them as they currently were. Instead, she visualized the black iron paned windows that would soon replace them.

They were one of the biggest splurges in the design, but in her opinion windows were well worth it. They were the divas in the opera of architectural style, as far as she was concerned.

She was back out to her car and wrestling a minifridge out of her trunk when Ian pulled up.

"Hey there. Hold on and I'll get that for you," he said, hopping out of his truck.

She happily handed it over and ran ahead to hold the door open. When he passed through she couldn't help but admire what she saw. Christine always said that one should never underestimate the importance of a good pair of jeans, and Juliette realized how true that statement was when she saw how well Ian wore his.

"Could you set that in the corner by the espresso maker over there? I'll be right back," she said. "I'm just going to grab one more thing out of my trunk."

She came back a couple of minutes later with a folding table tucked under one arm and a paper bag with handles in the other hand.

"What's all this?" Ian asked.

"Well, we couldn't exactly begin working on a *restaurant* without provisions, and if we're going to have provisions, then we might as well enjoy the good stuff. So I brought my kick-ass espresso maker from home and a minifridge to keep snacks, and of course, a table to keep my espresso maker on, because this little gem can't just languish on the dirty floor." She lovingly patted the top of the machine.

Juliette folded open the table legs and set it down.

"Sounds great," Ian said smiling at her. "If this wasn't already my favorite project, it would be now."

Juliette chuckled then jumped—startled by a loud rap at the door—and looked up to see who was knocking.

"There's Mark," Ian said, nodding to the front door. "Will you chuck me those keys so I can open the door for him?"

"Sure," Juliette said, throwing him the keys. "Mark's your construction partner, right?" she asked. "The one you told me about?"

"Yep, he's great. I think you'll get along well."

While Ian worked the lock, Juliette bent down to plug in the coffee maker.

"Hey," she heard what she guessed was Mark's voice. "So, this is the hottie's café. This is going to be a great job."

"Mark!" she heard Ian's sharp voice and saw his nod towards her just as the plug was pushed in and she stood up.

"Oh shit!" Mark laughed. "Sorry. I'm always putting my foot

in my mouth. And for the record, let me say that 'hottie' was my word, not Ian's."

Juliette laughed and walked over to shake his hand. She could feel herself blushing.

"No worries. He told me you were a hottie, too." She joked. "I'm Juliette, by the way."

"Mark," he responded, and stuck out his hand to shake hers.

Ian gave Mark a little shove. "Good start. Thanks for that."

"Good news, I have snacks," Juliette said, to steer them all away from the awkwardness. She reached into her bag and pulled out a basket of beignets she had made, and held them out.

Mark helped himself to one.

"Oh my God! What are these?" he said, still chewing with an expression of sheer ecstasy on his face.

Ian looked at Juliette and said with a wry smile on his face. "You'll have to excuse Mark. He's like a golden retriever puppy. It's still a mystery to us all as to how he found someone to marry him."

"It's all about the charm, bro," Mark said with his mouth still full. "You should try it some time."

Juliette laughed again. She immediately liked Mark. He was comfortable already and she liked the mischievous sparkle in his gray eyes.

"They're kind of something I invented." Juliette said. "I started with traditional beignets, which are basically like triangular doughnuts with powdered sugar sprinkled on top, then I piped a bit of custard with orange zest and a bit of nutmeg in there, and went lighter on the powdered sugar. And voilá, 'beignets Juliette' as my friends like to call them."

"They're amazing," Ian agreed, finishing his in two big bites and then licking his fingers. "I can tell this is going to be a dangerous job."

"All right," he clapped his hands once. "Let's get to work!" he smiled. "It's a great day for it. Our windows are going to be delivered later this afternoon, so let's get these old ones out."

And just like that, they were under way. Juliette loved every minute of it. Over the next couple of months, they settled into a routine. Ian and Mark arrived early and got started. Juliette took the breakfast shift at work and when she arrived in the early afternoon, she got to see what they had accomplished since she'd been in last. Ian put her to work while she was there as he'd promised.

The three of them got along famously. Mark was the jokester and Ian was the straight man with the wry sense of humor. It was obvious the two had been working together for years because their interactions were seamless.

When Juliette was there, they sought her opinion constantly. How tall did she want the counter exactly? They would move her in front of the space and have her simulate chopping and then decide together on the perfect height. They had her pace off the kitchen to make sure she liked the number of steps between each appliance and then would shift things around accordingly. They even had her think about where she wanted the light switches, so she could get to them easily when she entered and left.

Finally, after months of inside work, they broke through the side wall in order to open it up and incorporate the outside space. At last, Juliette got to live out the sledgehammer fantasy, although Gina wasn't kidding; they were surprisingly heavy. Juliette was no weakling, but it took her several tries before she busted even a tiny hole through.

At that point, she was happy to replace the hammer with a glass of champagne and let Ian and Mark finish the job. Watching them while she and Gina drank champagne was a treat. Ian wore a nice-fitting gray T-shirt that just said "BIKE" that she found particularly sexy for some reason. She was pleased to see that wielding the sledgehammer wasn't that easy for the guys either.

Sometimes Mark's wife, Lexi, and their sweet, little three-year-old girl, Lulu, would pop in at the end of the day. The two women hit it off instantly and Lulu quickly learned exactly where the snacks were kept, and was welcome to dip into the refrigerator any time. Other times Juliette's dad or Gina stopped by. Sometimes Christine and Saraya arrived to convince them all to dust off and head over to happy hour at their favorite sushi place.

Juliette realized one evening that Mark, Lexi, and Ian had become incorporated into her circle as if they had always been a part of it. She loved that about her friends. They were always willing to welcome people in, enjoying getting to know them.

But Juliette's favorite times were when she and Ian ended up working late together by themselves.

The late summer heat could be relentless during the day, but in the evening, with the windows and doors opened wide, the temperature cooled down to perfectly balmy. She wished she could freeze those moments of complete contentment.

Sometimes they worked without talking much, just listening to music. Ian had built Juliette a makeshift worktable and bench out of scrap wood. She loved it so much that she threatened to keep it as her desk once the project was finished. She brought in a cushion to sit on and used her laptop to research vendors and suppliers while Ian cut trim and hammered it into place.

She couldn't help her mind from drifting towards him. She thought she felt an undercurrent of chemistry, but he always kept it warmly friendly and close, yet professional.

She wasn't excited about the idea of more romantic rejection anyway, so she decided to shove away any feelings that may have been seeping in.

She forced herself to focus on the computer screen instead of thinking about Ian, but her curiosity suddenly got the better of her. "So, what's your story, Ian?" she looked up from the computer screen. "Any loves? You never talk about anyone."

"Not at the present moment," he answered offhandedly, and threw a scrap of trim he had just cut into a growing pile.

"Huh," she murmured, waiting for him to ask her, but instead he turned back to the saw and cut another piece of trim. The space seemed to get tighter and she was suddenly aware of herself.

"Man, it's so hot tonight," she changed the subject. "I wish there was somewhere to go swimming."

"Seriously?" Ian stopped what he was doing and turned back toward her. "Because if you really want to go swimming, we could."

"What do you mean?"

"Well, I grew up near here—right at the base of Mt. Diablo. Anyway, I know this sounds like a throwback to high school, but my parents are on vacation, so I've been staying at their house to take care of their dogs. They have a pool . . . "

"Count me in," she said without hesitation, and closed the lid to her laptop.

"It does sound pretty good about now. While we're at it, we could even steal their beer."

Juliette laughed, "Let's do it!" She sprang up from her seat and started closing up windows. Ian took off his tool belt, unplugged the power tools, and in minutes they were on their way out.

The warm evening air outside felt thick. It was perfect night-swimming weather.

"I'll swing by and get my suit and then come over," Juliette said, as Ian jotted the address on a scrap of paper and handed it to her.

"Call me if you get lost."

Juliette climbed behind the wheel. What was she doing? she asked herself. Nothing, she answered. Just going for a swim. She told herself not to make this into anything. They had been working together for months now. They could go swimming. It was no big deal.

So why did it feel like a big deal? Like they were crossing a line. What line? She rejected her own thoughts and told herself to relax.

"Wow," she said when he opened the door. "I didn't know you were a local boy. And you grew up with land. This is amazing." The house was a sprawling craftsman with a long porch and a three-car garage with a carriage house set off at an angle. Three dogs bound out to greet her—two large golden retrievers and a Welsh corgi.

"Hello sweeties," she greeted them with lots of petting, then looked up at Ian. "I love dogs. What are their names?"

"This is Alice, this one's Jessie," he said, pointing to the two goldens respectively, "and this little minx is Lily," he told her, pointing to the tricolored corgi who was wagging her nub of a tail with a big smile on her face.

"Hello, hello," she tried to keep herself from breaking out her doggie voice, but it was futile with three friendly dogs vying for attention.

Ian led her inside. They went through a casual living room and into a large kitchen with crisp white stone counter tops and walls the color of dark chocolate. He handed her a Corona with a wedge of lime.

She took a sip. "Heavenly, thanks. If I had a tail, I'd be wagging it about now myself."

"There's a bathroom off the kitchen there," he pointed, "where you can change into your swimsuit. I'll meet you outside in a couple of minutes."

Ian took the stairs two at a time, and she headed to the bathroom.

She had been forced to make a hasty decision: bikini or tankini, but she had decided on the former. She didn't run a few times a week for nothing. But still, all that pastry testing had taken a slight toll.

She heard a splash and walked through the French doors off the kitchen to join Ian.

She dove in and swam back and forth a couple of times to cool down her core, then moved to the steps to sit.

"This is great. I can't believe you grew up here."

"Don't be too impressed. We didn't move here until I was in middle school. Before that we lived in a tiny house where we were always all on top of each other. I have two brothers and a sister, and there was only one bathroom for all of us kids. Needless to say, my sister, who's the youngest, took charge of it as soon as she was big enough to close the door. It was crazy, but fun. My parents are both architects. Their dream was to build their own house, but it took them a long time to save up their pennies."

"Is that what made you become a contractor?"

"Kind of. I actually went to architecture school, too. But when I was home during the summers, I worked for a contractor my dad knew, and I fell in love with building. I like working with my hands. I love bringing projects to completion."

"Kind of like cooking."

"I've never thought of it that way, but yes, it must be."

Ian pulled himself up and out of the pool, toweled off and lay down on one of the chaise lounges. He tilted his beer back and sighed.

After a thoughtful pause he said, "Your project has been wonderful to work on. It's really coming along."

"I love working on it, too. And even though I'm excited to have it finished, I think I'll miss this phase."

"Have you come up with a name yet?"

"It's killing me, but I haven't. It's ridiculous. I'm tired of always thinking of it as 'my place' or 'my café.' I want it to have an actual name. "

"I don't know whether this would help, but maybe you should call it something in Italian like 'Taste' or 'Delicious' or something. You know, kind of like the way *tiramisu* really means 'pick me up'."

"Of course! Why didn't I think of that? *Gusto* in Italian means taste, but it can also mean 'to get pleasure from' or 'savor.' You're a genius. Do you think it should have an exclamation mark? No," she stopped herself. "Never mind. That would be overkill."

Ian smiled. "I like it. *Gusto*."

Juliette laid down on the lounge chair next to his. She breathed deeply and took a sip of her beer.

"That's all it took. A swim on a hot evening, a cold beer, and your brilliant idea. It's so simple. I feel like a moron for not coming up with it myself. I like the one word name. Thank you, Ian. Truly." She tapped her beer bottle again at his. "You're a godsend."

In that moment, she wished she could do more than just say thank you. Maybe rub olive oil all over his chest and shoulders and then let nature take its course.

Trying not to let him see her thoughts, yet digging around for more information from his often-reserved self, she decided to delve a little deeper into his past, but before she opened her mouth he said,

"You know the question you asked me when we were working earlier? Whether I'm seeing anyone?"

"Yes," she said casually, "So what *is* your story, romancewise? Is this when I'm going to learn about your skeletons?"

Ian laughed. "Definitely no skeletons. Well, maybe one or two." His mouth turned up slightly at one corner. "The thing is, I was engaged once, but that did *not* turn out well," he said, and took a long swig from his Corona.

"Sorry, I shouldn't have asked."

"It's ok. It was a long time ago. We went to college together and got engaged not long after we graduated. I got a construction job and she started grad school working on a doctorate in physics."

"Sheesh."

"Yeah, she definitely has some serious smarts but not so loyal as it turned out."

"What happened?"

"Well, I knew she loved this one class in particular—Experimental Physics. And she was always working late at the lab. So one night I decided to surprise her there with dinner, which as it turns out was a much bigger surprise than I intended. When I walked in, all sappy with wine and sandwiches from our favorite deli, she was doing an experiment all right, but it involved her lab partner, John, in a way I don't think was sanctioned in the syllabus."

"Oh shit."

"Yeah, on the lab table."

"No!"

"Oh yeah. Since then, I've pretty much limited myself to short relationships that involve alcohol and a sleepover, followed by an awkward breakfast the next morning, I'm sorry to say."

Juliette laughed, "You should be ashamed!"

"I am," he smiled. "But, you know . . . once bitten, twice shy."

Juliette mused, "And here I thought you were one of the nice ones."

Ian raised one eyebrow at her and looked into her eyes. Juliette couldn't keep herself from looking back and meeting his inviting look with a half smile and then ultimately a slow shake of her head before forcing herself to let the moment pass. It would have been so easy to allow something to happen.

She jokingly slapped herself in the face to lighten the moment, and then jumped back in the pool, hoping that Ian would not follow her in, because if he did, she wasn't sure she would have the willpower to stop herself.

When she climbed back out, she wrapped herself in a towel and laid back down on the lounge chair. She closed her eyes, thinking for a moment about her time in Italy, then opened them and turned towards Ian.

"I had my heart broken, too," she said. "Not as badly as what happened to you. I wasn't engaged or anything, although I thought we were heading in that direction."

"Your dad told me a little bit about it when I was working with him at his house."

"What?" Juliette sat up.

"Don't be mad at him, I *might* have been prying," Ian feigned a sheepish expression. "After we met at the hospital, I was curious about you. I'm not confessing to anything, but I *may* have asked a leading question or two."

"Really?" Juliette's heart skipped a beat.

"Maybe," Ian joked, keeping it light. "Anyway, tell me about what happened from your perspective."

Juliette leaned back, visualizing Roman.

"I just fell. Dropped like a ton of bricks. I don't know if it was because I was already so emotionally vulnerable or if it was just him and it would have happened either way, but within two months, I was visualizing myself staying in Italy, getting married, having little Italian babies, the whole thing. He was my instructor. An amazing cook. Funny, smart, nice, everything I wanted. But as it turns out, his *real* girlfriend was away on assignment for the newspaper she works for and I was simply someone to pass the time with."

"Ouch."

"You could say that. I don't think I've ever felt that kind of romantic beat down. And, I definitely don't want to feel it ever again."

"You can't close yourself off forever, you know."

Juliette laughed, "Says the man who sleeps around to avoid getting attached to anyone."

"Touché," Ian laughed.

"To heartbreakers," she raised her beer in a toast, "May they suffer," she smiled at him.

"I'll drink to that."

Before Juliette left for home, they talked and joked more, had another round of beers, and finally raided the fridge. It was a perfect night. One she knew she wouldn't forget.

Chapter 25

Catarina stood in line holding hands with Franco while waiting to register for her first painting class at Fort Mason. It was a rare warm, sunny day down by the water. She enjoyed watching the other people who waited in line to register for the class. There were both men and women of different ages, but none appeared to be Italian, which pleased Catarina. She was looking forward to meeting a greater variety of people than she had so far. She was elated about learning to paint, but two things were elbowing their way into her mind: one was that she had a secret notion that she was pregnant—which filled her with joy, terror, and excitement—all in equal portions. The first inkling she had that she may be with child was when the smell of coffee two days previously seemed unusually strong. She kept looking around for grounds that had burned on the stove, or something to account for the pungent smell. Suddenly remembered one of her sisters saying she had known she was pregnant with her second child as soon as the smell of coffee made her gag.

The moment the recollection and its implications struck, Catarina sucked in her breath, and instinctively moved her hand to her abdomen. She then quickly withdrew it and looked around furtively to see if anyone had noticed. At the time, Franco had been eating toast for breakfast and reading the paper, his father and brother bantered about the sport called baseball, which they were still trying to figure out, and Gabriella yelled at her son to find his sock. No one even noticed her sudden movements.

Although that should have been enough to preoccupy her, she also couldn't stop Gregorio from continuously creeping into her thoughts. She was becoming so annoyed with herself. She was happy. She loved her husband and was going to learn to paint, and might even soon become a mother; so why, in the name of *Dio*, could she not stop thinking about another man? It was her own fault, she knew, for continuing to seek him out. She knew she should leave well enough alone, so she resolved then and there to stop seeing him. She decided to tell him the next morning. She would go in for coffee—no, that wouldn't work. She would go in for lemonade—that suddenly sounded wonderfully refreshing—and tell him that she could no longer come in to talk to him. She had to dedicate herself to her husband and family. Enough was enough. She was resolved. Her determination grew while she and Franco spent the day together. After they were finished registering, Franco surprised Catarina with a trip to the De Young Museum, so she could see their collection of paintings. It was like nothing she had ever seen. She knew that vast museums existed in Italy's cities, but she had never visited one. She felt inspired walking through the galleries, spending time with the works of art.

All day she reminded herself about her plan to end her relationship with Gregorio, but she knew it wouldn't be easy.

"I'm going out to the market," Catarina told Isabella the next morning as she folded the ironing board back into the wall cabinet and put away the iron. "Do you need anything?" she asked.

"*Limoni, per favore,*" she said. Lemons, please. She patted her daughter-in-law's cheek. "Such a good girl." She smiled. "Such a blessing you are to us."

"*Grazie,*" Catarina answered, but she felt anything but a blessing as she walked down the street towards Flavio's in hopes of seeing Gregorio. The previous day's strong resolve had melted while she slept and the thought of severing ties was heartbreaking. She decided to stop at the produce market on the way to the restaurant to give herself more time, and as she pushed through the entrance door was surprised to see Gregorio himself walking to the adjacent exit door as she was entering. She had never seen him outside of Flavio's, and for some reason she instinctively acted as if she didn't know him. Gregorio picked up on her cue and walked away with only a quiet and brief, "*Buon giorno, Signora,*" spoken under his breath.

Catarina was flustered by running into him unexpectedly when she had just been fretting about whether to stop seeing him, but she gathered her emotions while picking out a half-dozen lemons to bring home.

She stalled, giving each lemon a good look and a little squeeze, and while she was doing so, she couldn't help but hear the women behind the counter of the small market gossiping with each other.

"There he goes," one said to the other. "There's something I don't like about him."

"Always trying to sweet talk us into putting a little extra into his bag without paying for it. He's slippery."

Catarina looked around the store. Were they talking about Gregorio? She didn't want to think so, but who else had just left? There were only other women doing the daily shopping.

"Tsk. I know the type. An oily charmer, that's what he is." The two women were still gossiping when Catarina approached the counter.

"Just lemons today, Catarina?"

"*Si, grazie.* Just these." She handed over the lemons to be weighed and then put them into her shopping bag.

"Are you ok, my dear? You look pale."

"I'm fine. Thank you, Signora Castilla." Catarina managed a smile for the shopkeeper. "It's just so cold today after the beautiful weather yesterday. I have a chill."

"Well, keep yourself warm. We don't want you getting sick."

"Yes, dear, stay nice and warm," added the other woman. "Tsk, this fog is enough to drive one mad, isn't it? So cold all the time." Catarina smiled warmly at them. She adored these two buxom Italian matrons.

"I'll be careful. Don't worry," she said and then continued on to Flavio's. Her mind reeled. She hated to think of anyone having such a low opinion of Gregorio. "An oily charmer." It made her heartsick. But underneath, she had to admit, she did see a hint of truth to what they said. She had seen him being overly charming when he was waiting tables. Especially to the women. There *was* a certain slickness she hadn't wanted to notice. She had smiled and shrugged it off before, but hearing Signora Castilla's remarks gave her a slap.

Had he just been charming her instead of having true feelings? Her heart sank and she felt her cheeks warm at the thought. She put one hand to her face to cool them.

She looked up and saw Gregorio leaning against a building a half block away. He gave her his rakish smile and a small wave.

Maybe it's better this way, she told herself. She could talk to him outside, instead of in the confines of the restaurant where anyone could overhear them.

When she caught up to him, he moved to walk beside her.

"*Amore mio,*" he whispered.

"Shh, don't call me that!" Catarina whispered back.

"But you are my love, Catarina."

"But I can't be, Gregorio," she paused and turned to face him. "In fact, I was coming to see you at Flavio's to talk to you." She looked down at the ground. "I can't keep coming to see you. I need to put an end to this, now. It's wrong and my behavior is disgracing my marriage and my family. I am a married woman. I love my husband. I can't see you anymore."

"This again?" Gregorio laughed. "Catarina, you're always telling me you should stop, but always coming back."

"This is different. I wanted to be friends, but I realize it's not possible because my feelings for you are too deep. I was being foolish and I'm sorry."

"You're serious?" Gregorio looked into her eyes. "Don't do this. Instead, run away with me. I asked you once before, but this time you have to. We can't live without each other." He put his hands on her shoulders.

"Listen," he continued. "I've been thinking about this for a while, I just hadn't talked to you about it yet. See this ring on your finger?" He held up her hand with Franco's ring. "It must have cost a fortune. We could sell it. We could leave here. We could go to New York, Chicago, anywhere. Even back to Italy."

"What?" Catarina stammered. "I can't," she said in a quavering voice. Her eyes were suddenly stinging and her entire body felt tensed, ready to flee. "I'm so sorry," she continued. "I've been stupid. I didn't mean for this to happen. I just couldn't seem to stay away from you. But I know now that I should have. I'm married to Franco. I love Franco, and I think I may be pregnant."

"You don't love him. Maybe you think you do, but you love *me*. You want to be with me. That's why you can't stay away." He grabbed her hand and pulled her down a small side street and before she realized what was happening, he was kissing her.

"Listen to me, Catarina. I don't care about the baby. We can raise it and your husband will never find out. We'll sell the ring and go back to Italy." His voice had taken on a tone of desperation. "We could go now. No one would ever find us."

Catarina's life with Franco was suddenly crystal clear before her eyes. It was a happy life and Franco was a good man. She knew she wanted her life to be with her husband—to grow old with him. She realized that she had come to love him for more than just companionship and duty, but with the depths of her heart. She couldn't believe she had been confused before, because now, the right decision was so obvious. It was as obvious and dazzling as the ring Franco had put on her finger with a promise to be a good and faithful husband.

Gregorio's character was suddenly clear to her and she realized she'd been foolish. He would not only take another man's wife, but steal her away and leave him to worry about her for the rest of his days. She would never do that to Franco and she was ashamed that she had betrayed her husband with her feelings for Gregorio. She realized that the shopkeepers were right. He was oily and she had been blind. She had come too close to ruining the best thing in her life, but now she would be free.

"I'm sorry I hurt you, Gregorio," she said, backing away. "I made a mistake and I hope you'll forgive me. But I love my husband and I am going back to him." She removed her hand from his tight grip and turned to leave.

"I'm not going to wait for you. And this time I'm not going to look for you. If you walk away from me, Catarina, then it's over between us."

"I'm truly sorry. Don't wait for me or look for me. Goodbye. I hope you'll live a happy life."

As she began to walk back towards home, she felt a tremendous sense of relief. She had heard the American saying "a weight lifted off your chest," and now she understood what it meant. She tried to compose herself before she walked through the front door, but as soon as she passed over the threshold and smelled the familiar smell of cooking and saw the two women of whom she'd become so fond, she began to cry and giggle at the same time. Isabella and Gabriella both looked at her in confusion.

"Are you all right?" Gabriella stopped spooning mashed bananas into the baby's mouth.

"What is it?" Isabella asked at the same time.

"It's nothing and everything," Catarina answered. Then she set down her lemons, burst into tears, and blurted, "I think I might be pregnant!" Saying it out loud and then having her mother- and sister-in-law throw their arms around her was exactly what she needed to soothe her turbulent feelings.

"*Oh, mio Dio!*" Isabelle shouted. "Another blessing on the way!" She wiped her eyes with her apron.

"Don't tell Franco yet, because I don't know for sure and I don't want him to be disappointed," Catarina requested.

"Of course, of course! Don't worry. We're used to keeping these secrets," Gabriella smiled in collusion with Isabella.

"It feels good to talk about it. I've been thinking for days that I may be pregnant, but didn't want to say anything just yet."

"Tell us your symptoms," said Isabella.

Catarina told them about the coffee smell, which they both nodded knowingly about, and the fact that her monthly was late.

"Only a week. Not unheard of," she admitted.

"Well, time will tell. But for now, you go wash your face and maybe take a little nap. You look like you could use it."

"That sounds like the best thing I could imagine right now," she said.

s she lay on the bed and dozed, she could hear laughter from the kitchen mixed with the sound of baby noises, chopping, and cooking. She sighed with deep relief, so grateful to be here at home instead of being on the street with Gregorio and making the worst decision of her life. A decision she would have never been able to undo.

She closed her eyes and drifted off to sleep.

When she awoke hours later, it was to the sound of her doorknob slowly turning.

"Hello," she said in a sleepy voice as her husband sat on the bed next to her.

He brushed the hair off of her face and she put her arms around his waist.

"Are you ok?" Franco asked. "Mama said you have been sleeping all afternoon and that I shouldn't disturb you."

"I'm fine," she smiled. "I just felt tired. I'm good now."

He bent down and kissed her forehead.

"Franco?"

"Yes?"

"I love you."

"I love you, too, *mia bella moglie*, beautiful wife," he said and lay down with his arms wrapped around her.

"Thank you for bringing me here and marrying me."

"You were always the one for me, Catarina."

"As it turns out," she smiled, "you were the one for me, too."

Chapter 26

JULIETTE, A DIFFERENT
KIND OF PAINTING, A STORY,
AND A LOSS

J uliette, donned in baggy, paint-splattered jean shorts and
an equally splattered white, V-neck T-shirt, pried open a can
of paint and poured it into the roller pan. Construction was to
the painting stage and Juliette had insisted on helping. She had been
painting walls since she was in third grade. In elementary school, she had
become tired of the bubble gum color she had chosen during the earnest
pink phase she'd gone through but her mother had been busy with the
shop and her father had been working on a paper he was writing about
some ancient civilization, so she had roped Nonna Catarina into coming
over and helping her. Together they chose a rich gray-green for the walls,
which was Juliette's favorite color for years. For the restaurant, she was

going with ochre. It would set off the brick sidewalls, and the black iron in the windows would stand out boldly against the warm brownish-yellow hue in the front.

She had climbed the ladder, roller brush in hand, when Ian yelled from below.

"Wait, Juliette," he waved thin plastic gloves. "I got these for you so you don't ruin your ring."

"You're so nice, but don't worry. I left it at home for once, so I wouldn't get paint all over it. Have I ever told you the story of my ring?" she asked.

"Nope. I just noticed that you always wear it."

"You're very observant, for a guy."

"I don't know whether to be appreciative of that comment or insulted for men in general."

Juliette laughed. "Take it as a compliment. That's how I meant it. Anyway, the ring has a very long history. It was actually given to my grandmother, Catarina Pensebene," she said with an Italian-accented flair, "when she arrived here as a mail-order bride from Italy."

Ian stopped shaking the can of paint he was about to open and looked up at her. "That's not your run-of-the-mill 'how we met' story."

"I know, right? My granddad gave it to her when she arrived here as a symbol that he would be a good and faithful husband. And he was. They were so sweet with each other. Even as a little girl, I could tell they loved each other so much. She arrived here when she was seventeen and he was twenty-six. How crazy is that? They were married almost sixty years. She told me the ring saved her life once."

"It's hard to imagine what would make a girl of that age leave her country and marry someone she didn't even know," Ian said.

"I've wondered the same thing many times, but Nonna always said that she had met him once when she was a small girl and that their families were friends—things were different then. She told me that her father wanted her to go because the war was coming and he wanted her away and safe, but the way she said it, I don't know . . . I could tell there was something more," she paused. "I never knew the whole story until I read her letters. They're fascinating. I'm almost done with them all."

"Anyway, when Nonna passed away, she left the ring to my mom. My mom was part of a huge Italian family. There were five boys—her older brothers—and then along came my mom years later. Nonna always said my mom was the pleasant surprise of her life. She was forty-two when Mom was born, which was a bit scandalous at the time."

"She sounds like an interesting woman."

"Yeah, she was. I miss her. That's why I wear the ring all the time. It's a way to keep her and my mom close to me," Juliette paused. "My nonna and granddad lived in San Francisco, but they bought a little house in Napa, where they would go to get out of the city. It's still in the family. If you want, I'll take you there sometime. We all get a weekend up there now and then and everyone congregates there on Thanksgiving. I have about a million cousins, as you can imagine. I love my uncles and aunts. It's crazy, but fun."

"It sounds great. I'd love to go."

"You'd like it from an architectural standpoint, too. It's been added on to a couple of times, but for the most part, it's as it was when it was built at the turn of the century."

"Count me in." Ian smiled, holding her eyes for a long moment.

When she went back to painting, she could picture him there with her family. Her uncle Dante always hosed down a big patch on the side of the orchard so they could play mud football. It was ridiculously filthy and fun.

They worked together silently for a while—both ignoring the growing chemistry between them.

Several hours of painting, in addition to the shift she'd pulled as a barista earlier in the morning, had worked some kinks into Juliette's neck, so she decided to call it a night and left Ian to finish up. As she drove up the hill to her in-law studio, she noticed that the sky was turning the golden hue that told her fall was just around the corner, and realized she'd noticed the same thing while she was walking out of the restaurant with her mom just before the accident. How could that have been almost a year ago?

She pulled into her driveway and stopped short.

Her front door was ajar.

Her mind raced. Had she forgotten to lock the door? She tried to remember locking it behind her when she left. Had she? Of course she had. In fact, she remembered locking it, then having to go back for her cell phone, which she'd left on the table. She'd come back out and had definitely locked it again.

She parked the car and walked cautiously to the door.

"Hello?" she paused, listening. "Dad? Gina?"

She gently opened the door wider and made a bunch of noise. Her heart was racing.

"Not today, not today," she whispered. "Not the *one* day when my only entirely irreplaceable item is not on my finger."

She peeked in and saw that the cottage had been ransacked but she didn't hear any noises coming from inside, so she cautiously walked in with her heart hammering in her chest. She had hidden the ring in the paper towel tube, putting it back on the holder with the ring inside. She had thought it was ingenious, but when she saw the roll on the floor, her heart lurched.

"No! No! No!" she yelled, and grabbed her phone to call the police.

She raced up to the main house to see if it had been broken into as well, and it had.

Once the officers were on the way, she sat down on the porch with her head in her hands.

She reached for the phone again and dialed.

"Dad," she cried. "My studio had been broken into, and they took Nonna's ring."

"What?"

"It's gone." She choked on a sob. "Why *today* of all days?"

"Are you home?"

"This is exactly why I never take it off."

"Are you safe?"

"Why was I so stupid? I could have just worn a plastic glove, like Ian said"

"Are the police on the way?"

She didn't care about the stuff she had, when it came right down to it. Only the ring. It was her connection to her mother and grandmother. It was the perfect flawless stone Franco had given Catarina.

"Juliette!" Alexander yelled. "Are you at home?"

"Yes," she exhaled, and dejectedly sat down on her front stoop.

"Hold tight, Sweetie. I'll be there soon."

"Ok."

"Call Gina, too,"

"I will," she said.

Juliette took a deep breath and exhaled before dialing again.

"Hi Gina," she said more calmly when her sister was on the line. "Are you driving?"

"No, why?"

"Because I have some terrible news. My studio was broken into and Nonna Catarina's ring was stolen."

"What? Why would anyone break into your place when there's a ton of big, nice houses so close by?"

"They broke into the Scotts' house, too. My guess is that they just hit mine as an afterthought. Shit," she added. "I've got to call them. They don't even know that they've been burglarized yet."

"I'm coming over. Have you talked to Dad?"

"Yeah, he's on the way."

"You'll get the ring back, don't worry."

"That would be a miracle."

"I'll make you a new one. Just like it."

"You're sweet, but it wouldn't be the same," Juliette said dejectedly.

"I know. Jeez, I'm so sorry. I can't believe it. I . . . "

"I know, me too," Juliette looked at her empty finger. "Listen, I have to call the Scotts and the sheriff should be here any minute, so I should go, but I'll see you when you get here."

The evening was spent going over what little she knew of what happened, first with the Scotts who owned the in-law studio she lived in and then with the police. They followed her as she recreated getting home and exactly what she did from there. They took a report of everything that she found missing and gave her a copy with their cards so she could contact them if she realized other things were missing as well.

"Sometimes you won't even notice until you reach for something that isn't there," the officer told her. "If that happens, even months from now, contact us, because you never know which item is going to turn up and give us the unexpected lead."

"What about the ring?" she asked the officer. "What are the chances of finding it?"

"Truthfully, the chances are slim," he said. "I'm sorry. But don't give up hope. You never know."

After the police were gone, they surveyed the mess before cleaning up.

"It really creeps me out that someone was pawing through my drawers and searching through my stuff. They used a crowbar on the front door, for God's sake."

"I know, Sweets, you told us."

"Sorry. I'm just upset. How could someone just come into my home and take my things? I hate that. I feel so . . . I don't even know how I feel, but I can tell you it's awful." She plunked down on her couch.

"I'm going to make tea," her dad said.

"Thanks Dad, but you stay on the couch and put your leg up. I'll make tea," Juliette said, to give herself something to do.

"While you do that," Gina said, "I'm going to get us a shot of lemoncello, unless the fuckheads stole that, too."

"Gina!"

"Sorry Dad, but how could they do this to Juliette? Besides, I can let fly with an F-bomb once in a while," Gina told their dad. "And, while we're waiting for tea," she poured them each a cordial of the liquid sunshine, "let's drink this."

"Cheers," they all said.

"Here's to catching the *fuckheads*," added Juliette's dad in a mock British tone.

Juliette laughed for the first time since she drove up to her studio.

"Absolutely," she said, and tossed back her shot. "I'll drink to that."

Both her father and Gina had wanted to spend the night, but once they had cleaned up the mess, Juliette found herself wanting to be alone. The police had left her with a special metal bar that would temporarily lock her door until she could get the broken one repaired.

But when it was time to change her clothes and get into bed, she felt on edge—as if she were being watched, or at any moment the door was going to burst open again with the sound of splintering wood.

She washed her face with her phone sitting right next to the sink, in case she had to quickly dial 911. She then closed herself into her room and hastily changed into her pajamas. Her heart was racing so she tried to make herself calm down with some deep breathing.

She had taken two deep breaths and then almost screamed out loud when the neighbor's dog barked.

Her hands were shaking as she walked through the studio turning off the lights and making sure everything was locked up. Once she clicked off the last light, she ran and jumped onto her bed in the same way she used to when she was a little girl afraid of monsters hiding in her room.

She turned her bedside table lamp on and picked up the box of Catarina's letters because she knew she wouldn't be falling asleep anytime soon.

The last letter had revealed the secret of Gregorio. When she read it, Juliette had felt a renewed kindred spirit with her grandmother. The thought that they had both fallen for cads somehow helped.

Catarina had gotten over Gregorio, and that fact had helped Juliette close the door on her feelings for Roman. Catarina had chosen to make an amazing life even when she had to leave the hope of Gregorio behind when she first arrived. Later, she got the benefit of closure when she met him and got to know of his deceitfulness. Juliette thought about that. Maybe knowing that Roman had been untrustworthy was actually a blessing in disguise. Better to have been heartbroken now then end up with a selfish, dishonest husband later. She wanted someone who was salt of the earth, like her dad and grandfather. Ian's face flashed through her mind as she picked up the next letter and began to read. Catarina's words kept her company, and thinking in Italian helped her focus on something other than burglars pawing through her things.

And then, in spite of her jumpiness, she slept.

Chapter 27

"One of the most difficult things I'm learning about painting," Catarina told Franco, "is knowing when I'm finished. *Capisci?*"

"*Si, capisco,*" her husband said with an indulgent smile.

She had moved the landscape she was working on from room to room in their new apartment to view it in different lights. She wanted to add a bit of vermilion when the painting was in the living room and then she added a brush stroke or two of eggplant when it was in the bedroom. Finally, she asked Franco to hold it up directly in front of the window so she could see it yet again. She felt that it needed something, but what? She thought perhaps more texture in the sky. She wished she would become a better painter faster, but she knew that she had years and years of practice ahead of her before she would be able to paint anything that truly pleased her. But she didn't mind. She loved taking painting classes and learning skills slowly but surely.

She bit the end of the brush handle and considered her work, completely forgetting that her husband was holding the large canvas painting until his arms began to tremble. She had already reused the canvas numerous times, because spending their hard-earned money on paints and art supplies was an expense they could barely afford.

"*Oh, mio Dio!* Franco, I'm sorry. Here, put it down." She tried to take it from him, but her large, pregnant belly got in the way.

Catarina had been painting more and more since she received news that the war had reached the border towns in northern Italy. Her father had been right. Hundreds of thousands of young Italian men were forced to fight for a cause she was still confused about. Why did politics have to come to shedding blood?

When she received the letter from her mother with the news that Mateo had been forced to leave home to fight, the conflict became much more real to her. She couldn't imagine her witty, humorous, gangly brother with a weapon in his hand. She prayed he would somehow be able to stay out of it. She asked the Virgin for a miracle. She heard news of young men coming home missing limbs or being terribly scarred and permanently damaged. She was terrified for Mateo's safety, and her family was living on scant provisions because they were required to give their surplus to the occupying soldiers. She hated to think of Mateo in danger and her family hungry, but painting the landscapes of her youth made her feel a connection to home. She wanted to send money, but her mother insisted that the mail was unreliable and that whatever she sent would probably not make it. Her family was even considering moving to her aunt's farm to wait out the fighting because it was tucked further away in the countryside.

For now, she painted the sunlight of Italy, the vines, the olive orchards. She prayed that Mateo and her sisters' husbands would stay safe and that she and Franco could go visit as soon as the conflict ended. She felt a need to hold her family in her arms.

The piece she was working on featured the stone wall, bordered in lavender, that separated her family's kitchen garden from the vineyard in the foreground, and the vines gently sloping uphill in the background. It was the wall she had sat on, contemplating her future, the evening before she left to marry Franco. On the canvas the image didn't look as accurate as it did in her mind's eye because her talents were still taking shape. But for her, it was home.

Catarina had made friends in her painting classes. She and Franco had taken to hosting small groups of them for dinner in the apartment they rented shortly after Catarina became pregnant. She loved those evenings because her painting friends came from all different backgrounds, each with varying levels of artistic proficiency, and each with an interesting perspective on life. Most were men, who came to dinner with their wives or girlfriends, but there was one other woman she'd met in her class. She had the most amazing views about life and Catarina was entranced with her perspective. She talked about wanting to vote in elections and knew about politics, an entirely foreign concept to a young woman raised in a strictly patriarchal Italian family.

Franco enjoyed Catarina's new friends, and because of their artistic viewpoints he began to see himself as a jewelry designer rather than a merchant. Catarina insisted he was an artist in his own right and maintained that the ring he created for her was proof of his exceptional talent.

"I f it wasn't for this incessant worrying about my family," she said to Franco as they cleaned up one evening after their guests had left, "life would be perfect."

"I think that's how life is, *mi amore*. You have to focus on the best of it and sweep aside the worry and sorrow because there's nothing you can do about it anyway."

"I know," she wrapped her arms around him. "You're right, but it's difficult."

"Go put your feet up now. They're swelling to the size of pumpkins. I'll finish these dishes."

He took the serving platter she was carrying to the sink out of her hands and gently nudged her toward the couch.

"If you want to, you can read your book," he suggested, "it's there on the side table."

Catarina was slogging through *Ethan Frome* by Edith Wharton. She was continually trying to improve her reading and she found this novel compelling in spite of its level of difficulty, the horrible bleakness of the plot, and the constant need to stop and ask Franco for the definition of words.

"I'm too tired to think in English," she said. "I think I'll just lie here and talk to you while you finish. You spoil me too much, Franco. Some day when Mama comes to visit, I'm going to have to show her that I'm a good wife. Otherwise she'll see that I have gotten soft here in America."

"You haven't gotten soft," he said from the kitchen, "just round!"

"Well, that she would approve of!" she laughed and patted her pregnant middle. "If it's a boy, would you mind if we named him after my brother?" she asked.

"Mateo?"

"I feel like somehow that will help keep him safe. He'll want to be sure to meet a nephew named after him. He's just that arrogant," she teased.

O ver the next months, the letters from her mother became increasingly worrisome. Even though the fighting remained in the north, everyone in the country was forced to live in fear while waiting for news about their sons and husbands, and wondering whether the battles would move south. The Pensebenes said rosaries everyday for Mateo. There had been no news of him after the second short, scrawled letter her family had received in the months after he left.

At least Catarina and Franco had a welcome distraction. Baby Mateo was born. He was the perfect foil to her worries, temporarily taking her mind off of the fear she felt for her family. She was happy to be able to send them good news to celebrate in spite of their circumstances.

Overwhelmed by love for him, Catarina felt Mateo was a perfect little boy. He looked like his father and she was surprised by how much time she could spend simply gazing at him.

Catarina tucked a blanket under the baby's chin and hugged her newborn tight. She understood for the first time just how difficult

it must have been for her mother to send her off to marry Franco—
knowing she might never see her again. And then to have to send Mateo
off to battle. How hard that would be for her parents. She resolved
again to go see her family as soon as the war was over even though the
journey was so long.

E very day she opened the mailbox with a mixture of hope
and dread. She was desperate to hear news that her family
was safe, but each day that she unlocked the box and found
it empty was one more in which she could visualize Mateo alive and
sitting around with other soldiers making jokes and eating rations.
She hoped it was true. Maybe he was being housed on a farm where
the farmer had a beautiful daughter and he was madly in love and
helping out around the farm instead of wading through mud and blood
on a smoke-filled battlefield, which is where she saw him in her darker
moments. She made up different scenarios every day. While she tended
the baby and snuck in painting time while he slept, she fretted over the
fate of her beloved brother.

It was easier to pass the time when Franco was home. When
he came back from work each evening, he rolled up his shirtsleeves
and carried their son around the apartment making cooing sounds and
getting baby smiles, while she cooked dinner. He made faces at Mateo
while telling Catarina stories of the day. She told him about all the
mesmerizing things their son did while he was at work, but the best
time of the day was the very end. The three of them would prop up
in bed. Catarina fed Mateo while Franco read to her in English.

One night, after the dishes were put away and they were snuggled
in bed, Franco pulled a letter out of his pocket instead of picking the

book up off of the bedside table.

"Catarina, my love, I have some bad news for you." He took her hand. "Your babbo sent my father a letter."

She looked from the baby to her husband and silently shook her head, imploring him to stop. He had been quiet and ashen all evening, but had insisted he was fine when she asked if he was ill. Now she could see her husband bite the inside of his cheek as he did whenever he struggled to stay composed.

"It's Mateo, Catarina," Franco said. And then paused and looked away for a moment, because he wanted to stay strong for his wife. He gained control and then looked back. "He was killed in battle," he forced the words out, knowing that each one would rip a piece of his wife's heart to pieces.

"No, Franco," she said, shaking her head and trying to force back tears, trying to deny what her husband told her. "You're wrong. There's a mistake. He's fine. I would know. I would feel it. Don't you think I would feel it?" she rushed her words out. Her shoulders began to shake and she had to hold the baby tightly to stop herself from dropping him. The sobs began even as her words of denial continued.

"Besides," she fought on, "why would your parents know first? My parents would write to *me*."

"They wanted to make sure you didn't get the news when you were home alone," he said, and gently pried baby Mateo from Catarina so he could take his wife into his protective embrace.

"How can he be gone from us?" she cried. "I look out at the moon at night and I think about the fact that he can see the same moon. We're not so far away from each other. But now? I can't imagine being alive, here, and being without him in this world."

Catarina stopped trying to fight the truth and allowed herself to sob. Franco held her tightly and rocked them both.

"My brother," she cried.

"I know," Franco soothed.

"Did the letter say what happened?"

"He was in Caporetto. There was fighting, and his battalion was advancing when there was an explosion. It was a bomb. One of his friends crawled to him, but it was too late. At least it was fast. He didn't suffer. They sent his personal things to your parents with a letter."

"Here," he handed her the letter. Through her tears, she could see that it had already been folded and unfolded several times. She wondered how many times both he and his father had read the news.

She saw her father's handwriting and as she read the words herself she had to accept the truth.

She looked up at Franco when she finished reading.

"*Oh, mio Dio!*," she sobbed. "I hate this war, the violence. It's all so senseless."

Franco brushed aside her hair and as he did, Catarina remembered her brother bowing as they passed the beautiful, shy Bianca, whom he swore to someday marry.

"Oh, Mateo," she said and handed the letter back to Franco, buried her face in her hands, and began to cry again.

Chapter 28

"My God, what happened to you?" Ian asked, when Juliette came in the next morning with extremely swollen eyes. "Did you have an allergic reaction to something?"

"I wish it were something that simple. No, it's something much worse. My studio got broken into and my ring was stolen."

"No!" He put the plans he was looking at down and came and wrapped her in a hug.

She sniffed and wiped her nose with her sleeve. "Sorry, I don't want to get snot on you."

"Don't worry, you can get as much snot on me as you need to. See this sleeve?" He held up his arm. "You can even use it to blow your nose."

Juliette laughed in spite of herself.

"Tell me what happened. Here, sit down. Today I'll make the coffee."

"That sounds good. I was supposed to go to work this morning, but I called in sick. I was too freaked out to get a good night's sleep. The burglars broke in right through my front door. It made me feel like anyone could just waltz in at any time, you know?"

"Just . . . boom? Right through?" Ian's contractor's mind was already working on getting her door secured.

"I can't believe I lost the ring."

"You didn't *lose* the ring, some scumbags came in and took it."

"I know that in theory, but I still feel like I let them down. Mom and Nonna, I mean. They took care of the ring. They didn't let it fall into the hands of a bunch of thieves. I can't believe this happened. My God, Ian," a thought suddenly occurred to her. "They were probably in my cottage while I was telling you the story of it. *Why* did I leave it at home? I could have used gloves like you said."

"Juliette, you couldn't possibly have known. You were trying to keep it from getting covered in paint. Your mom and Catarina wouldn't be mad at you. They loved you. They would never hold this against you. Come here," Ian wrapped her in a hug again. "Listen, we're not going to work today."

"No?"

"Definitely not. First of all, you're going to lie down, right here on the floor. Wait, actually I'll sweep first." He moved away from her, swept up a spot and grabbed the pillow off her bench to place under her head. "And I'm going to get a cold towel to put across your eyes, and you're going to rest them while I go to the drugstore to get some eye drops."

"It's that bad?"

"Well, let me put it this way: you look like a boxer who went one round too many. But still cute, of course."

She lay down, and he tucked the pillow beneath her head and placed one of his clean paint rags that he rinsed with cold water across her eyes.

"You rest while I get the drops, then when we get back we're going to get in the truck and go to the most restful spot around. It's my favorite place."

"And where would that be?"

"Pacific Grove. Have you been there?"

"You mean down by Monterey?"

"Exactly."

"Isn't that, like, two hours away?"

"It doesn't matter. There's a great path along the ocean where we can watch otters and seals, and there are lots of restaurants. We'll bring our coffee and drink it on the way."

"Sounds perfect," she sighed, releasing some of the tension. "And my eyes are feeling better already, even from this cool rag."

"Good. I'll be back in a few."

"Wow, that was fast," Juliette said when she heard the back door open again just moments later.

"Whoa girl, what happened to you?" Instead of Ian, she heard Mark's voice, so she peeked out from under the cloth.

"I had a bad night," she said.

"It must have been a doozie."

"It was, but not the kind of doozie you're thinking of. Someone broke into my place and stole a bunch of my stuff."

"Shit, no wonder you're down on the floor. Do you need help getting up?"

"No, Ian's getting eye drops and then he's whisking me away for the day. I'm afraid you're going to be on your own."

"What? Where are you going?"

"He said Pacific Grove is the place to go to lick wounds. Something about peaceful ocean walks."

Mark raised his eyebrows at that one, but Juliette couldn't see because she was still lying with the cloth on her eyes.

"What a show-off. Whisking you away, huh? Well, then, I guess I'll have to settle for putting more cool water on your cloth. Hand it over."

"Geez, you guys are amazing. Do you give this treatment to all your clients?"

"Only the ones who feed us fancy Italian pastries, make us amazing coffee, treat my daughter like a princess, introduce us to the best sushi place in town, and get robbed."

"So yes, pretty much all your clients."

"Exactly."

She took the cloth off of her face and handed it to Mark. "My eyes are feeling better already. Hey, I can even open them beyond puffy slits. Look."

"Come on Juliette, you always look great. Don't worry about it."

"Thanks for the sympathy compliment."

"No problem. It usually works on Lexi." He walked to the

bathroom to rinse out the cloth with more cool water. Juliette took it from him and lay back down while Mark strapped on his tool belt and put his lunch in the fridge.

Ian's return was announced when she heard Mark say, "Hey, I heard what happened to our girl."

In spite of her depressed state, she couldn't help but like being called "their girl." When she decided to go ahead with *Gusto*, she never would have guessed that she would make such good friends in the bargain.

"Ok, Juliette, let's see." Ian crouched down beside her.

She sat up again and took off the cloth.

"Better already." He took out the eye drops. "Tilt." He lifted her chin and dropped three drops neatly in each eye.

"Impressive work. Were you a pothead in your youth?"

"No, I was not. But I do have a sister who pretty much made me her slave during any emotional upset."

"Good deal for her."

"I think you're good to go," Ian said, tilting her chin up again and looking into her eyes. He smiled at her and rubbed his knuckles against her cheek.

"Thank you," she spontaneously kissed his cheek. "You're very good to me."

"I aim to please, Ma'am." Ian drolled, but kept his eyes locked on hers.

"All right," Juliette got up off the floor. "*I'll* make the coffee while you confer with Mark about the day's agenda, since we're cruelly ditching him."

"What, you don't trust my coffee skills?"

"I don't know what you're talking about, " Juliette looked at him, all innocence. "I'm just trying to be helpful."

The day lived up to Ian's promise. The sleepy seaside town was peaceful. They walked along the cliff path and spotted more ocean life than Juliette had ever seen. Ian took her hand as they scrambled over rocks to peek into tide pools, and they went out for a huge lunch at a place called Aliotti's where Juliette had the best piece of quiche Lorraine she'd ever tasted. They stopped off for tea in a tucked-away garden, which turned out to be Juliette's favorite part of the day.

Only once did they even talk about the ring.

"I'm curious," Ian told her. "Yesterday, when you were telling me the story of your ring, you said that your grandmother told you it saved her life once. What was that about?"

"Actually, I just read about it in one of her letters to her friend. It turns out that when she was on the ship, coming from Italy to New York, she met another man and fell for him. Hard. In fact, he asked her to skip out on her promise to marry my grandfather, but she refused."

"Gutsy. I don't know that I would have blamed her if she had. After all, she was only a teenager and she was going to marry some guy she didn't know."

"She said that back then, a promise was a promise. And then she met Granddad, and she came to love him, too. So then, more than a year later, she ran into the other guy again and guess what? He had come to San Francisco in search of her. He hoped she hadn't gone through with the wedding because he was sure she loved him, too. Anyway, she said she wasn't proud of her behavior, but she struck up a secret friendship with him."

"Then what?" Ian was completely hooked.

"Well, he still loved her, and she was confused because she loved Granddad, but she still had feelings for this other guy. But then he did something that made her know that Granddad was the man for her."

"What?"

"He suggested they hock the ring and use the money to run away together. He wanted Nonna to leave right then, and not even tell Granddad that she was going. Just disappear. Can you imagine what that would have done to Granddad? To have your wife just gone with no idea of what happened?" Juliette paused. "Anyway," she continued, "Nonna wrote that it was like someone threw a bucket of icy water over her and she realized that the other man was deceitful and no good. She would never do that to Granddad because he was such a wonderful man who had been nothing but good and loyal to her. And that's when she realized that she not only loved her husband, but was in love with him as well."

"So the ring saved her life."

"Uh-huh."

"Look, I know you already know this, but even though it's not on your finger, the ring will always be a part of you—even if you only had it a short time. It's part of your life story because it was part of theirs."

"I do know and I'll try to remind myself of that. Thank you for everything. For taking me here and, I don't know . . . "

"Don't worry about it. Besides," he smirked, "I'm going to add all this to your bill." He stood up and pulled her up.

"Very funny." She paused. "You know what, Ian Matthews? You're a good person."

"Yeah, well, don't let it get around. It'll ruin my bad boy reputation," he smiled. "Come on," Ian reached out, took her hand and pulled her off the bench she was sitting on, "we better head back. I want to take a look at your door before it gets dark."

They stopped by *Gusto* so Juliette could pick up her car and then drove up the hill to her place. Ian walked around it to make sure everything looked secure and took a closer look at the front door.

"The bar lock looks good, but I'll stop by tomorrow to repair the dead bolt so you can use it until you get a new door. As long as you have your dead bolt thrown, it should be fine. See how they busted the jam?" he asked and pointed to the splintered wood.

"It feels creepy knowing people just barged right in."

"Call me if you need me, ok? And, if you get freaked out, you could always borrow one of my parents' dogs for a while. Or, hey, all three of them." He smiled and kissed her on the cheek and then headed to his truck.

"Wait!" Juliette yelled. "Which one barks the most?"

"Lily, why? Do you want me to get her?"

"Do you think your parents would mind?"

"Not at all. And Lily loves an adventure. I'll go pick her up and be right back."

"Thank you," she said, liking the idea of Lily being there with her.

As he drove away, she sighed. Then she went inside, washed her face, made a cup of tea, and waited while Ian went to get her temporary sleeping companion.

Chapter 29

CATARINA, A DEEP, DEEP SLEEP
AND VINE-COVERED HILLS

I n spite of the fact that it was summer, it had been cold and
drizzly since Catarina heard the news that her brother was dead.
It was exactly as it should have been, in her opinion.

She put baby Mateo in the pram and strolled to her in-laws' house
most mornings since she had gotten the news. In her depressed state,
every task, from changing the baby's diapers to feeding him, seemed
to be insurmountably difficult.

Franco's mother kept up a steady stream of chatter in an attempt
to pull her daughter-in-law out of her overwhelming sadness. Catarina
responded to her questions and listened, but Isabella could see that the
sparkle was missing from her daughter-in-law's eyes.

When the second week slipped into the third, Isabella decided it was time to do something a little bit more drastic, so when Catarina arrived with Mateo, she stopped the two at the doorstep and took the pram handle from Catarina.

"Listen to me," she said, wheeling the stroller back and forth, but not inviting Catarina in. "I used to hear the saying 'life is for the living' and I thought pfft, what a stupid thing to say. But, in this case," she paused, "I think it is exactly what I need to say to you. So, today I'm taking Mateo, and I'm sending you home. You just fed him, right? He'll be fine for a few hours without you. Go home, pick up a paintbrush and start to paint again. You can't stop living your life because your brother had to stop living his."

"I'm living my life. What are you talking about? It's . . . "

Isabella held up her hand to stop Catarina from saying more.

"I'm your mother-in-law and you will do what I say. Go home. Paint. And listen to me. This is what my mother said to me before she passed: she said, 'Isabella, have lots of good adventures, be happy, and live your life, and then when you get to heaven, you can tell me all about it.' She didn't want me to ruin my only chance to have fun while I'm here."

Catarina's eyes welled up but she nodded. "*Va bene*," she said and kissed Mateo goodbye. "I'll be back for you soon," she whispered.

"Not a minute before four," Isabelle said with a stern look.

"I understand," she acquiesced and turned to trudge back home. Catarina dearly wished she could mourn with her parents and sisters. She thought of them living in the barn at her aunt's farm waiting out the war, their own vineyard abandoned for now.

But when she got back to her apartment, she didn't pick

up a paintbrush. Instead she climbed back into her unmade bed and
went to sleep. The blankets were heavy and she dozed off immediately.
The cocoon of oblivion felt good. She woke briefly after an hour, rolled
over, and went back to sleep. It was as if the more she slept the wearier
she became. Rolling over and catching sight of the clock again at 1:13,
she let herself sink back to sleep for another half hour. Finally, she
forced herself to get up and splashed water on her face. She brushed
her teeth and hair, looking in the mirror.

"Oh Mateo," she said aloud.

She could almost see him waiting for her with laughter in his
eyes when she emerged from the Carlucci's front door on market day.
She saw him waving goodbye to her from the dock as the ship gradually pulled away. It was the last time she had laid eyes on her brother,
and she could feel the tears on her cheeks yet again. The supply never
seemed to end. But this time, she tried to focus on a happy memory of
him, so she could keep him alive in her mind instead of dwelling on
the fact that he was gone.

She splashed cool water on her face again and pulled herself
together before she left her apartment to retrieve Mateo.

Stopping at the market, she picked up some flowers for herself
and for Isabella.

"Thank you," she said and handed the flowers to her when she
opened the door.

"You look a little better maybe," she said, patting her daughter-
in-law's cheek. "Come in and I'll put these in some water. Let's have
some coffee."

She and the baby were back home and she was rolling pasta sheets when Franco got back from work. He picked up Mateo and twirled him and then gave his wife a kiss on the lips.

"I have a surprise for you," he said.

She looked up from her rolling pin. "What kind of surprise?" she felt her heart lift a little bit at the prospect of something exciting.

"A weekend away. There's a town I've heard about that I think will remind you of Italy. I got the entire weekend and Monday off from work, and we're going to take the train in the morning."

"Where? And what about the baby?" she looked over at their son.

"The town's called Napa, and we'll bring him. It will be sunny and warm. I think you'll love it there. There are vineyards, hills, and hot weather. We'll find a hotel to stay in. Come on, a change of scene will do you good."

"You don't need to coax me," she smiled at her husband, in what felt like the first time in a long, long time. "It sounds wonderful already."

"Do you remember the last time we took a train?" he asked.

"I'll never forget. It's when I started to fall in love with you," she said matter-of-factly, but hearing the words was music to his ears. He had been hit hard the second she had walked through the door at Ellis Island in New York, even though she was dirty and exhausted. He had recognized her the second she stepped into the sunlight and his chest had immediately tightened at the realization that the young girl who had captured his imagination had truly come to marry him.

Now, more than two years later, they were on another train, with their infant son between them.

Even before the train reached the station, Catarina

could feel the pent-up emotion in her chest loosen further. Franco had been right, seeing the open sky and the hillsides covered in vines gave her the nostalgic feeling of returning to Italy. She hadn't known all this existed just a short trip from San Francisco. Not long after they boarded the train, fog had given way to sunshine, and then, as they traveled northeast, the air warmed. By the time they stepped onto the train platform less than an hour later in Napa, she had to take off her sweater and remove an extra blanket she'd wrapped around Mateo. It felt good to be hot for a change.

Catarina breathed in the heavy, warm air scented with the essence of dirt, ripe grapes, and roses that were planted at the ends of the rows of vines. She paused, closed her eyes, and inhaled again to pull every last trace of the familiar fragrance into her lungs. She wanted to seal it inside her body so she could bring it back to the city at the end of the weekend.

They gathered their bags and then walked two short blocks to a hotel Franco had heard about. Catarina wished she had her paints and canvas with her. She would have loved to stand outside and paint what she actually saw rather than try to paint memories. The realization that she could grow as a painter here seeped into her mind. The subject that interested her most was painting outdoor landscapes, but in San Francisco she was too limited by buildings when what she longed for were open green spaces.

When they reached their room, Franco threw open windows to let in the fresh, hot air. Catarina set the sleeping Mateo on the bed.

"We should have brought his sleeping basket," she said.

"Don't worry," Franco said, "I have a plan."

He removed a deep drawer from a dresser in the corner of the room and placed a pillow from the bed inside. He set it by the side of the bed, and turned to his wife."

"*Fantastico*!" she laughed. "You are a genius."

"*Grazie*," he smiled and then wrapped his arms around his wife. "I have another surprise, too."

"What?"

"There's a town a little further north that has a hot spring. We're going to buy bathing costumes and bathe in the mineral waters. I've heard it's very hot and that if you soak in it, you are guaranteed to stay healthy."

"What is mineral water? I don't know that I like the sound of it. It sounds dirty and brown."

"I'm not exactly sure, to be honest, but I think it's just hot water like a bath. We're going to love it."

"What will we do with Mateo?"

"We'll take turns with him. There is a time for the men to bathe and a time for the women to bathe. And there's a room with chairs and a fireplace where people can wait while their companions go in the water."

"How do you know about this?"

"From a customer at the shop. He said we'll love it. That it's just the thing."

Catarina couldn't imagine it and wasn't sure what "just the thing" meant exactly, but the next morning, after spending an afternoon and evening strolling and looking into the shops in Napa and reveling in the pleasure of a warm summer evening, they boarded the train to go to Calistoga.

The scenery on the short trip was beautiful and lush and when they left the train they found themselves in a tiny town, with very few shops. Fortunately one of them had clothes and textiles for men and women, where they were each able to purchase a bathing costume. Catarina wasn't used to showing her legs and laughed at how silly she felt.

"It will be like going into the bath wearing my dressing gown," she said.

Franco laughed at his, too. "You'll still look beautiful," he said.

When they arrived at Pacheteau Baths, it was exactly as Franco had heard. They bought tickets at a white stucco building that was surrounded by cottages for guests who were staying the night. They walked across the garden to a walled pool.

When they passed through the gate Catarina gasped. "It's larger than our kitchen garden in Italy," she whispered to Franco. "I was expecting a large bath tub, but this is like a small pond!"

He was also stunned. "It must be at least fifteen meters across!" he whispered back.

In the water, women and girls of all ages frolicked and chatted. One end was extremely shallow, like entering the water from a beach, so Catarina passed the baby to Franco and gingerly waded in.

When her feet were completely submerged she turned to smile at him, "It's hot! It's wonderful, *meravigliosa!*

"*Va bene,*" he smiled. "I'll be in there with Mateo," he nodded toward a large open room with a fireplace and couches that opened onto the pool area, "but don't go in too far. I don't want you to sink."

"I promise. I'll stay where I can stand. Oh Franco, you're going to love it." She said, wiggling her toes in the warm, silky water, and wading in further. Once she was up to her knees she decided to lie down. The water smelled vaguely earthy, but looked perfectly clear. She felt buoyant, so she ventured a bit deeper, but she sank under the water, so she moved back to where she could lie in the water, with her head out.

She tilted her head back so her ears were submerged. She could hear her heart beating and her own breathing. She stared up at the incredibly blue sky and for the first time since she left Perdifumo to begin her trip to marry Franco, she felt like she was where she belonged. She had come to love San Francisco, her husband, and her new family, but this new place, with the sunshine, hot air, and vine-covered hills, felt right.

She swayed her arms back and forth in the water and thought about her parents. The farm would be left abandoned until the end of the war. Her brother was gone, and she couldn't even visit until the fighting ended. They were so far away, but she was desperate to be with them again.

Right then, she decided that she would coax them to come here. They could live here in the Napa Valley. They could buy a small house and some land, and her parents could grow grapes and olives just like they did at home. Her sisters and their husbands could have the farm in Italy, if there was anything left when the family returned home. But Catarina resolved right then to send for her parents.

And we can visit them on the weekends," Catarina explained to Franco later that afternoon, after he had taken his turn with the men bathing, while Catarina dried off and played with Mateo in front of the fire. She felt relaxed and warm deep into her core. They lay a sleepy Mateo on a blanket on the lawn near the pool while they played a new game called shuffleboard.

She felt the warm sun on her arms while she pushed the puck along with the cue. She missed the number she was aiming for by a considerable distance and sighed.

"I'm not very good at this," she shook her head.

"Apparently I'm not either," Franco said, making a face, when his puck also missed the mark.

"Do you think we could get them to come? If we could get the visas and sponsor them?" he asked.

"I don't know. But, if you're willing to try it, I'll write to them. Losing Mateo has been a terrible blow—especially to Babbo, since Mateo was his only son."

"My father can write, too." Franco said, pushing another puck along.

"I think they would love it here."

"I'm amazed we never came to Napa when I was a boy." Franco looked around. "I would like our children to have time away from the fog of the city. Maybe we could save up and buy a little house here whether we can get your parents to come or not. Then the kids could have the outdoors to run around like we did when we were children."

"Kids? Franco, we only have one so far," she smiled at her sleepy boy and bent down to kiss his plump cheek.

He put down the shuffleboard stick and wrapped his arms around his wife and kissed her.

"One so far, but I'm sure there will be more, no?"

Catarina chuckled and kissed her husband back.

"And I could paint landscapes here, too. I could stand in the fields and paint what I see instead of what I remember."

"It sounds good."

"It does," she nodded.

Franco had been right to bring her there. She felt refreshed. Bathing in the warm, silky mineral water had been restorative. Between having the baby and Mateo dying, she had been focused on getting through each moment of her day. She had not been able to think about the future. Now she became determined to bring her parents to her. They would love this place and after everything they'd been through since she'd left, she was sure that they could heal here in a way that they may not have been able to at home.

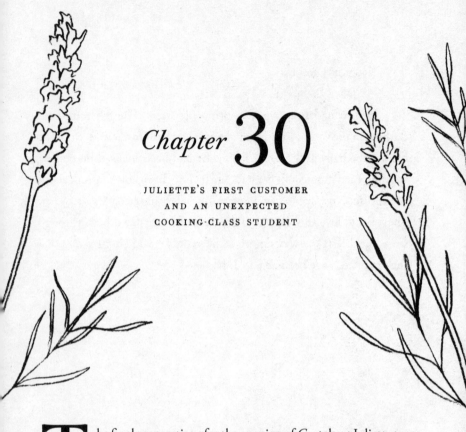

Chapter 30

JULIETTE'S FIRST CUSTOMER
AND AN UNEXPECTED
COOKING-CLASS STUDENT

The final preparations for the opening of *Gusto* kept Juliette too busy to think about her woes. Appliances were in place, the painting was complete, the floor tiles were gleaming and she was down to placing tables, chairs, lights, and putting the finishing touches on the patio. She had even set an opening date, created a website, blanketed the city with flyers, placed ads for her first group of cooking students, and had a mostly full class signed up. She gave notice at her temporary coffee-house job with a promise to invite everyone to the opening.

Juliette was practically living at *Gusto* and came home only to fall into bed, so she had long since returned Lily to Ian's family, but missed her happy companionship. Now, after going full tilt, by the time she got back to her studio she was so tired she couldn't worry about being afraid to sleep.

She hired two cooks, two counter helpers, and four servers, all whom came in to help with the final preparations.

The day before *Gusto* was due to open, she threw a party for her friends and family to help her celebrate. Ian and Mark were there earlier in the day to finish up the last details, helping her to hang art and arrange the tables, and then they were gone. She knew she would miss their presence in her daily life, but at least they'd be there that evening. She pushed the thought of missing Ian especially to the back of her mind, and forced herself to focus on the thousands of tasks she had still to do.

The guests arrived and the champagne flowed freely all evening. The patio lights were on and the inside décor looked even better than she could have hoped. She had bought a long, high table that separated the entry from the rest of the room and she put the huge urn she lugged home from Lucca on one end and filled it with olive branches. It looked perfect paired with the large landscape that Catarina had once painted, gracing the biggest of the brick walls.

Juliette absentmindedly twisted the bare finger where her ring used to rest. Weeks had passed and there was still no sign of it. She had finally accepted that it was gone forever. But the life lessons aren't gone, she reminded herself. Chase your dreams. Choose happiness. That's what her mom and Nonna would both say today. She hoped they would be proud.

She caught sight of Ian from across the room and gave him

a smile. She felt sparkling tonight. Her hair was down and wavy and she was wearing a dress she'd bought just for the occasion. For once he wasn't seeing her covered in dust or flecks of paint or up to her elbows in the food she was preparing.

Juliette circulated the room, filling glasses until she approached him.

"You look beautiful," he said.

"Thank you," she smiled. "You clean up well yourself."

"Are you happy with it?" Ian asked, looking around the room.

"It's even better than I imagined. You realized my vision and them some," she said. "We did this." She nodded and took his arm.

"Yes, we did."

"Ahem," Mark had steered Lexi over to them.

"We *all* did," Juliette amended with a smile.

"Absolutely," Ian agreed, and they clinked their glasses together.

The evening gave way to multiple toasts, compliments on the food, and at last a final farewell with wishes for a fantastic opening in the morning. Before she turned the lights out behind her, she took one last look around and grinned. She could hardly believe it was truly happening after all this time, all the plans, the dreams.

Juliette was up by five a.m. after a short and restless night's sleep. She managed to get in her morning run before showering and heading to *Gusto*. She had to get rid of some of her nervous energy. Her hair was up in a twist, she had a half apron on, and was putting pastries under the glass when the three employees scheduled to work that morning made their way in one-by-one. She unlocked the door, propped one side open and turned the sign around for the very first time at seven thirty. And then they all waited.

The minutes ticked by. Juliette went into the office to pretend to work because she couldn't stand to wait in desperation up front. And then it happened. She could hear a voice inside ordering something. She tried to focus on sending an email to Christine with her ear cocked to the side to help her hear the order. And then she recognized the voice. It wasn't a regular customer. It was her Dad. She smiled and got up from her desk.

"Hey you."

"Hey yourself."

"Am I your first customer?"

"The honor is yours," she said, as Cheryl, who worked behind the counter, passed him a slice of breakfast frittata and then expertly turned the knobs on the espresso maker to make her dad's latte.

Before she could say another word, two women wearing yoga clothes with rolled-up yoga mats slung over their shoulders came in and ordered tea.

"It smells so good in here," one of them commented. "We walk by here almost every morning and we've been watching the progress. It looks terrific!"

"Thanks! Welcome." They took their tea to one of the tables by the window and Juliette's heart did a leap in her chest. She spontaneously brought over a plate of tiny marzipan cakes she'd made.

"Here, try these," she said. "They're nice with tea. Let me know how you like them. I thought it would be fun to experiment on my favorite customers and you two are already on the list."

The morning passed by quickly with more customers than she could have hoped for with only a few lulls here and there. They filled

huge baskets with foccacia, sourdough, and pugliese bread for sandwiches and they prepped the line with all the fixings for lunch. A huge
black chalkboard hung behind the counter, filled with every possible
sandwich concoction and salad item that one could dream of. She'd
had an art student from the local college do all the lettering in colorful
chalk and she loved the results.

She had created matching order forms with boxes to check off
with a place for a name, so when the lunch rush came (and please God,
she prayed, let it come), customers could move through the line, place
their order, pay, and then hang out until their order was up. Daily
specials of soup, salad and pasta were on a separate board, and of
course, dessert items were placed conspicuously by the cash register.

Juliette was behind the counter making sandwiches when
a familiar order came in. Before she saw the name, she knew whom
the sandwich was for. It was Ian's favorite from the days when she was
testing combinations on both Ian and Mark: foccacia bread with black
olive tapenade, olive oil, balsamic vinegar, roasted red peppers, gem
lettuce and roasted turkey. She turned around and there he was.

"Any chance you can join me?"

Juliette looked at the short line and the efficiency with which
her assistants were working and decided she could sneak away for
a few minutes.

"I'd love to," she smiled. "Grab a table and I'll join you in
a few minutes."

"So far so good," he said when Juliette got to the table. Ian looked
around and saw that more than half the tables were full, with
more people taking their food to go.

"Yeah, I'm trying not to get too excited, but it's busier than I even hoped. Everyone says there's a honeymoon period, but still," she paused. "And my first cooking class starts tomorrow. It's more than three quarters full."

"I was wondering about that, actually. Any chance I could score a spot in the group? Now that I'm not going to be here on a daily basis with the perk of being your guinea pig, I'm going to have to learn to cook a few things myself. I've been spoiled and I can't stand going back to eating boxed fettuccini and frozen food from Trader Joe's."

Juliette smiled. "Of course you can join the group. In fact, I would love to have you there."

"Great. Then it's a date."

She peeked at the line, which was growing, and got up to go.

"Hey," she said, "looks like I'm needed behind the counter, but I'll see you tomorrow," she smiled. "I'm glad you're coming."

The next evening's cooking class began with introductions. It reminded her of the first cooking class in Lucca and the adrenaline rush of having to introduce herself in Italian. It felt so long ago. Roman occasionally sent sweet or witty texts to keep in touch. She was sometimes tempted to pop a note back with some flirty intercontinental text banter but she held herself in check and instead responded with something nice and chatty, but reserved. It had taken months to get over him and she didn't want to allow herself to be vulnerable to more heartbreak.

She recently received a report from Odessa that Roman had been seen having a heated argument with his girlfriend in the central piazza. She had to admit to a slight sense of pleasure at hearing that tidbit of news but tried not to be petty. It had been a wonderful chapter of her life even if it had ended badly.

As the class progressed, she was pleased because the group was a fun and interesting hodgepodge of pupils. By the end of the evening, she felt it had been a success in spite of a mishap or two. She supposed the kinks would soon be worked out. The prosciutto pinwheels in puff pastry they made to go with the salt-encrusted shrimp with roasted red pepper sauce had been a hit. They came out of the oven golden brown and fragrant. When they bit into them they were the perfect combination of flaky, salty, and tangy. Her students were proud, and Juliette was excited and energized by their enthusiasm.

Ian had been game to take on any task she delegated to him. The switch in their roles was fun. She found herself glancing at him throughout the evening. More often then not he would feel her gaze, meet it, and smile.

At the end of class, the group sat on the stools around the worktable to peel the crispy shrimp and dip them in the pepper sauce. Juliette poured each of them a glass of chilled Viognier to accompany the food. To end the class, she poured espresso and set out individual-sized tiramisus as a sweet to finish off the flavors. She sat down with them and dipped a spoon into her own dessert.

"Mmmmm," she moaned at the taste of the creamy and spongy concoction that was one of her favorites. "Remember," she told the class, "you should love what you cook because it's just as much effort to cook bad food as it is good food."

Ian lingered to help Juliette clean up, after the rest of the class headed home. She soaped the wine glasses, dipped them into a cold-water rinse, and then handed them to Ian to dry.

The conversation started out about cooking and the classes she had taken in the past, but gradually shifted onto the subject of her class in Lucca and Roman.

"Do you still miss him?" Ian asked, glancing at Juliette while he dried the glasses she passed to him.

"Funny you should ask, because I was just thinking about him tonight when we were all introducing ourselves. It reminded me of my first class there. But, no, I don't miss him in the sense that I'm pining away for him or anything. How about you, do you miss your ex fiancée?"

"God no, I got over her a long time ago. Now when she does enter my mind I'm just happy I dodged a bullet. I would never cheat and I expect loyalty in return."

"I feel the same way. That's how it should be."

Ian had been working beside her, looking at the glass he was drying rather than at her. When he was done, he set it down and turned to her.

"Well, it looks like we're done, so I guess I'll let you get home."

"I'll let you out," Juliette nodded towards the entrance to the café that had long since been locked up.

"Thanks for coming tonight," she said, leaning against the door frame. "It was great to have you in my class," she paused, an idea occurring to her. "Hey, if you want to come every week, I'll let you in for free if you stay and help me do the dishes afterwards."

"You drive a hard bargain, but consider it a deal," he looked into her eyes for a lingering moment. "I'll see you next week," he said, "if not sooner. I'm addicted to your coffee, so I might have to stop by on my way to work."

"I think I could stand that. I'll even make it a double."

"Excellent," he said and gave her a quick kiss on the cheek. "I'll see you then."

"See you then." She gave a little wave before she locked the door behind him and sighed.

Chapter 31

Catarina squeezed Franco's hand.

"I'm almost afraid to see them," she said. "I'm worried they will have aged and gotten frail."

"They may have, my darling. I'm trying to remember how long it's been since we visited."

"Let's see," she said. She had taken to thinking about time in relation to how many boys she had. "We brought Mateo, who was four, and Carlo—but he was just a baby. I think we conceived Dante while we were there," she added, and smiled mischievously at Franco.

"I think you're right," he wrapped his arm around her neck and kissed her cheek.

"I'm sure they're exhausted," he said, thinking again about her parents.

"I know we were."

"And we were young when we went through immigration. Think about them." A picture of her mother's sturdy-but-aging body flashed through Catarina's mind along with the memory of herself when she entered the country years before. It seemed so long ago now. She was thirty-four now and had been in the United States as long as she had lived in Italy.

It had been many years since she first saw Napa, resolving to coax her parents into coming to California. Finally she had. The war had raged on and finally ended. As soon as she and Franco could, they had taken a ship back to Italy to help her parents, sisters, and brothers-in-law to get the vineyard and orchard back in order. The vines were wretchedly overgrown and the olive trees were in desperate need of pruning. The kitchen garden had to be planted from scratch.

Franco and Catarina were no longer used to that type of work and each night they felt every single one of their muscles as they drifted off to sleep in Catarina's old room. But for Catarina it had been good to be back with her family where she was needed.

She was surprised at how poverty-stricken the village seemed. Had it been like that when she was growing up? She couldn't remember anymore. To her, it had simply been home.

The act of waiting in line at the well each day to draw water was almost intolerable to her after simply turning the faucet on and watching the water pour forth at their apartment in San Francisco. Everything in this rural part of southern Italy took much more effort.

Having the chance to see Maria Nina and her other old friends was joyous. She invited everyone over for a picnic in the orchard and it felt almost like old times. Most of all she enjoyed showing off her husband and sons. She was proud of her family.

She was especially happy to have them by her side when she encountered Signor Carlucci walking up the street while she strolled with Franco, Mateo, and Carlo to the market on an errand for her mother.

"Catarina Pensebene," he had said as they walked by. "I would recognize those blue eyes anywhere." He had the same lecherous look on his face that she remembered and it gave her a chill to think about what had passed between them so many years before.

She was surprised by his appearance. Her mother had included the news in one of her letters that he had become very ill during the war. He was stooped and had the countenance of an old man, even though she estimated he must have only been sixty years old.

"Signor Carlucci," she said with her iciest voice. "I would not have recognized you, if you hadn't stopped me. I'm afraid time has not treated you well." She then gave him a nod, without stopping. And, after he passed, she leaned back and spit in the road.

"Catarina!" Franco whispered, shocked. "What was that about? You were so rude." He couldn't imagine what would cause his good-natured wife to act so disrespectfully to anyone.

"I worked for his family before I left Italy. He was terrible to me. I was the maid. He tried to rape me," she whispered over her son's heads. She had never spoken of what had happened to anyone except her mother.

"What?" Franco stopped and took her arm protectively. His

face darkened.

"Don't worry. I bashed his nose in and ran," Catarina said, still proud of protecting herself.

"Why didn't you ever tell me?"

"The only person I ever told was my mother. After he attacked me I quit working for them. It was around the same time your marriage proposal came, and I left."

"I have half a mind to bash his nose in again, for good measure."

Catarina squeezed her husband's arm. "He's not worth it," she told him, smiling at her husband and tousling her sons' hair.

Throughout their visit, Catarina and Franco talked to her parents about Napa and how much the area reminded them of Perdifumo, and as the end of their visit drew near, they finally admitted to trying to lure them to move there.

"We bought some land there," Franco said in an offhand manner while they were drinking a small *degistivo* after dinner. "But we don't have anyone in mind yet to tend it. We can only get up on the weekends."

"The soil is so rich, Babbo," Catarina chimed in. "If only you could see it."

"We plan to build a little house there," Franco continued. "A place where the boys can run and play in the fresh air. They need to get out of the city sometimes and get a sense of living like this," he spread his arms wide to indicate the countryside where the Pensebene home was.

"If only you could come," Catarina slipped in. "Mama, you

would love it there. And we'll put in running water. That's when there are pipes that go right to the house. Can you imagine? Franco had to teach me how to use them when I first arrived."

"Running water? I don't understand," her mother asked.

"It pours out of the faucet. It's like having a full pitcher available all the time and all you have to do is tilt it and water pours out."

"Humph," she smiled. "Such wonders."

"Do you think maybe you would consider coming?" Catarina asked her parents.

"It's so far for a visit," answered Babbo.

"Maybe you could come and live there," Catarina raised her eyebrows, tentatively asking the question.

"This is my home. How could I leave the land where my son is buried?" Her eyes searched her daughter's, looking for understanding.

"Mama, no matter where you are, Mateo will be with you, because he's in your heart. And you could help me care for little Mateo," she put her hand on her son's head and mussed up his brown curls, "and Carlo."

"Maybe a fresh start would do us good, Celestina," Catarina's father took baby Carlo, kissing his cheek and handing him to his wife.

"Let's think on it," she said. "We'll think on it, ok?"

"*Grazie*, Mama, Babbo," Catarina said. "*Ti amo*. I just want you with us."

They talked about every aspect while Catarina and Franco were still there. There were no definite decisions made, but they were at least hopeful that Emiliano and Celestina were softening to the idea by the time Catarina and Franco returned to San Francisco.

It took almost another year of letters in order to finally convince her parents to leave Italy for California, and then many more months of visa clearances and sponsorship commitments before they booked passage on a ship.

In the meantime, Catarina and Franco added Dante to the family, but he was too young to make the trip to New York to meet Catarina's parents. Instead he, along with his older brothers, stayed with Isabella and Vittorio.

T he train trip to New York was a second honeymoon for them.

"More like a first honeymoon," Franco corrected when Catarina said as much.

"True, it was before we got married. *Oh, mio Dio*, Franco. I was so young. Just a girl. But when I think back, I wasn't frightened."

"You seemed older than your years to me."

"And now we've been together for such a long time. I hope you're not tired of me."

"Never," he said and then nudged her as he caught sight of Emiliano and Celestina coming through the doors and walking towards them.

"Mama! Babbo!" Catarina yelled and waved, running to them, and she kept her arms around them until they squirmed free like children.

Franco caught up with them, took the baggage out of their hands, and gave them each a welcoming hug. "Come," he said, leading them to the ferry. "Let's get you a meal and some sleep. We have a room waiting at the hotel where Catarina and I first stayed when she arrived. You'll like it."

"And you can have a bath, Mama. Wait until you soak in the tub that fills itself up. I'll show you how it works."

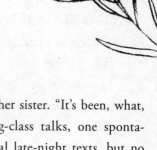

Chapter 32

"He's killing me," Juliette told her sister. "It's been, what, three weeks of post-cooking-class talks, one spontaneous sushi meal, and several late-night texts, but no actual moves."

"Maybe he's giving you space."

"Maybe, but here's the thing. I'm kind of terrified to say this, but I think he's everything I've been looking for. You know?"

Gina dragged a small table over to her couch, sat down with her cup of tea, and took a good, long look at her sister.

"Nothing that's going to gradually wear you down?" she asked. "No annoying habits?"

"No, that's the thing. He's great. Funny, smart, nice . . . God, so nice. He's good through and through."

"Handsome," Gina chimed in. "By the way, does he have a brother?"

"Yes," Juliette smiled mischievously. "As a matter of fact, he does."

"Hmmm."

"I want him to love me in spite of all of my flaws. I want him not to mind all the random stuff that's hard to love."

"Well, of course *I* know what I think is unlovable about you, but what do *you* think are things that might give a man pause?" Gina nudged her sister playfully.

"Let's see, having to be in the same family as you, for one thing." She gave Gina a wry smile, then continued, "Really, though, stuff like the fact that I like boring, comfortable underwear, and that I look like a wreck when I wake up."

"Don't forget that you sleep with your mouth open and drool."

"Thanks for that, and yes, that's exactly what I mean. Also, I talk too much and often too loudly. Why can't I just shut up?"

"We've been asking ourselves that for years," Gina laughed and rolled her eyes.

"It's just so strange. I haven't even kissed this guy but I keep seeing the future. But then I get scared. After all, not that long ago, I thought Roman was the perfect man for me. And look how that turned out."

"Yeah, I get that." Gina smiled. "But I think sometimes we love people differently. And even though you loved Roman, it doesn't mean you can't love Ian too."

"I see what you're saying. It's just unexpected."

"Seriously Juliette, I wouldn't worry. Because if there's one thing in the world you are most definitely not, it's impetuous. Remember, this is said by the woman who knows you best—including how long you mulled over opening a restaurant and of course, how long you insisted on staying in Girl Scouts when we all knew you had kind of hated it from the time you were in second grade."

"That's true, Girl Scouts was a drag," Juliette admitted.

"My point is that I wouldn't worry about whether it's too soon or anything else. Just go with it," Gina told her.

"It'll be ok, right?" asked Juliette.

"Exactly. Plant some flowers."

Juliette was mulling over a plan of action about how to break through the barrier with Ian while reading the newspaper on Saturday morning. She was sitting in one of her favorite breakfast joints, Café Dora, enjoying eggs, when the man himself breezed in with a beautiful woman. She had blond, silky hair the color of hay and eyes as green as his own. She wore loose, faded jeans and a perfectly white, long-sleeved T-shirt that Juliette envied. Her jeans were hanging off of her slim hips in an equally enviable way.

After a quick intake of breath, Juliette instinctively held up the paper so she was hidden. She felt heartbroken. If this was one of his morning-after women then she was definitely not up to his standards.

She wasn't sure whether to fold the paper down and nonchalantly wave as if she didn't have a care in the world, or stay crouched awkwardly at her table behind the *New York Times* Style section.

She peeked out and saw him grab the mystery woman by the back of her neck and playfully shake her while they stood at the counter and ordered. The blond shook her head and smiled at him in a way that spoke volumes about how comfortable they were with each other. This didn't seem like some awkward post-hook-up breakfast—but why would he not tell her if he was seeing someone?

As Juliette gagged down the bite that had been in her mouth since they came in, she heard Ian say, "To go, please," so she knew she would be put out of her misery soon and decided to take the coward's way out and stay hidden.

The door chimed as they left. Juliette lowered the paper and with a trembling hand she picked up her coffee cup and took a sip.

Over the next few days, she didn't say a word to anyone about seeing Ian and his beautiful *whatever*. But she couldn't get the vision of them out of her mind. Did she have to be so pretty? He had looked happy and at ease.

Juliette felt blindsided. Why hadn't he ever said anything about her? It's not like they hadn't talked about their love lives.

And what about the chemistry between the two of them? And why was he texting her and coming around all the time? Was this a Roman situation all over again? She wondered whether she was losing her ability to judge people.

She was dying of embarrassment. She wondered if she had given away her feelings. Did he feel kind of sorry for her? Had he been too gentlemanly to say anything? She wondered if that's why he hadn't brought the mystery woman up.

She was tormented and wished more than anything he wouldn't come to cooking class that week. It would help to have a little break from him so she could face seeing him with an insouciant, "we're just old friends" attitude. She sighed, took a deep breath, and wished for the thousandth time that she did yoga. Then she could be all *namaste* about it. Instead she went home, put on her running shoes, and headed for the trail.

She spent the rest of the weekend depressed, and devoured not only the better part of a chocolate cake but two trashy romance novels to boot. And when Monday rolled around she wasn't feeling much better. She managed to get herself out of bed and threw her hair into a messy bun, drank an espresso instead of going for a morning run and then dragged herself to work feeling bloated.

Juliette was grumpy, confused, and holed up in her office when her barista poked her head around her office door with a huge bouquet of deep burgundy peonies.

"Look who got flowers!" she raised her eyebrows at Juliette. "Have you been keeping secrets from us?"

Juliette looked up from her computer. "Are you sure those are for me? I don't know anyone who would be sending flowers to me these days."

"The note says 'Juliette', all right." She said handing over the little envelope. "Here, let's see who they're from."

Juliette looked at her name on the white square, which confirmed that they were indeed for her. She tore it open and involuntarily sucked in her breath in surprise.

"You look shocked. Who is it?" She peered at the note in Juliette's hand and read it out loud: "*Juliette, I need to talk to you. Please call me.* Who's Roman?" she asked.

"An old boyfriend."

CATARINA'S RING

"Great name. Sounds sexy," she raised her eyebrows at her with a twinkle in her eye.

"He *is* that," Juliette admitted. "But I have no idea why he would be sending flowers to me now."

"Maybe he misses you and wants to get back together."

"Highly unlikely. He lives in Italy and has a girlfriend," she looked up at her and then tossed the note onto her desk.

"Are you going to call him?"

"I don't know. I guess I will. It's weird."

"Well, not to make generalizations, but guys are weird. They are a complete mystery to me. I can never figure them out."

"I hear you," Juliette commiserated, thinking about Ian and the woman he was with in addition to Roman's sudden gesture. "I have absolutely no idea what goes on in their minds."

One thing she did know, though, was that she didn't want to talk to Roman while she was at work, but with the nine-hour time difference she didn't want to wait too long either.

She stayed busy ordering food and checking invoices for a while, but curiosity got the better of her, so after the lunch rush she decided to leave her crew to hold down the fort while she popped home to give him a call.

Phone clutched in her hand, Juliette paced the living room for a few minutes wondering if this could be some sort of divine timing. Just when it seemed that nothing was going to happen with Ian, Roman was getting back in touch. Would she even want him back at this point? And what would it mean? She stopped at the window and looked out at the crimson fall leaves clinging to the tree branches in front of her cottage. She realized she was jumping to huge conclusions based on a few flowers. Still, she couldn't help but read into the gesture. She wouldn't know until she talked to him, though, so she closed her eyes, inhaled deeply and dialed.

"*Pronto?*" Roman picked up immediately. "Juliette?"

"*Si, sono io.*"

"*Ciao. Grazie per aver chiamato,*" Roman said. Her heart was pounding and her palms were sweating just hearing his voice.

"You're welcome. Thank you for the beautiful flowers. They're gorgeous."

"*Avevo bisogno di sentire la tua voce.*"

"*Perché?* Why do you need to hear my voice?

"Because, Juliette, I miss you. I think I made a terrible mistake."

"*Cosa stai dicendo?*" she asked, completely confused. "What are you saying?"

"I'm saying I miss you. Do you miss me? Would you ever consider coming back?"

"I don't understand. It's been so many months. Why now? And what about your girlfriend?"

"I don't know, Juliette," he sighed. "It's never been the same with her since I met you. I keep comparing the two of you and missing you."

Juliette closed her eyes and leaned her forehead against the cool windowpane. She couldn't believe this was happening. She had longed to hear those words for weeks when she returned home and then finally gave up hope. Her heart was pounding and she felt light-headed and confused.

"Even if I wanted to, Roman, I don't see how we could make it work now. I just opened my restaurant here. You have your own cooking school there."

"Just think about it. *Per favore.*"

"but . . . "

"Don't say anything now. Don't make any decisions. Just think about it and I'll call you in a couple of days."

"Listen, Roman, I don't . . . "

He cut her off again, "Promise me you'll think about it. I miss your beautiful face, your laughter, you were good for me."

"I promise I'll think about it, but for now let's just catch up. What have you been up to?" Juliette asked.

"What I've been up to is the same as always. Teaching, sometimes working at the restaurant in Florence, going to the market, wondering about you."

Juliette could visualize Lucca. It was the fall again, close to when she first arrived.

"I can imagine the chestnut trees," she said, "and the market. Have you seen Odessa and Antonello lately?"

"I see Odessa often, but she's decidedly cooler to me than before you two became friends."

Juliette chuckled at that, pleased by her friend's loyalty.

"I miss her. And Antonello. Do you see him?"

"Only once in a while. Sometimes hanging around the cheese stall with Odessa, but that's it."

"And how's class? Any new recipes you want to share?"

"Stop trying to change the subject. I want to talk about us, not recipes."

Juliette sat down on the side of her bed. Confusion swept over her. She could visualize Roman but Ian kept intruding in her mind.

The way his eyes crinkled around the edges when he smiled and the way he took her hand when they were walking around the tide pools in Pacific Grove. But she also had a film reel of him and the blond from the café running through her mind. She sighed.

"I don't know what to say, Roman. You broke my heart, you lied to me, and then you let me go."

"I know and I'm so sorry. *Mi dispiace.* If I could go back in time and do it differently I would, but all I can do now is try to mend my mistake, no?"

"That's one of the frustrating things about life, isn't it? We can only go forward and I have worked so hard to go forward without you. I loved you even when you didn't love me. But I don't know now."

"I'll make it up to you. Can I come visit? If I could see you I could convince you. I made a mistake, Juliette. You have to forgive me. I miss you."

Juliette knew it would be so easy to allow herself to get swept back up with him, but she had to be realistic. She was in California. He was in Lucca. They both had businesses, but she also knew it wasn't just that. No matter what was happening between Ian and the other woman, she had fallen for him.

"Life is so complicated," she said. And then a thought occurred to her and she had to ask. "I have one question."

"Anything, *bella*. What do you want to know?" Roman said.

"Have you and Maddelena broken up or is she just away on assignment again?"

"I . . . ah . . . ," he hesitated. "She *is* away, but that's not why now. I've been thinking about you. About us."

"*Davvero*? Really?" Juliette's heart was pounding, "And how long ago did she leave?"

"Two weeks, but I swear, it's not what you're thinking. I promise you, and now you have to promise me. You'll think about it?"

"I'll think about it," Juliette said, but the answer to her question about Maddelena told her everything she needed to know.

"*Ti amo*, Juliette."

"*Ciao*, Roman," Juliette answered and then put her head in her hands.

Ti amo? Now *ti amo* after all the time she had hoped and dreamed he would tell her he loved her before? Especially when she was already a wreck about Ian and the blond. She threw herself onto the couch. "Why now?" she asked herself. But the answer to the later question was painfully obvious to her. *Of course* now, because Maddelena had left again. And then it suddenly occurred to her. Yes, Roman was handsome, witty, and loveable, but utterly unable to be alone.

After so many years of dating but not falling in love with anyone, she felt raw and exposed having loved two very different men in a row.

She looked at the clock and sighed. She should get back to work, but she couldn't quite bring herself to get off the couch. She spied the shoebox of letters, which had been all but abandoned since the opening of *Gusto*. There was only one letter left unread. It was from someone whose name she didn't recognize.

"Humm," Juliette looked it over. The postmark was from New York, dated 1918—the same year the correspondence abruptly stopped. It was from Maria's sister-in-law, bearing tragic news. Catarina's confidant and friend had died in the influenza epidemic and she was returning the letters Maria had saved to her dear friend.

"No!" Juliette cried out, feeling like she too had lost a friend.

"Poor Nonna." She rubbed her fingers gently across the written page. She imagined the tiny smears in the ink were a result of Catarina's tears.

Sometimes life is too hard, Juliette sighed, thinking of Roman and Ian both. But she knew what Catarina would say to that. *Plant flowers, plant flowers*, she said to herself, then got up off the couch and went back to work.

Juliette was careful to keep her tone light and upbeat when cooking class rolled around that week. She hadn't yet called Roman back because she couldn't bring herself to have the conversation she knew she needed to have.

For now, in class she tried to be upbeat, popping into the small groups she'd formed to demonstrate the best way to cut an onion or to show her students the fabulous whisk she loved that seemed to add air to eggs more quickly than standard wire whisks.

She met Ian's eye once or twice and gave him a brief smile. Aside from that she didn't seek him out. Once everyone was gone he collected the large metal bowls while she put away the baking sheets, but for the first time ever she had nothing to say.

"How was your weekend?" Ian broke the silence.

"Good, good," she replied, determined to keep it light.

"Have you been busy? I texted you a couple of times the last couple of days, but you never replied."

"Sorry, yeah, it's been a crazy week. And I didn't want to intrude."

"Why would you be intruding? I'm the one who was texting you."

"That's true," she smiled. "But . . . well, here's the thing. I happened to see you out with a woman on Saturday morning, so I know you're seeing someone and I didn't want to be, you know," she stammered, "someone you feel you have to text to be nice."

Ian stopped collecting bowls and just looked at her.

"Is that really what you think?"

"I don't know. I never seem to know what to think. Is this something new? Whenever I ask you about your love life, you're always vague."

"Would it bother you if I was seeing someone?" he asked.

"Well, I mean, I would be happy for you, of course," she tried to muster a fake smile.

She took a deep breath and leaned against the stainless steel countertop. She pinched the skin on her finger where the ring used to be, wishing it was there to urge her on. She knew Catarina would suggest she go for it.

"But, yes, to be honest," she looked up at him with searching eyes. "Yes, it would bother me."

Ian walked over to her and took her face in his hands. "I'm so glad to hear that, because I'm crazy about you, Juliette. The woman you saw me with is my sister. I think I've mentioned her before, haven't I? Well, her schmuck of a boyfriend broke up with her so she flew home from Seattle for the weekend so she could take some time away and regroup."

"Your sister?"

"My sister. And I'm afraid I was hardly any help to her because all weekend she had to listen to me talk about you. And how to . . . "

That's as far as he got before their lips met.

"I can't believe it was your sister. You have no idea what I've been going through."

"Well let me assure you," Ian said and kissed her again. The kiss intensified, and then when they finally broke apart, he pulled her to him and wrapped his arms around her again.

"I texted you because I thought it would be nice to introduce you two."

"Oh my God. I'm such an idiot. But an incredibly happy idiot." She tucked her face into the space above his collarbone and inhaled his scent. She loved the way he smelled like fresh wood and something uniquely him. He released her and they stepped back and looked at each other and smiled ridiculously goofy smiles at each other. It felt perfect. He took his fingers and entwined them with hers. His fingers were long, slender and elegant. His hands looked more like a concert pianist's than a carpenter's.

He smiled a quick, eye-crinkling smile at her, then pulled her back to him and kissed her again in a way that made her never want to stop. Juliette rubbed her hands along his arms as she had been wanting to do for weeks—even months. She slipped her hand into the sleeve of his shirt and held his wrist. She liked the feeling of his skin under her fingertips.

They pulled apart breathless and giddy. Juliette refilled their wine glasses and they both hopped up and sat on the counter, sipping wine, holding hands.

"I'm so relieved," she told him. "When you walked into Café Dora with such a beautiful woman, I thought, 'well, shit'. " She smiled sheepishly. "And you know me, I hardly ever swear."

Ian laughed. "Glad to know I can evoke a strong response."

"You know that saying, 'My heart stopped'?" she asked. "It turns out it's true. That happens. Anyway, instead of waving and saying hello, I hid behind my newspaper like a coward."

"I've been in stages between smitten and desperate for months. The smitten stage started the day we met. The desperate has developed more recently."

"You haven't said a word. Why did you wait so long?" she asked.

"Let's see. For starters, I was working for you and it's never a good idea to mix business and romance. When that all ended, I thought I should give you some time because I wasn't sure how you felt and I wanted you to know that I'm not fooling around here. This is the real deal. I'm seriously in love with you," he paused. "Look Juliette, when I walked in and saw my fiancée with her lab partner, I was indescribably hurt and angry. I felt stupid for trusting her. Now, I'm glad it happened." He locked eyes with her then pulled her to him and kissed her again.

"I love you too!" she giggled joyfully, almost unable to believe this was happening. "When it's right, it's right. In fact I had a bit of a revelation about that very thing this weekend," she said. "To love someone and have that person love you back seems impossibly perfect."

He kept his eyes on her eyes. "Exactly."

"That night we went swimming at your parents."

"Nearly killed me."

"Me too," she smiled and kissed him again.

"Come on," he hopped down and took her hand. "Let's go."

"Your place or mine?"

"Oh yours, definitely. It's closer."

Chapter 33

CATARINA, AND FINALLY, A DAUGHTER

"Tell me the story of how you picked my name, Mama."

"Again? You've heard it so many times."

"I know, but it's my favorite."

Catarina lifted her daughter onto her lap and ran her fingers through her dark curls. Her eyes were the same blue as Celestina's and her own.

"Ok, darling. It began when I was in the hospital, and the nurse handed a sweet little baby girl to me. And I said to your papa, 'I can't believe after all these boys, we got a girl.'"

"Then what happened?"

"Then the nurse said, 'How many sons do you have?' And Papa

said, "Five. We have five wonderful boys. Our youngest is already ten and our oldest is practically old enough to have children of his own, and then along comes this special surprise.'"

"And I said . . . "

" . . . we have to think of a name," piped in her daughter's voice, because she already knew all the lines in the story by heart.

"That's right. And I told the nurse, 'We were sure we would have another boy, so we haven't picked a name for this little angel.'"

"And then Papa started naming all the girl names he could imagine. He suggested Isabella after his mother, and Celestina after mine. He suggested Maria Nina, after my best friend in Italy, and he even suggested Olive, which seemed like a silly name to me. I said, 'No, no, no' to all of them because none of them was just right for you."

"Especially Olive."

"Yes, especially Olive. What was Papa thinking?"

"So, how did you decide on my name?"

"I had been in the hospital for three long days, and still no name. And Papa brought all of your brothers to visit their new little sister. And he said, 'No one leaves this room until we decide on a name.'"

"So that's when he took off his hat?"

"Exactly. He took off his hat and tore up a piece of paper, and everyone in the room wrote down their favorite name. And then Papa put all the bits of paper in the hat and held it up. I dipped my hand in, and that's when I pulled out the best name of all."

"Amilia!"

"That's right. Amilia. And we all said, 'Yes! That's the best name of all.'"

"And who had put that one on the paper?"

"Well, you already know the answer to that, silly. It was me."
She leaned over and gave her little girl a kiss on her sweet,
smooth cheek.

"I love that story, Mama."

"I know. I love it, too. Now, should we get back to work?"

"Yes," she said, and jumped off of her mother's lap.

They were each working on a painting in Catarina's studio. She
had a full-size easel for herself and a pint-size easel for her four-year-
old daughter.

Catarina was painting a field of flowers and Amilia was
painting a kitten.

Catarina stood back from her work and chewed on the end
of her paintbrush while she contemplated her next step. She glanced
over at Amilia and smiled when she saw her step back and put the end
of her paint brush in her mouth as well, emulating her mother's gesture
exactly. She pretended she hadn't noticed and casually began to fan
her face with her other hand. She had to suppress a smile when she saw
Amilia do the same.

"Hummm," said Catarina. "What do you think my
painting needs?"

"A dash of pink, Mama,"

"Excellent idea, darling girl. Coincidentally, that's the very color
I think your painting needs as well."

Catarina reached for a tube of fuchsia and dabbed a blob on her
pallet. She dipped it down in front of Amilia, like a tray full of treasures
and let her daughter dab her brush in the pigment.

She put a dash of pink on the tip of the kitten's nose.

"Perfect," she said.

Catarina dipped her own brush onto the palette as well and carefully added the hue to the petals of some flowers.

"Mama?" Amilia asked.

"Yes," Catarina responded offhandedly.

"Where's your sparkly ring?"

"I put it away while I work with oil paints, so it doesn't get ruined. Why do you ask?"

"Because I like to look at the sparkles."

"It's pretty, isn't it? Papa gave it to me when I came here to marry him."

"He did?"

"Yes, so I take special care of it. Someday it will be yours, and when it is, you can always look at it and remember how much Papa and I loved each other and how much we loved you." She dabbed a tiny dot of pink onto Amilia's nose and smiled at her. "Now get back to work," she said. "That kitty isn't going to paint itself."

"I might want to be a real painter, someday. Or maybe a jewelry maker, like Papa."

"That's a fine idea. But who knows, you may want to do something you think up all by yourself. You can be anything you want to be, Amilia. Just remember to always choose to do what makes you happy. That's how you'll know it's right."

"Is that what you did, Mama?"

"*Certamente*," Catarina smiled thinking back to the journey that began so long ago.

"Absolutely."

Chapter 34

JULIETTE AND THE
UNEXPECTED KEY TO HER HEART
DURING A RAINSTORM

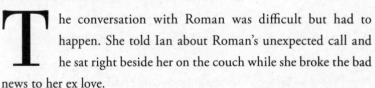

T he conversation with Roman was difficult but had to happen. She told Ian about Roman's unexpected call and he sat right beside her on the couch while she broke the bad news to her ex love.

The fact that he had no idea what they were saying, since Juliette and Roman were speaking in Italian, made it easier for everyone.

After Juliette hung up she laid down with her head on Ian's lap and looked into his face while he stroked her hair.

"That was hard," she said.

"Do you have regrets?" Ian asked, worry lines showing around his eyes.

"None," she lifted her head to kiss him. "But it was still difficult. Thanks for being here. I hope it wasn't too awkward for you."

"Not at all," Ian joked. "I always hang out with my girlfriends when they break up with their boyfriends."

Juliette laughed and playfully kissed him again. "I wasn't breaking up with him. Just officially ending that chapter of my life. I couldn't be any happier, though. I can hardly believe how lucky I am. There I was, brokenhearted, and then in you walked and swept me off my sad, lonely feet."

"And don't you ever forget it," he smiled against her lips as he flipped her around so he was lying on top of her.

Juliette smiled at the memory of that day months later as she looked through the windows of *Gusto* at the rain coming down in sheets. Cold, wet weather usually got her down after a while, but not this year. Getting *Gusto* off to a successful start and spending all her free time with Ian kept her in high spirits through the gray, rainy winter months. Even now in April, when everyone was ready for the warmer days of spring, she didn't mind the unusual torrents that kept coming.

She was at her desk mulling over a produce order when Ian walked through the door, dripping wet. He looked like the cat who ate the canary.

"Hey, you," Juliette said, getting up to give him a kiss. "This is a nice surprise."

"Hey, yourself," he wrapped his arms around her.

"You're soaking wet!" she laughed and untangled herself from his sopping clothes. "Do you want a towel?"

"That would be great, thanks," he said, helping himself to one from the pile delivered from the laundry service. He dried off his face and shook his hair.

Juliette laughed, getting hit with drops of flying water.

"You're like one of your parents' dogs. What are you doing here in the middle of the day anyway? Did you knock off work early?"

"I was called away on an errand and I couldn't bring myself to go back to work. I had to see you."

"I like the sound of that."

Ian pulled her in for a quick kiss. He kissed her again harder, gently kicking closed the office door behind him so they were alone. Taking her hands, he smiled at her and took a deep breath.

"When you came into my life, it became right. It became whole. I feel like we're perfect together. I love it that I can just be myself and you can be yourself. We bring out the best in each other. You've become my best friend as well as my lover," he paused. "You're it for me, Juliette. I can't imagine life without you in it. I want to wake up with you every morning and grow old and wrinkly with you."

"Are you proposing to me?" Juliette asked, a surprised grin on her face.

"Yes, I am. Will you marry me? Could you stand to be with me for the rest of your days?"

"Yes!" Juliette threw her arms around him. "I could definitely stand it. In fact, I can't picture my life any other way."

"Thank God!" He kissed her again, "I was planning to propose over a romantic dinner, but then I was thinking that it should be right here. After all, this is where it all happened, right?"

"There couldn't be a better place."

"And now the surprise," Ian said.

"That wasn't the surprise?"

"Nope, that was just the prelude," he grinned at her and took an unassuming white box out of the pocket of his jacket.

"Ever since your cottage was burglarized," Ian told her, "I've been on the lookout for your ring. Catarina's ring, I should say."

"What do you mean?" Juliette asked, her eyes locked on Ian's.

"The police said that the best shot to find it would be to scour pawn shops and that it might eventually turn up."

Juliette looked at the box in his hand. She couldn't imagine it could possibly contain her ring, but she couldn't suppress a glimmer of hope.

Ian opened the lid and there it was, sitting on top of a layer of white cotton, perfectly intact.

"Is it . . . ?"

He nodded.

"Even though it's yours already, I hope you'll do me the honor of wearing it as an engagement ring. Or I can get you a different one if you want," he told her, "I just thought this one would have so much more meaning,"

"I never thought I'd see it again," she whispered. "I can't believe you got it back. I would love to wear it as our ring, Ian. I can't think of anything more perfect."

She held out her hand and he slid it on her finger where Juliette looked at it, tears slipping down her cheeks in spite of her smile.

"You wouldn't believe how many pawnbrokers I now know on a first-name basis. I've looked at pretty much every pawnshop in California and Nevada and have e-mailed the photos around to more than I can count. I was afraid it was futile. Then yesterday, I got a call from Anthony, one of the guys I've talked to a couple of times in Grass Valley, who was sure a ring that had just come in was yours."

"You never said anything to me." She looked up to meet his eyes.

"I didn't want to get your hopes up." He ran a finger across her cheek.

"You're the most amazing man in the world. I can't believe you did this for me."

"After hearing the history, I couldn't stand to think of it out there without you."

"Did you get it today?"

"Yep, and then once I had it, I couldn't wait to give it to you. That's when my plan for the romantic dinner flew out the window. I drove straight here. It's a good thing you weren't in the middle of the lunch rush."

"You can tear me away from making sandwiches to propose anytime," she smiled. Then a thought occurred to her.

"You know," Juliette said with a gleam in her eye, "this means we're going to have to have a daughter to pass it on to."

"I was actually thinking about the very same thing on the way here, and don't worry, we will, but for now, you're *all* mine."

Juliette knew she should call her dad, sister, and friends to tell them her exciting news, but at the moment she was content snuggling at home with Ian and listening to the rain pattering the window. She held up her hand and looked at Catarina's ring sparkling on her finger. Ian rolled onto his side, looked at her in the dim evening light, and entwined his fingers with hers.

"What are you thinking about?" he asked.

"About love and how when you least expect to find it, you do."

"I remember the first time I saw you. You were distraught and so alone, and when I held your hand it felt completely right even though falling in love was the very last thing on my mind in that moment. I felt an intense sense of protectiveness over you."

"I think God has a way of making beautiful things happen from terrible situations if we're open to it."

"Then when you were in Italy, I would casually ask your dad about you. He was always happy to talk about what you were up to. When I heard about Roman, I told myself not to be disappointed. After all, I didn't even really know you, but it was odd because I felt like I did already."

"Really?"

"Yeah. Then when you came home and I got to know you, I knew you were the one for me. You're lovely inside and out, Juliette. I have loved you all along."

"Well, you certainly played it cool, mister."

"I had to because I didn't want to scare you away. You were a bit skittish after everything you'd been through, so I made do with spending time with you, which was not exactly a hardship because you're smart and funny. And I won't even mention the pastries, which were really the coup de grace." Ian paused and stared up at the ceiling for a minute.

"What is it?" Juliette asked.

"Do you remember when you told me the story about your grandmother and that guy who wanted her to leave your grandfather for him?"

"Of course, Gregorio."

"It's interesting, isn't it? The fact that sometimes we have to love the wrong people in order to figure out who the right people are. Like Gregorio for Catarina, Roman for you, my ex fiancée for me. But in the end, we all got to the right place."

"That's true. I like thinking about it that way. So," she snuggled closer to him, "what do you want to do now?" Juliette asked, lazily.

"Well, for the moment, I intend to keep you right where you are. And then I guess we'll be planning a wedding."

"I know exactly where I want to have it," she told him.

"Where?"

"In Napa. At Nonna and Granddad's house."

"That sounds perfect," Ian said.

"It'll be like they're there with us."

"I think they will be."

Juliette twirled Catarina's ring around on her finger. It felt both familiar and new at the same time. Just like her life. She knew the best part was just beginning.

ACKNOWLEDGEMENTS:

First and foremost, thank God for blessing me with amazing friends and family (Dad, Mary, Bill, Kathy, my late-and-much-loved Mom, and Michael) who have encouraged me along this journey, and for giving me an extra helping of tenacity, because I've definitely needed it in this life. A huge thanks also to the following beloved friends who have read this manuscript (sometimes twice!) and have given me excellent feedback, insight, a stern talking to when needed, someone to laugh with (and cry with when the going got tough), and a sounding board when I was stuck: Julie Wold for early encouragement; Alexandra Matisoff-Li—one of the gracious ones who read it twice; my sister, Cheryl Duncan, who pushed me to add more layers of detail, and then more layers of detail again; Chris Boral and Terri Stanfield—who did early reads and urged me to keep going; Erika Mailman and Annie Barrows—who read later rounds and gave me great feedback and a much-needed vigorous shaking; Beth Weber who bolstered me with cocktails when I was ready to throw in the towel; Kim Carpenter who had the exact right suggestions in the eleventh hour; Leslie Jonath who graciously read it even though she doesn't like reading fiction; Sarah Rosenberg who has been an amazing champion to me in all things publishing; Maria Carr and her lovely daughters who brought the perfect aesthetic to the cover photo; to Elysse Ricci Achuff for the beautiful design; and finally and most importantly a huge thank you to my husband, Matt McGuinness, whose never ending love and support of me is the greatest gift in my life.

To read more about the author, visit her blog at lisamcguinnesswrites.com.